THE
CURIE
SOCIETY

THE CURIE SOCIETY

ASTRA INCLINANT

TM

This book is dedicated to women who devote
their lives and minds to the sciences—now,
in the past, and in the future. You are trailblazers.
Your heroics are often unseen, but we see you!

Editor: Joan Hilty

Editorial Assistant: Laura Martin

Produced By: Einhorn's Epic Productions

Book Production: Pageturner Graphic Novels

Book Producer & Designer: Pete Friedrich

Creative Director: Ryan McCann

Art Assistant, Portrait and Blueprint
Illustrations: Annette Fanzhu

CSHQ Historical Illustration: Pia Guerra

Additional Lettering: Deron Bennett

MITP Production Editor: Liz Agresta

MITP Production Manager: Janet Rossi

Library of Congress Control Number: 2020945814
ISBN: 978-0-262-53994-4

Created by Heather Einhorn and Adam Staffaroni

THE CURIE SOCIETY

Janet Harvey
Writer

Sonia Liao
Artist

Johanna Taylor
Colorist

Morgan Martinez
Letterer

The MIT Press
Cambridge, Massachusetts
London, England

Einhorn's Epic Productions
New York, New York

"Nothing in life is to be feared, it is only to be understood.
Now is the time to understand more,
so that we may fear less."
–Marie Curie

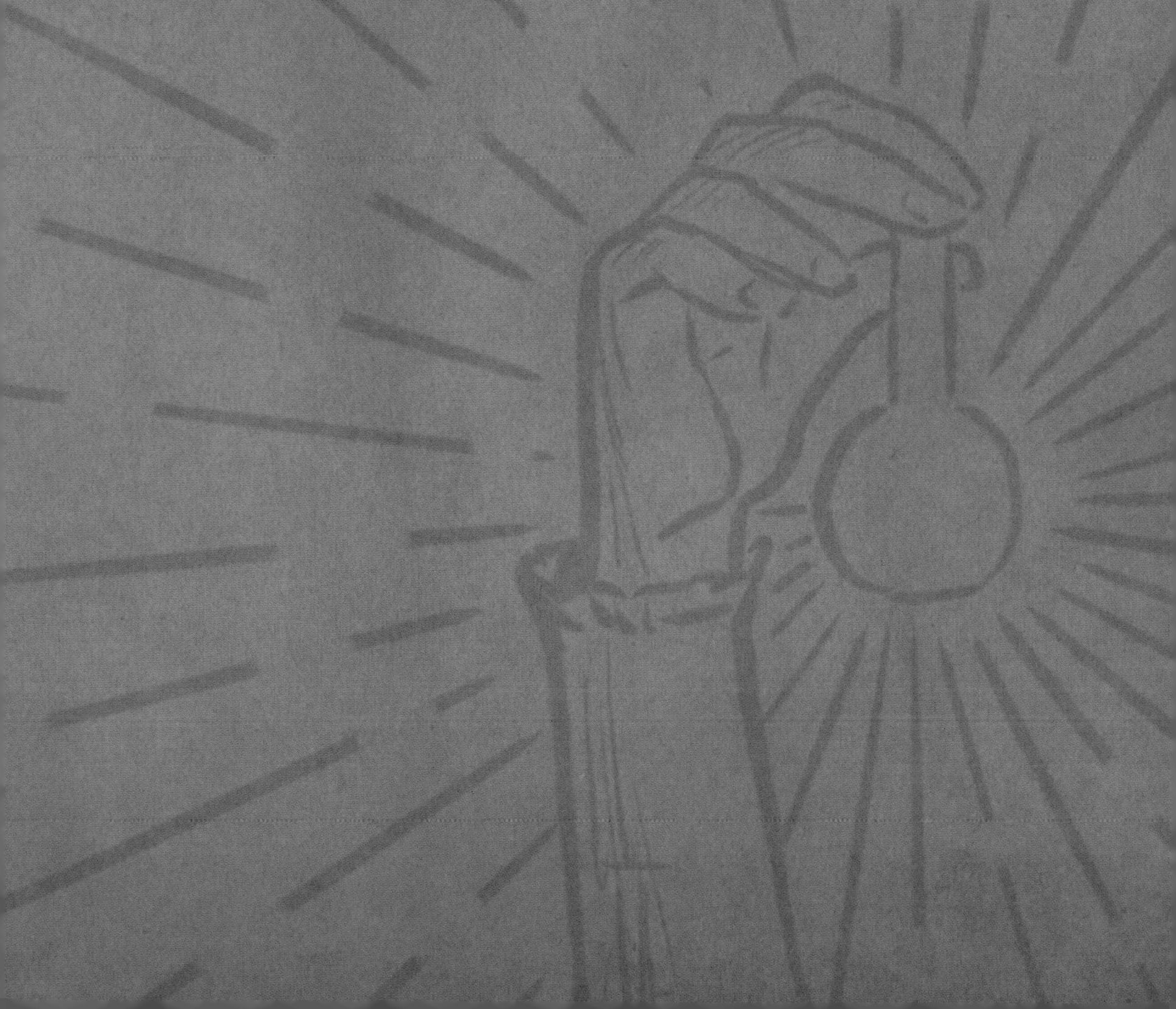

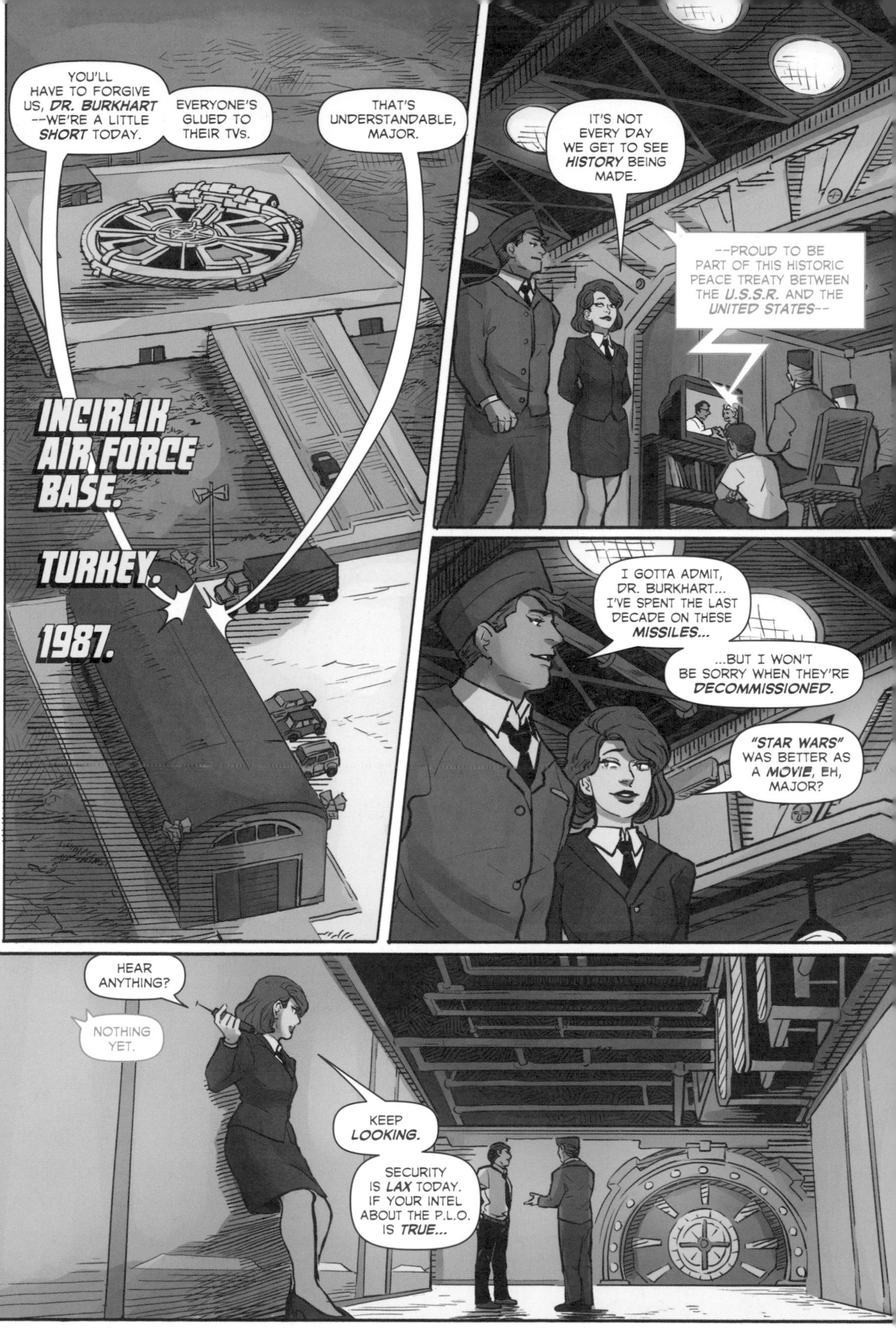
YOU'LL HAVE TO FORGIVE US, DR. BURKHART --WE'RE A LITTLE SHORT TODAY.
EVERYONE'S GLUED TO THEIR TVs.
THAT'S UNDERSTANDABLE, MAJOR.
INCIRLIK AIR FORCE BASE.
TURKEY.
1987.
IT'S NOT EVERY DAY WE GET TO SEE HISTORY BEING MADE.
--PROUD TO BE PART OF THIS HISTORIC PEACE TREATY BETWEEN THE U.S.S.R. AND THE UNITED STATES--
I GOTTA ADMIT, DR. BURKHART... I'VE SPENT THE LAST DECADE ON THESE MISSILES...
...BUT I WON'T BE SORRY WHEN THEY'RE DECOMMISSIONED.
"STAR WARS" WAS BETTER AS A MOVIE, EH, MAJOR?
HEAR ANYTHING?
NOTHING YET.
KEEP LOOKING.
SECURITY IS LAX TODAY. IF YOUR INTEL ABOUT THE P.L.O. IS TRUE...

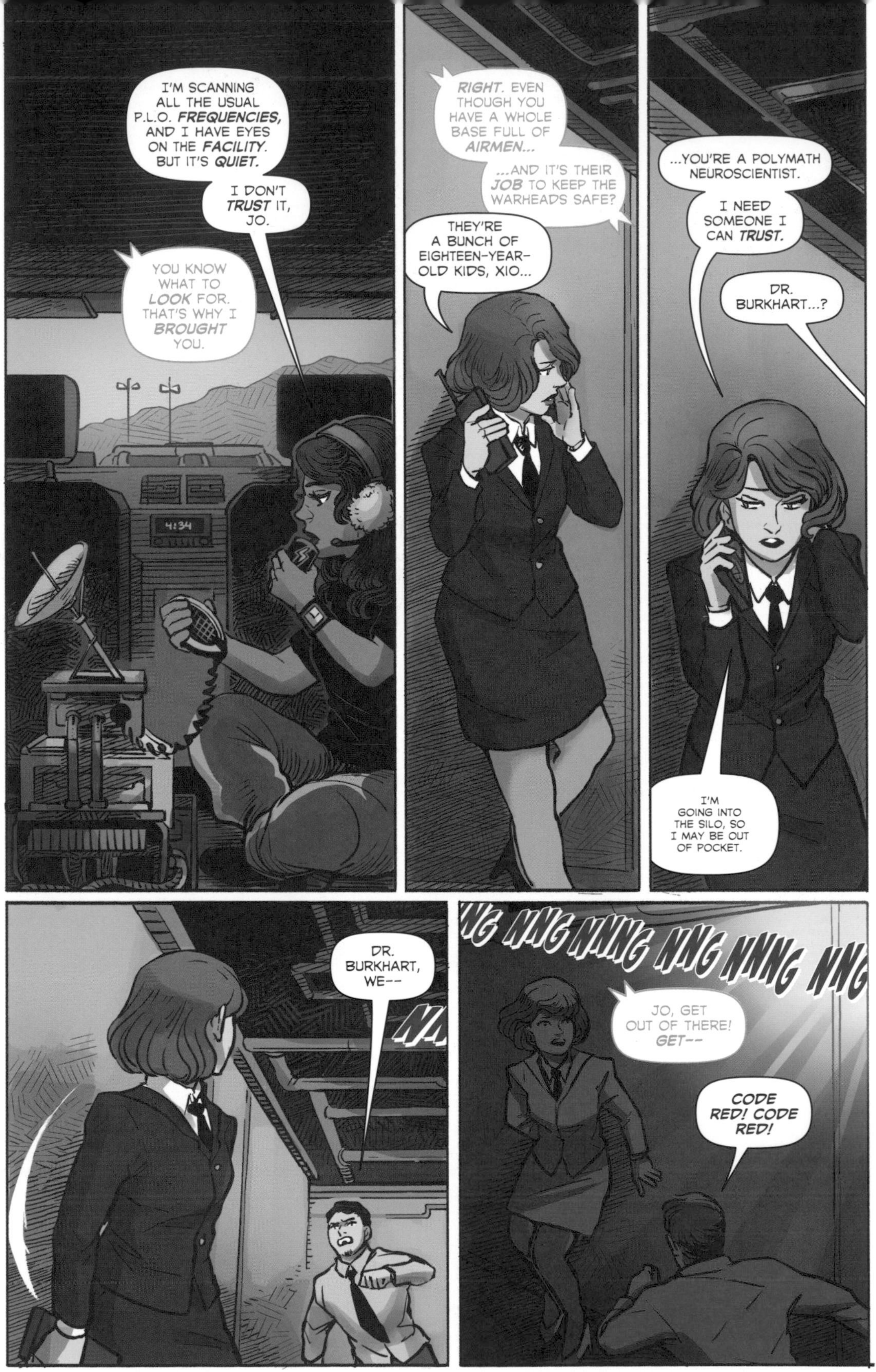
I'M SCANNING ALL THE USUAL P.L.O. FREQUENCIES, AND I HAVE EYES ON THE FACILITY. BUT IT'S QUIET.
I DON'T TRUST IT, JO.
YOU KNOW WHAT TO LOOK FOR. THAT'S WHY I BROUGHT YOU.
4:34
RIGHT. EVEN THOUGH YOU HAVE A WHOLE BASE FULL OF AIRMEN...
...AND IT'S THEIR JOB TO KEEP THE WARHEADS SAFE?
THEY'RE A BUNCH OF EIGHTEEN-YEAR-OLD KIDS, XIO...
...YOU'RE A POLYMATH NEUROSCIENTIST.
I NEED SOMEONE I CAN TRUST.
DR. BURKHART...?
I'M GOING INTO THE SILO, SO I MAY BE OUT OF POCKET.
DR. BURKHART, WE--
NNG NNG NNNG NNG NNG NNNG NNG
JO, GET OUT OF THERE! GET--
CODE RED! CODE RED!

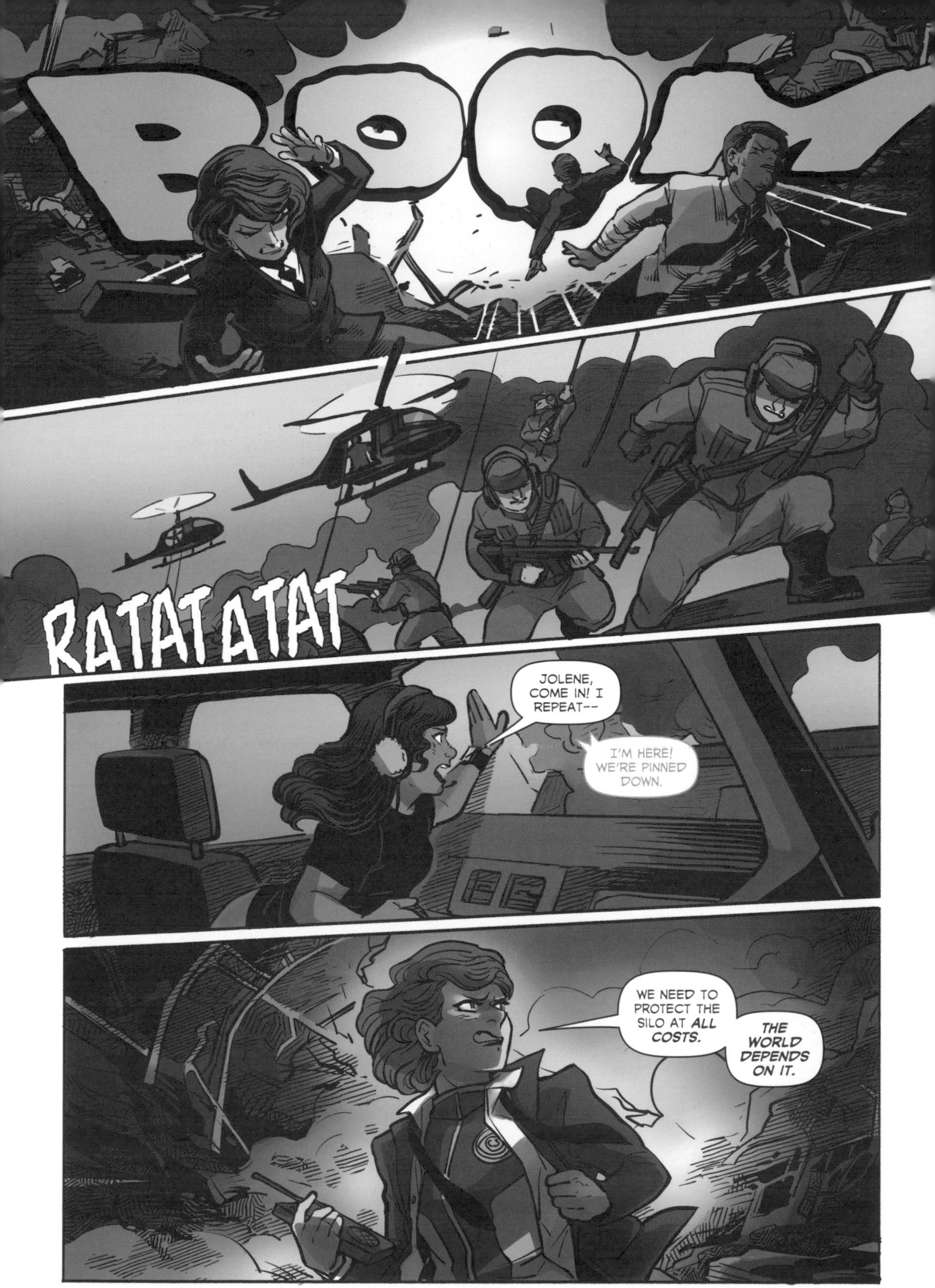
BOOM
RATATATAT
JOLENE, COME IN! I REPEAT--
I'M HERE! WE'RE PINNED DOWN.
WE NEED TO PROTECT THE SILO AT *ALL COSTS.*
THE WORLD DEPENDS ON IT.

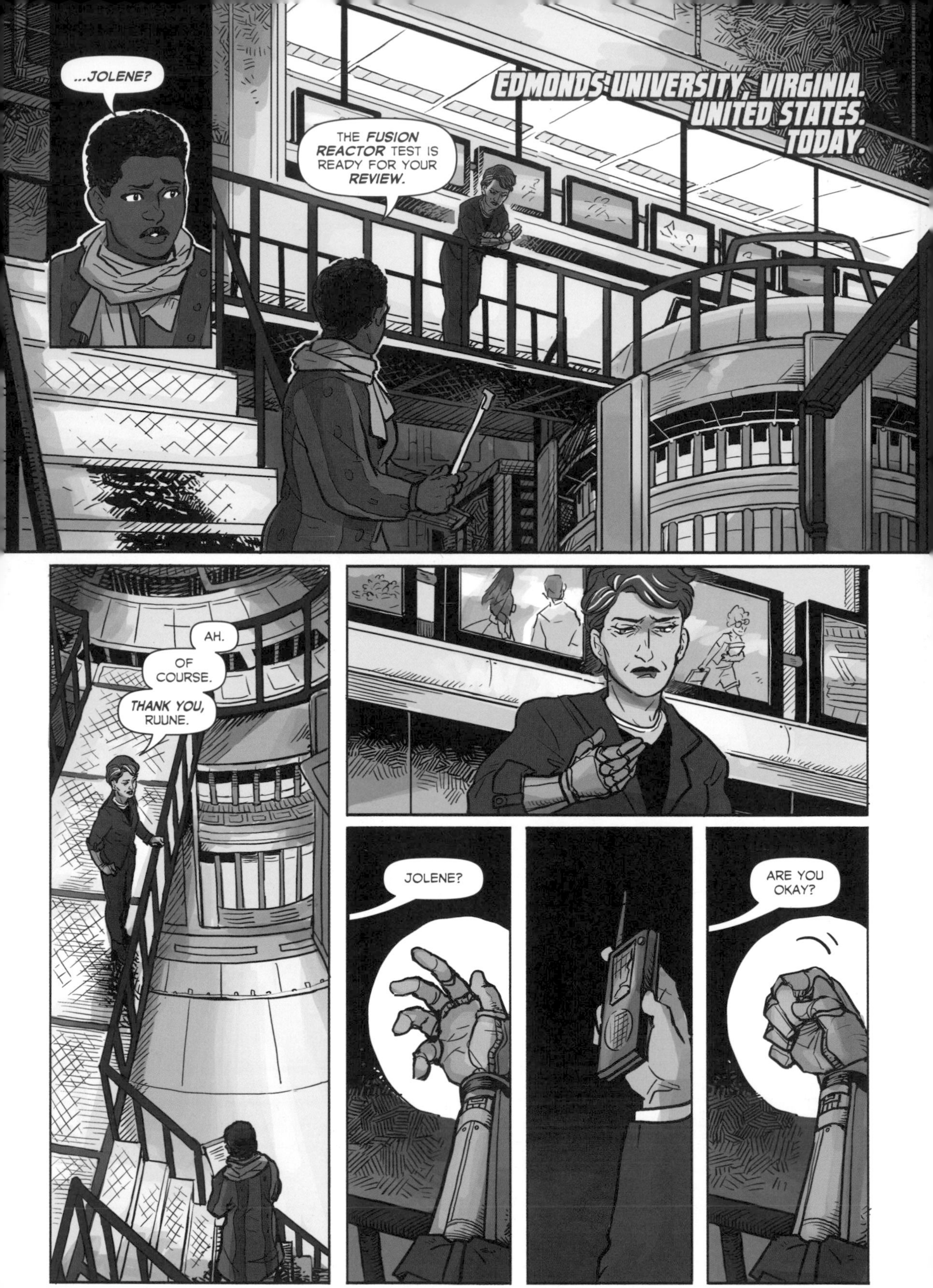

EDMONDS UNIVERSITY, VIRGINIA.
UNITED STATES.
TODAY.
...JOLENE?
THE FUSION REACTOR TEST IS READY FOR YOUR REVIEW.
AH.
OF COURSE.
THANK YOU, RUUNE.
JOLENE?
ARE YOU OKAY?

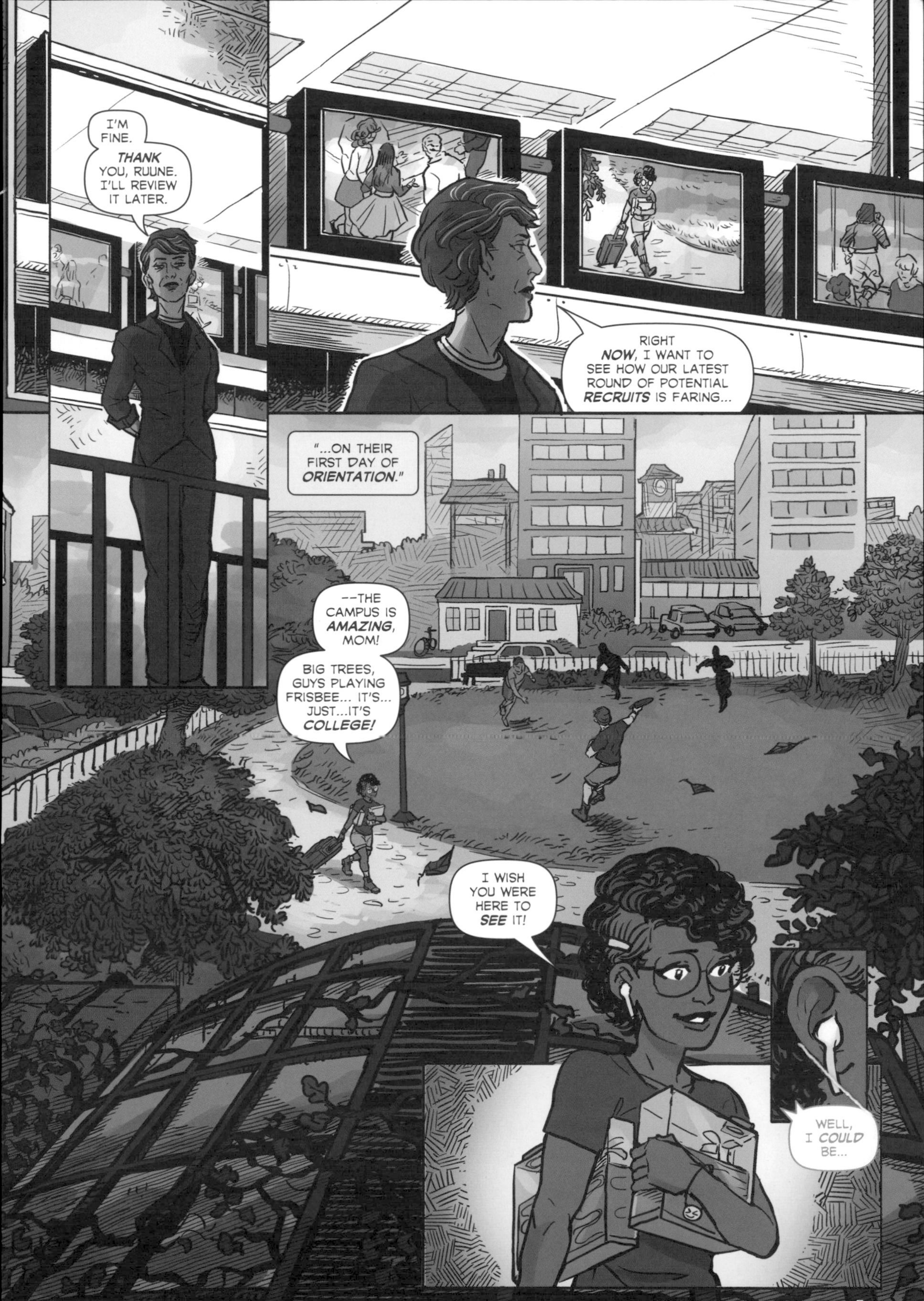
I'M FINE. THANK YOU, RUUNE. I'LL REVIEW IT LATER.
RIGHT NOW, I WANT TO SEE HOW OUR LATEST ROUND OF POTENTIAL RECRUITS IS FARING...
"...ON THEIR FIRST DAY OF ORIENTATION."
--THE CAMPUS IS AMAZING, MOM!
BIG TREES, GUYS PLAYING FRISBEE... IT'S... JUST...IT'S COLLEGE!
I WISH YOU WERE HERE TO SEE IT!
WELL, I COULD BE...

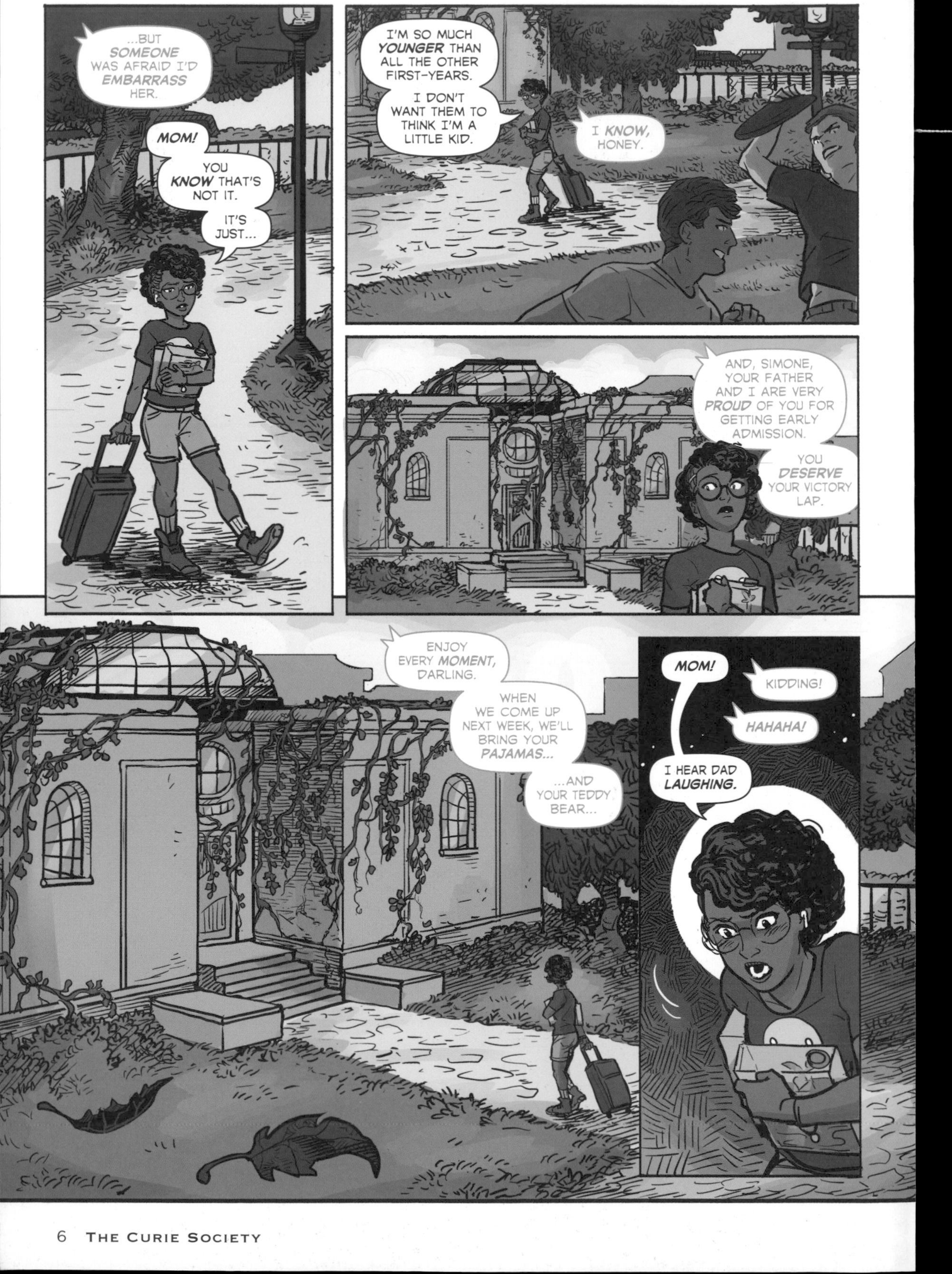
...BUT SOMEONE WAS AFRAID I'D EMBARRASS HER.
MOM!
YOU KNOW THAT'S NOT IT.
IT'S JUST...
I'M SO MUCH YOUNGER THAN ALL THE OTHER FIRST-YEARS.
I DON'T WANT THEM TO THINK I'M A LITTLE KID.
I KNOW, HONEY.
AND, SIMONE, YOUR FATHER AND I ARE VERY PROUD OF YOU FOR GETTING EARLY ADMISSION.
YOU DESERVE YOUR VICTORY LAP.
ENJOY EVERY MOMENT, DARLING.
WHEN WE COME UP NEXT WEEK, WE'LL BRING YOUR PAJAMAS...
...AND YOUR TEDDY BEAR...
MOM!
KIDDING!
HAHAHA!
I HEAR DAD LAUGHING.

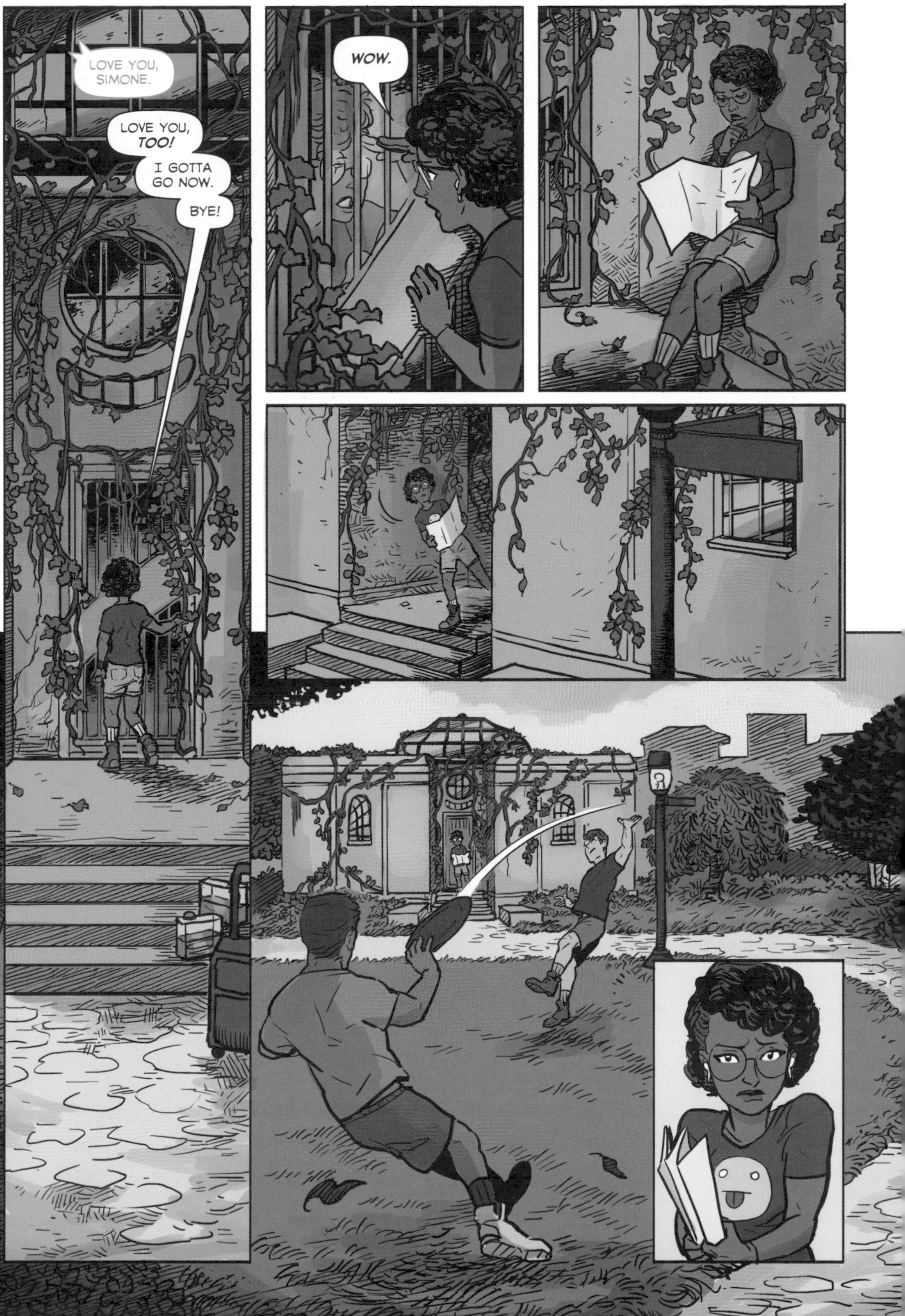
LOVE YOU, SIMONE.
LOVE YOU, TOO!
I GOTTA GO NOW.
BYE!
WOW.

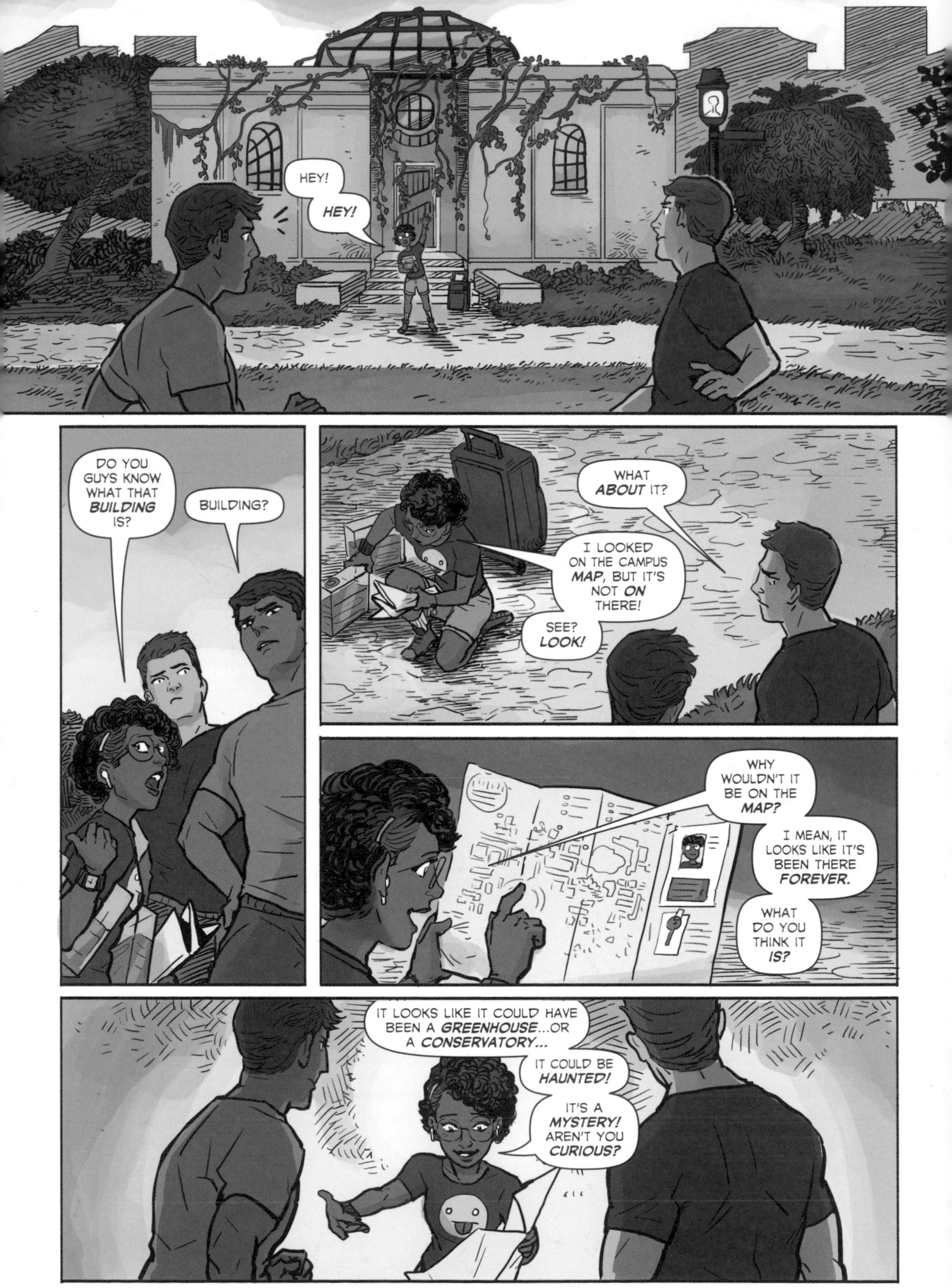

HEY!
HEY!
DO YOU GUYS KNOW WHAT THAT BUILDING IS?
BUILDING?
WHAT ABOUT IT?
I LOOKED ON THE CAMPUS MAP, BUT IT'S NOT ON THERE!
SEE? LOOK!
WHY WOULDN'T IT BE ON THE MAP?
I MEAN, IT LOOKS LIKE IT'S BEEN THERE FOREVER.
WHAT DO YOU THINK IT IS?
IT LOOKS LIKE IT COULD HAVE BEEN A GREENHOUSE...OR A CONSERVATORY...
IT COULD BE HAUNTED!
IT'S A MYSTERY! AREN'T YOU CURIOUS?

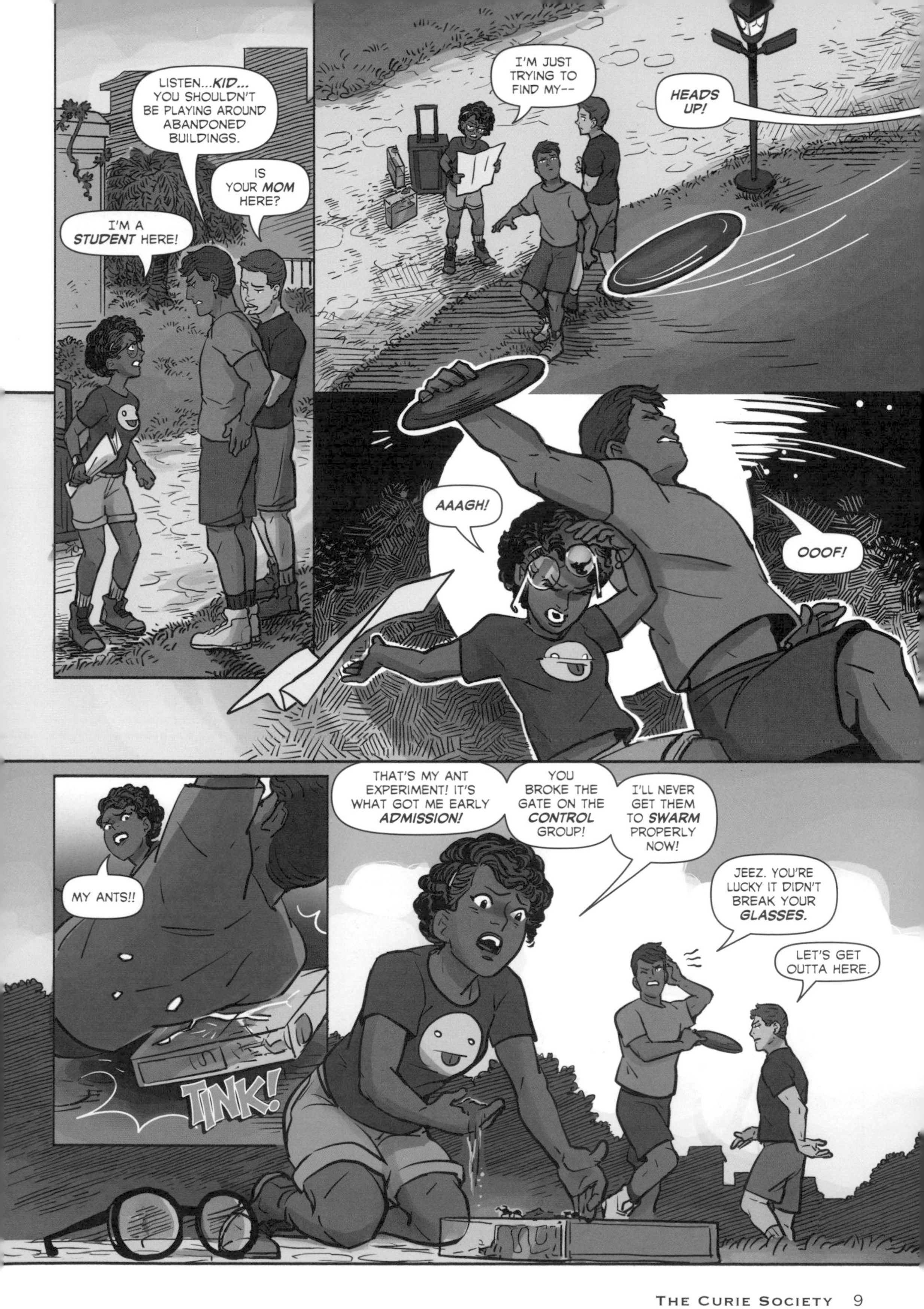
LISTEN...KID... YOU SHOULDN'T BE PLAYING AROUND ABANDONED BUILDINGS.
IS YOUR MOM HERE?
I'M A STUDENT HERE!
I'M JUST TRYING TO FIND MY--
HEADS UP!
AAAGH!
OOOF!
MY ANTS!!
TINK!
THAT'S MY ANT EXPERIMENT! IT'S WHAT GOT ME EARLY ADMISSION!
YOU BROKE THE GATE ON THE CONTROL GROUP!
I'LL NEVER GET THEM TO SWARM PROPERLY NOW!
JEEZ. YOU'RE LUCKY IT DIDN'T BREAK YOUR GLASSES.
LET'S GET OUTTA HERE.

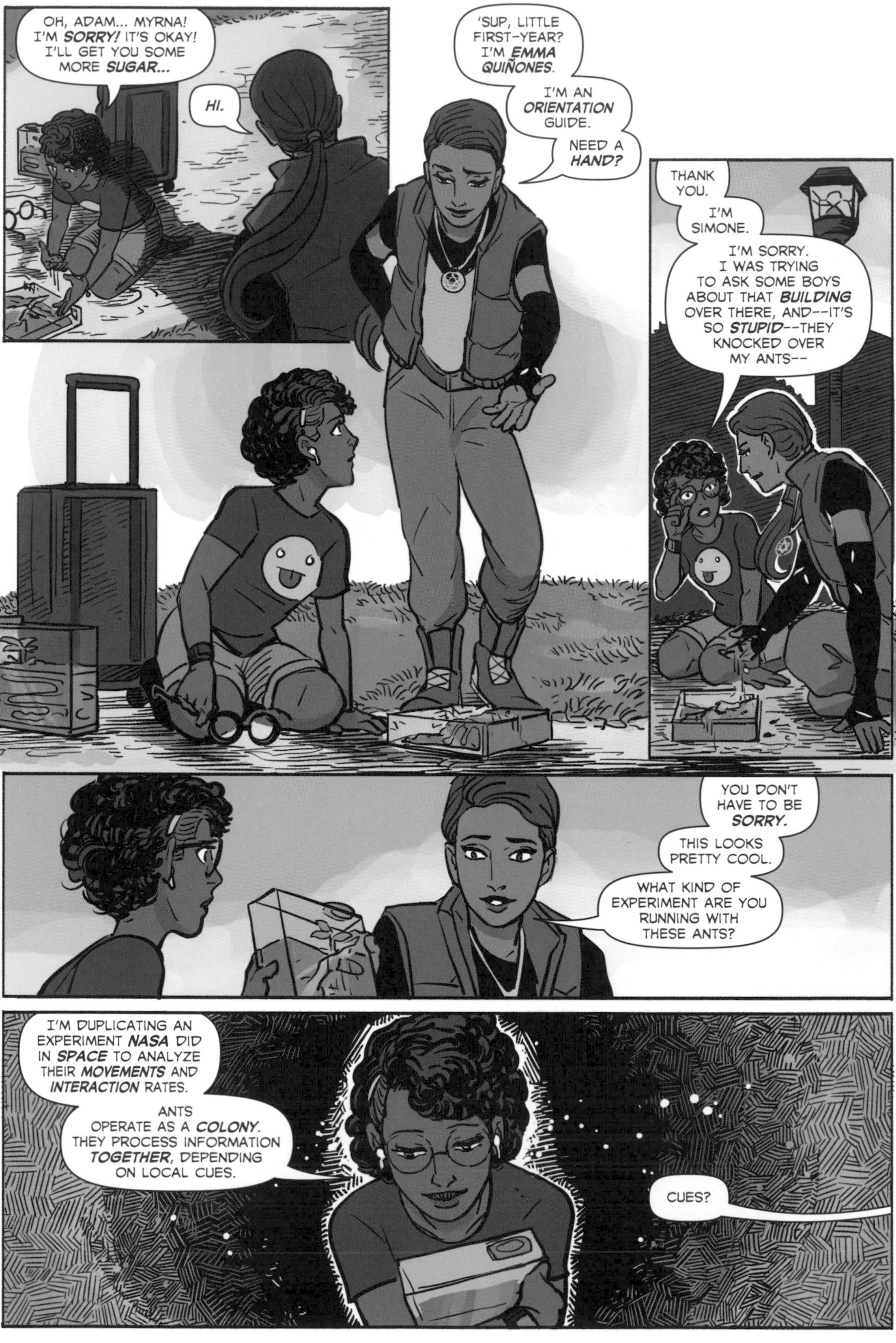
OH, ADAM... MYRNA! I'M SORRY! IT'S OKAY! I'LL GET YOU SOME MORE SUGAR...
HI.
'SUP, LITTLE FIRST-YEAR? I'M EMMA QUIÑONES.
I'M AN ORIENTATION GUIDE.
NEED A HAND?
THANK YOU.
I'M SIMONE.
I'M SORRY. I WAS TRYING TO ASK SOME BOYS ABOUT THAT BUILDING OVER THERE, AND--IT'S SO STUPID--THEY KNOCKED OVER MY ANTS--
YOU DON'T HAVE TO BE SORRY.
THIS LOOKS PRETTY COOL.
WHAT KIND OF EXPERIMENT ARE YOU RUNNING WITH THESE ANTS?
I'M DUPLICATING AN EXPERIMENT NASA DID IN SPACE TO ANALYZE THEIR MOVEMENTS AND INTERACTION RATES.
ANTS OPERATE AS A COLONY. THEY PROCESS INFORMATION TOGETHER, DEPENDING ON LOCAL CUES.
CUES?

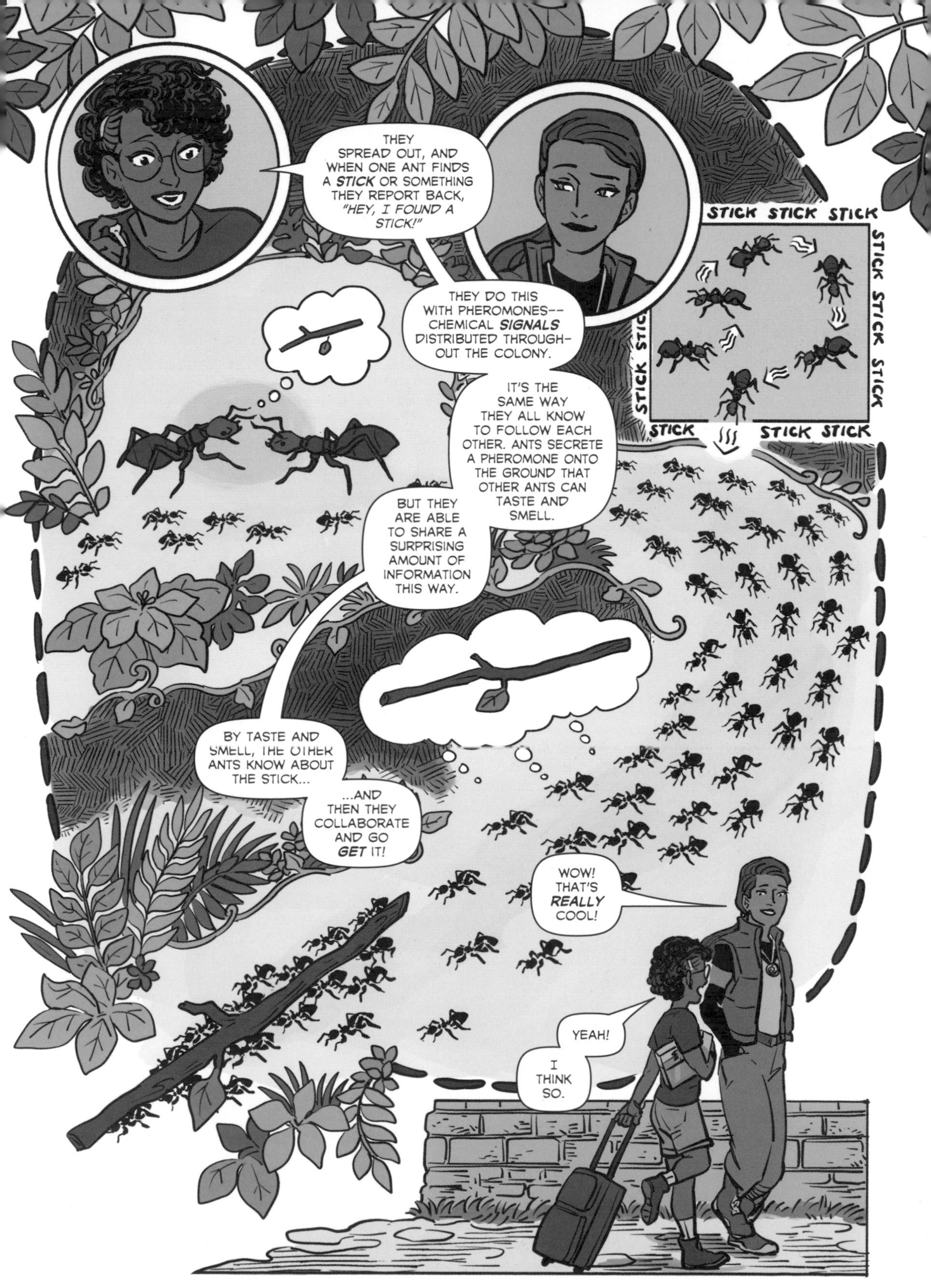
THEY SPREAD OUT, AND WHEN ONE ANT FINDS A STICK OR SOMETHING THEY REPORT BACK, "HEY, I FOUND A STICK!"
THEY DO THIS WITH PHEROMONES-- CHEMICAL SIGNALS DISTRIBUTED THROUGH-OUT THE COLONY.
STICK STICK STICK STICK STICK STICK STICK STICK STICK STICK STICK
IT'S THE SAME WAY THEY ALL KNOW TO FOLLOW EACH OTHER. ANTS SECRETE A PHEROMONE ONTO THE GROUND THAT OTHER ANTS CAN TASTE AND SMELL.
BUT THEY ARE ABLE TO SHARE A SURPRISING AMOUNT OF INFORMATION THIS WAY.
BY TASTE AND SMELL, THE OTHER ANTS KNOW ABOUT THE STICK...
...AND THEN THEY COLLABORATE AND GO GET IT!
WOW! THAT'S REALLY COOL!
YEAH!
I THINK SO.

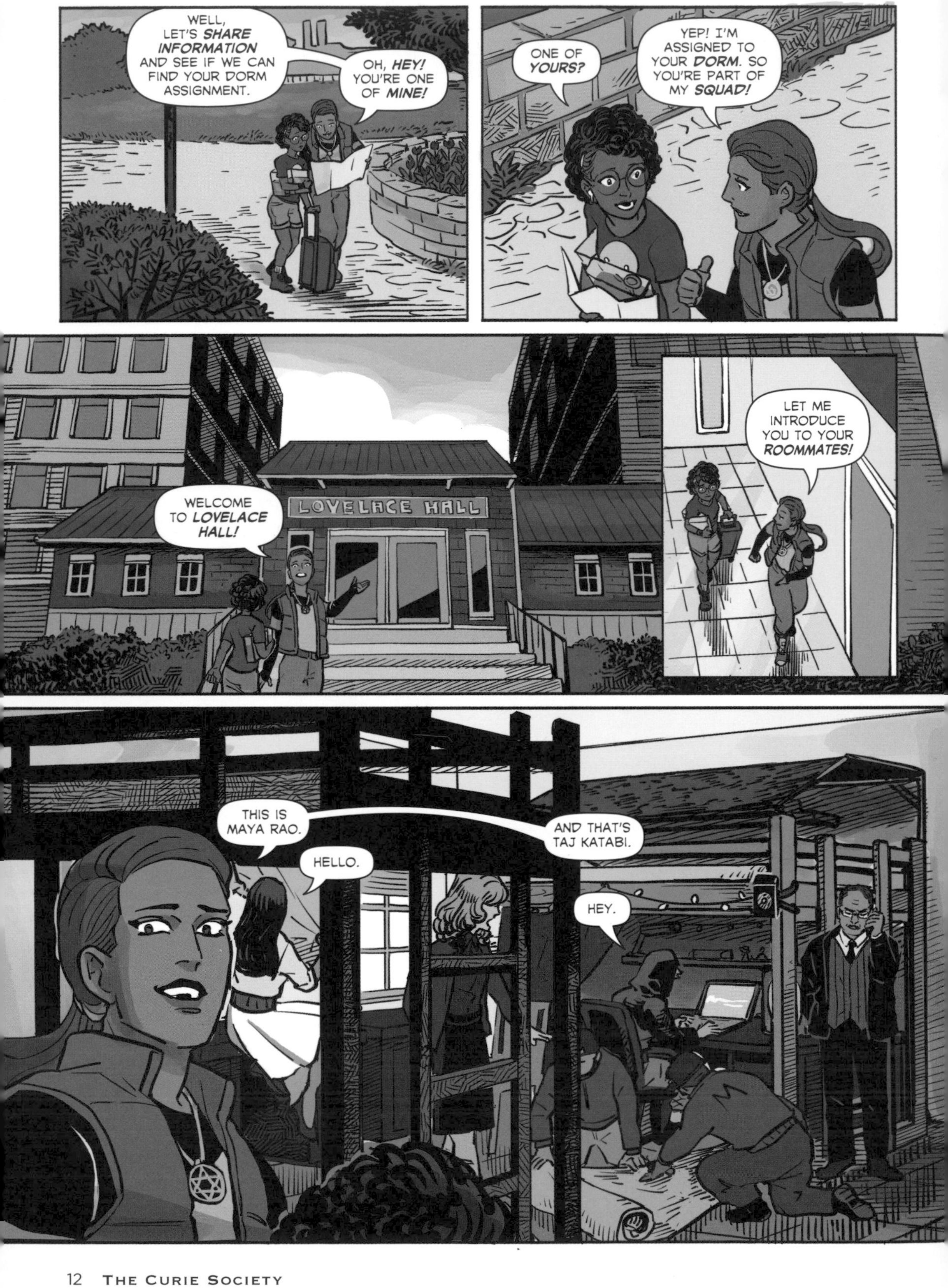
WELL, LET'S SHARE INFORMATION AND SEE IF WE CAN FIND YOUR DORM ASSIGNMENT.
OH, HEY! YOU'RE ONE OF MINE!
ONE OF YOURS?
YEP! I'M ASSIGNED TO YOUR DORM. SO YOU'RE PART OF MY SQUAD!
LOVELACE HALL
WELCOME TO LOVELACE HALL!
LET ME INTRODUCE YOU TO YOUR ROOMMATES!
THIS IS MAYA RAO.
AND THAT'S TAJ KATABI.
HELLO.
HEY.

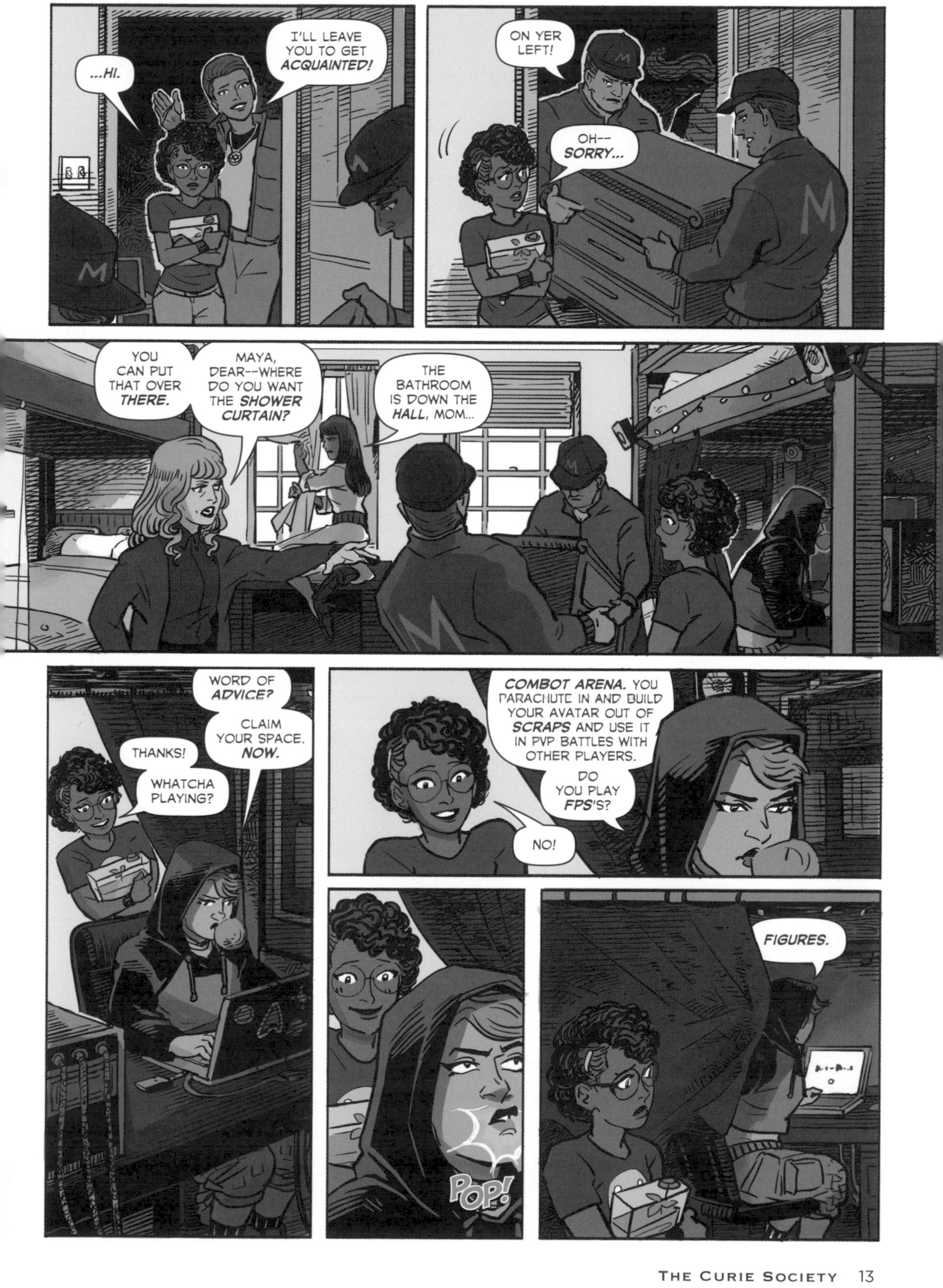
...HI.
I'LL LEAVE YOU TO GET ACQUAINTED!
ON YER LEFT!
OH-- SORRY...
YOU CAN PUT THAT OVER THERE.
MAYA, DEAR--WHERE DO YOU WANT THE SHOWER CURTAIN?
THE BATHROOM IS DOWN THE HALL, MOM...
WORD OF ADVICE?
CLAIM YOUR SPACE. NOW.
THANKS!
WHATCHA PLAYING?
COMBOT ARENA. YOU PARACHUTE IN AND BUILD YOUR AVATAR OUT OF SCRAPS AND USE IT IN PVP BATTLES WITH OTHER PLAYERS.
DO YOU PLAY FPS'S?
NO!
POP!
FIGURES.

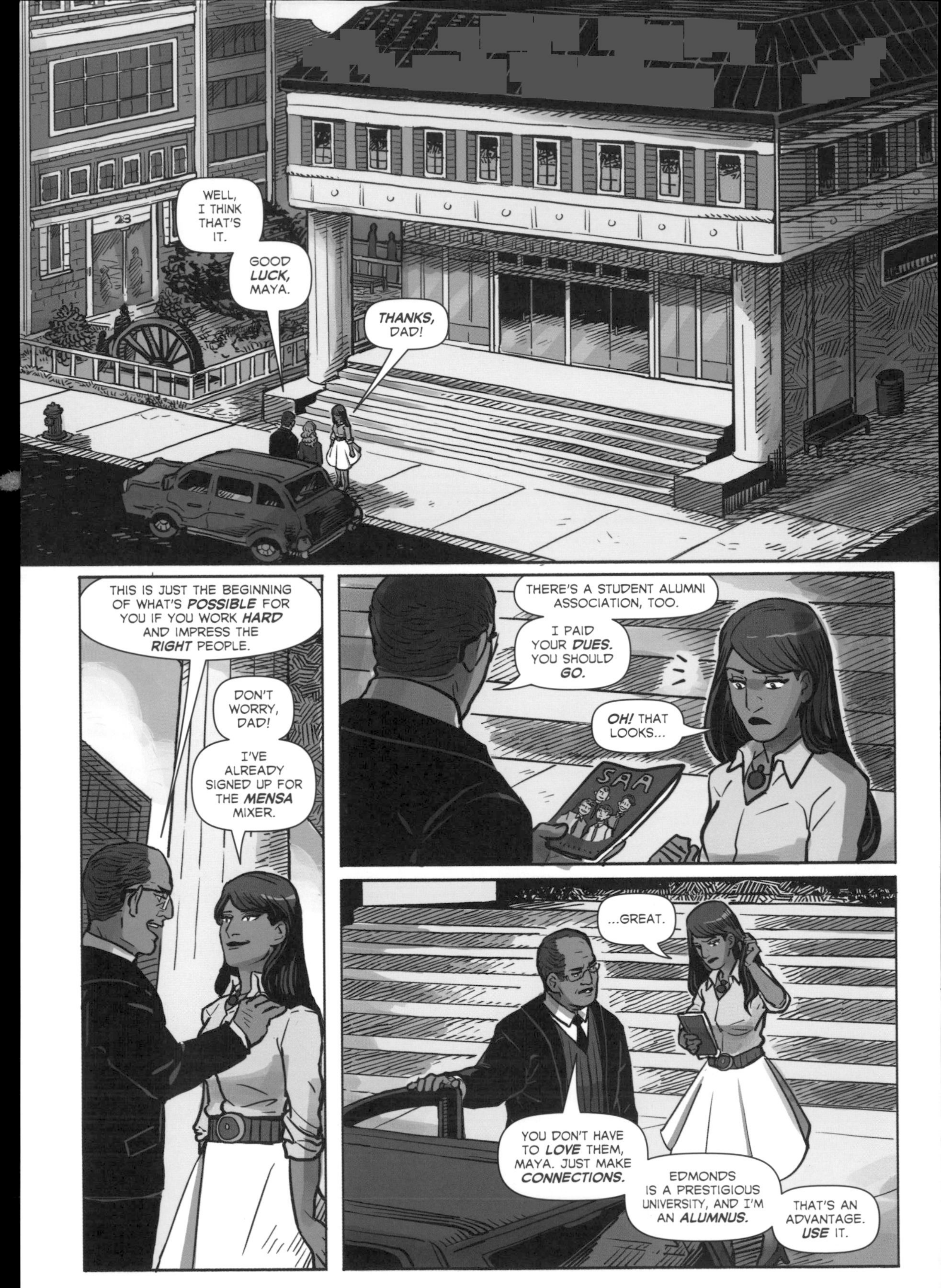
WELL, I THINK THAT'S IT.
GOOD *LUCK,* MAYA.
THANKS, DAD!
THIS IS JUST THE BEGINNING OF WHAT'S *POSSIBLE* FOR YOU IF YOU WORK *HARD* AND IMPRESS THE *RIGHT* PEOPLE.
DON'T WORRY, DAD!
I'VE ALREADY SIGNED UP FOR THE *MENSA* MIXER.
THERE'S A STUDENT ALUMNI ASSOCIATION, TOO.
I PAID YOUR *DUES.* YOU SHOULD *GO.*
OH! THAT LOOKS...
SAA
...GREAT.
YOU DON'T HAVE TO *LOVE* THEM, MAYA. JUST MAKE *CONNECTIONS.*
EDMONDS IS A PRESTIGIOUS UNIVERSITY, AND I'M AN *ALUMNUS.*
THAT'S AN ADVANTAGE. *USE* IT.

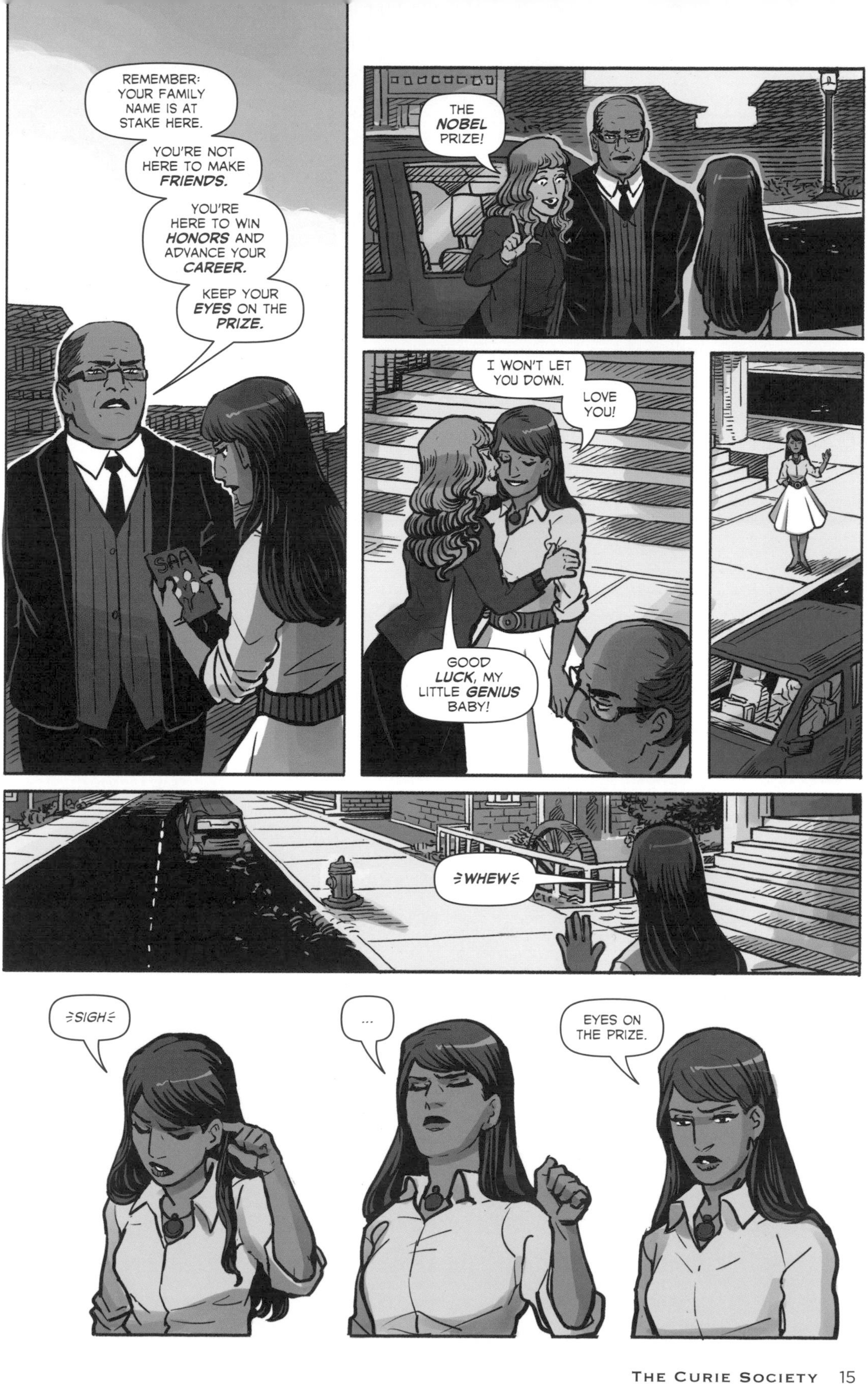
REMEMBER: YOUR FAMILY NAME IS AT STAKE HERE.
YOU'RE NOT HERE TO MAKE **FRIENDS.**
YOU'RE HERE TO WIN **HONORS** AND ADVANCE YOUR **CAREER.**
KEEP YOUR **EYES** ON THE **PRIZE.**
SAA
THE **NOBEL** PRIZE!
I WON'T LET YOU DOWN.
LOVE YOU!
GOOD **LUCK**, MY LITTLE **GENIUS** BABY!
WHEW
SIGH
...
EYES ON THE PRIZE.

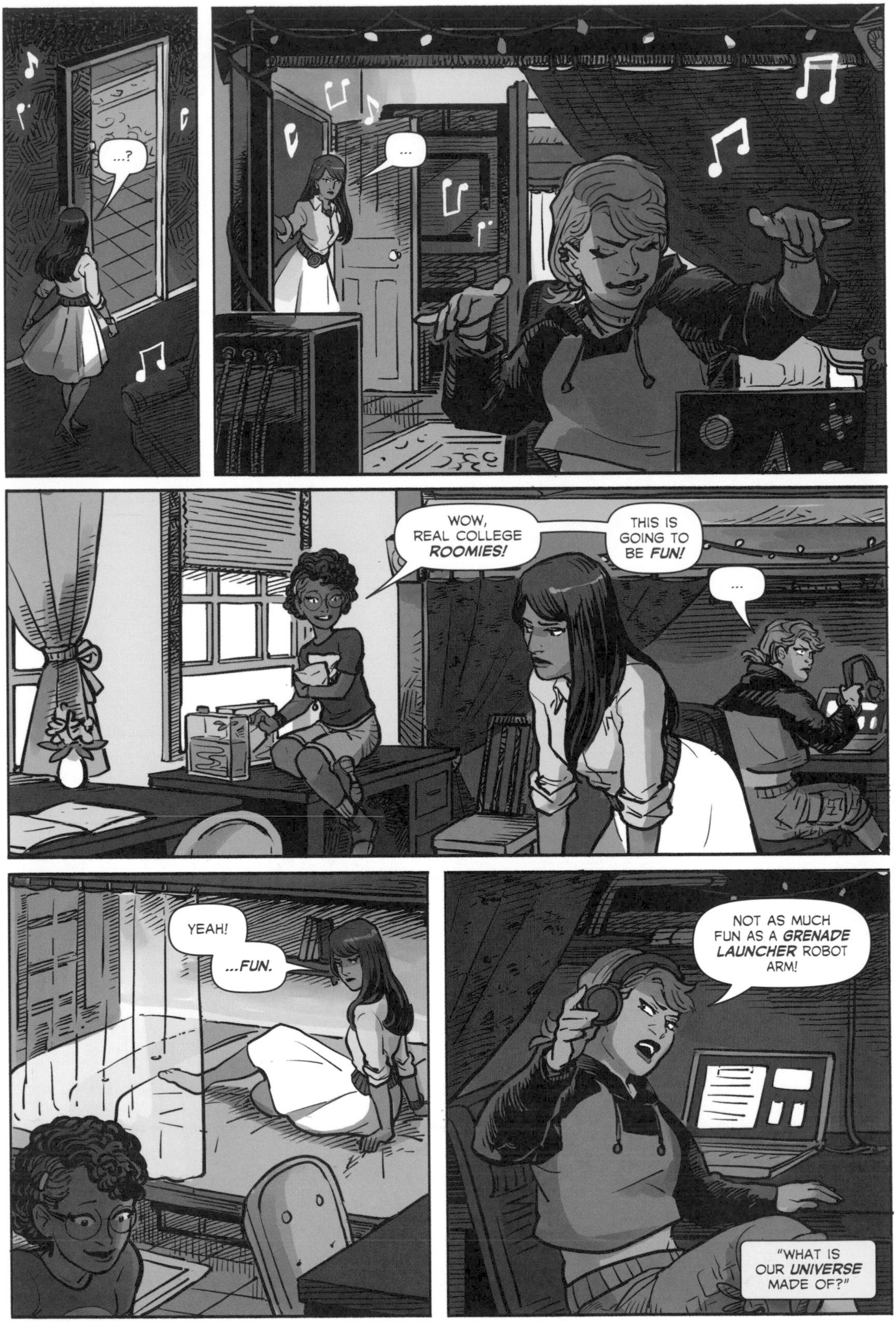
...?
...
WOW, REAL COLLEGE ROOMIES!
THIS IS GOING TO BE FUN!
...
YEAH!
...FUN.
NOT AS MUCH FUN AS A GRENADE LAUNCHER ROBOT ARM!
"WHAT IS OUR UNIVERSE MADE OF?"

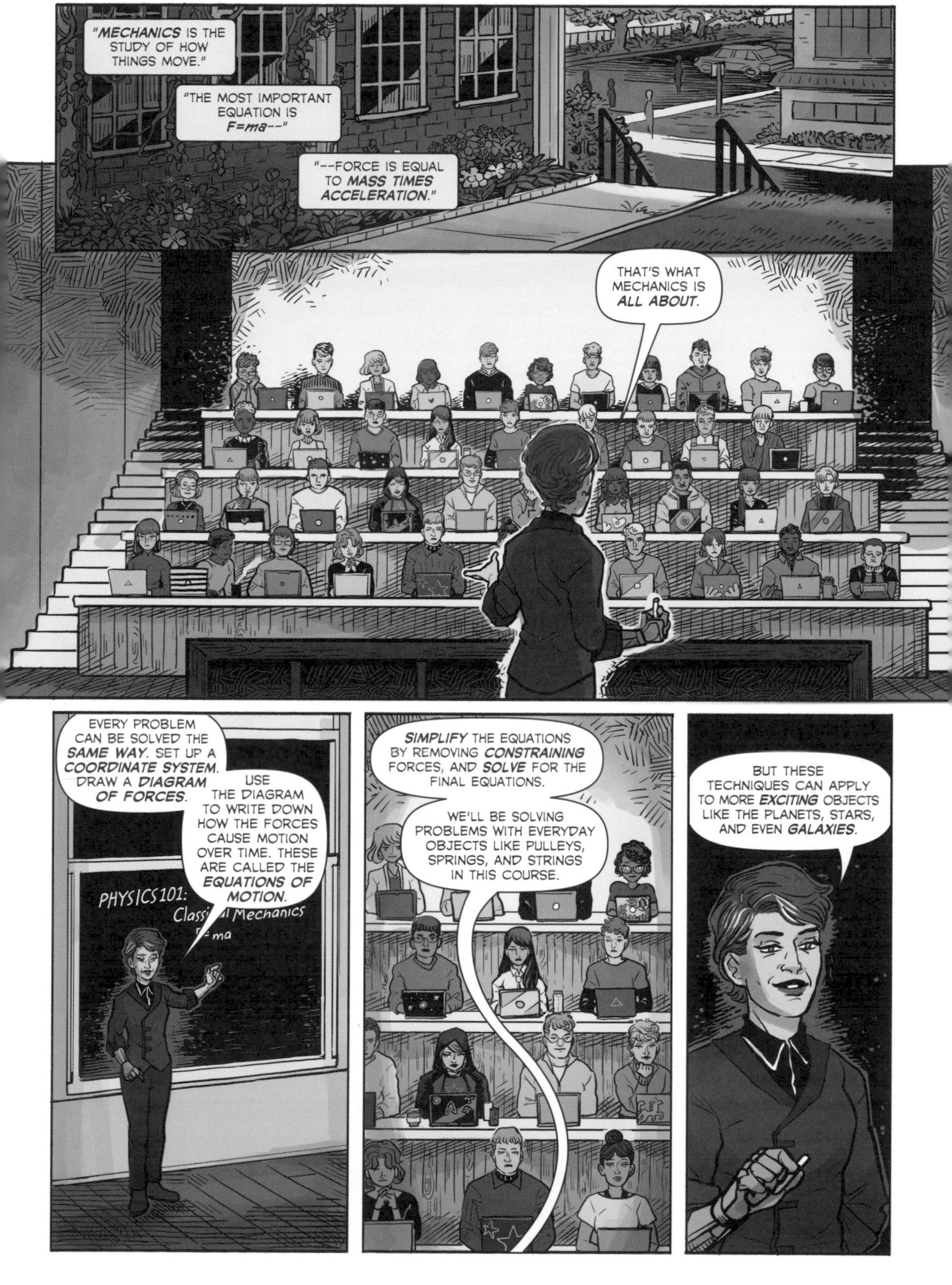
"MECHANICS IS THE STUDY OF HOW THINGS MOVE."
"THE MOST IMPORTANT EQUATION IS F=ma--"
"--FORCE IS EQUAL TO MASS TIMES ACCELERATION."
THAT'S WHAT MECHANICS IS ALL ABOUT.
EVERY PROBLEM CAN BE SOLVED THE SAME WAY. SET UP A COORDINATE SYSTEM. DRAW A DIAGRAM OF FORCES.
USE THE DIAGRAM TO WRITE DOWN HOW THE FORCES CAUSE MOTION OVER TIME. THESE ARE CALLED THE EQUATIONS OF MOTION.
PHYSICS 101:
ma
SIMPLIFY THE EQUATIONS BY REMOVING CONSTRAINING FORCES, AND SOLVE FOR THE FINAL EQUATIONS.
WE'LL BE SOLVING PROBLEMS WITH EVERYDAY OBJECTS LIKE PULLEYS, SPRINGS, AND STRINGS IN THIS COURSE.
BUT THESE TECHNIQUES CAN APPLY TO MORE EXCITING OBJECTS LIKE THE PLANETS, STARS, AND EVEN GALAXIES.

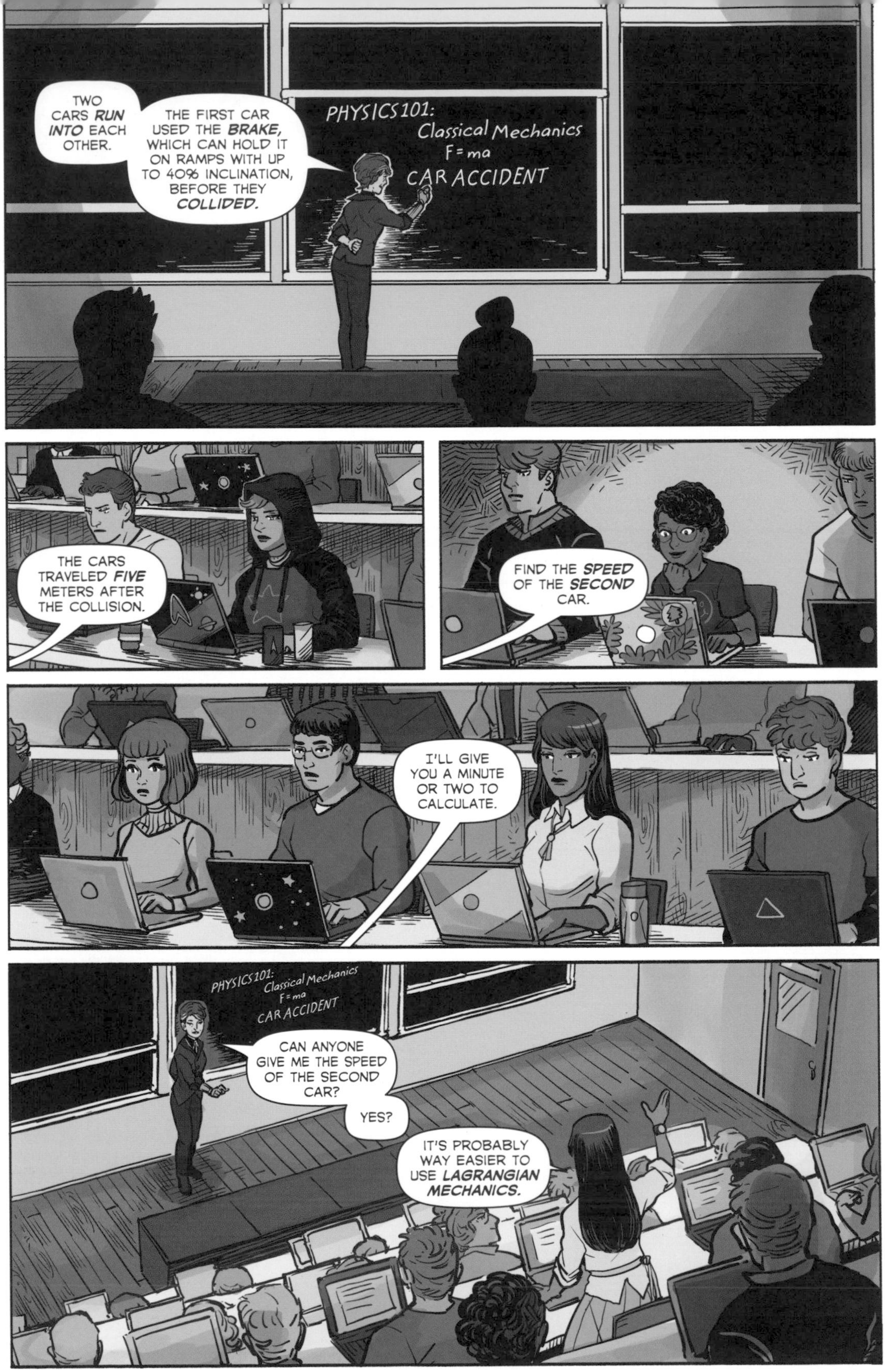
PHYSICS 101:
Classical Mechanics
F = ma
CAR ACCIDENT
TWO CARS **RUN INTO** EACH OTHER.
THE FIRST CAR USED THE **BRAKE,** WHICH CAN HOLD IT ON RAMPS WITH UP TO 40% INCLINATION, BEFORE THEY **COLLIDED.**
THE CARS TRAVELED **FIVE** METERS AFTER THE COLLISION.
FIND THE **SPEED** OF THE **SECOND** CAR.
I'LL GIVE YOU A MINUTE OR TWO TO CALCULATE.
PHYSICS 101:
Classical Mechanics
F = ma
CAR ACCIDENT
CAN ANYONE GIVE ME THE SPEED OF THE SECOND CAR?
YES?
IT'S PROBABLY WAY EASIER TO USE **LAGRANGIAN MECHANICS.**

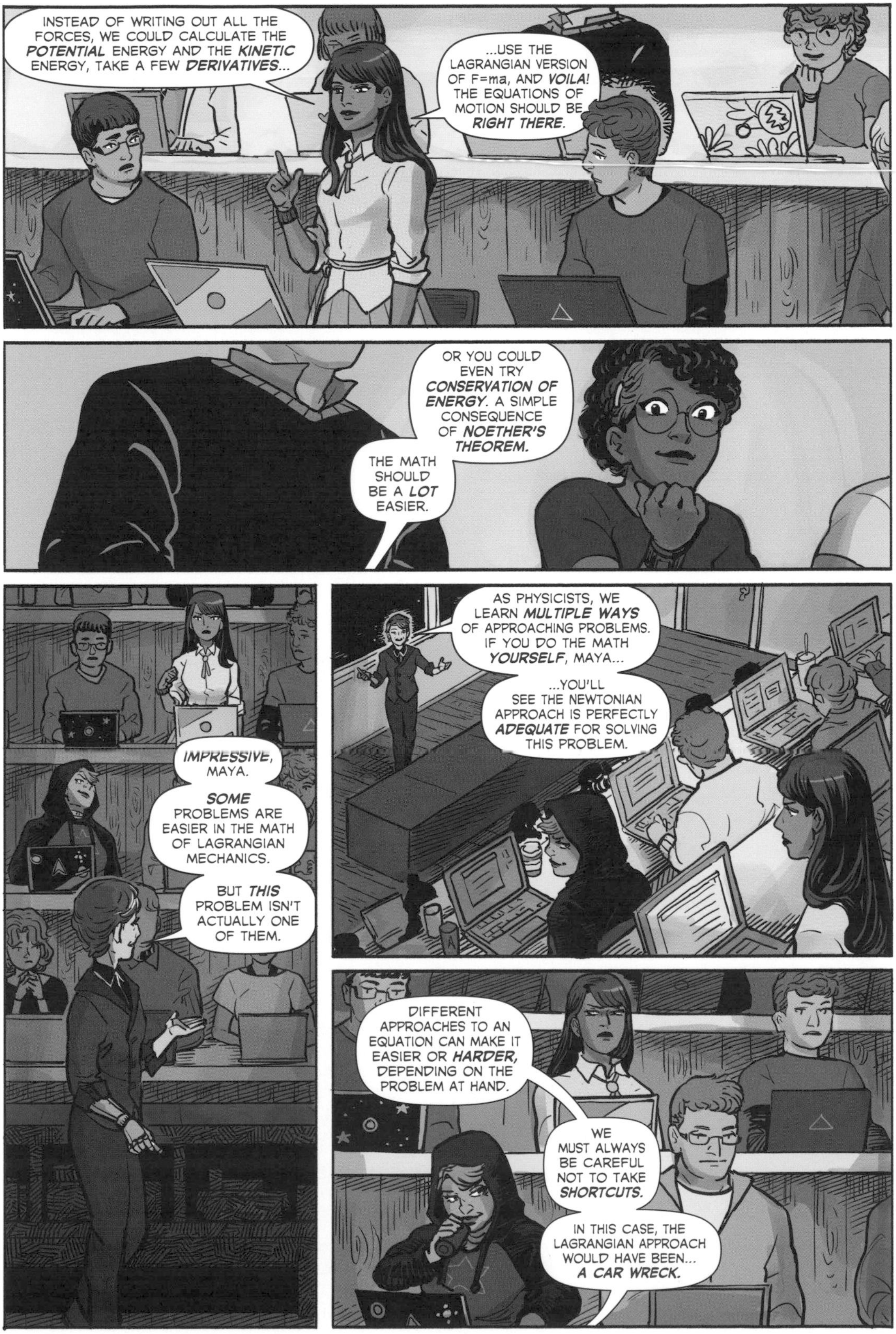
INSTEAD OF WRITING OUT ALL THE FORCES, WE COULD CALCULATE THE POTENTIAL ENERGY AND THE KINETIC ENERGY, TAKE A FEW DERIVATIVES...
...USE THE LAGRANGIAN VERSION OF F=ma, AND VOILA! THE EQUATIONS OF MOTION SHOULD BE RIGHT THERE.
OR YOU COULD EVEN TRY CONSERVATION OF ENERGY. A SIMPLE CONSEQUENCE OF NOETHER'S THEOREM.
THE MATH SHOULD BE A LOT EASIER.
IMPRESSIVE, MAYA.
SOME PROBLEMS ARE EASIER IN THE MATH OF LAGRANGIAN MECHANICS.
BUT THIS PROBLEM ISN'T ACTUALLY ONE OF THEM.
AS PHYSICISTS, WE LEARN MULTIPLE WAYS OF APPROACHING PROBLEMS. IF YOU DO THE MATH YOURSELF, MAYA...
...YOU'LL SEE THE NEWTONIAN APPROACH IS PERFECTLY ADEQUATE FOR SOLVING THIS PROBLEM.
DIFFERENT APPROACHES TO AN EQUATION CAN MAKE IT EASIER OR HARDER, DEPENDING ON THE PROBLEM AT HAND.
WE MUST ALWAYS BE CAREFUL NOT TO TAKE SHORTCUTS.
IN THIS CASE, THE LAGRANGIAN APPROACH WOULD HAVE BEEN... A CAR WRECK.

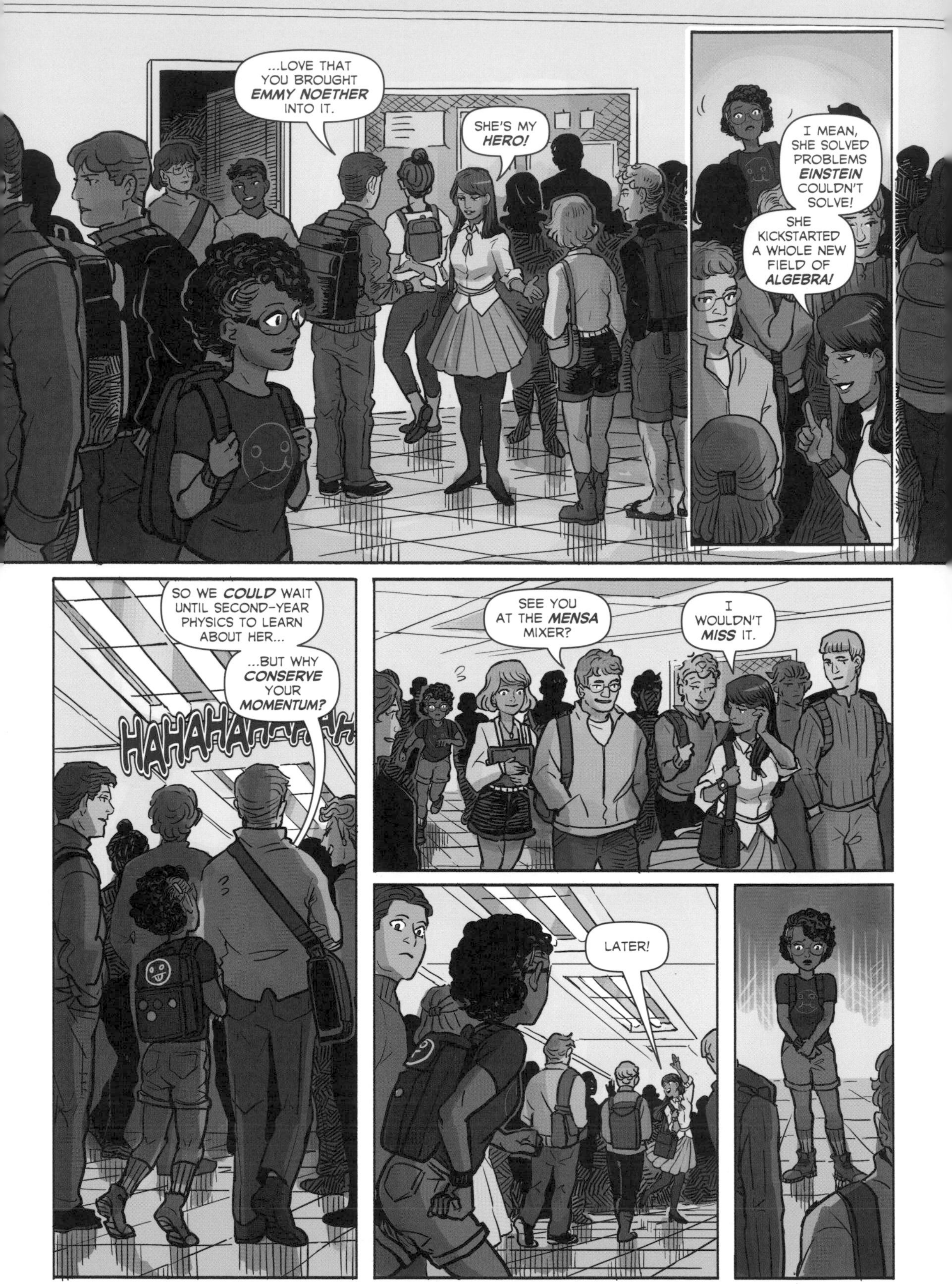

...LOVE THAT YOU BROUGHT **EMMY NOETHER** INTO IT.
SHE'S MY **HERO!**
I MEAN, SHE SOLVED PROBLEMS **EINSTEIN** COULDN'T SOLVE!
SHE KICKSTARTED A WHOLE NEW FIELD OF **ALGEBRA!**
SO WE **COULD** WAIT UNTIL SECOND-YEAR PHYSICS TO LEARN ABOUT HER...
...BUT WHY **CONSERVE** YOUR **MOMENTUM?**
HAHAHAHAHAH
SEE YOU AT THE **MENSA** MIXER?
I WOULDN'T **MISS** IT.
LATER!

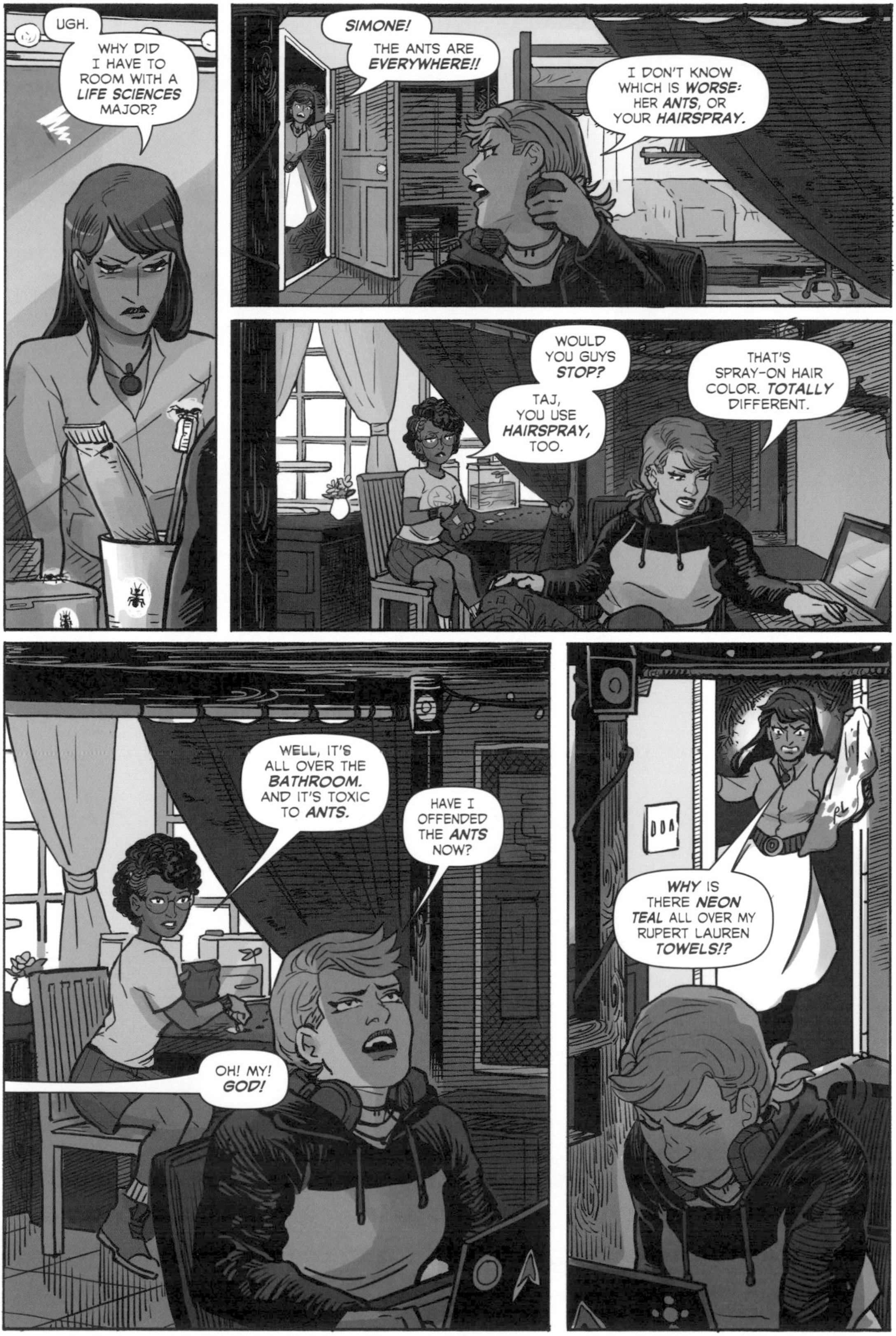
UGH.
WHY DID I HAVE TO ROOM WITH A *LIFE SCIENCES* MAJOR?
SIMONE!
THE ANTS ARE *EVERYWHERE!!*
I DON'T KNOW WHICH IS *WORSE:* HER *ANTS*, OR YOUR *HAIRSPRAY.*
WOULD YOU GUYS *STOP?*
TAJ, YOU USE *HAIRSPRAY,* TOO.
THAT'S SPRAY-ON HAIR COLOR. *TOTALLY* DIFFERENT.
WELL, IT'S ALL OVER THE *BATHROOM.* AND IT'S TOXIC TO *ANTS.*
HAVE I OFFENDED THE *ANTS* NOW?
OH! MY! *GOD!*
WHY IS THERE *NEON TEAL* ALL OVER MY RUPERT LAUREN *TOWELS!?*

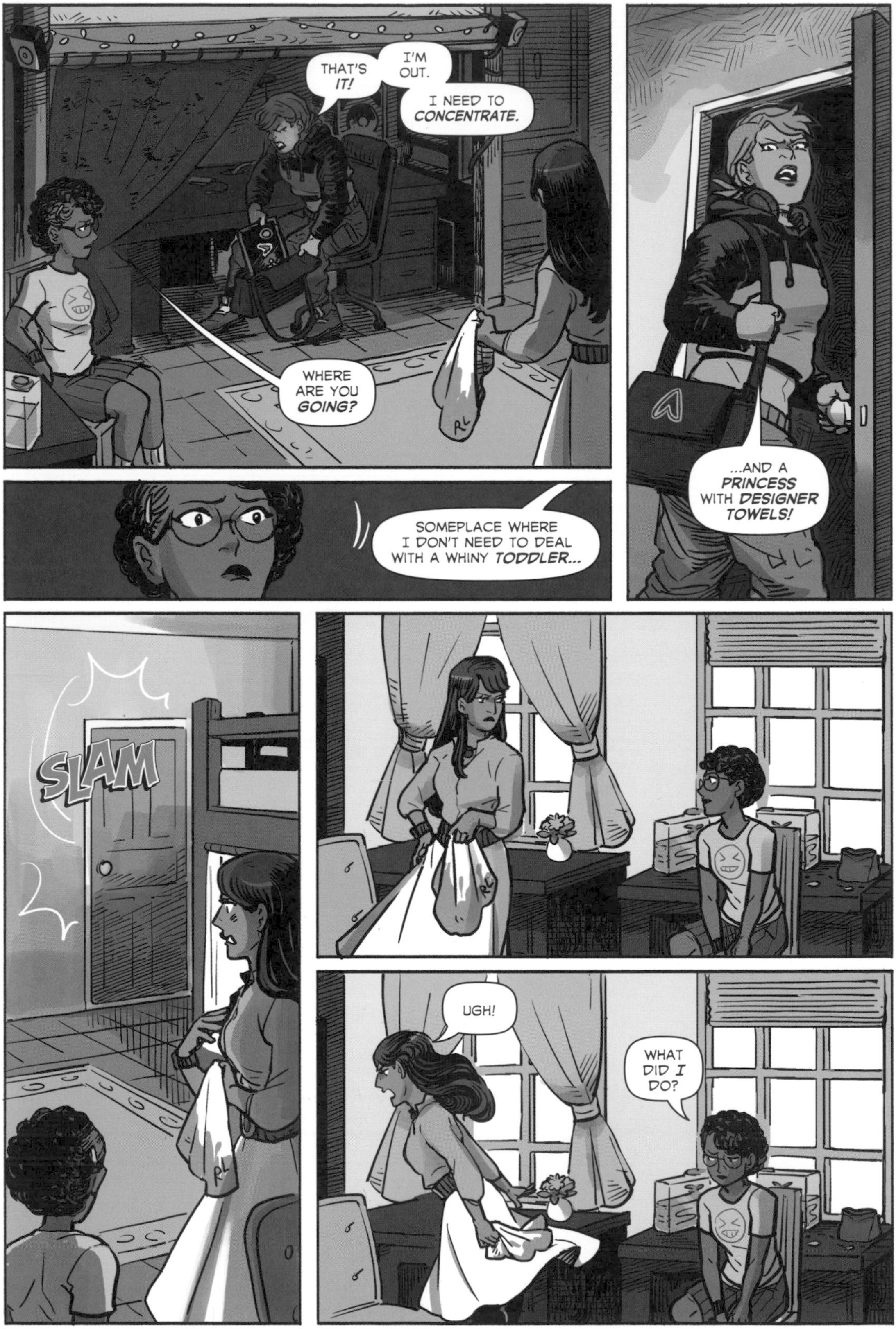
THAT'S *IT!*
I'M OUT.
I NEED TO *CONCENTRATE.*
WHERE ARE YOU *GOING?*
SOMEPLACE WHERE I DON'T NEED TO DEAL WITH A WHINY *TODDLER...*
...AND A *PRINCESS* WITH *DESIGNER TOWELS!*
SLAM
UGH!
WHAT DID *I* DO?

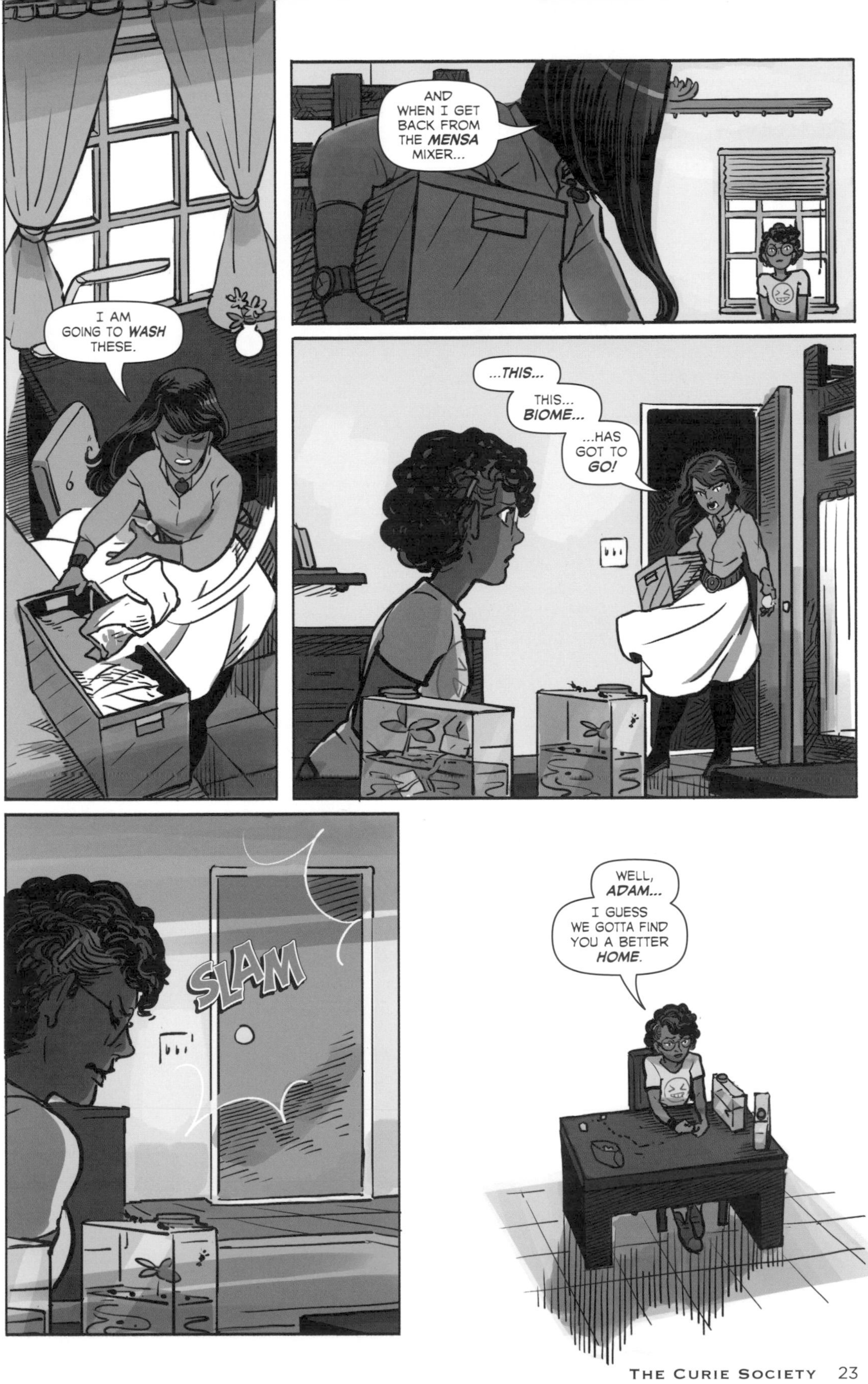
I AM GOING TO *WASH* THESE.
AND WHEN I GET BACK FROM THE *MENSA* MIXER...
...*THIS*...
THIS... *BIOME*...
...HAS GOT TO *GO!*
SLAM
WELL, *ADAM*...
I GUESS WE GOTTA FIND YOU A BETTER *HOME*.

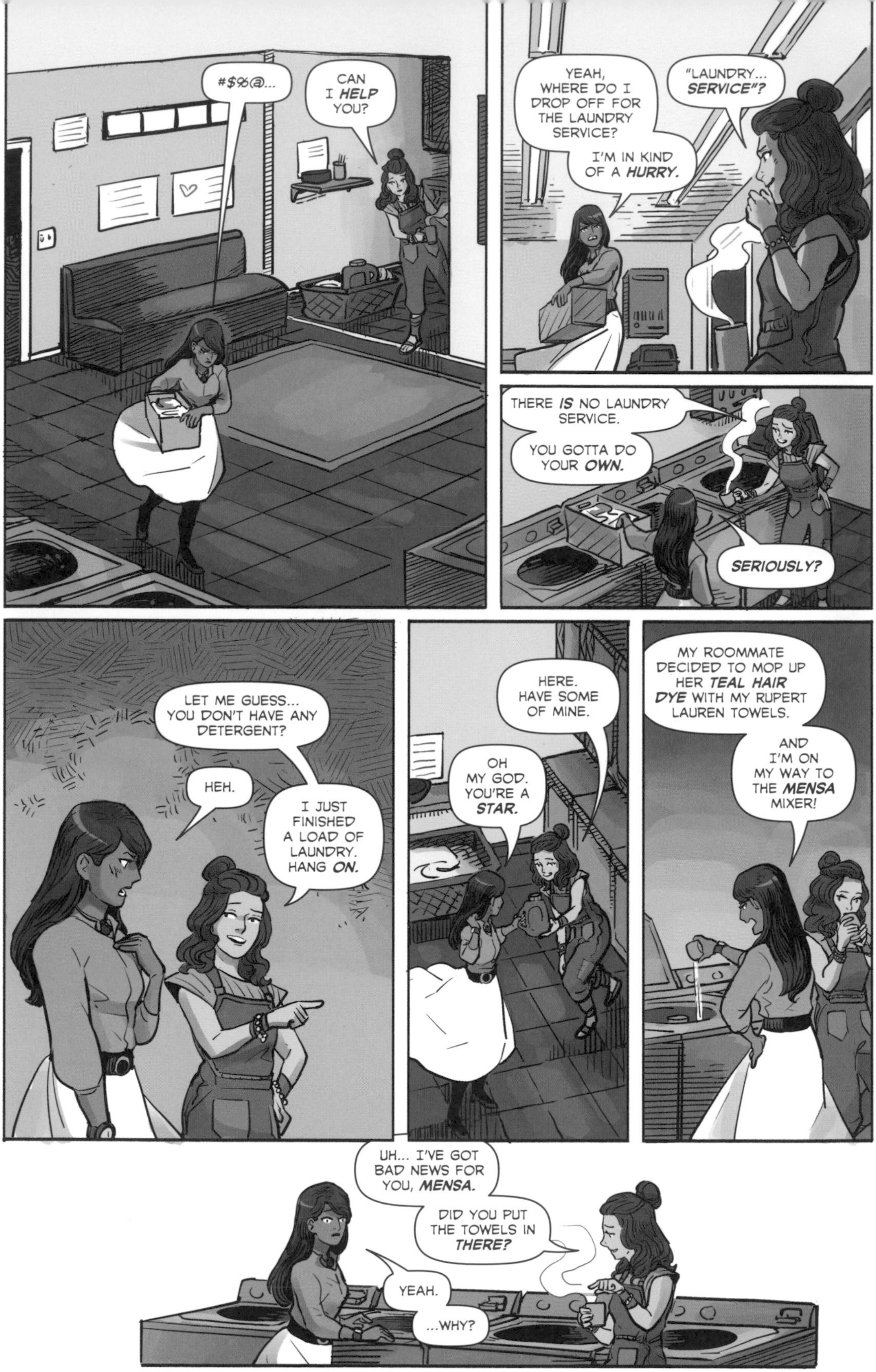

#$%@...
CAN I HELP YOU?
YEAH, WHERE DO I DROP OFF FOR THE LAUNDRY SERVICE?
I'M IN KIND OF A HURRY.
"LAUNDRY... SERVICE"?
THERE IS NO LAUNDRY SERVICE.
YOU GOTTA DO YOUR OWN.
SERIOUSLY?
LET ME GUESS... YOU DON'T HAVE ANY DETERGENT?
HEH.
I JUST FINISHED A LOAD OF LAUNDRY. HANG ON.
HERE. HAVE SOME OF MINE.
OH MY GOD. YOU'RE A STAR.
MY ROOMMATE DECIDED TO MOP UP HER TEAL HAIR DYE WITH MY RUPERT LAUREN TOWELS.
AND I'M ON MY WAY TO THE MENSA MIXER!
UH... I'VE GOT BAD NEWS FOR YOU, MENSA.
DID YOU PUT THE TOWELS IN THERE?
YEAH.
...WHY?

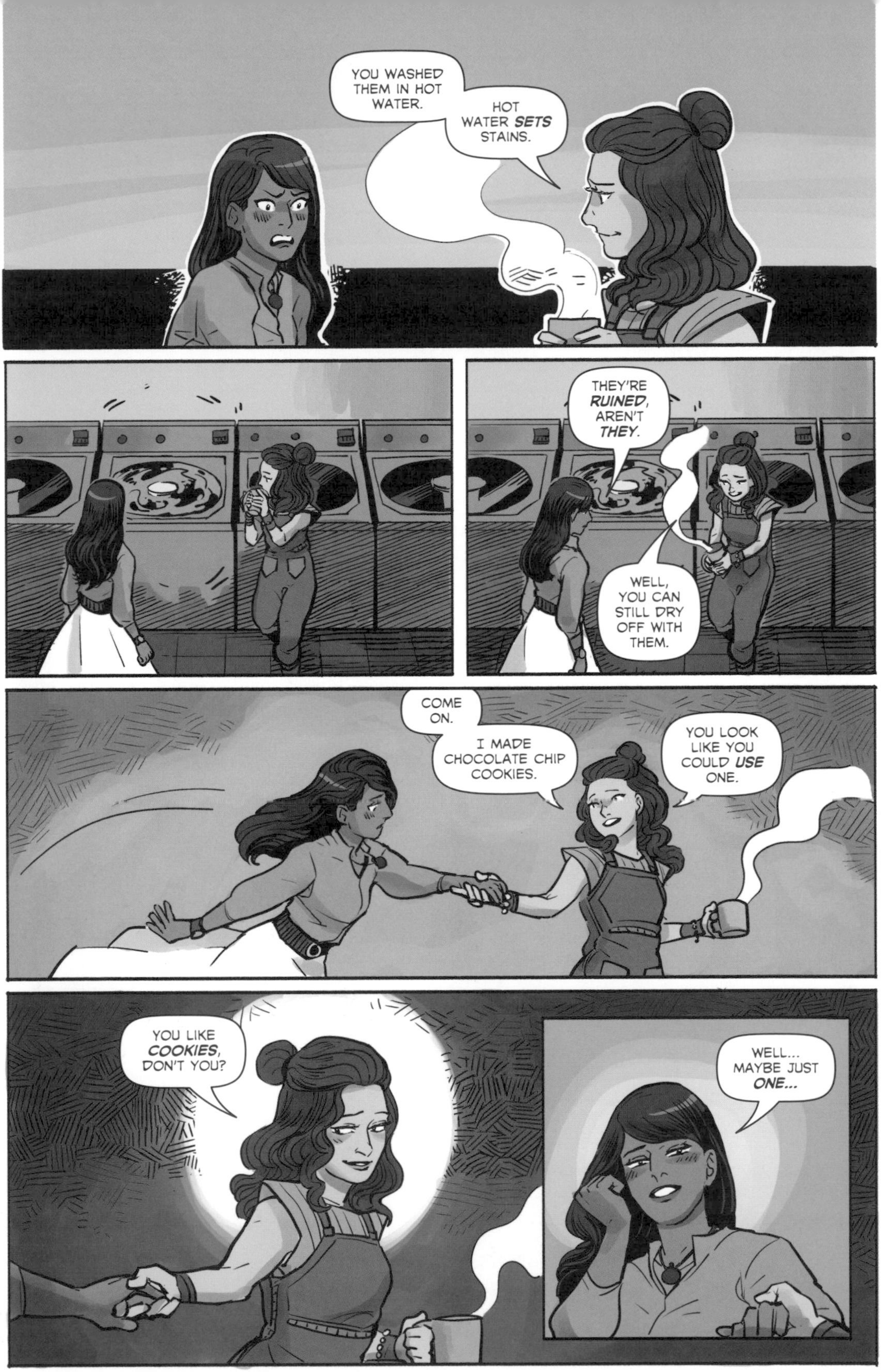
YOU WASHED THEM IN HOT WATER.
HOT WATER *SETS* STAINS.
THEY'RE *RUINED*, AREN'T *THEY*.
WELL, YOU CAN STILL DRY OFF WITH THEM.
COME ON.
I MADE CHOCOLATE CHIP COOKIES.
YOU LOOK LIKE YOU COULD *USE* ONE.
YOU LIKE *COOKIES*, DON'T YOU?
WELL... MAYBE JUST *ONE...*

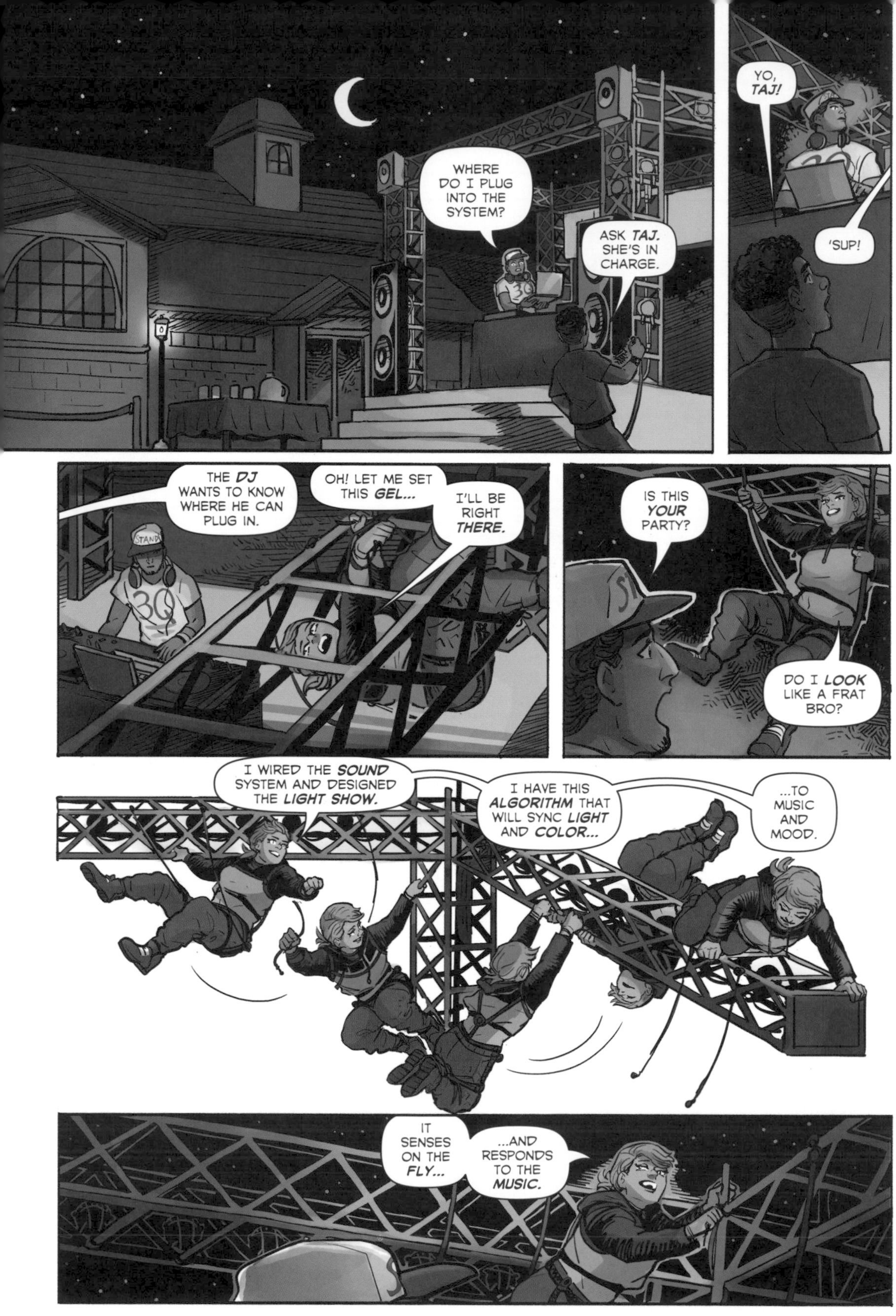
WHERE DO I PLUG INTO THE SYSTEM?
ASK TAJ. SHE'S IN CHARGE.
YO, TAJ!
'SUP!
THE DJ WANTS TO KNOW WHERE HE CAN PLUG IN.
OH! LET ME SET THIS GEL...
I'LL BE RIGHT THERE.
IS THIS YOUR PARTY?
DO I LOOK LIKE A FRAT BRO?
I WIRED THE SOUND SYSTEM AND DESIGNED THE LIGHT SHOW.
I HAVE THIS ALGORITHM THAT WILL SYNC LIGHT AND COLOR...
...TO MUSIC AND MOOD.
IT SENSES ON THE FLY...
...AND RESPONDS TO THE MUSIC.

HANG ON A SEC--

GOTTA GET THIS ONE--

BE CAREFUL!

DON'T WORRY. I USED TO *TAG BRIDGES* IN DETROIT.

COMPARED TO *THAT?*

CHUNK

HMMMNNMMMMMMMMNNMMMM

THIS IS *EASY.*

FIRE.

STAND

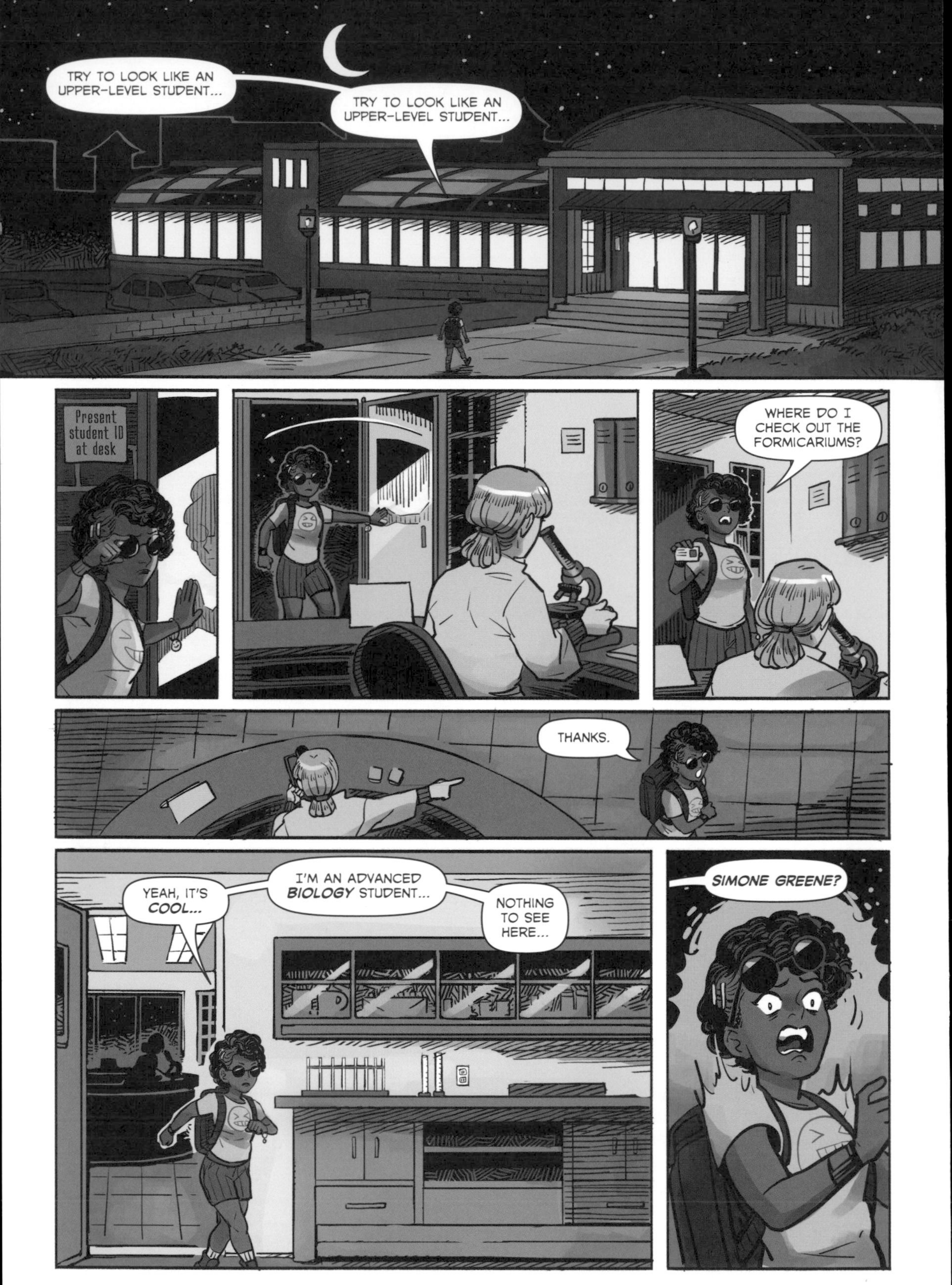

TRY TO LOOK LIKE AN UPPER-LEVEL STUDENT...
TRY TO LOOK LIKE AN UPPER-LEVEL STUDENT...
Present student ID at desk
WHERE DO I CHECK OUT THE FORMICARIUMS?
THANKS.
YEAH, IT'S *COOL...*
I'M AN ADVANCED *BIOLOGY* STUDENT...
NOTHING TO SEE HERE...
SIMONE GREENE?

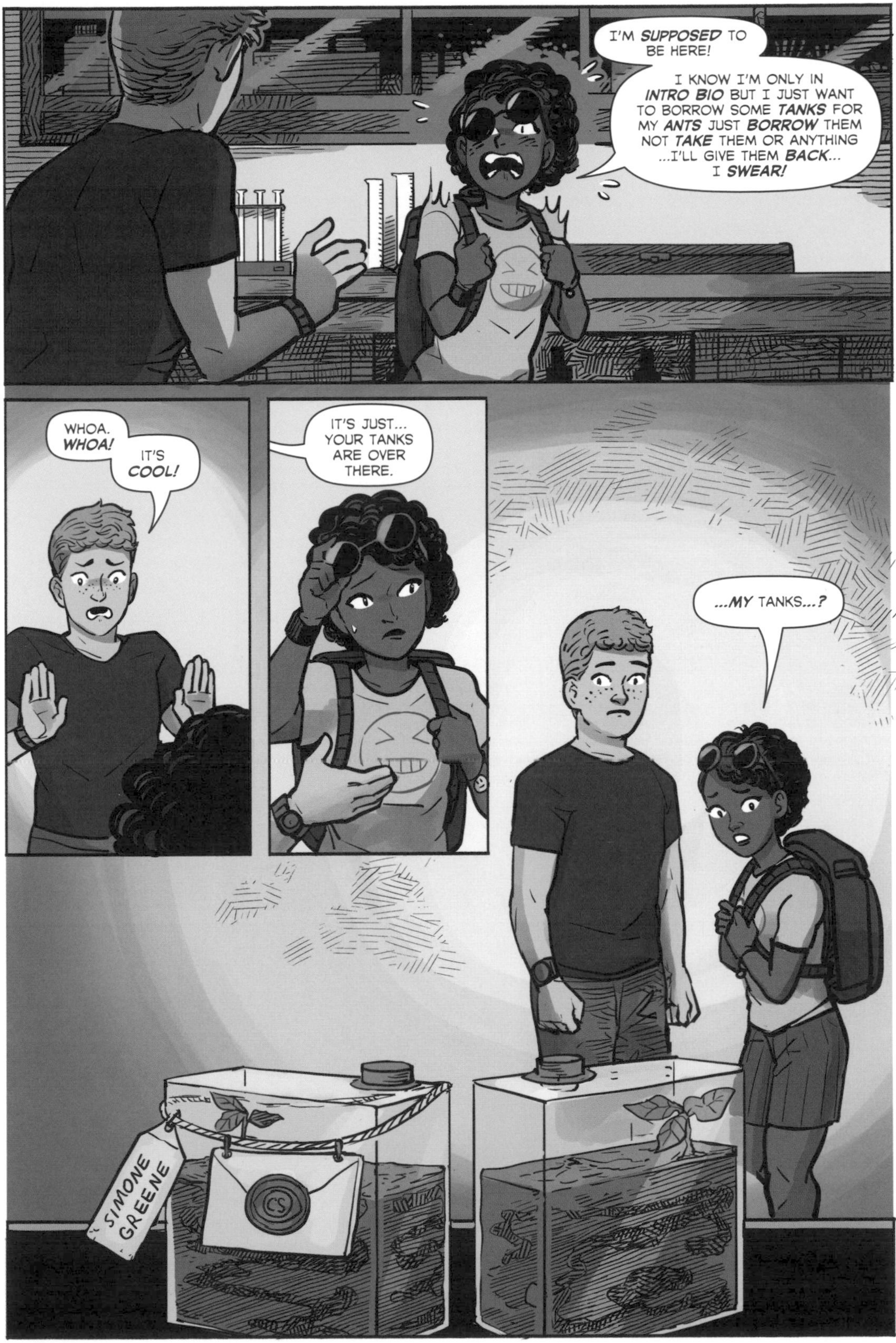
I'M SUPPOSED TO BE HERE!
I KNOW I'M ONLY IN INTRO BIO BUT I JUST WANT TO BORROW SOME TANKS FOR MY ANTS JUST BORROW THEM NOT TAKE THEM OR ANYTHING ...I'LL GIVE THEM BACK... I SWEAR!
WHOA. WHOA!
IT'S COOL!
IT'S JUST... YOUR TANKS ARE OVER THERE.
...MY TANKS...?
SIMONE GREENE
CS

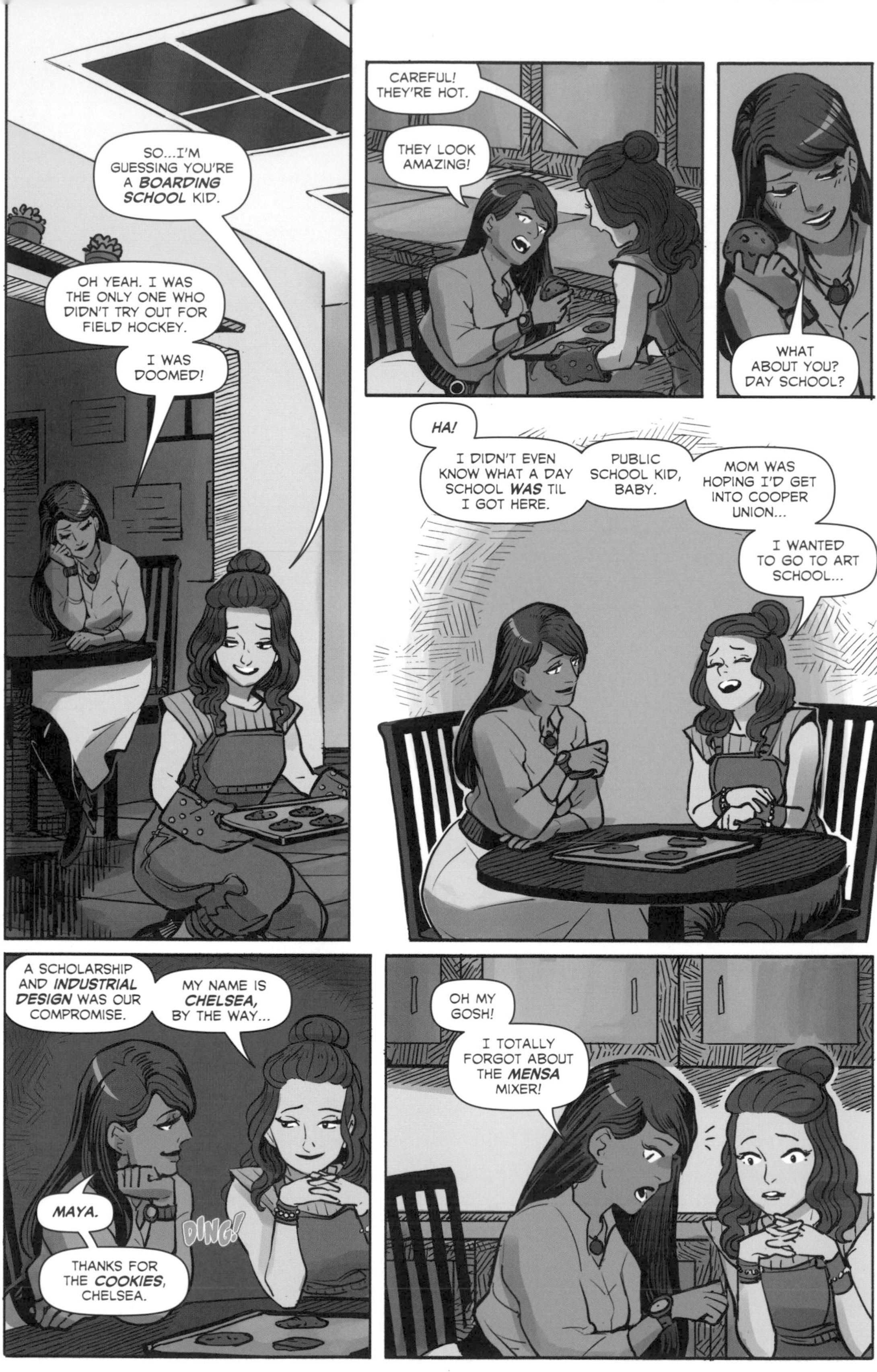
SO...I'M GUESSING YOU'RE A BOARDING SCHOOL KID.
OH YEAH. I WAS THE ONLY ONE WHO DIDN'T TRY OUT FOR FIELD HOCKEY.
I WAS DOOMED!
CAREFUL! THEY'RE HOT.
THEY LOOK AMAZING!
WHAT ABOUT YOU? DAY SCHOOL?
HA!
I DIDN'T EVEN KNOW WHAT A DAY SCHOOL WAS TIL I GOT HERE.
PUBLIC SCHOOL KID, BABY.
MOM WAS HOPING I'D GET INTO COOPER UNION...
I WANTED TO GO TO ART SCHOOL...
A SCHOLARSHIP AND INDUSTRIAL DESIGN WAS OUR COMPROMISE.
MY NAME IS CHELSEA, BY THE WAY...
MAYA.
DING!
THANKS FOR THE COOKIES, CHELSEA.
OH MY GOSH!
I TOTALLY FORGOT ABOUT THE MENSA MIXER!

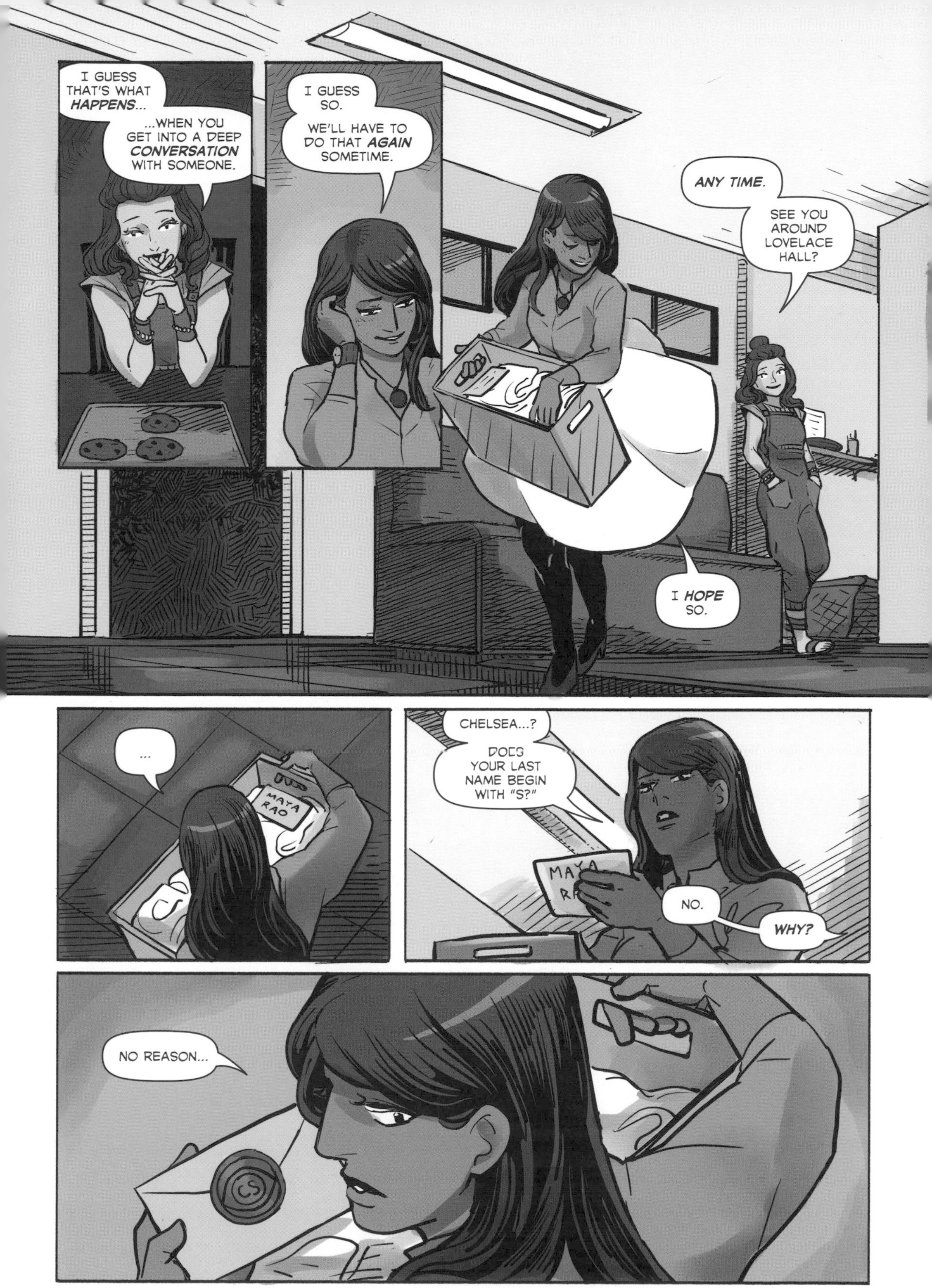
I GUESS THAT'S WHAT **HAPPENS**...
...WHEN YOU GET INTO A DEEP **CONVERSATION** WITH SOMEONE.
I GUESS SO.
WE'LL HAVE TO DO THAT **AGAIN** SOMETIME.
ANY TIME.
SEE YOU AROUND LOVELACE HALL?
I **HOPE** SO.
...
MAYA RAO
CHELSEA...?
DOES YOUR LAST NAME BEGIN WITH "S?"
MAYA RA
NO.
WHY?
NO REASON...
CS

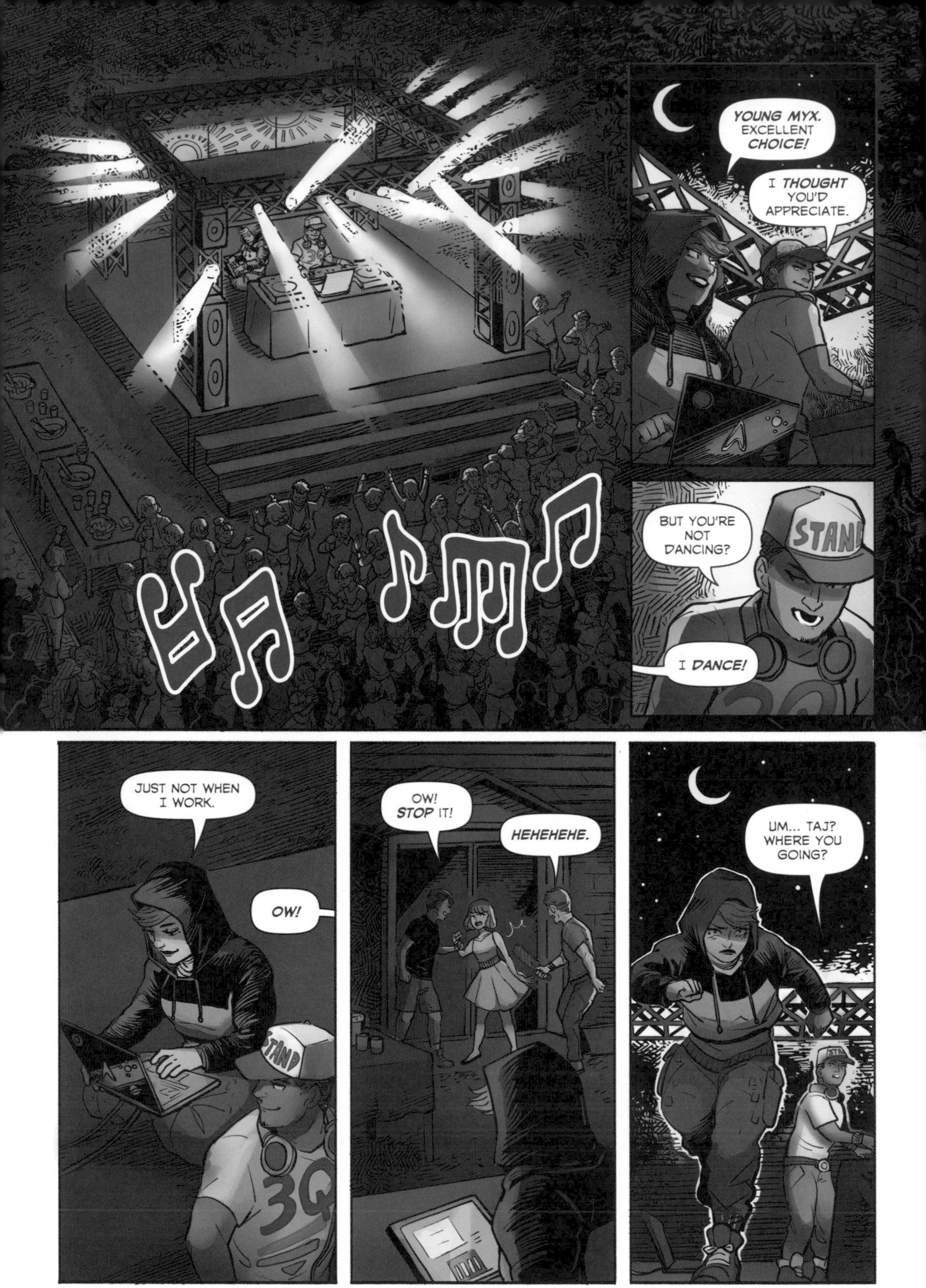
YOUNG MYX. EXCELLENT CHOICE!
I THOUGHT YOU'D APPRECIATE.
STAND
BUT YOU'RE NOT DANCING?
I DANCE!
JUST NOT WHEN I WORK.
OW!
STAND
3Q
OW! STOP IT!
HEHEHEHE.
UM... TAJ? WHERE YOU GOING?

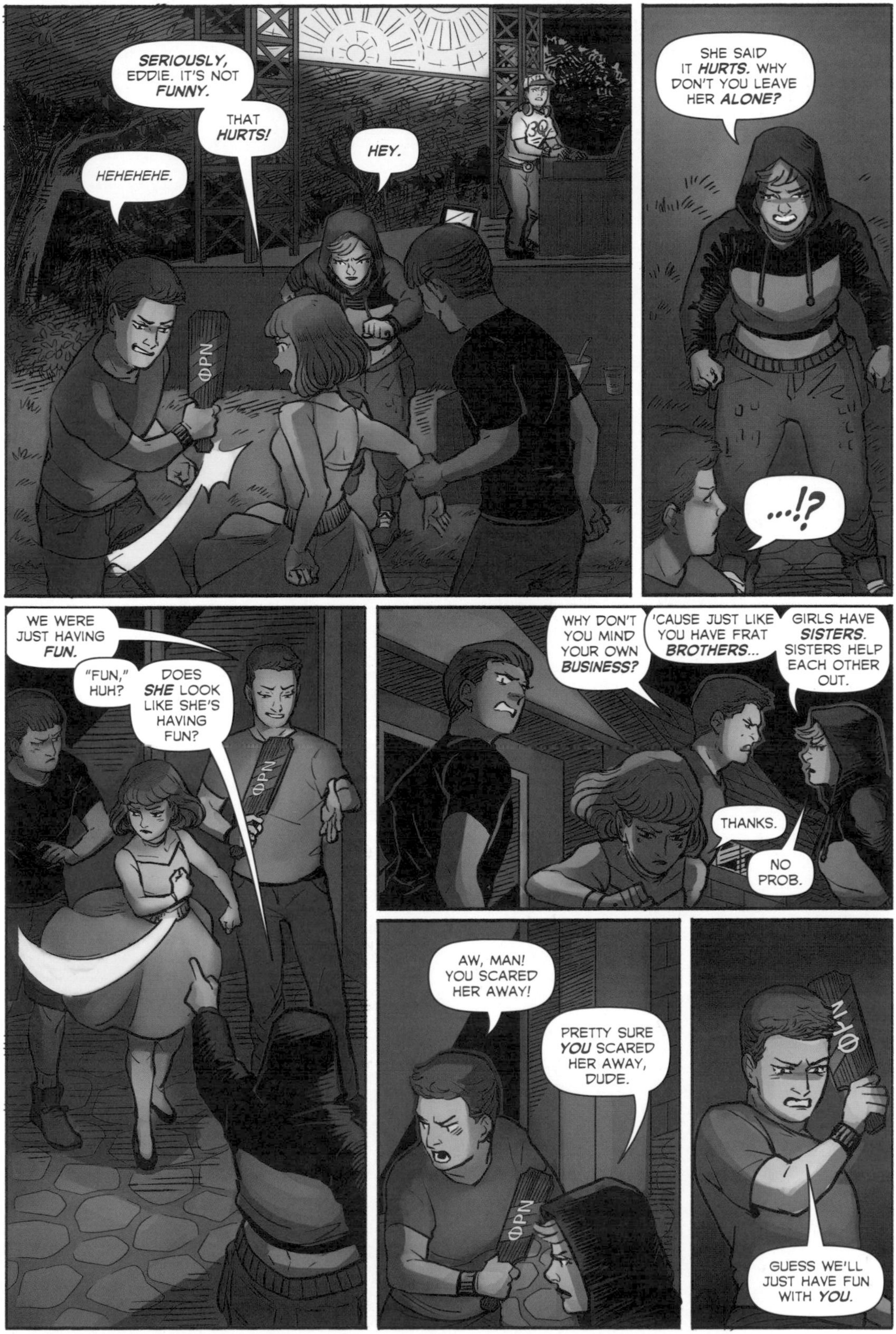
SERIOUSLY, EDDIE. IT'S NOT FUNNY.
THAT HURTS!
HEHEHEHE.
HEY.
SHE SAID IT HURTS. WHY DON'T YOU LEAVE HER ALONE?
...!?
WE WERE JUST HAVING FUN.
"FUN," HUH?
DOES SHE LOOK LIKE SHE'S HAVING FUN?
WHY DON'T YOU MIND YOUR OWN BUSINESS?
'CAUSE JUST LIKE YOU HAVE FRAT BROTHERS...
GIRLS HAVE SISTERS. SISTERS HELP EACH OTHER OUT.
THANKS.
NO PROB.
AW, MAN! YOU SCARED HER AWAY!
PRETTY SURE YOU SCARED HER AWAY, DUDE.
GUESS WE'LL JUST HAVE FUN WITH YOU.

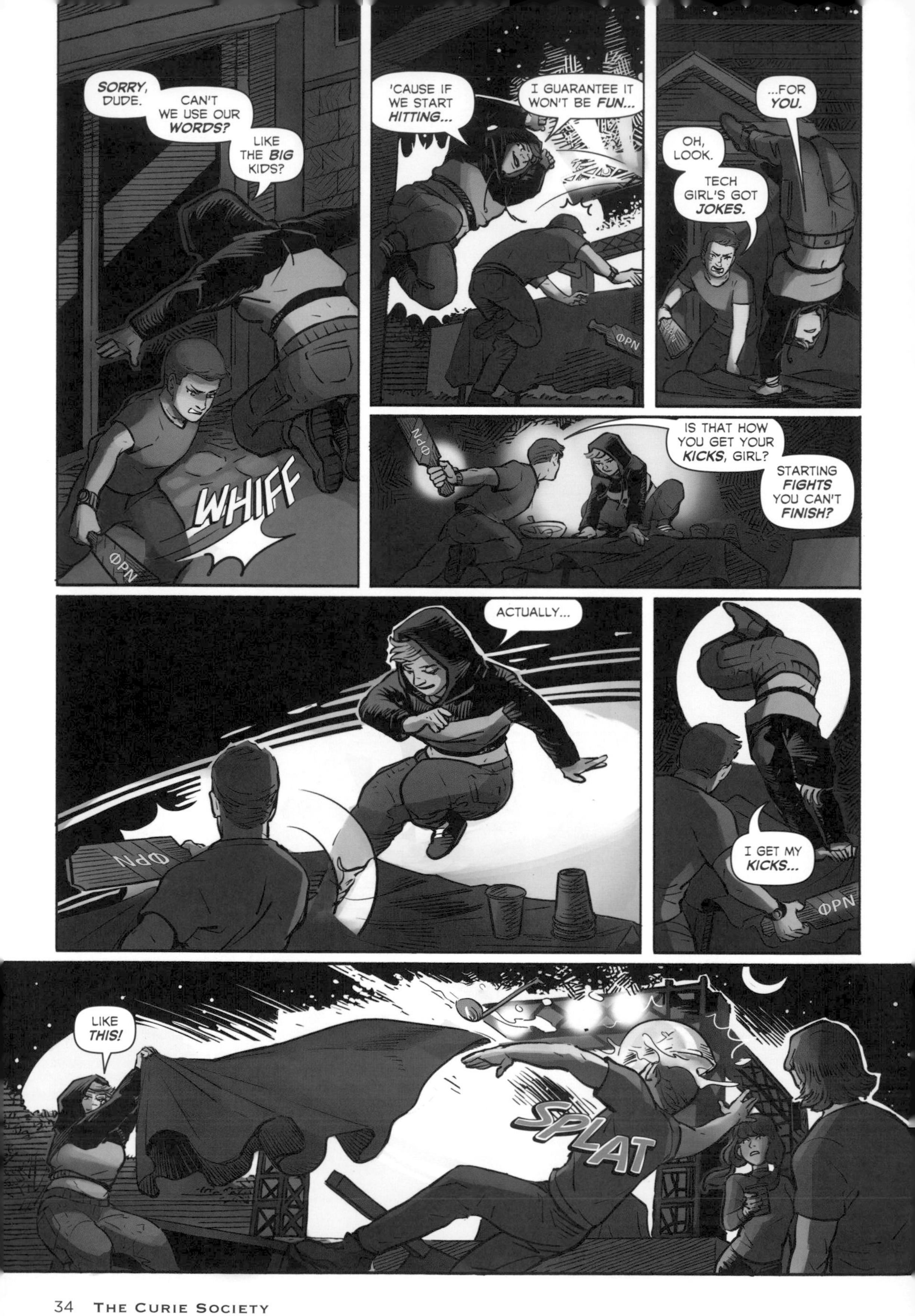
SORRY, DUDE.
CAN'T WE USE OUR WORDS?
LIKE THE BIG KIDS?
WHIFF
'CAUSE IF WE START HITTING...
I GUARANTEE IT WON'T BE FUN...
...FOR YOU.
OH, LOOK.
TECH GIRL'S GOT JOKES.
IS THAT HOW YOU GET YOUR KICKS, GIRL?
STARTING FIGHTS YOU CAN'T FINISH?
ACTUALLY...
I GET MY KICKS...
LIKE THIS!
SPLAT

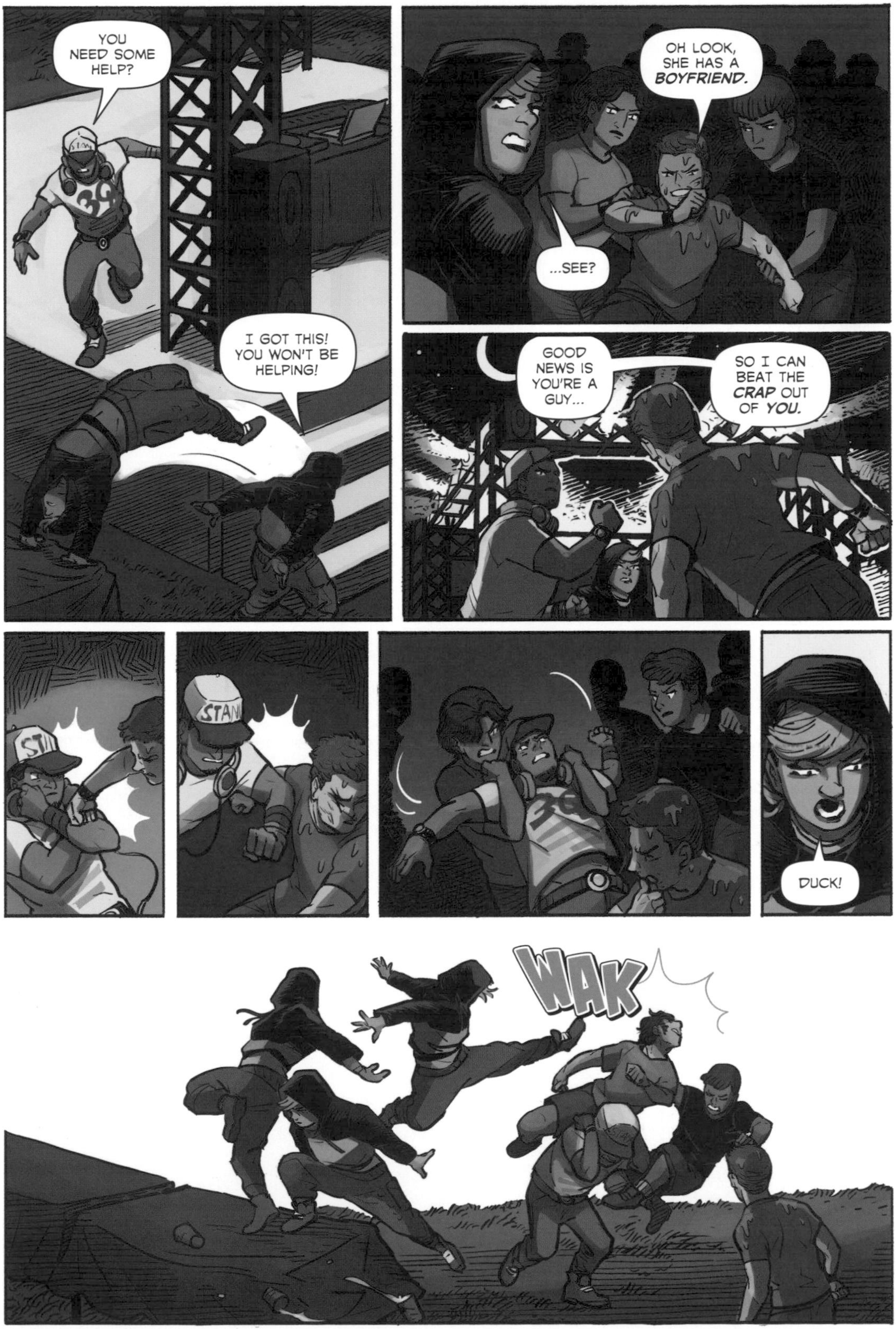
YOU NEED SOME HELP?
I GOT THIS! YOU WON'T BE HELPING!
OH LOOK, SHE HAS A *BOYFRIEND.*
...SEE?
GOOD NEWS IS YOU'RE A GUY...
SO I CAN BEAT THE *CRAP* OUT OF *YOU.*
DUCK!
WAK

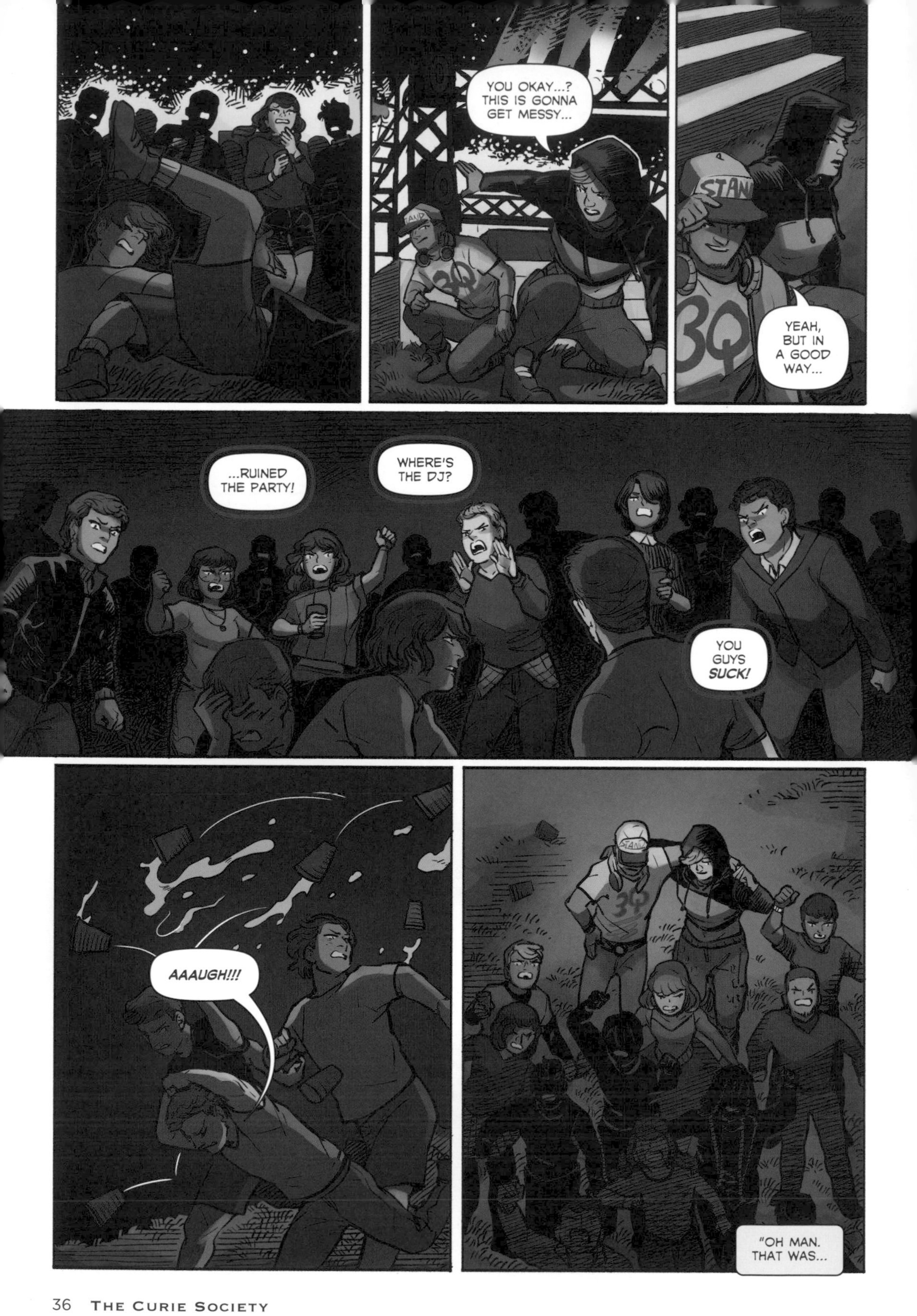
YOU OKAY...? THIS IS GONNA GET MESSY...
STAND
YEAH, BUT IN A GOOD WAY...
...RUINED THE PARTY!
WHERE'S THE DJ?
YOU GUYS **SUCK!**
AAAUGH!!!
"OH MAN. THAT WAS...

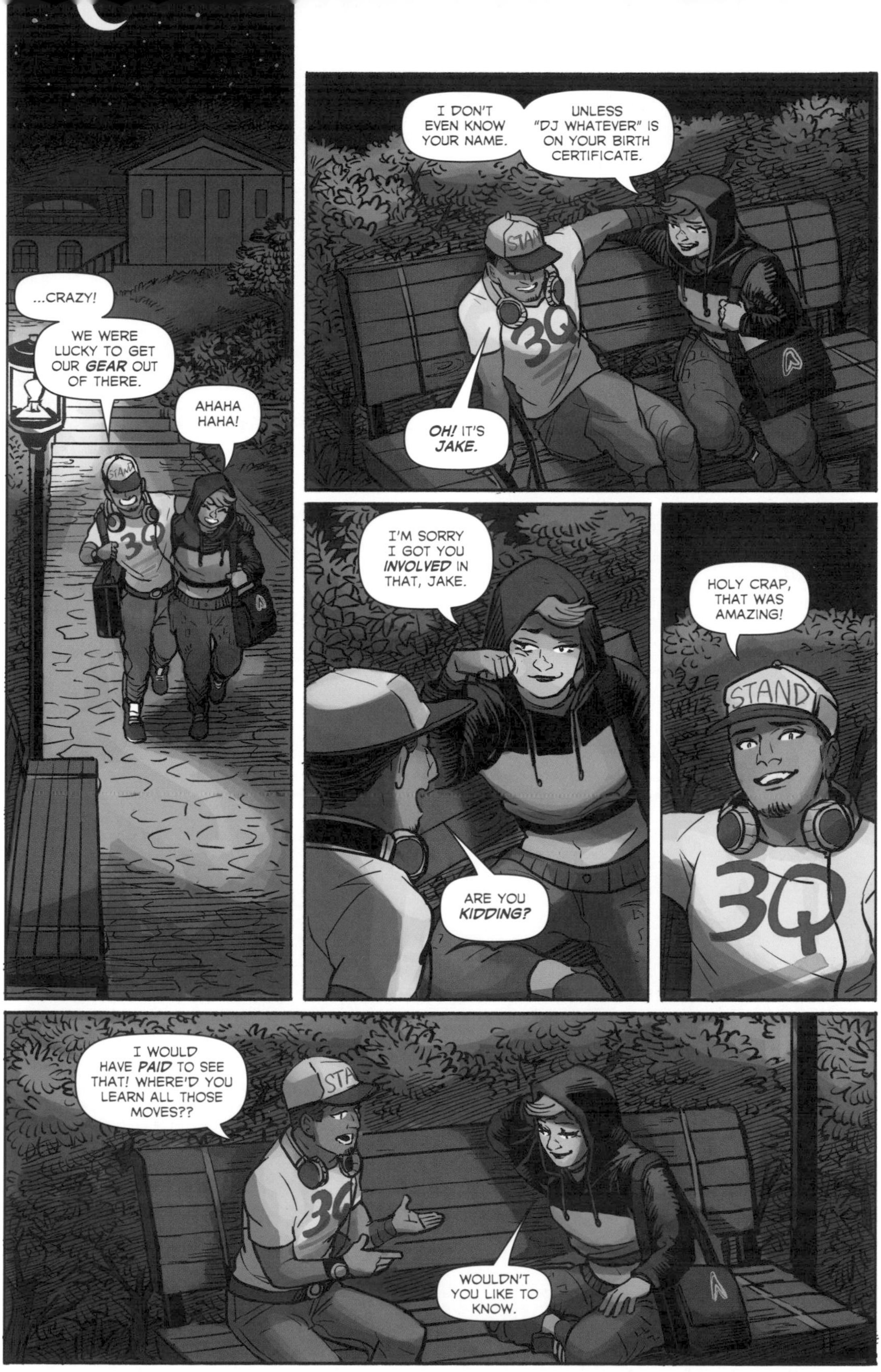
...CRAZY!
WE WERE LUCKY TO GET OUR *GEAR* OUT OF THERE.
AHAHA HAHA!
I DON'T EVEN KNOW YOUR NAME.
UNLESS "DJ WHATEVER" IS ON YOUR BIRTH CERTIFICATE.
OH! IT'S *JAKE.*
I'M SORRY I GOT YOU *INVOLVED* IN THAT, JAKE.
ARE YOU *KIDDING?*
HOLY CRAP, THAT WAS AMAZING!
I WOULD HAVE *PAID* TO SEE THAT! WHERE'D YOU LEARN ALL THOSE MOVES??
WOULDN'T YOU LIKE TO KNOW.

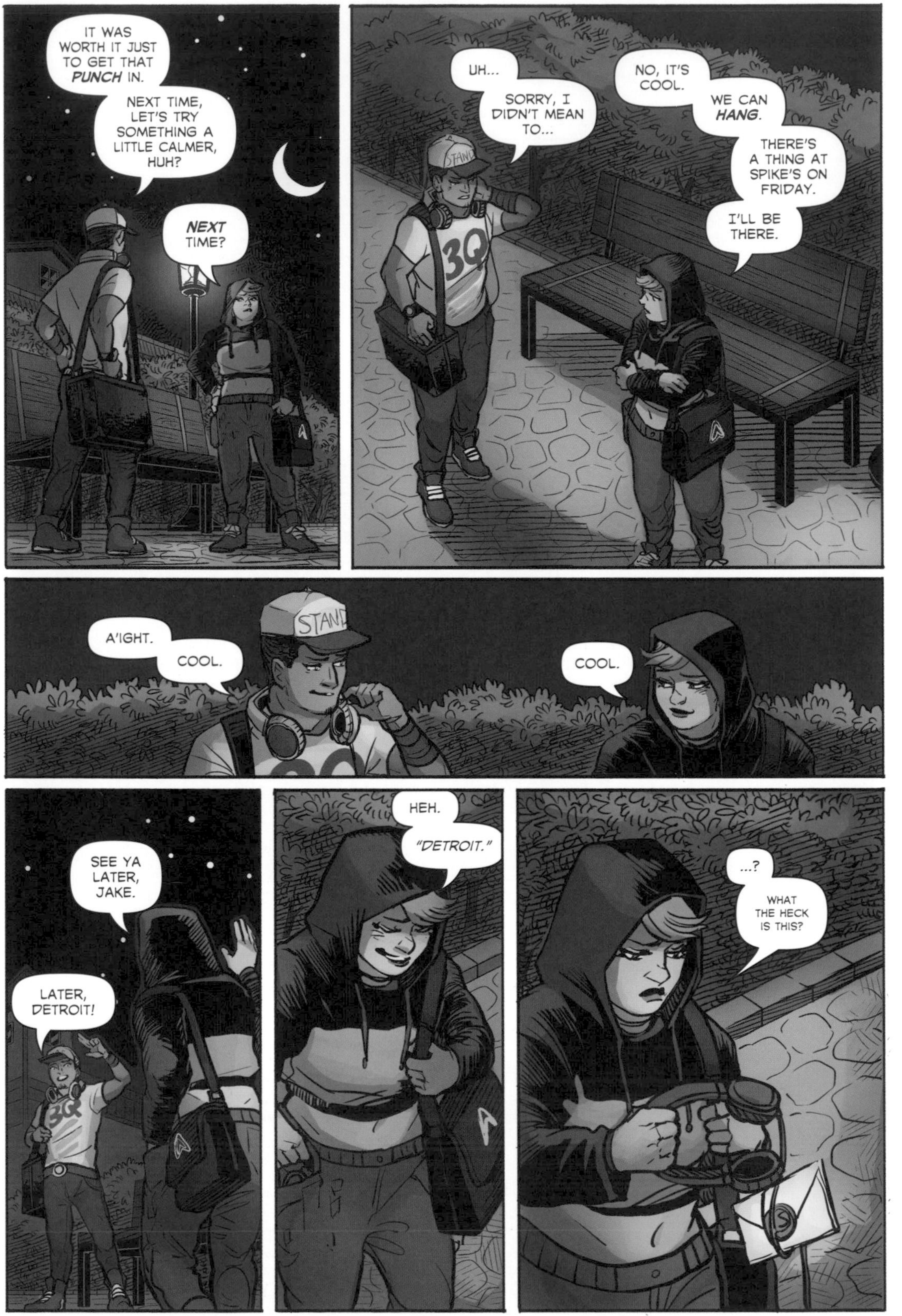
IT WAS WORTH IT JUST TO GET THAT *PUNCH* IN.
NEXT TIME, LET'S TRY SOMETHING A LITTLE CALMER, HUH?
NEXT TIME?
UH...
SORRY, I DIDN'T MEAN TO...
NO, IT'S COOL.
WE CAN *HANG*.
THERE'S A THING AT SPIKE'S ON FRIDAY.
I'LL BE THERE.
STAND
3Q
A'IGHT.
COOL.
COOL.
SEE YA LATER, JAKE.
LATER, DETROIT!
HEH.
"DETROIT."
...?
WHAT THE HECK IS THIS?

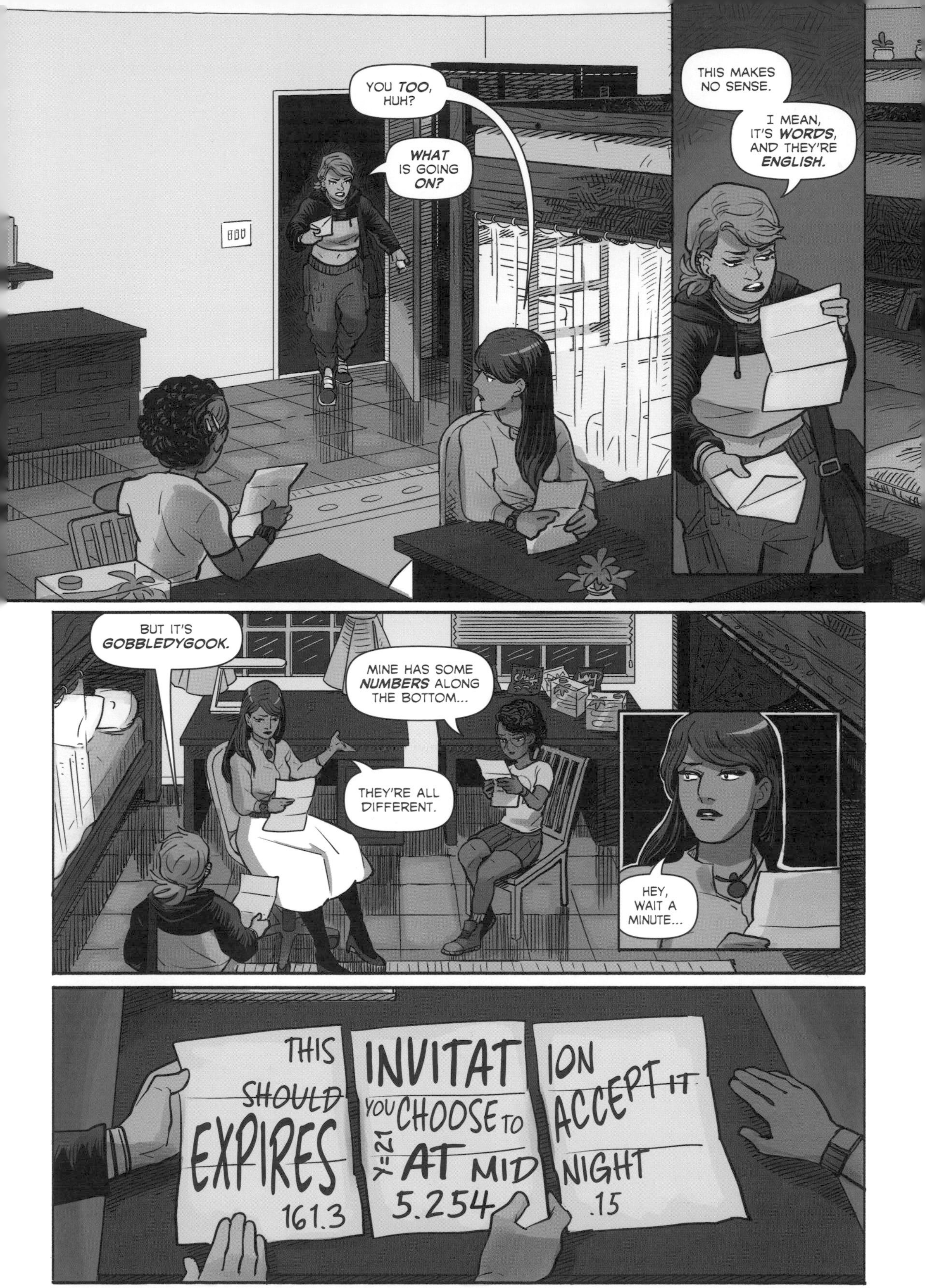
YOU TOO, HUH?
WHAT IS GOING ON?
THIS MAKES NO SENSE.
I MEAN, IT'S WORDS, AND THEY'RE ENGLISH.
BUT IT'S GOBBLEDYGOOK.
MINE HAS SOME NUMBERS ALONG THE BOTTOM...
THEY'RE ALL DIFFERENT.
HEY, WAIT A MINUTE...
THIS INVITAT ION
SHOULD YOU CHOOSE TO ACCEPT IT
EXPIRES AT MID NIGHT
161.3 5.254 .15
Y-21

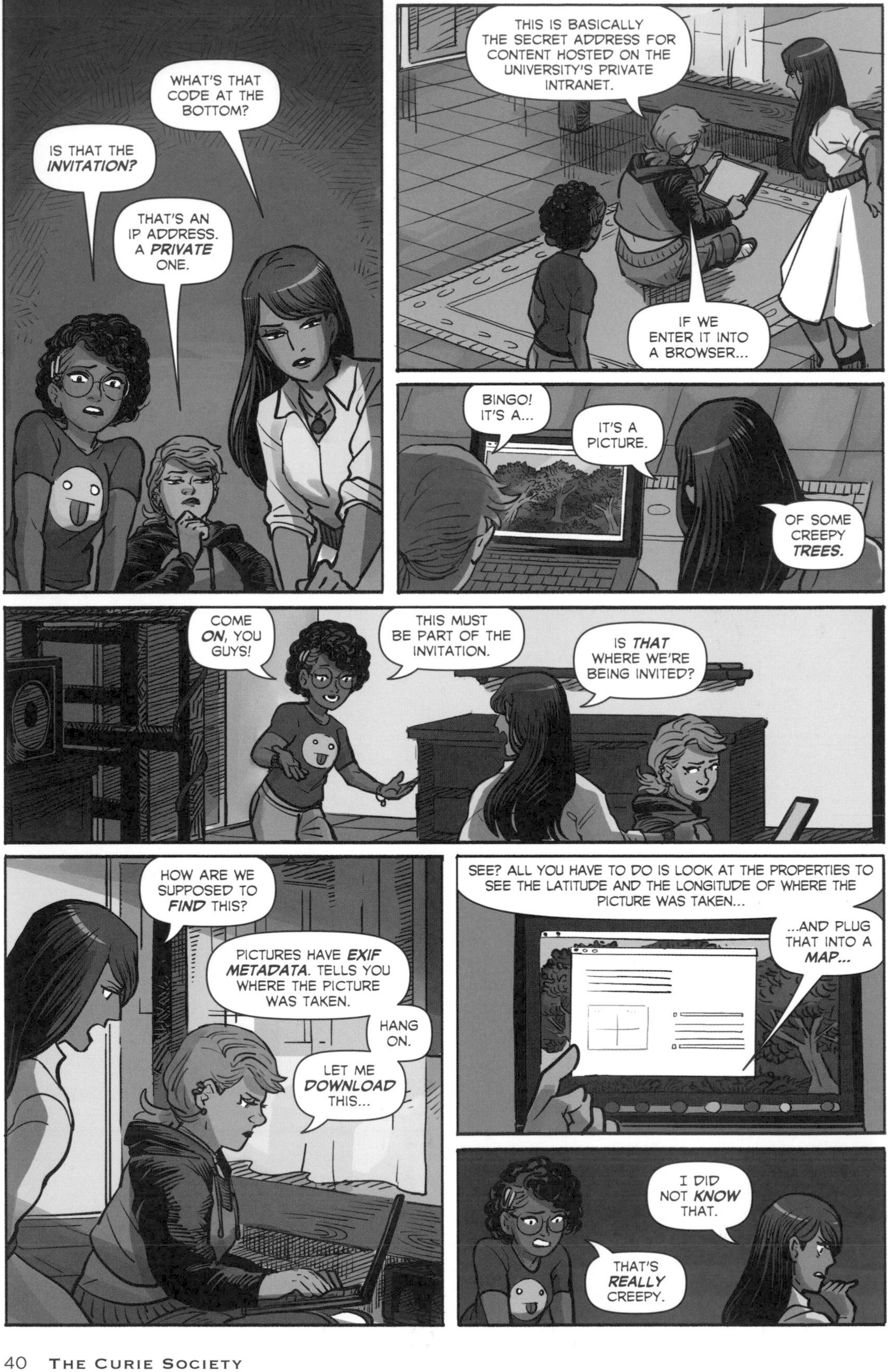

IS THAT THE INVITATION?
WHAT'S THAT CODE AT THE BOTTOM?
THAT'S AN IP ADDRESS. A PRIVATE ONE.
THIS IS BASICALLY THE SECRET ADDRESS FOR CONTENT HOSTED ON THE UNIVERSITY'S PRIVATE INTRANET.
IF WE ENTER IT INTO A BROWSER...
BINGO! IT'S A...
IT'S A PICTURE.
OF SOME CREEPY TREES.
COME ON, YOU GUYS!
THIS MUST BE PART OF THE INVITATION.
IS THAT WHERE WE'RE BEING INVITED?
HOW ARE WE SUPPOSED TO FIND THIS?
PICTURES HAVE EXIF METADATA. TELLS YOU WHERE THE PICTURE WAS TAKEN.
HANG ON.
LET ME DOWNLOAD THIS...
SEE? ALL YOU HAVE TO DO IS LOOK AT THE PROPERTIES TO SEE THE LATITUDE AND THE LONGITUDE OF WHERE THE PICTURE WAS TAKEN...
...AND PLUG THAT INTO A MAP...
I DID NOT KNOW THAT.
THAT'S REALLY CREEPY.

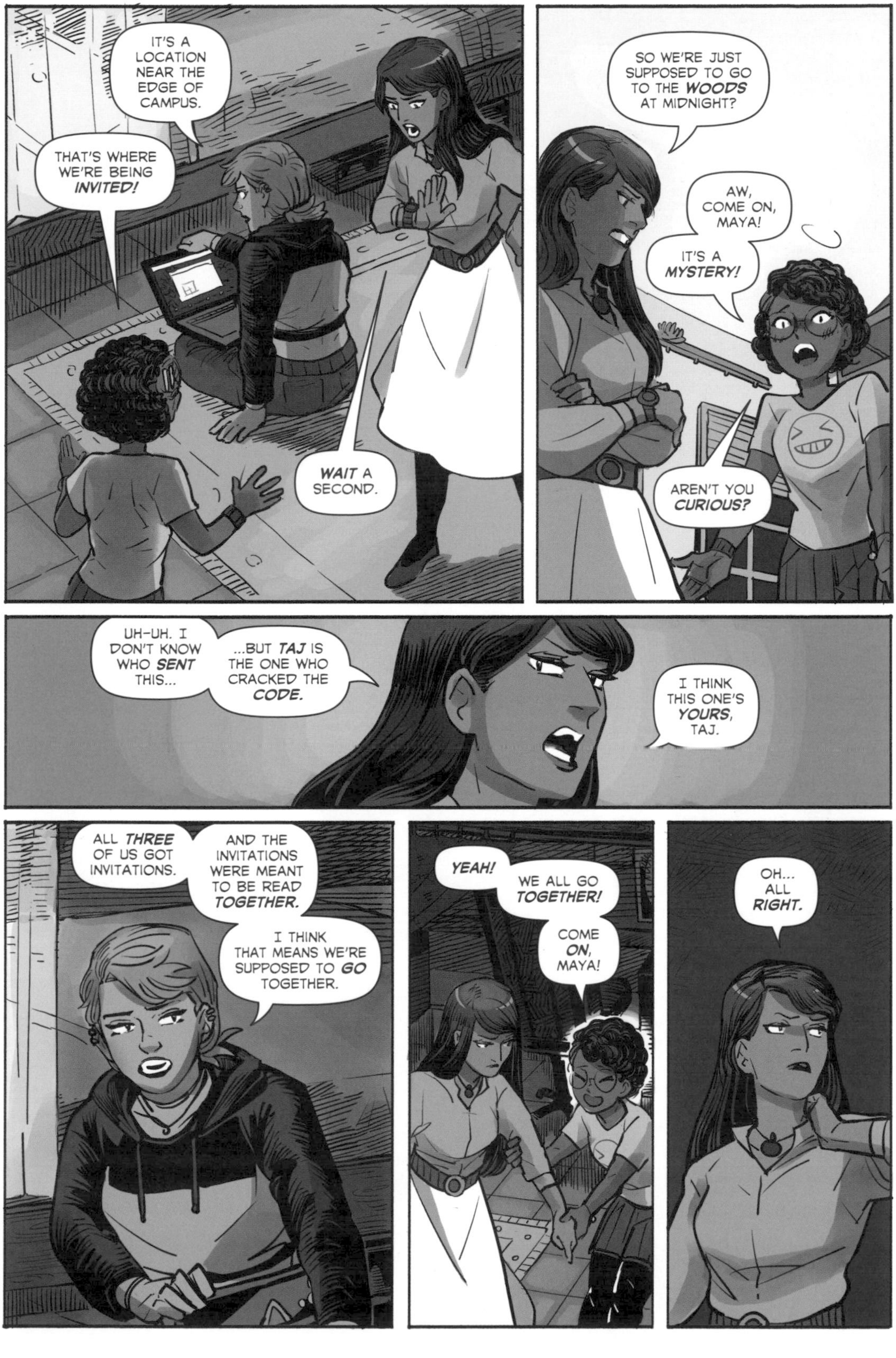
IT'S A LOCATION NEAR THE EDGE OF CAMPUS.
THAT'S WHERE WE'RE BEING *INVITED!*
WAIT A SECOND.
SO WE'RE JUST SUPPOSED TO GO TO THE *WOODS* AT MIDNIGHT?
AW, COME ON, MAYA!
IT'S A *MYSTERY!*
AREN'T YOU *CURIOUS?*
UH-UH. I DON'T KNOW WHO *SENT* THIS...
...BUT *TAJ* IS THE ONE WHO CRACKED THE *CODE.*
I THINK THIS ONE'S *YOURS*, TAJ.
ALL *THREE* OF US GOT INVITATIONS.
AND THE INVITATIONS WERE MEANT TO BE READ *TOGETHER.*
I THINK THAT MEANS WE'RE SUPPOSED TO *GO* TOGETHER.
YEAH!
WE ALL GO *TOGETHER!*
COME *ON*, MAYA!
OH... ALL *RIGHT.*

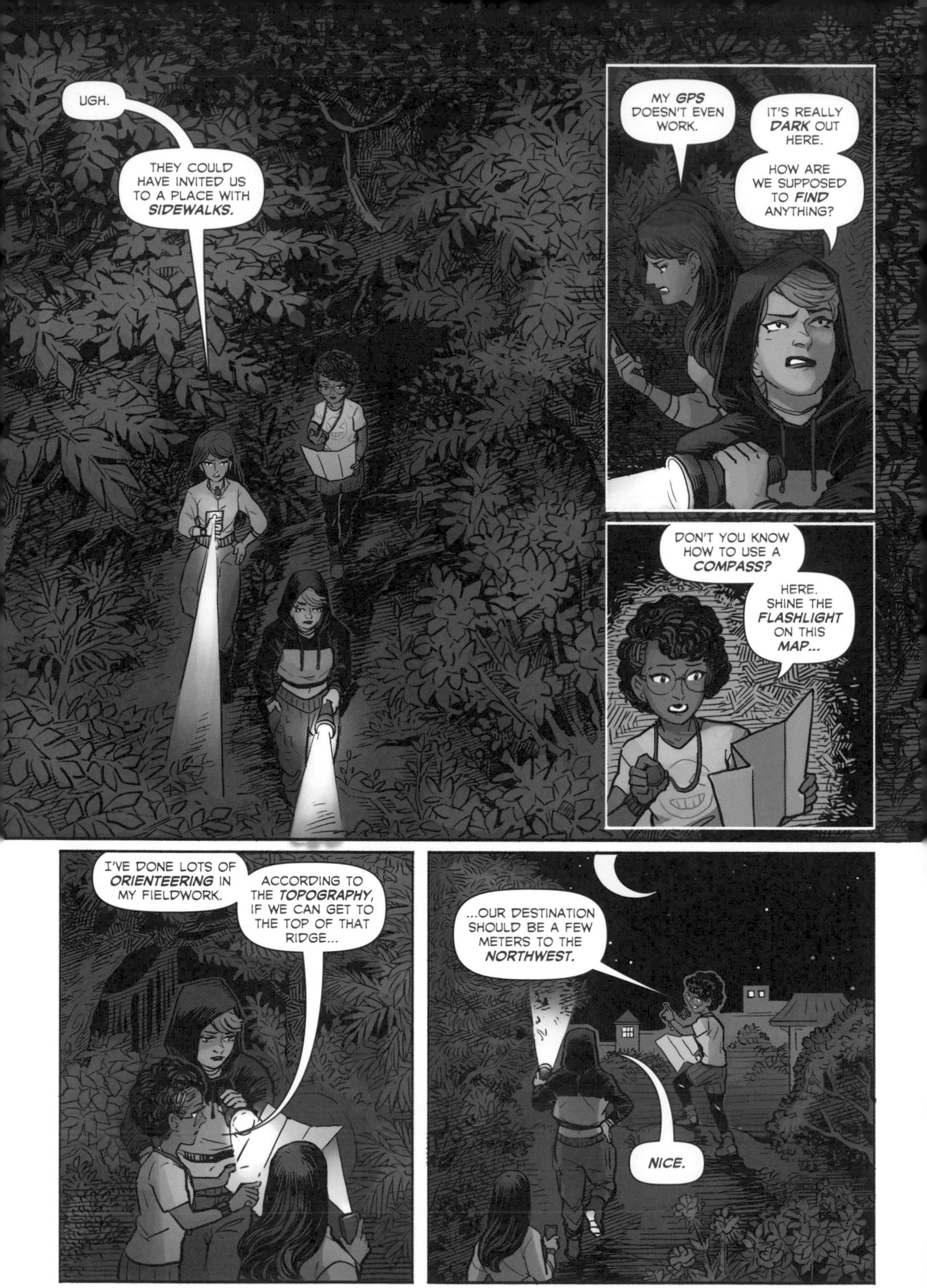
UGH.
THEY COULD HAVE INVITED US TO A PLACE WITH SIDEWALKS.
MY GPS DOESN'T EVEN WORK.
IT'S REALLY DARK OUT HERE.
HOW ARE WE SUPPOSED TO FIND ANYTHING?
DON'T YOU KNOW HOW TO USE A COMPASS?
HERE. SHINE THE FLASHLIGHT ON THIS MAP...
I'VE DONE LOTS OF ORIENTEERING IN MY FIELDWORK.
ACCORDING TO THE TOPOGRAPHY, IF WE CAN GET TO THE TOP OF THAT RIDGE...
...OUR DESTINATION SHOULD BE A FEW METERS TO THE NORTHWEST.
NICE.

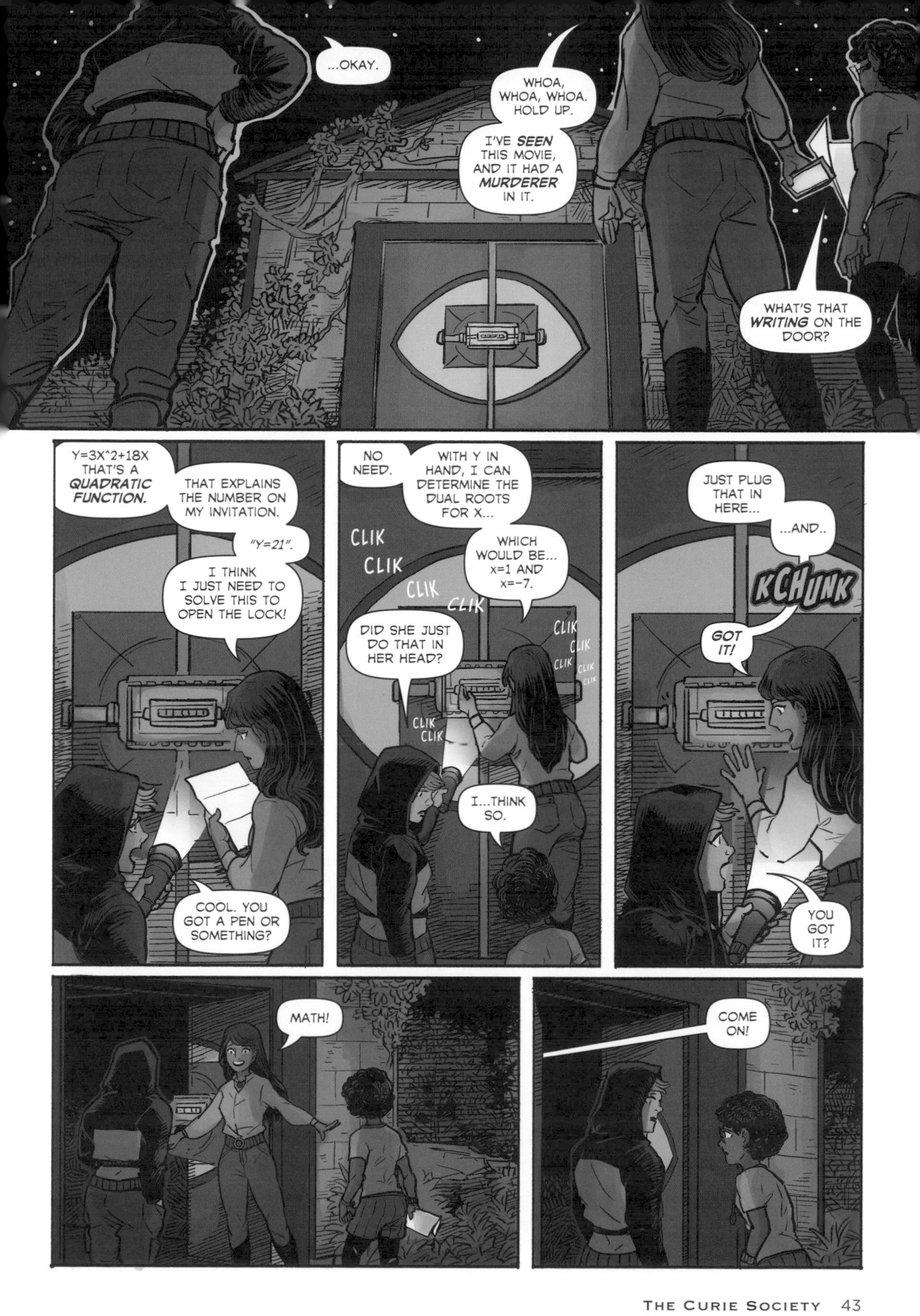
...OKAY.
WHOA, WHOA, WHOA. HOLD UP.
I'VE SEEN THIS MOVIE, AND IT HAD A MURDERER IN IT.
WHAT'S THAT WRITING ON THE DOOR?
Y=3X^2+18X THAT'S A QUADRATIC FUNCTION.
THAT EXPLAINS THE NUMBER ON MY INVITATION.
"Y=21".
I THINK I JUST NEED TO SOLVE THIS TO OPEN THE LOCK!
COOL. YOU GOT A PEN OR SOMETHING?
NO NEED.
WITH Y IN HAND, I CAN DETERMINE THE DUAL ROOTS FOR X...
CLIK CLIK CLIK CLIK
WHICH WOULD BE... x=1 AND x=-7.
CLIK CLIK CLIK CLIK CLIK
DID SHE JUST DO THAT IN HER HEAD?
CLIK CLIK
I...THINK SO.
JUST PLUG THAT IN HERE...
...AND..
KCHUNK
GOT IT!
YOU GOT IT?
MATH!
COME ON!

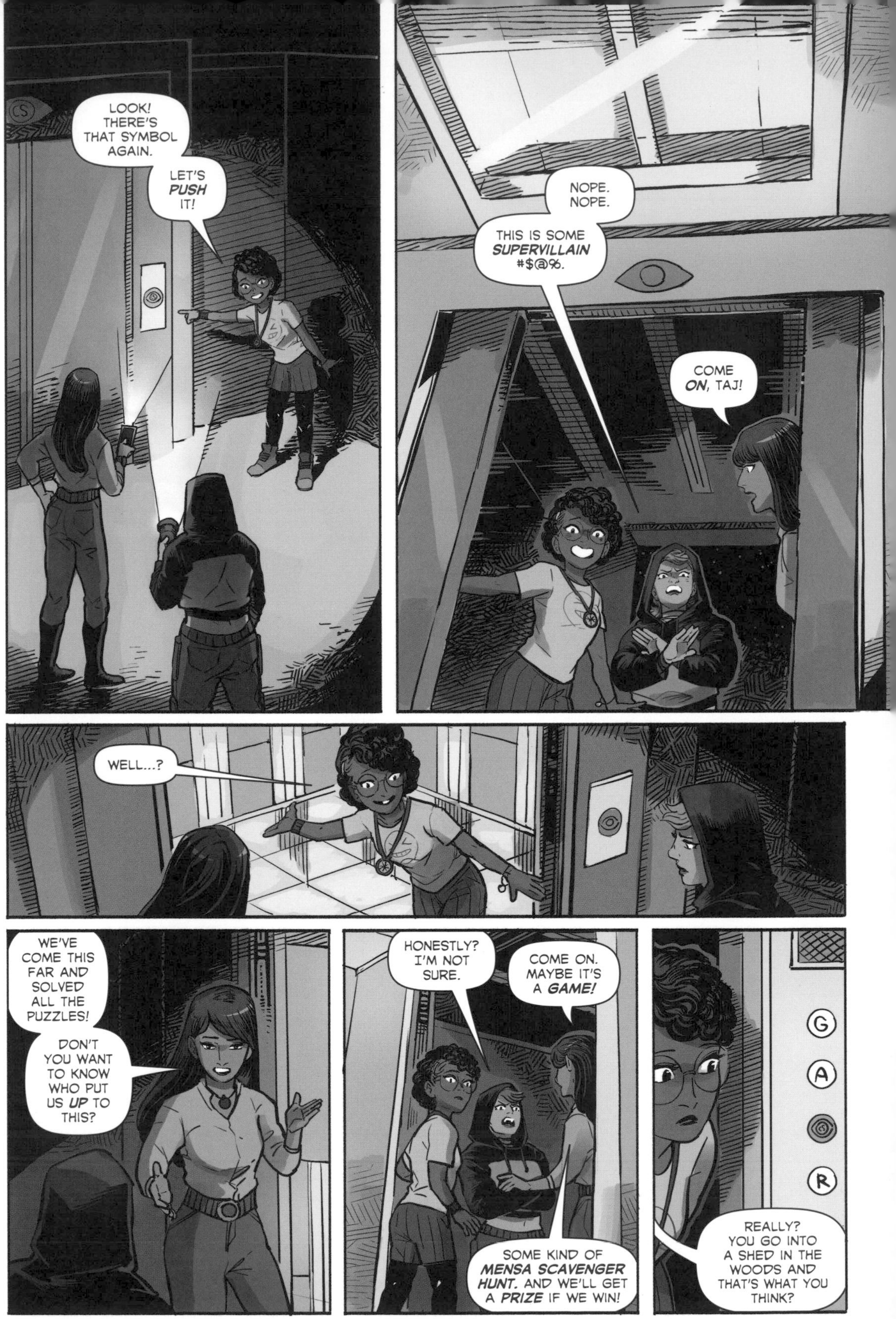

LOOK! THERE'S THAT SYMBOL AGAIN.
LET'S PUSH IT!
NOPE. NOPE.
THIS IS SOME SUPERVILLAIN #$@%.
COME ON, TAJ!
WELL...?
WE'VE COME THIS FAR AND SOLVED ALL THE PUZZLES!
DON'T YOU WANT TO KNOW WHO PUT US UP TO THIS?
HONESTLY? I'M NOT SURE.
COME ON. MAYBE IT'S A GAME!
SOME KIND OF MENSA SCAVENGER HUNT. AND WE'LL GET A PRIZE IF WE WIN!
G
A
R
REALLY? YOU GO INTO A SHED IN THE WOODS AND THAT'S WHAT YOU THINK?

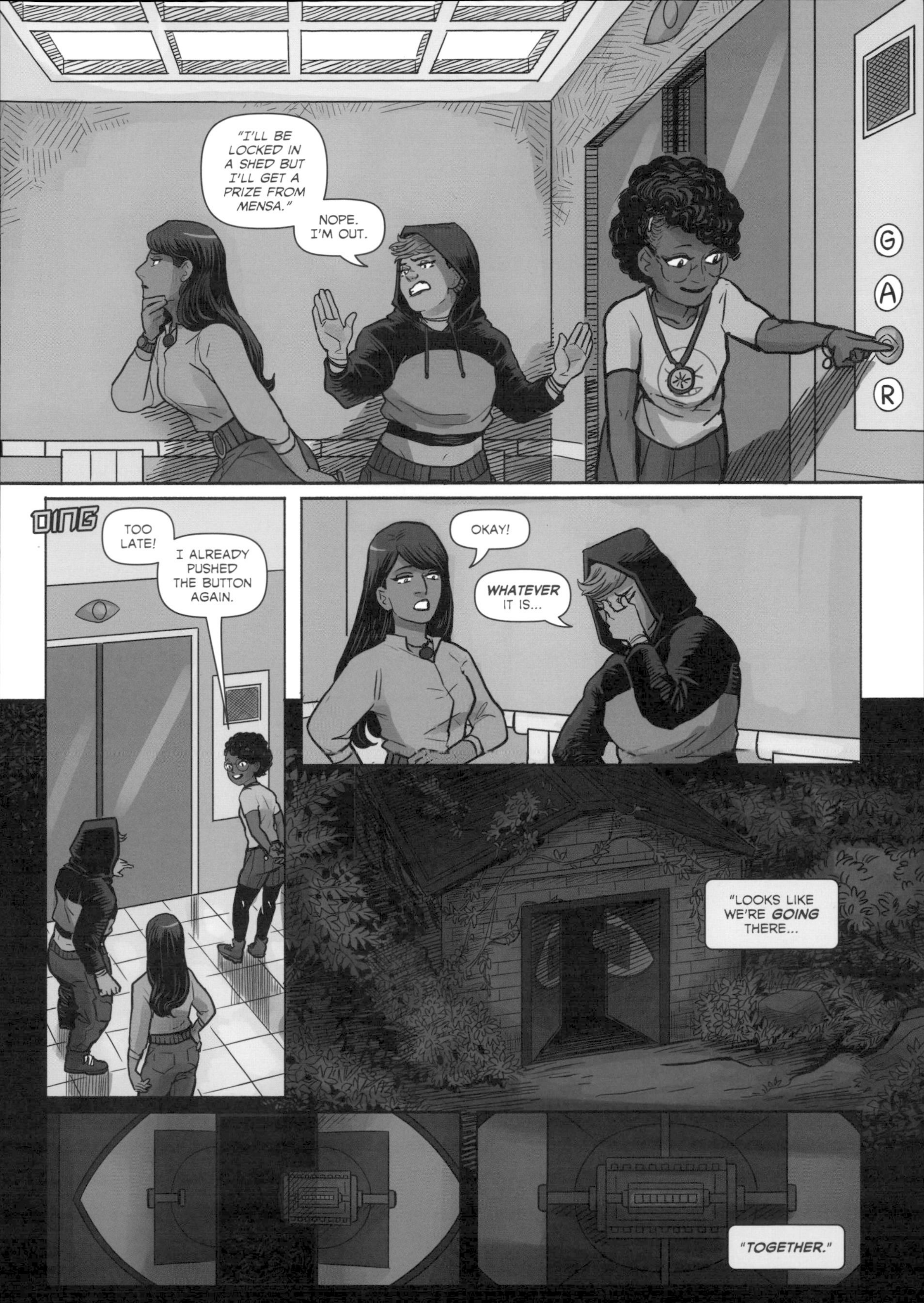
"I'LL BE LOCKED IN A SHED BUT I'LL GET A PRIZE FROM MENSA."
NOPE. I'M OUT.
G
A
R
DING
TOO LATE!
I ALREADY PUSHED THE BUTTON AGAIN.
OKAY!
WHATEVER IT IS...
"LOOKS LIKE WE'RE *GOING* THERE...
"TOGETHER."

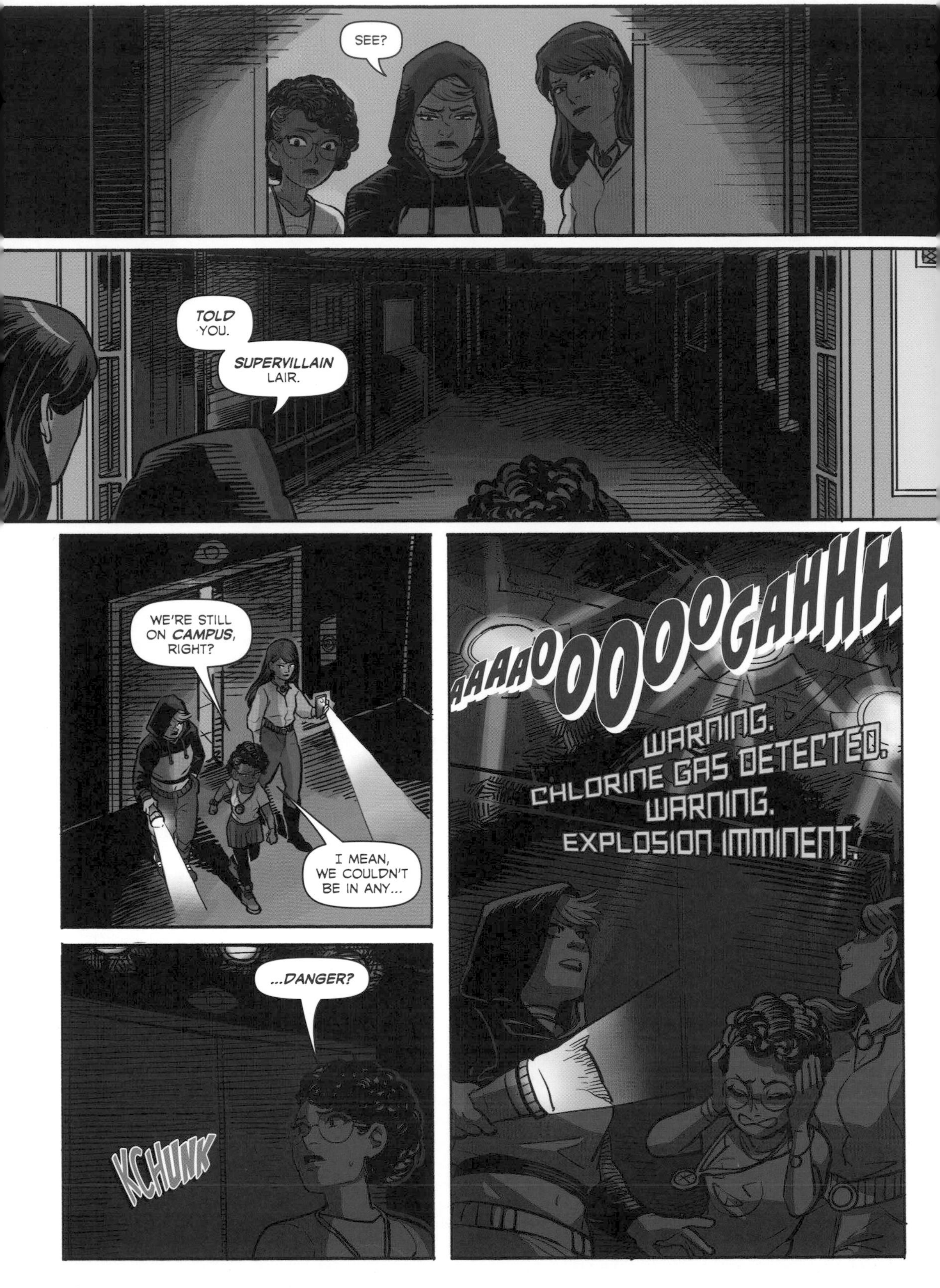
SEE?
TOLD YOU.
SUPERVILLAIN LAIR.
WE'RE STILL ON CAMPUS, RIGHT?
I MEAN, WE COULDN'T BE IN ANY...
...DANGER?
KCHUNK
AAAAOOOOOGAHHH
WARNING.
CHLORINE GAS DETECTED.
WARNING.
EXPLOSION IMMINENT.

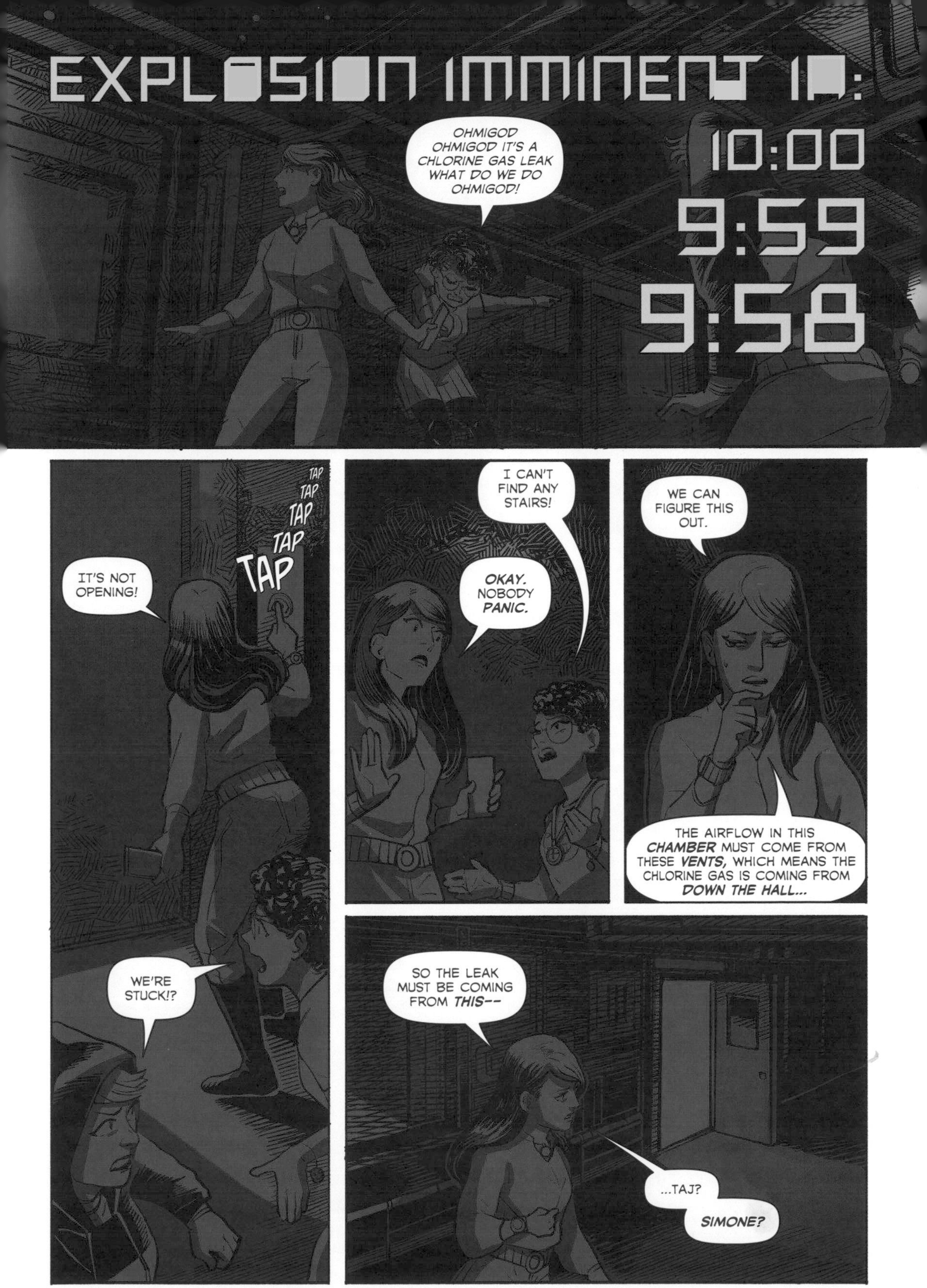
EXPLOSION IMMINENT IN:
10:00
9:59
9:58
OHMIGOD OHMIGOD IT'S A CHLORINE GAS LEAK WHAT DO WE DO OHMIGOD!
TAP TAP TAP TAP TAP
IT'S NOT OPENING!
WE'RE STUCK!?
I CAN'T FIND ANY STAIRS!
OKAY. NOBODY PANIC.
WE CAN FIGURE THIS OUT.
THE AIRFLOW IN THIS CHAMBER MUST COME FROM THESE VENTS, WHICH MEANS THE CHLORINE GAS IS COMING FROM DOWN THE HALL...
SO THE LEAK MUST BE COMING FROM THIS--
...TAJ?
SIMONE?

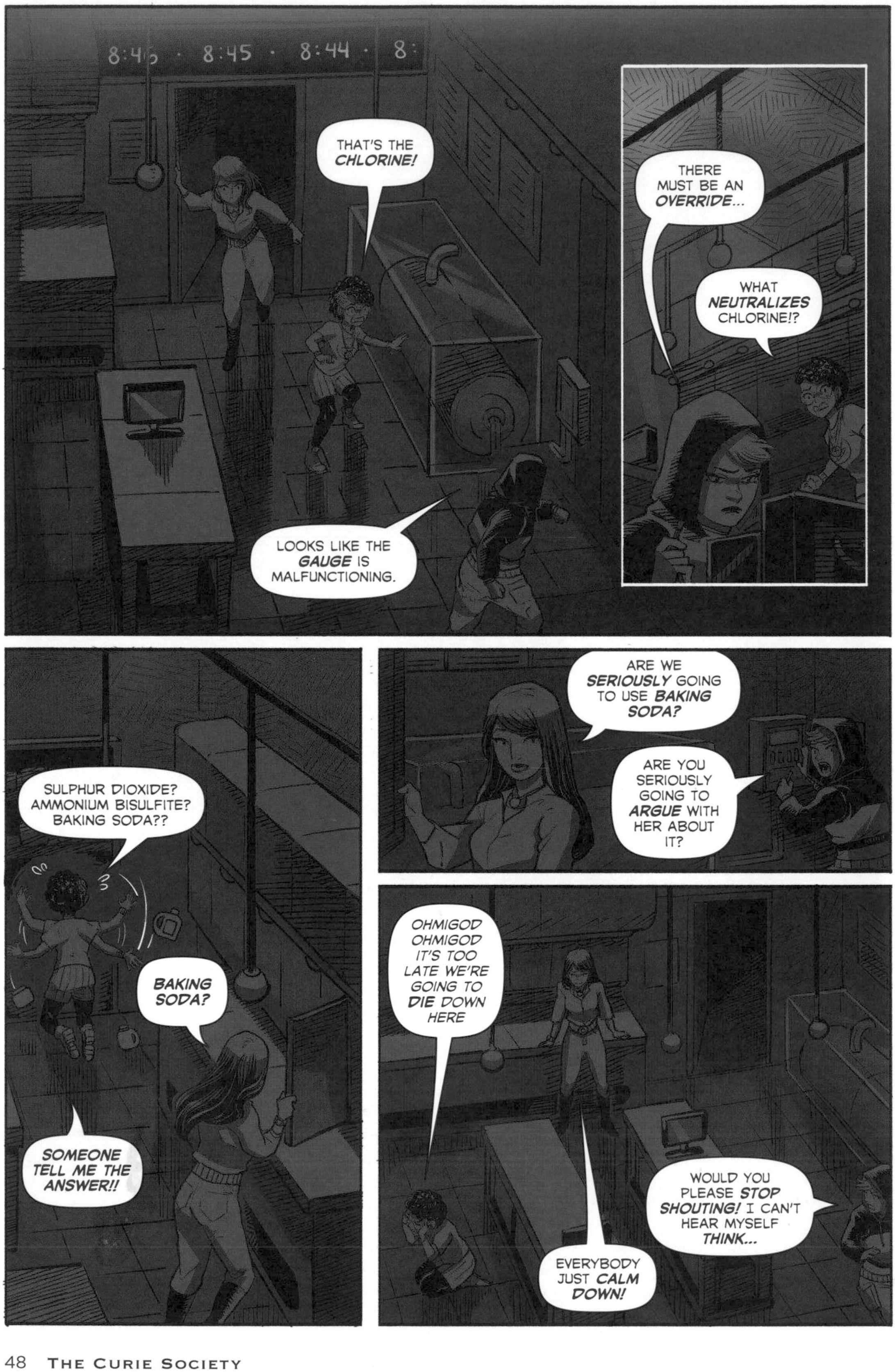
8:46 · 8:45 · 8:44 · 8:
THAT'S THE CHLORINE!
LOOKS LIKE THE GAUGE IS MALFUNCTIONING.
THERE MUST BE AN OVERRIDE...
WHAT NEUTRALIZES CHLORINE!?
SULPHUR DIOXIDE? AMMONIUM BISULFITE? BAKING SODA??
BAKING SODA?
SOMEONE TELL ME THE ANSWER!!
ARE WE SERIOUSLY GOING TO USE BAKING SODA?
ARE YOU SERIOUSLY GOING TO ARGUE WITH HER ABOUT IT?
OHMIGOD OHMIGOD IT'S TOO LATE WE'RE GOING TO DIE DOWN HERE
EVERYBODY JUST CALM DOWN!
WOULD YOU PLEASE STOP SHOUTING! I CAN'T HEAR MYSELF THINK...

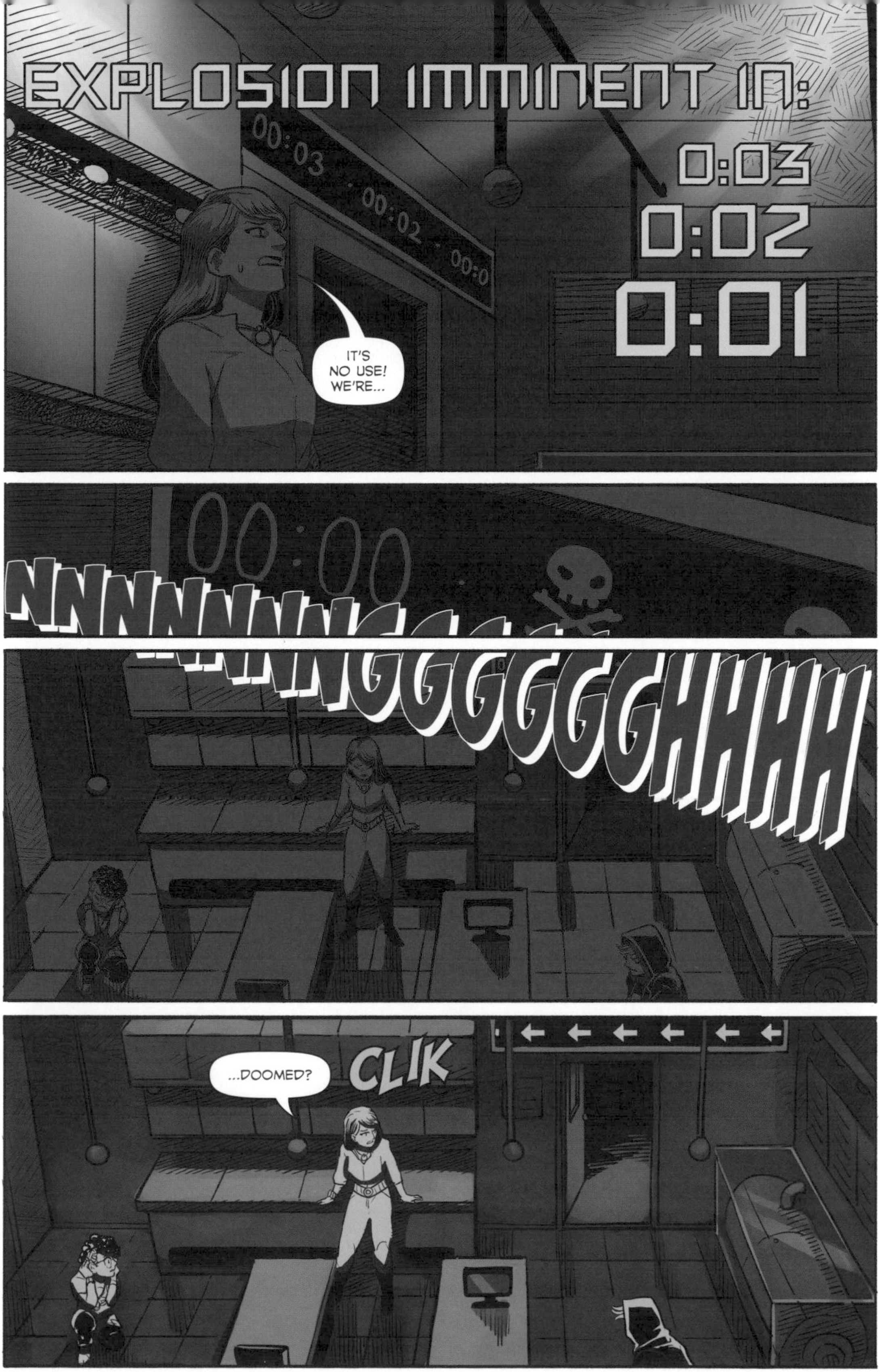
EXPLOSION IMMINENT IN:
0:03
0:02
0:01
IT'S NO USE! WE'RE...
NNNNNNNNNNNGGGGGGGGGHHHHH
...DOOMED?
CLIK

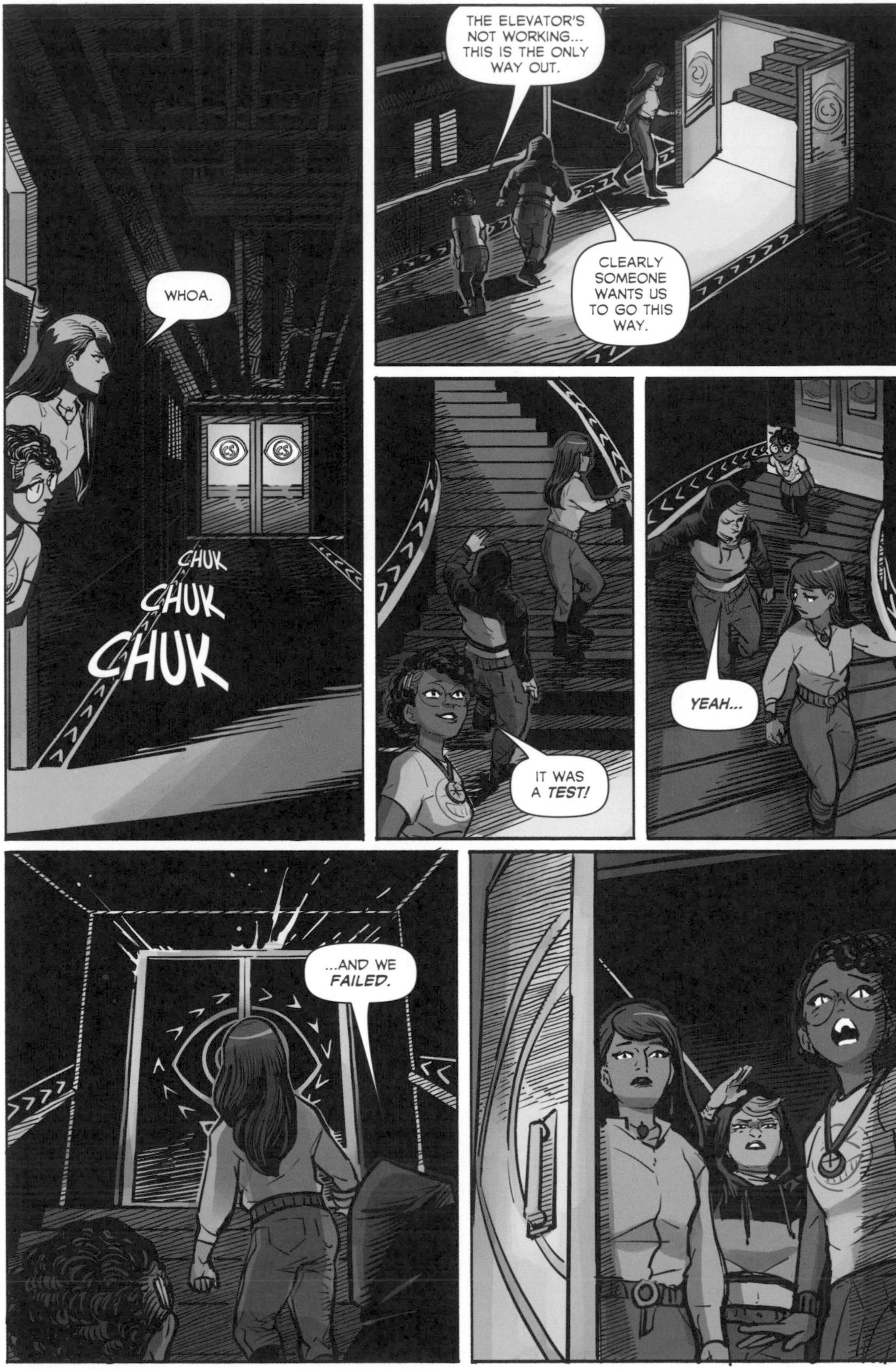
WHOA.
CHUK
CHUK
CHUK
THE ELEVATOR'S NOT WORKING... THIS IS THE ONLY WAY OUT.
CLEARLY SOMEONE WANTS US TO GO THIS WAY.
IT WAS A *TEST!*
YEAH...
...AND WE *FAILED.*

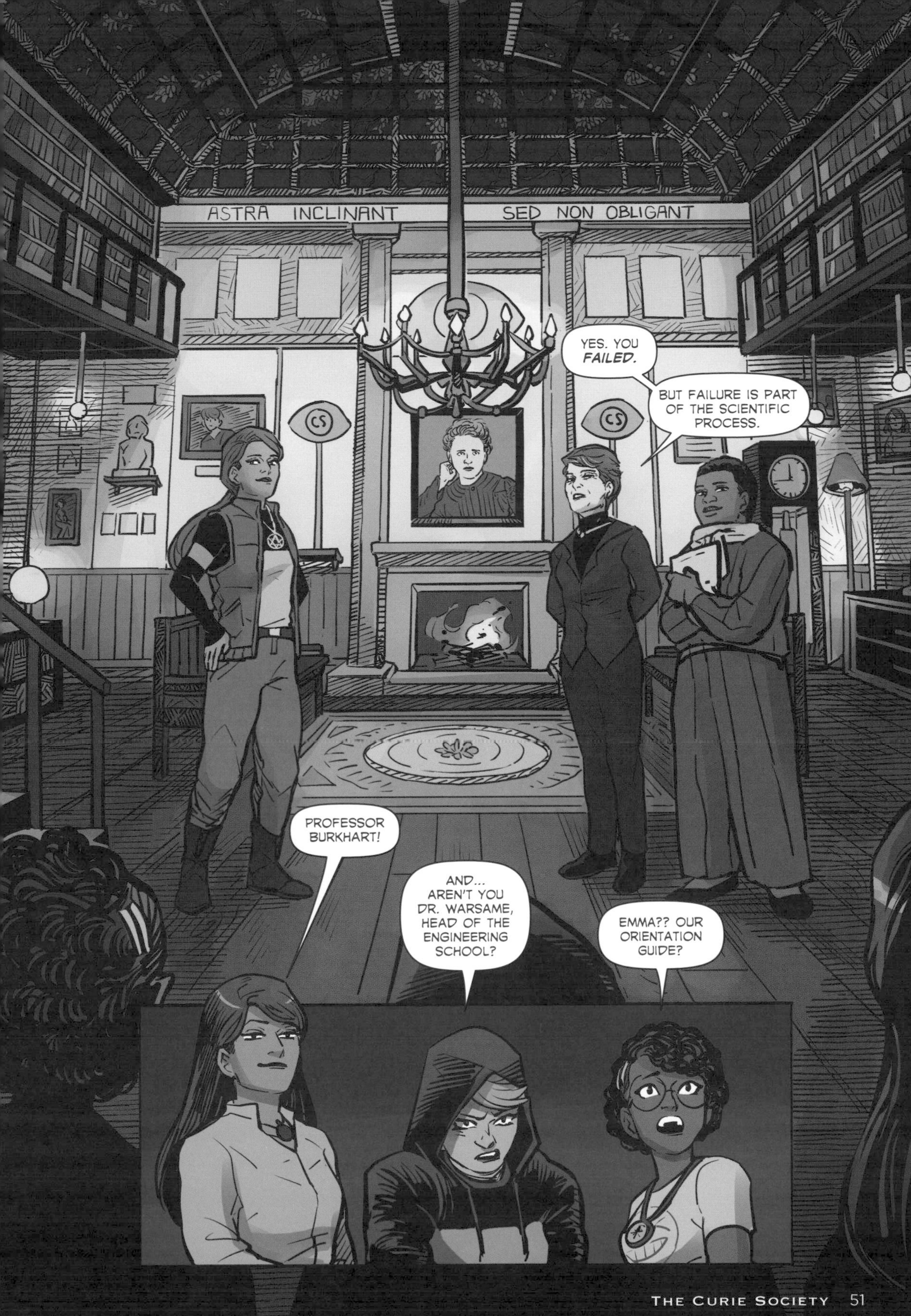
ASTRA INCLINANT SED NON OBLIGANT
CS
CS
YES. YOU *FAILED.*
BUT FAILURE IS PART OF THE SCIENTIFIC PROCESS.
PROFESSOR BURKHART!
AND... AREN'T YOU DR. WARSAME, HEAD OF THE ENGINEERING SCHOOL?
EMMA?? OUR ORIENTATION GUIDE?

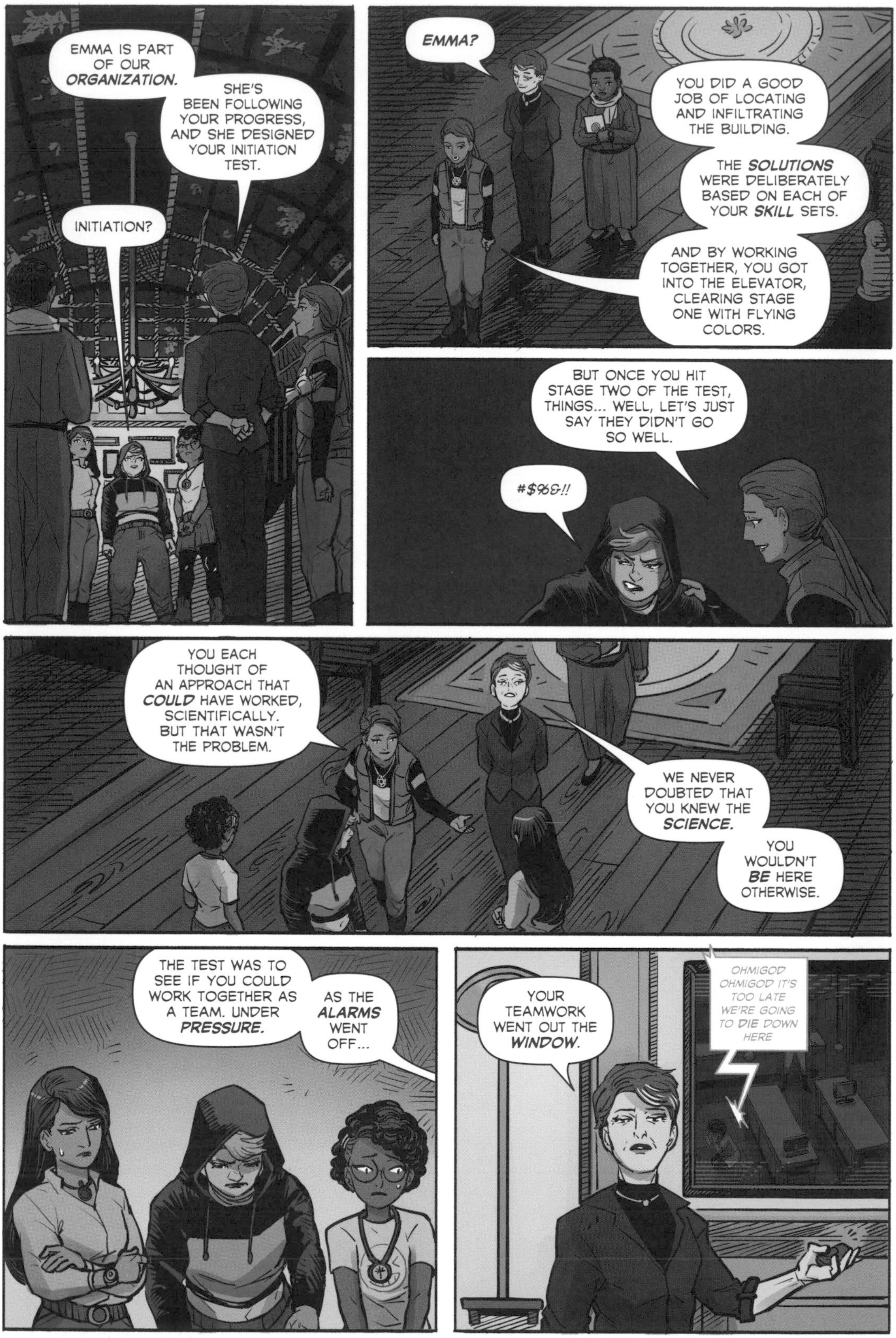
EMMA IS PART OF OUR ORGANIZATION.
SHE'S BEEN FOLLOWING YOUR PROGRESS, AND SHE DESIGNED YOUR INITIATION TEST.
INITIATION?
EMMA?
YOU DID A GOOD JOB OF LOCATING AND INFILTRATING THE BUILDING.
THE SOLUTIONS WERE DELIBERATELY BASED ON EACH OF YOUR SKILL SETS.
AND BY WORKING TOGETHER, YOU GOT INTO THE ELEVATOR, CLEARING STAGE ONE WITH FLYING COLORS.
BUT ONCE YOU HIT STAGE TWO OF THE TEST, THINGS... WELL, LET'S JUST SAY THEY DIDN'T GO SO WELL.
#$%&!!
YOU EACH THOUGHT OF AN APPROACH THAT COULD HAVE WORKED, SCIENTIFICALLY. BUT THAT WASN'T THE PROBLEM.
WE NEVER DOUBTED THAT YOU KNEW THE SCIENCE.
YOU WOULDN'T BE HERE OTHERWISE.
THE TEST WAS TO SEE IF YOU COULD WORK TOGETHER AS A TEAM. UNDER PRESSURE.
AS THE ALARMS WENT OFF...
YOUR TEAMWORK WENT OUT THE WINDOW.
OHMIGOD OHMIGOD IT'S TOO LATE WE'RE GOING TO DIE DOWN HERE

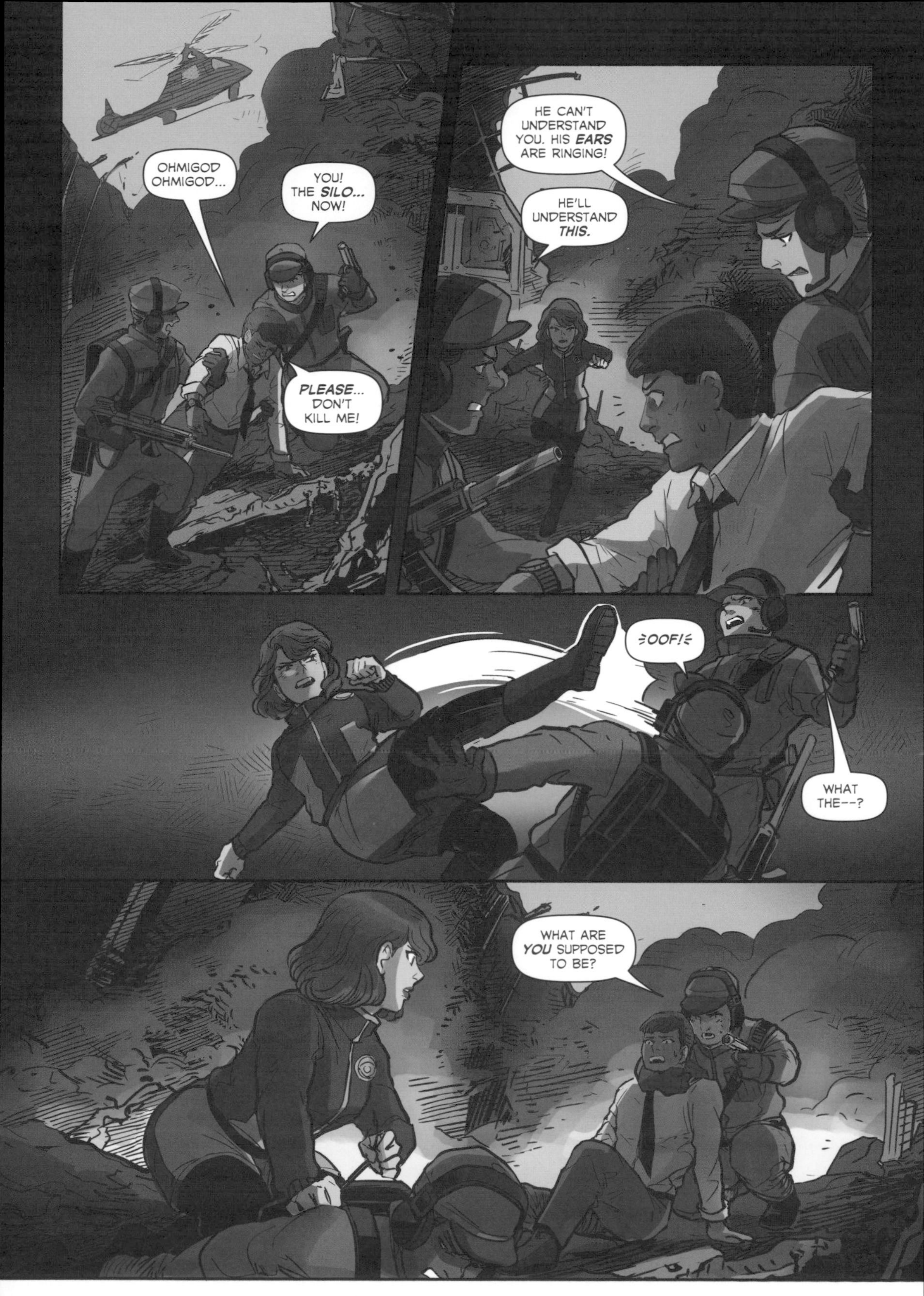
OHMIGOD OHMIGOD...
YOU! THE SILO... NOW!
PLEASE... DON'T KILL ME!
HE CAN'T UNDERSTAND YOU. HIS EARS ARE RINGING!
HE'LL UNDERSTAND THIS.
OOF!
WHAT THE--?
WHAT ARE YOU SUPPOSED TO BE?

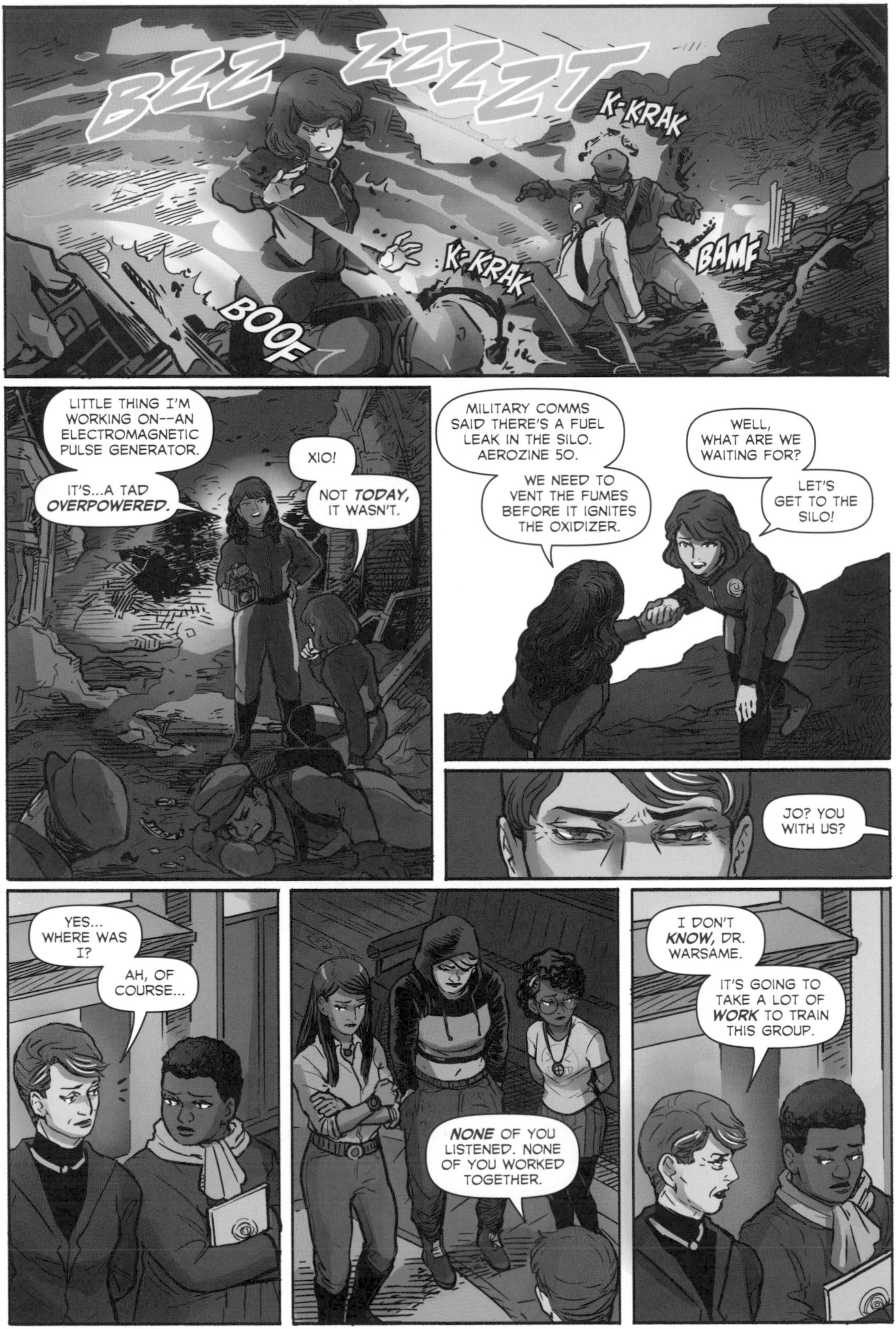
BZZ ZZZZZT
K-KRAK
K-KRAK
BAMF
BOOF
LITTLE THING I'M WORKING ON--AN ELECTROMAGNETIC PULSE GENERATOR.
IT'S...A TAD *OVERPOWERED.*
XIO!
NOT *TODAY,* IT WASN'T.
MILITARY COMMS SAID THERE'S A FUEL LEAK IN THE SILO. AEROZINE 50.
WE NEED TO VENT THE FUMES BEFORE IT IGNITES THE OXIDIZER.
WELL, WHAT ARE WE WAITING FOR?
LET'S GET TO THE SILO!
JO? YOU WITH US?
YES... WHERE WAS I?
AH, OF COURSE...
NONE OF YOU LISTENED. NONE OF YOU WORKED TOGETHER.
I DON'T *KNOW,* DR. WARSAME.
IT'S GOING TO TAKE A LOT OF *WORK* TO TRAIN THIS GROUP.

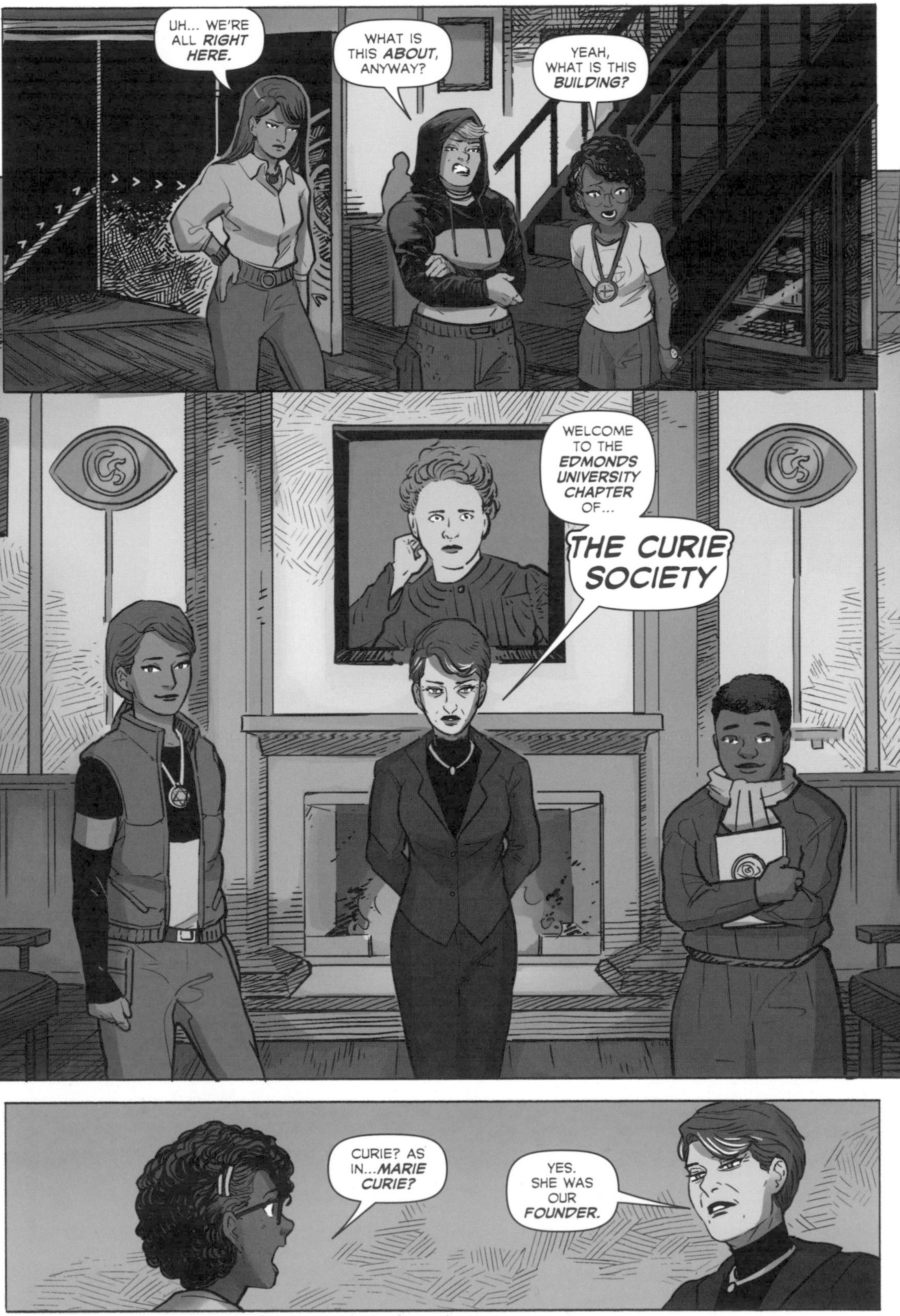
UH... WE'RE ALL RIGHT HERE.
WHAT IS THIS ABOUT, ANYWAY?
YEAH, WHAT IS THIS BUILDING?
WELCOME TO THE EDMONDS UNIVERSITY CHAPTER OF...
THE CURIE SOCIETY
CURIE? AS IN... MARIE CURIE?
YES. SHE WAS OUR FOUNDER.

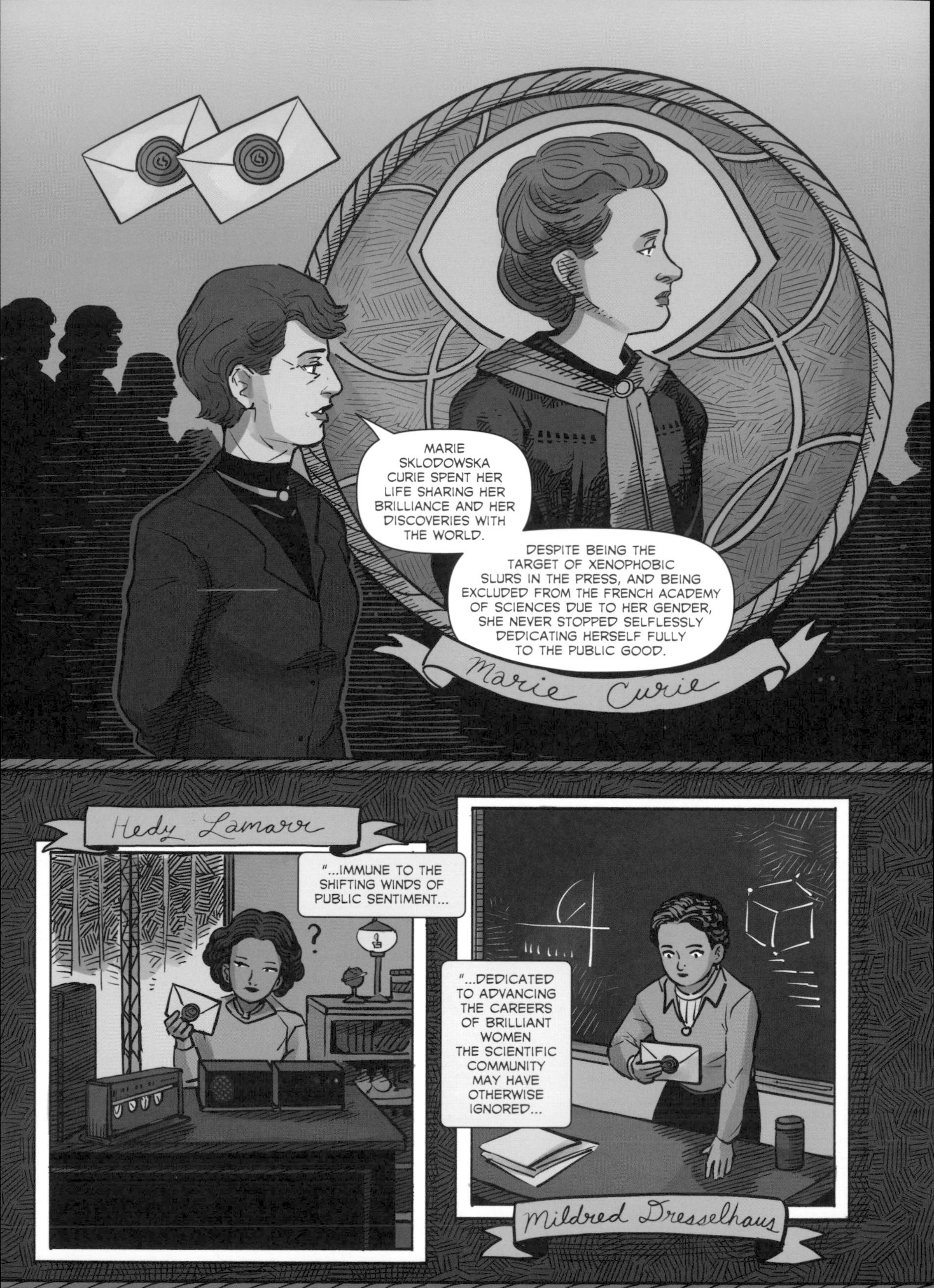
MARIE SKLODOWSKA CURIE SPENT HER LIFE SHARING HER BRILLIANCE AND HER DISCOVERIES WITH THE WORLD.
DESPITE BEING THE TARGET OF XENOPHOBIC SLURS IN THE PRESS, AND BEING EXCLUDED FROM THE FRENCH ACADEMY OF SCIENCES DUE TO HER GENDER, SHE NEVER STOPPED SELFLESSLY DEDICATING HERSELF FULLY TO THE PUBLIC GOOD.
Marie Curie
Hedy Lamarr
"...IMMUNE TO THE SHIFTING WINDS OF PUBLIC SENTIMENT...
?
"...DEDICATED TO ADVANCING THE CAREERS OF BRILLIANT WOMEN THE SCIENTIFIC COMMUNITY MAY HAVE OTHERWISE IGNORED...
Mildred Dresselhaus

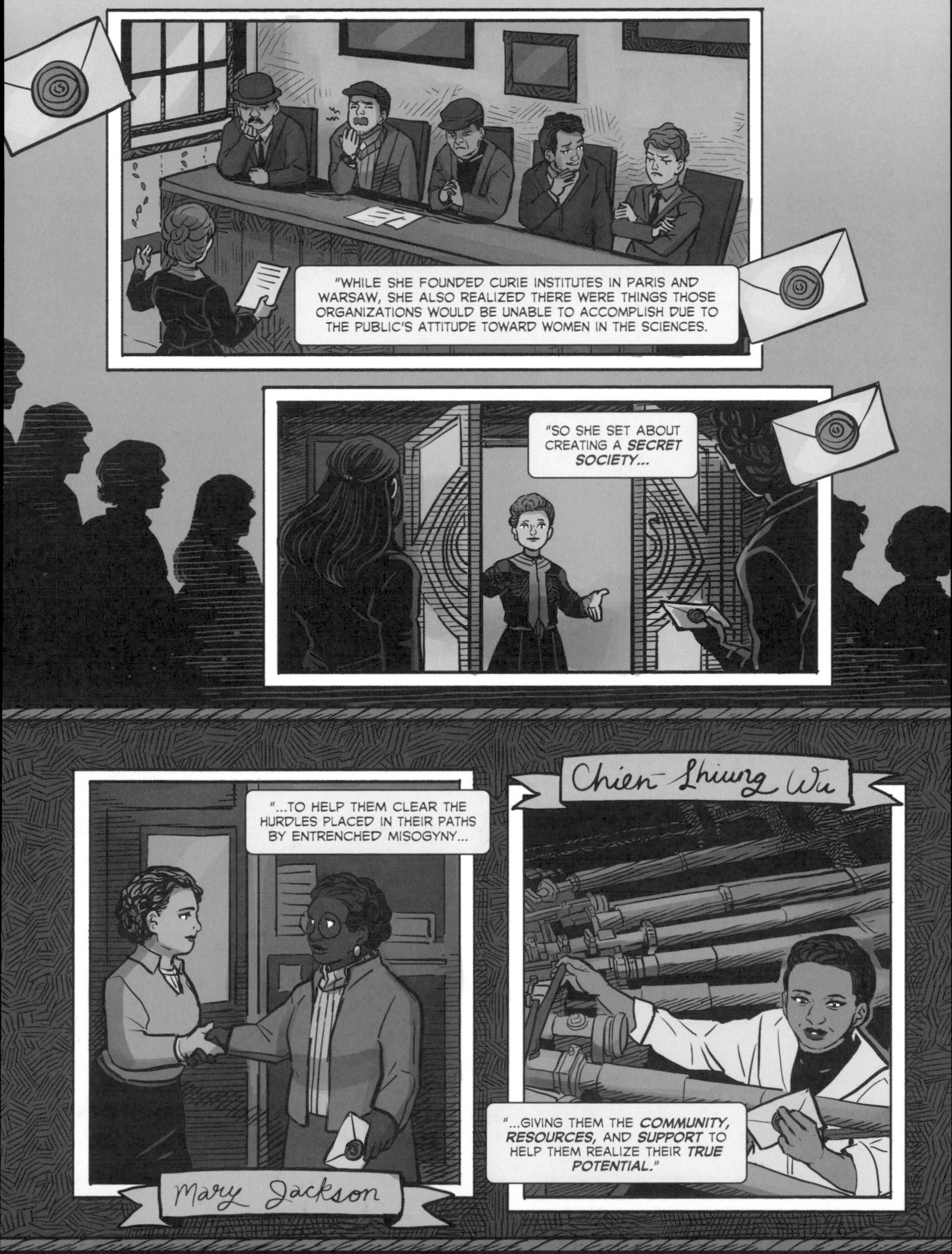
"WHILE SHE FOUNDED CURIE INSTITUTES IN PARIS AND WARSAW, SHE ALSO REALIZED THERE WERE THINGS THOSE ORGANIZATIONS WOULD BE UNABLE TO ACCOMPLISH DUE TO THE PUBLIC'S ATTITUDE TOWARD WOMEN IN THE SCIENCES.
"SO SHE SET ABOUT CREATING A *SECRET SOCIETY*...
"...TO HELP THEM CLEAR THE HURDLES PLACED IN THEIR PATHS BY ENTRENCHED MISOGYNY...
Mary Jackson
Chien-Shiung Wu
"...GIVING THEM THE ***COMMUNITY, RESOURCES,*** AND ***SUPPORT*** TO HELP THEM REALIZE THEIR ***TRUE POTENTIAL.***"

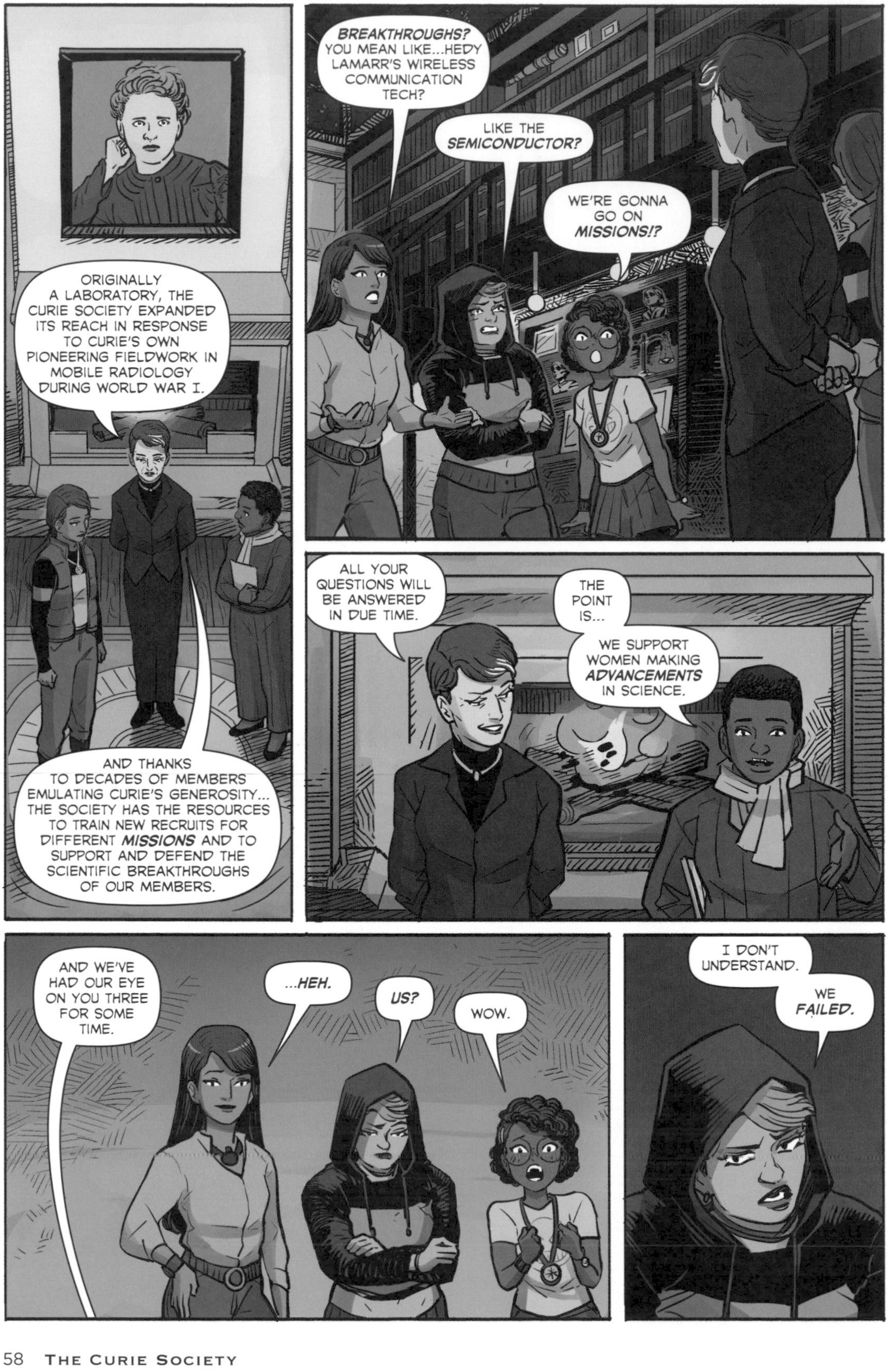

ORIGINALLY A LABORATORY, THE CURIE SOCIETY EXPANDED ITS REACH IN RESPONSE TO CURIE'S OWN PIONEERING FIELDWORK IN MOBILE RADIOLOGY DURING WORLD WAR I.
AND THANKS TO DECADES OF MEMBERS EMULATING CURIE'S GENEROSITY... THE SOCIETY HAS THE RESOURCES TO TRAIN NEW RECRUITS FOR DIFFERENT MISSIONS AND TO SUPPORT AND DEFEND THE SCIENTIFIC BREAKTHROUGHS OF OUR MEMBERS.
BREAKTHROUGHS? YOU MEAN LIKE...HEDY LAMARR'S WIRELESS COMMUNICATION TECH?
LIKE THE SEMICONDUCTOR?
WE'RE GONNA GO ON MISSIONS!?
ALL YOUR QUESTIONS WILL BE ANSWERED IN DUE TIME.
THE POINT IS...
WE SUPPORT WOMEN MAKING ADVANCEMENTS IN SCIENCE.
AND WE'VE HAD OUR EYE ON YOU THREE FOR SOME TIME.
...HEH.
US?
WOW.
I DON'T UNDERSTAND.
WE FAILED.

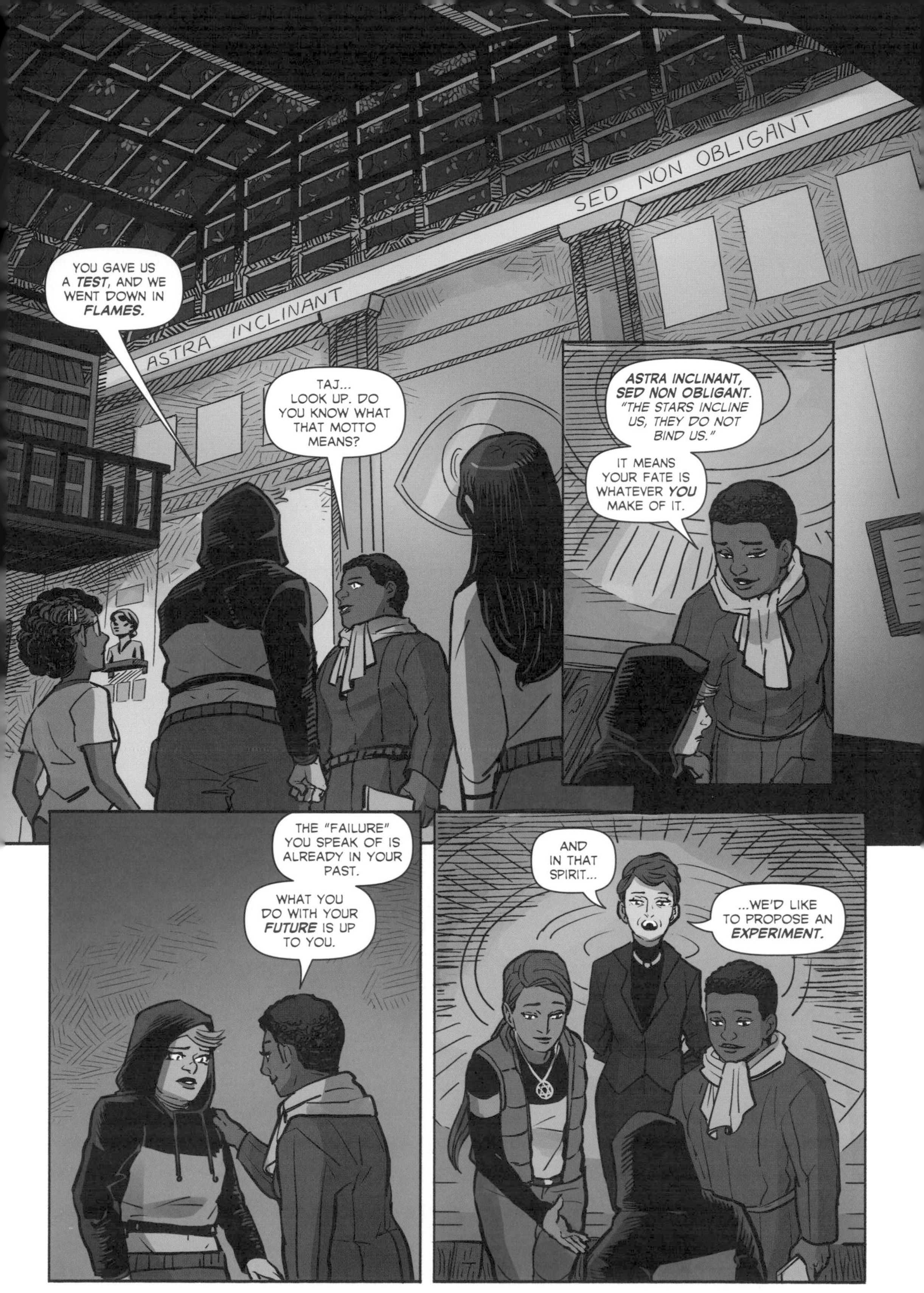
ASTRA INCLINANT
SED NON OBLIGANT
YOU GAVE US A TEST, AND WE WENT DOWN IN FLAMES.
TAJ... LOOK UP. DO YOU KNOW WHAT THAT MOTTO MEANS?
ASTRA INCLINANT, SED NON OBLIGANT. "THE STARS INCLINE US, THEY DO NOT BIND US."
IT MEANS YOUR FATE IS WHATEVER YOU MAKE OF IT.
THE "FAILURE" YOU SPEAK OF IS ALREADY IN YOUR PAST.
WHAT YOU DO WITH YOUR FUTURE IS UP TO YOU.
AND IN THAT SPIRIT...
...WE'D LIKE TO PROPOSE AN EXPERIMENT.

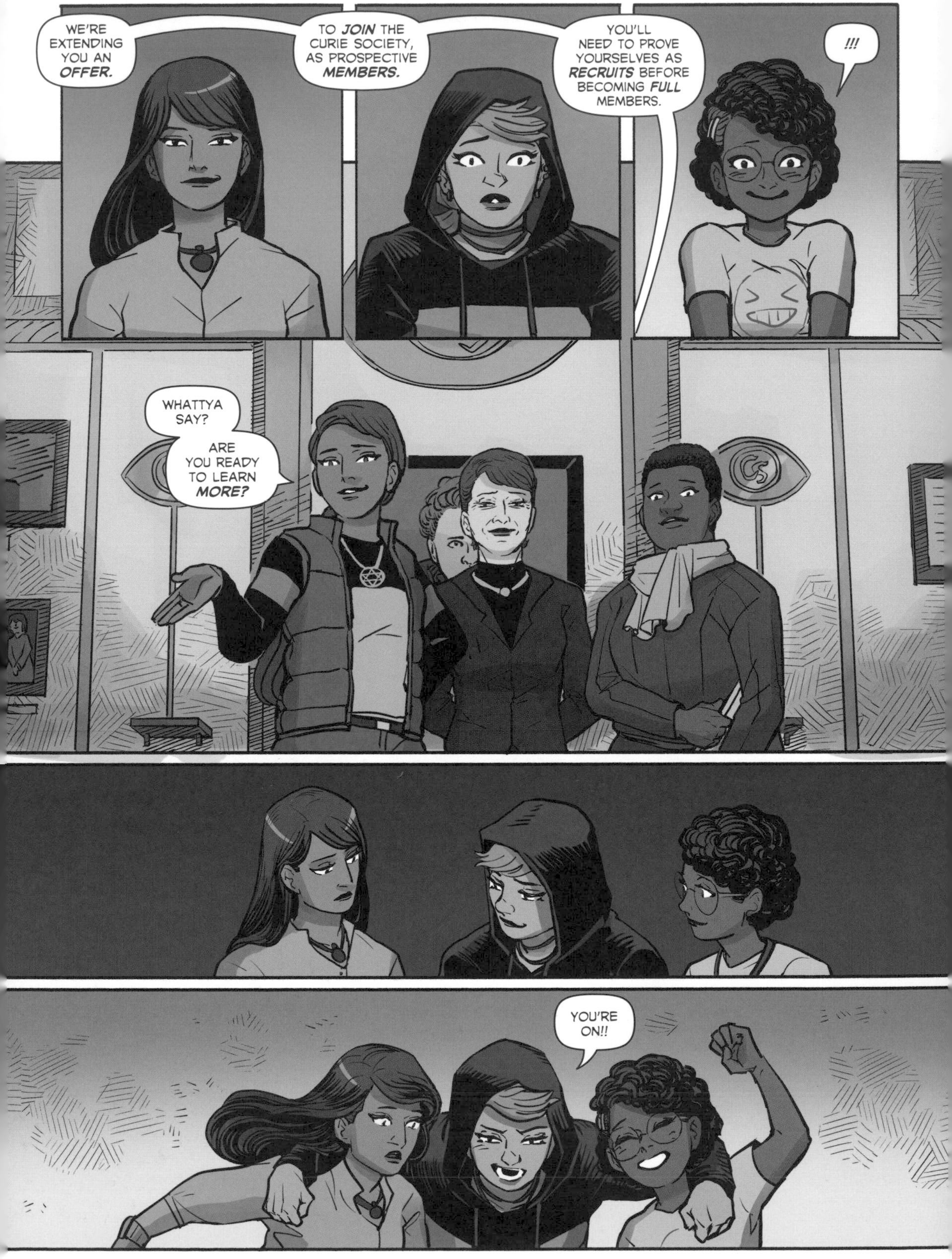
WE'RE EXTENDING YOU AN *OFFER.*
TO *JOIN* THE CURIE SOCIETY, AS PROSPECTIVE *MEMBERS.*
YOU'LL NEED TO PROVE YOURSELVES AS *RECRUITS* BEFORE BECOMING *FULL* MEMBERS.
!!!
WHATTYA SAY?
ARE YOU READY TO LEARN *MORE?*
YOU'RE ON!!

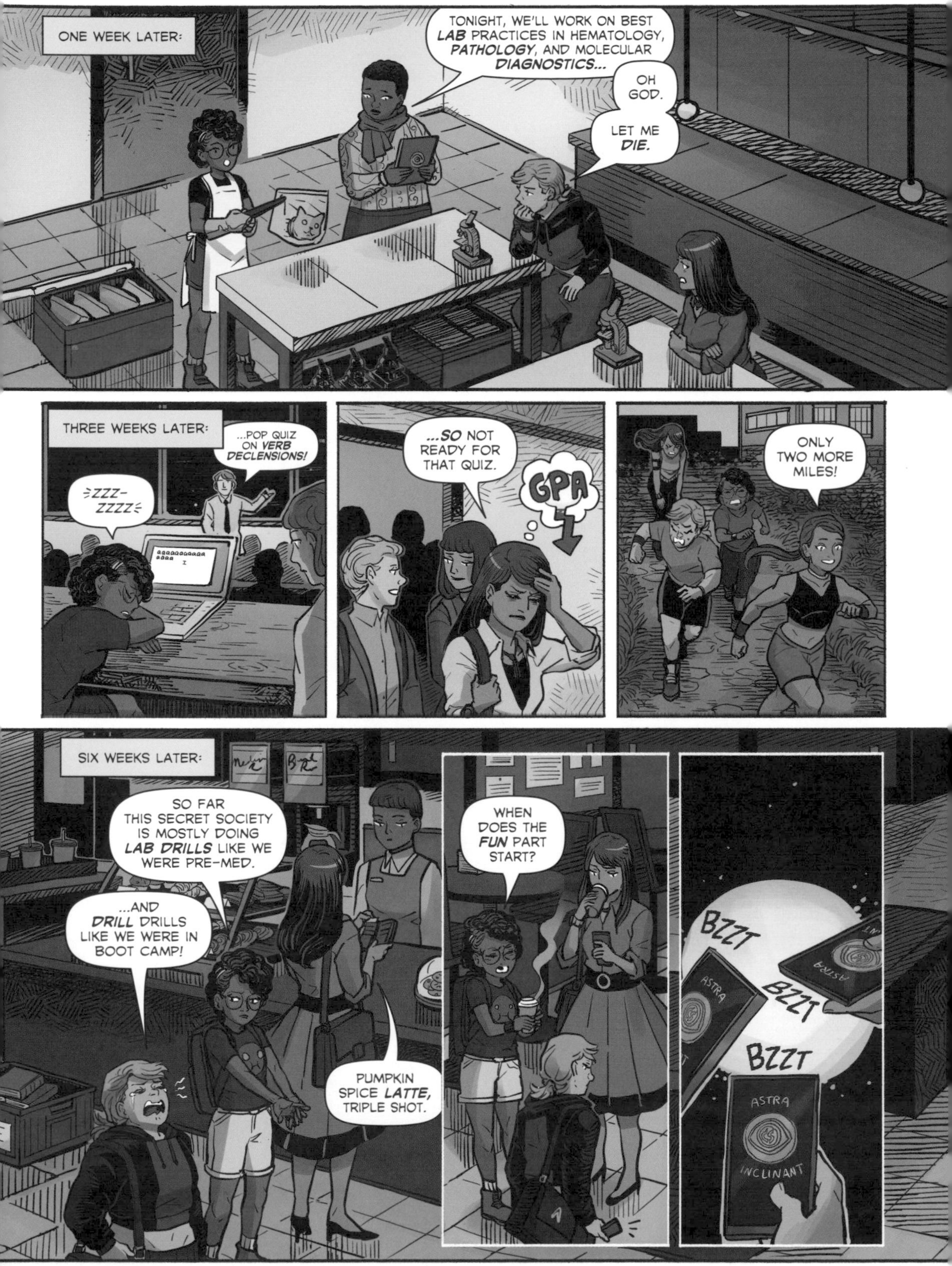
ONE WEEK LATER:
TONIGHT, WE'LL WORK ON BEST LAB PRACTICES IN HEMATOLOGY, PATHOLOGY, AND MOLECULAR DIAGNOSTICS...
OH GOD.
LET ME DIE.
THREE WEEKS LATER:
...POP QUIZ ON VERB DECLENSIONS!
ZZZ-ZZZZ
...SO NOT READY FOR THAT QUIZ.
GPA
ONLY TWO MORE MILES!
SIX WEEKS LATER:
SO FAR THIS SECRET SOCIETY IS MOSTLY DOING LAB DRILLS LIKE WE WERE PRE-MED.
...AND DRILL DRILLS LIKE WE WERE IN BOOT CAMP!
PUMPKIN SPICE LATTE, TRIPLE SHOT.
WHEN DOES THE FUN PART START?
BZZT
BZZT
BZZT
ASTRA
ASTRA
ASTRA
INCLINANT

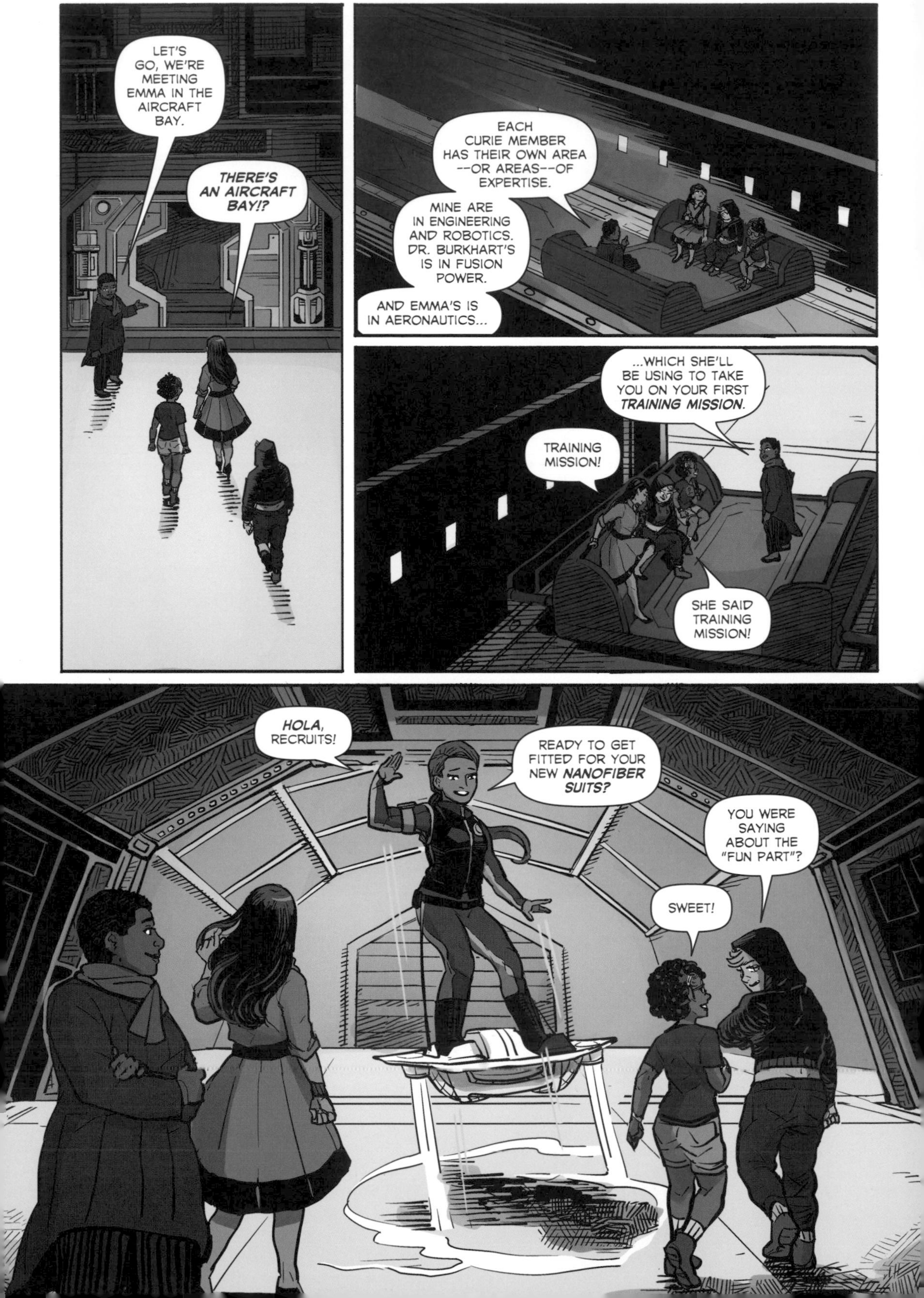
LET'S GO, WE'RE MEETING EMMA IN THE AIRCRAFT BAY.
THERE'S AN AIRCRAFT BAY!?
EACH CURIE MEMBER HAS THEIR OWN AREA --OR AREAS--OF EXPERTISE.
MINE ARE IN ENGINEERING AND ROBOTICS. DR. BURKHART'S IS IN FUSION POWER.
AND EMMA'S IS IN AERONAUTICS...
...WHICH SHE'LL BE USING TO TAKE YOU ON YOUR FIRST TRAINING MISSION.
TRAINING MISSION!
SHE SAID TRAINING MISSION!
HOLA, RECRUITS!
READY TO GET FITTED FOR YOUR NEW NANOFIBER SUITS?
YOU WERE SAYING ABOUT THE "FUN PART"?
SWEET!

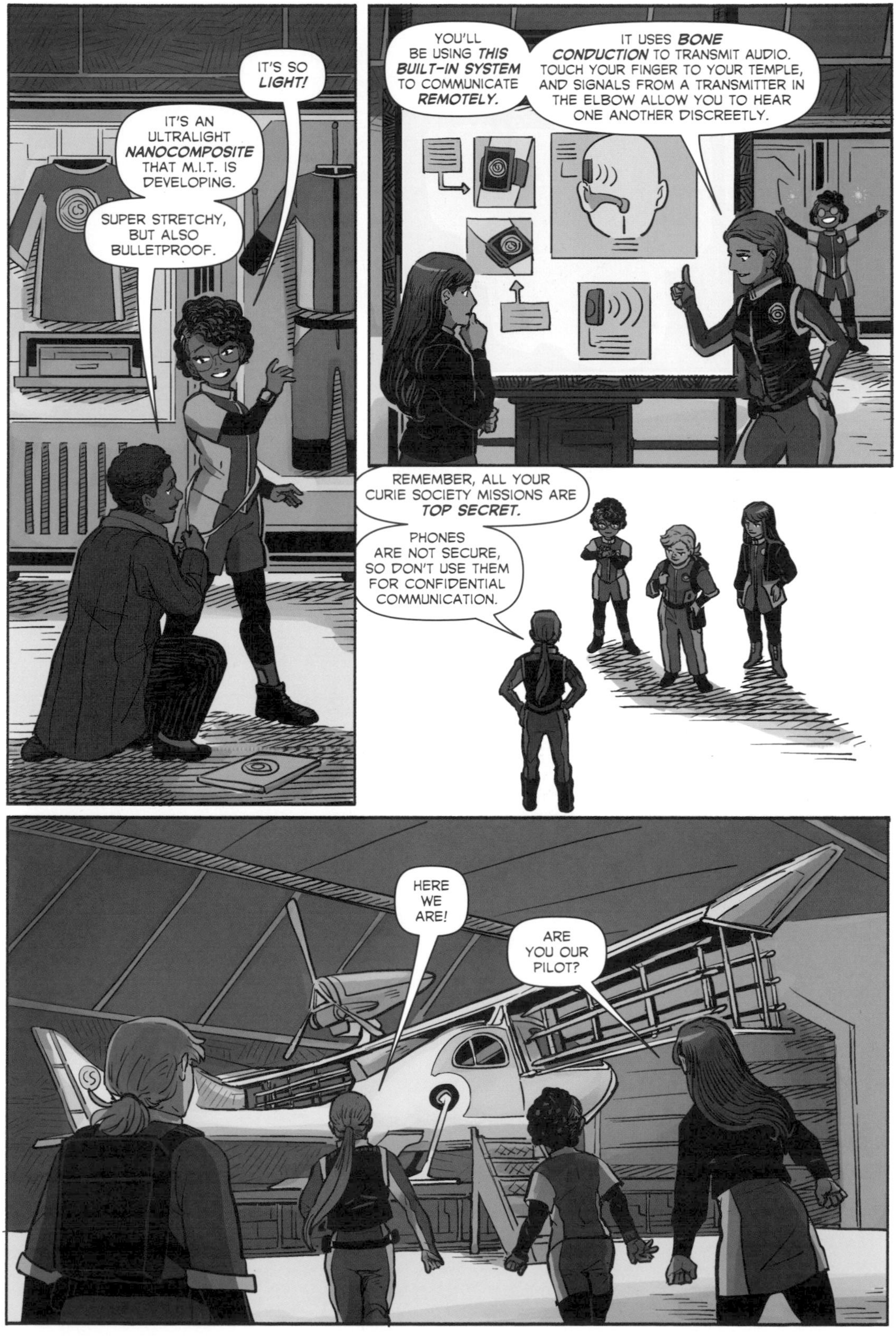
IT'S SO LIGHT!
IT'S AN ULTRALIGHT NANOCOMPOSITE THAT M.I.T. IS DEVELOPING.
SUPER STRETCHY, BUT ALSO BULLETPROOF.
YOU'LL BE USING THIS BUILT-IN SYSTEM TO COMMUNICATE REMOTELY.
IT USES BONE CONDUCTION TO TRANSMIT AUDIO. TOUCH YOUR FINGER TO YOUR TEMPLE, AND SIGNALS FROM A TRANSMITTER IN THE ELBOW ALLOW YOU TO HEAR ONE ANOTHER DISCREETLY.
REMEMBER, ALL YOUR CURIE SOCIETY MISSIONS ARE TOP SECRET.
PHONES ARE NOT SECURE, SO DON'T USE THEM FOR CONFIDENTIAL COMMUNICATION.
HERE WE ARE!
ARE YOU OUR PILOT?

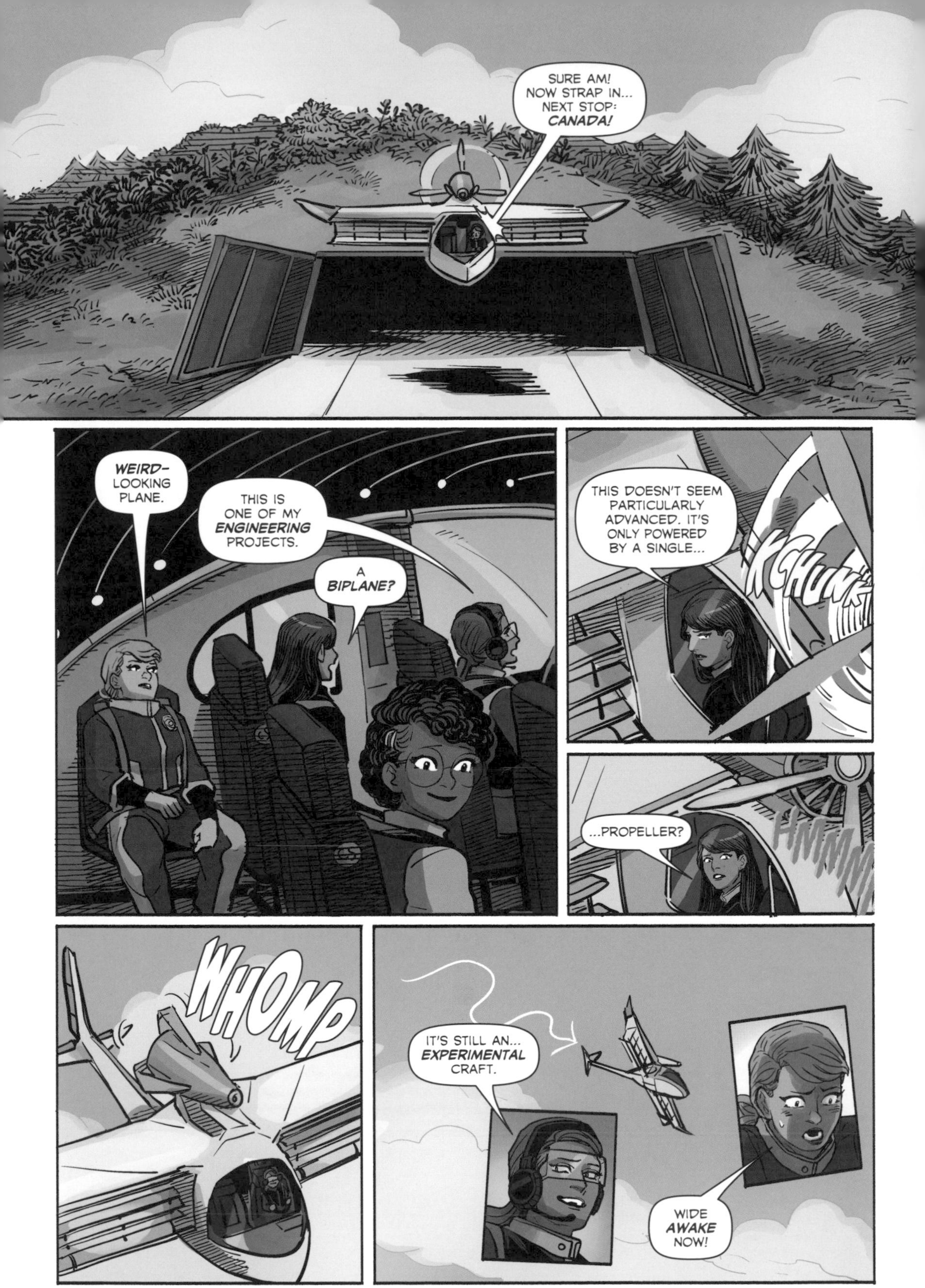
SURE AM! NOW STRAP IN... NEXT STOP: *CANADA!*
WEIRD-LOOKING PLANE.
THIS IS ONE OF MY *ENGINEERING* PROJECTS.
A *BIPLANE?*
THIS DOESN'T SEEM PARTICULARLY ADVANCED. IT'S ONLY POWERED BY A SINGLE...
KCHUNK
...PROPELLER?
HMMM
WHOMP
IT'S STILL AN... *EXPERIMENTAL* CRAFT.
WIDE *AWAKE* NOW!

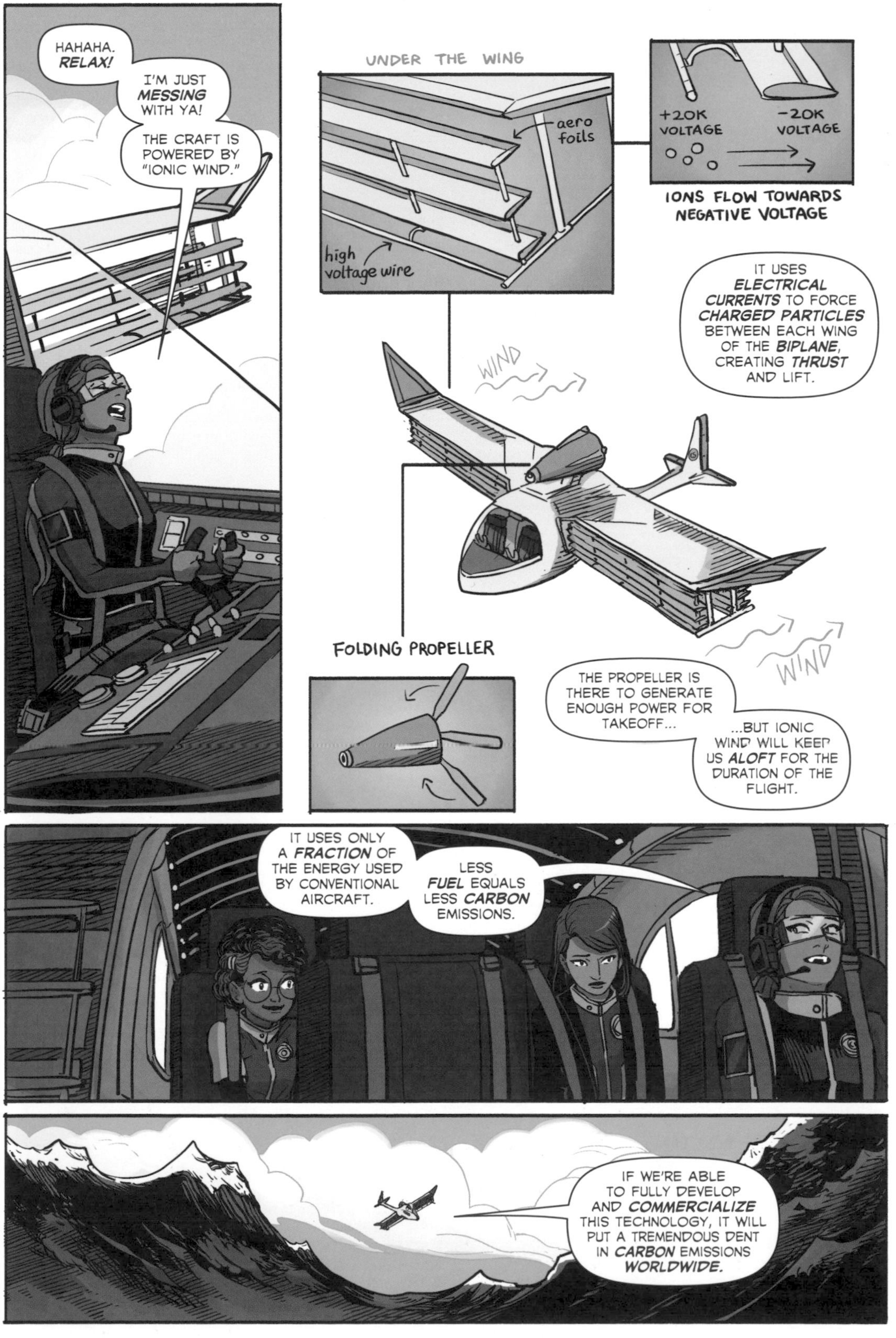
HAHAHA. RELAX!
I'M JUST MESSING WITH YA!
THE CRAFT IS POWERED BY "IONIC WIND."
UNDER THE WING
aero foils
high voltage wire
+20K VOLTAGE
-20K VOLTAGE
IONS FLOW TOWARDS NEGATIVE VOLTAGE
IT USES ELECTRICAL CURRENTS TO FORCE CHARGED PARTICLES BETWEEN EACH WING OF THE BIPLANE, CREATING THRUST AND LIFT.
WIND
WIND
FOLDING PROPELLER
THE PROPELLER IS THERE TO GENERATE ENOUGH POWER FOR TAKEOFF...
...BUT IONIC WIND WILL KEEP US ALOFT FOR THE DURATION OF THE FLIGHT.
IT USES ONLY A FRACTION OF THE ENERGY USED BY CONVENTIONAL AIRCRAFT.
LESS FUEL EQUALS LESS CARBON EMISSIONS.
IF WE'RE ABLE TO FULLY DEVELOP AND COMMERCIALIZE THIS TECHNOLOGY, IT WILL PUT A TREMENDOUS DENT IN CARBON EMISSIONS WORLDWIDE.

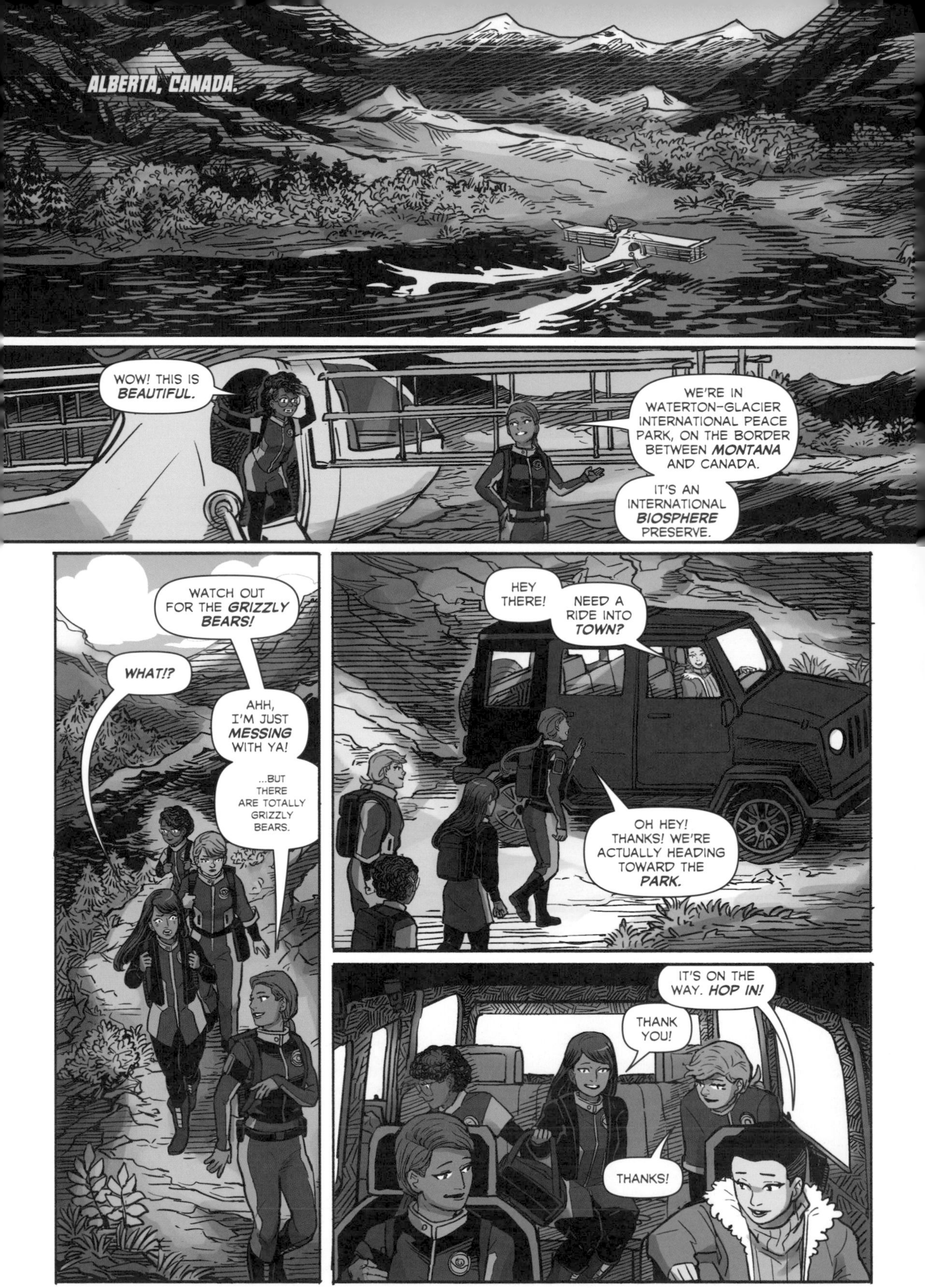

ALBERTA, CANADA.
WOW! THIS IS *BEAUTIFUL.*
WE'RE IN WATERTON-GLACIER INTERNATIONAL PEACE PARK, ON THE BORDER BETWEEN *MONTANA* AND CANADA.
IT'S AN INTERNATIONAL *BIOSPHERE* PRESERVE.
WATCH OUT FOR THE *GRIZZLY BEARS!*
WHAT!?
AHH, I'M JUST *MESSING* WITH YA!
...BUT THERE ARE TOTALLY GRIZZLY BEARS.
HEY THERE!
NEED A RIDE INTO *TOWN?*
OH HEY! THANKS! WE'RE ACTUALLY HEADING TOWARD THE *PARK.*
IT'S ON THE WAY. *HOP IN!*
THANK YOU!
THANKS!

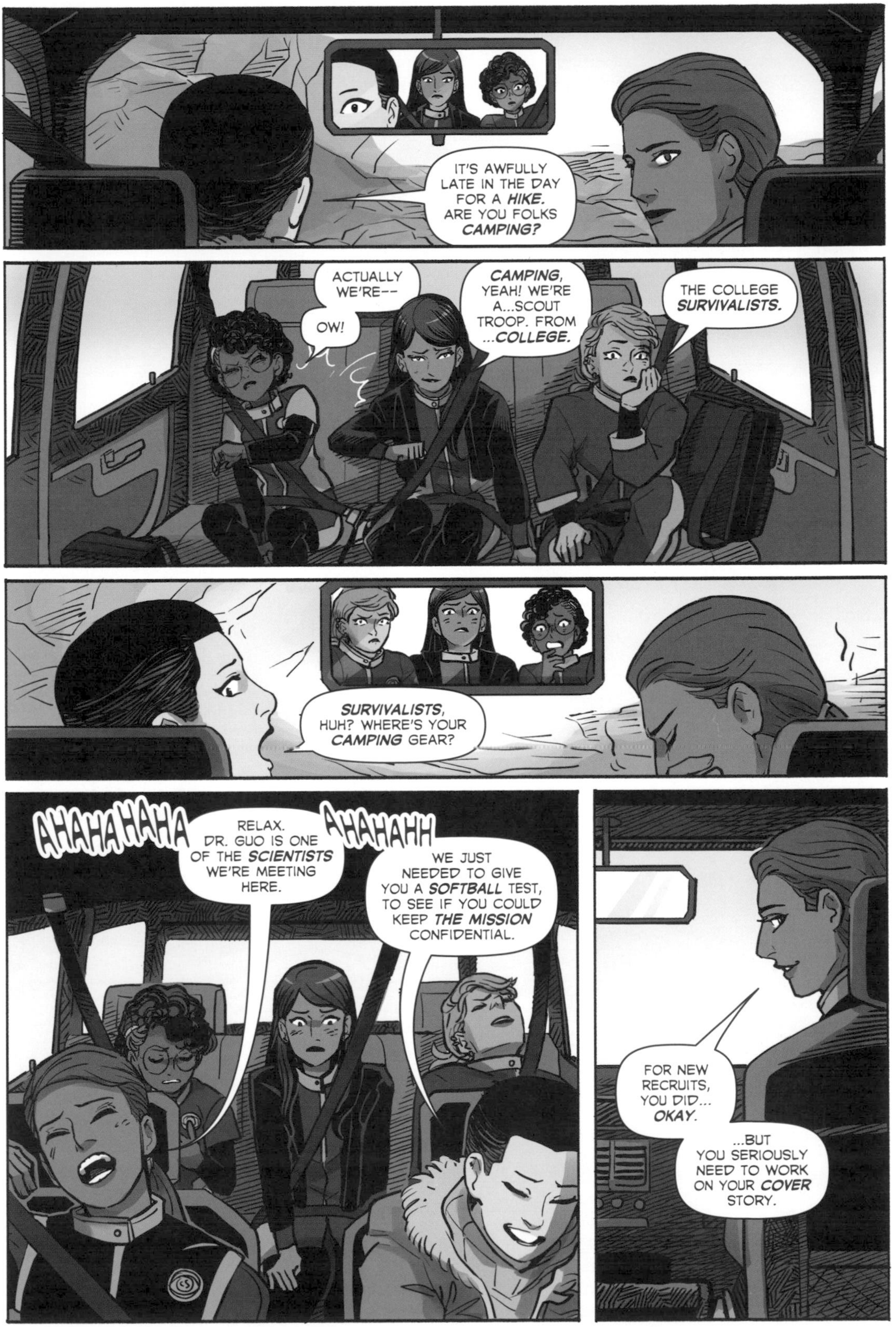

IT'S AWFULLY LATE IN THE DAY FOR A HIKE. ARE YOU FOLKS CAMPING?
ACTUALLY WE'RE--
OW!
CAMPING, YEAH! WE'RE A...SCOUT TROOP. FROM ...COLLEGE.
THE COLLEGE SURVIVALISTS.
SURVIVALISTS, HUH? WHERE'S YOUR CAMPING GEAR?
AHAHAHAHA
RELAX. DR. GUO IS ONE OF THE SCIENTISTS WE'RE MEETING HERE.
AHAHAHH
WE JUST NEEDED TO GIVE YOU A SOFTBALL TEST, TO SEE IF YOU COULD KEEP THE MISSION CONFIDENTIAL.
FOR NEW RECRUITS, YOU DID... OKAY.
...BUT YOU SERIOUSLY NEED TO WORK ON YOUR COVER STORY.

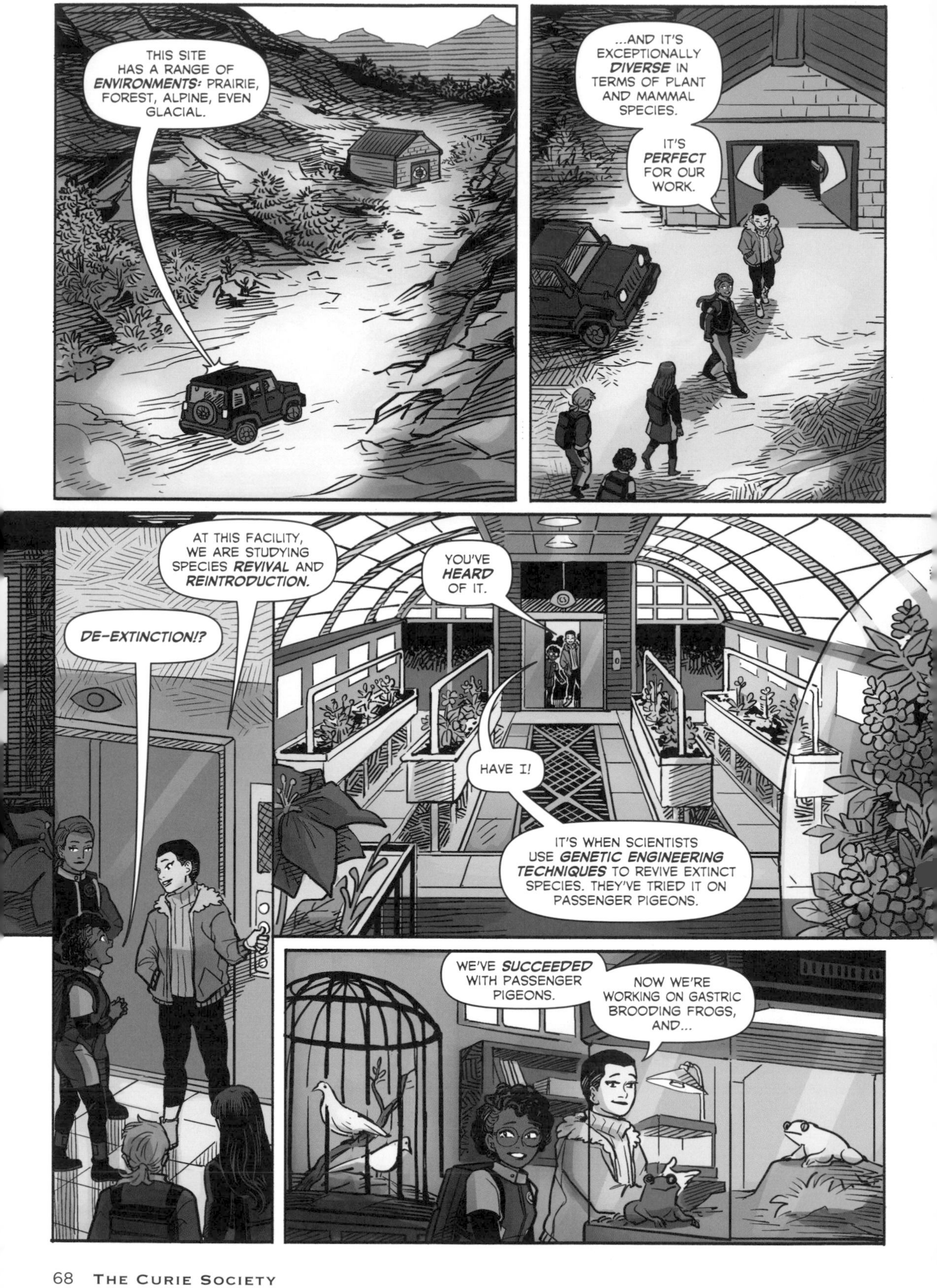
THIS SITE HAS A RANGE OF ENVIRONMENTS: PRAIRIE, FOREST, ALPINE, EVEN GLACIAL.
...AND IT'S EXCEPTIONALLY DIVERSE IN TERMS OF PLANT AND MAMMAL SPECIES.
IT'S PERFECT FOR OUR WORK.
AT THIS FACILITY, WE ARE STUDYING SPECIES REVIVAL AND REINTRODUCTION.
DE-EXTINCTION!?
YOU'VE HEARD OF IT.
HAVE I!
IT'S WHEN SCIENTISTS USE GENETIC ENGINEERING TECHNIQUES TO REVIVE EXTINCT SPECIES. THEY'VE TRIED IT ON PASSENGER PIGEONS.
WE'VE SUCCEEDED WITH PASSENGER PIGEONS.
NOW WE'RE WORKING ON GASTRIC BROODING FROGS, AND...

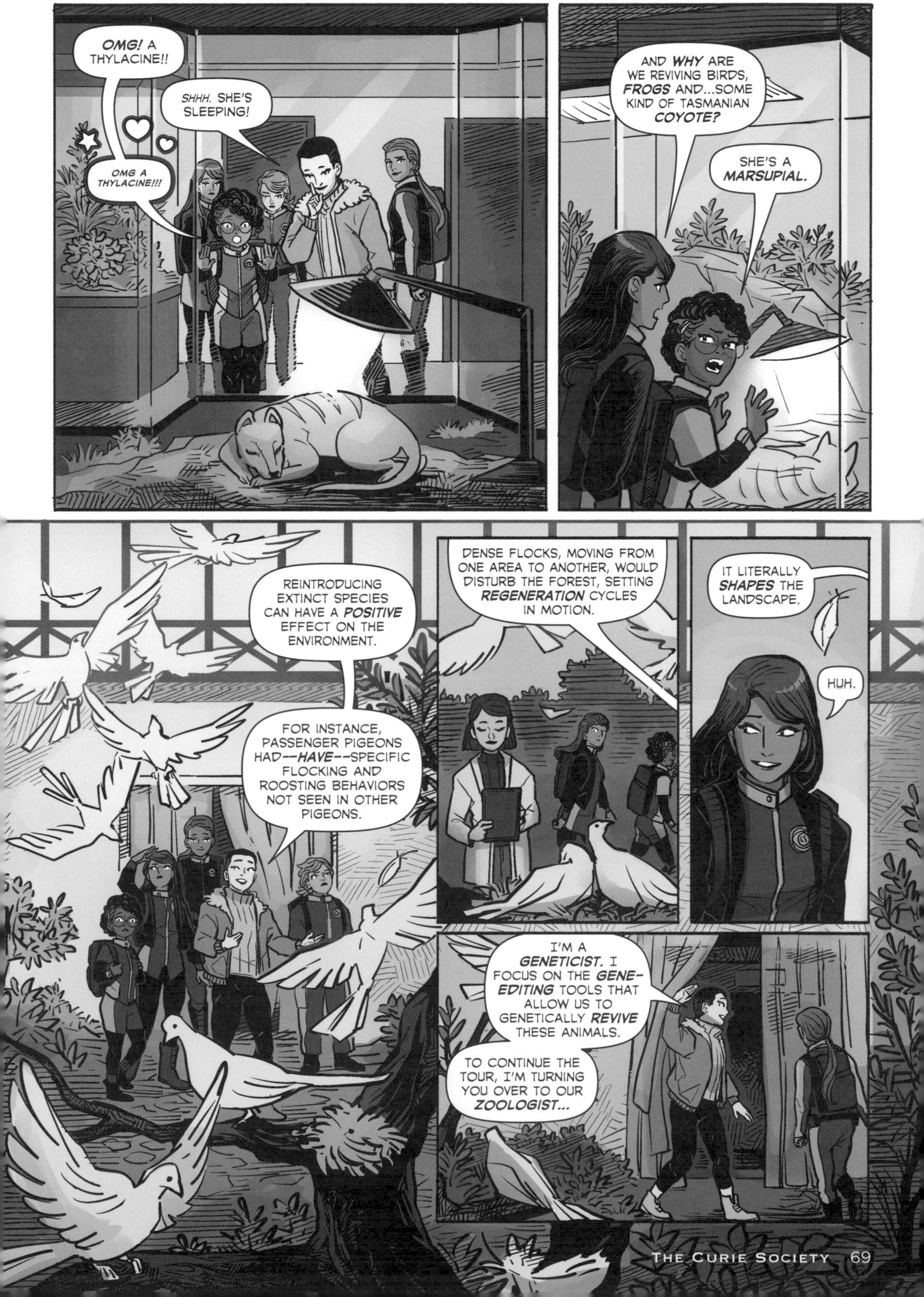
OMG! A THYLACINE!!
SHHH. SHE'S SLEEPING!
OMG A THYLACINE!!!
AND WHY ARE WE REVIVING BIRDS, FROGS AND...SOME KIND OF TASMANIAN COYOTE?
SHE'S A MARSUPIAL.
REINTRODUCING EXTINCT SPECIES CAN HAVE A POSITIVE EFFECT ON THE ENVIRONMENT.
FOR INSTANCE, PASSENGER PIGEONS HAD--HAVE--SPECIFIC FLOCKING AND ROOSTING BEHAVIORS NOT SEEN IN OTHER PIGEONS.
DENSE FLOCKS, MOVING FROM ONE AREA TO ANOTHER, WOULD DISTURB THE FOREST, SETTING REGENERATION CYCLES IN MOTION.
IT LITERALLY SHAPES THE LANDSCAPE.
HUH.
I'M A GENETICIST. I FOCUS ON THE GENE-EDITING TOOLS THAT ALLOW US TO GENETICALLY REVIVE THESE ANIMALS.
TO CONTINUE THE TOUR, I'M TURNING YOU OVER TO OUR ZOOLOGIST...

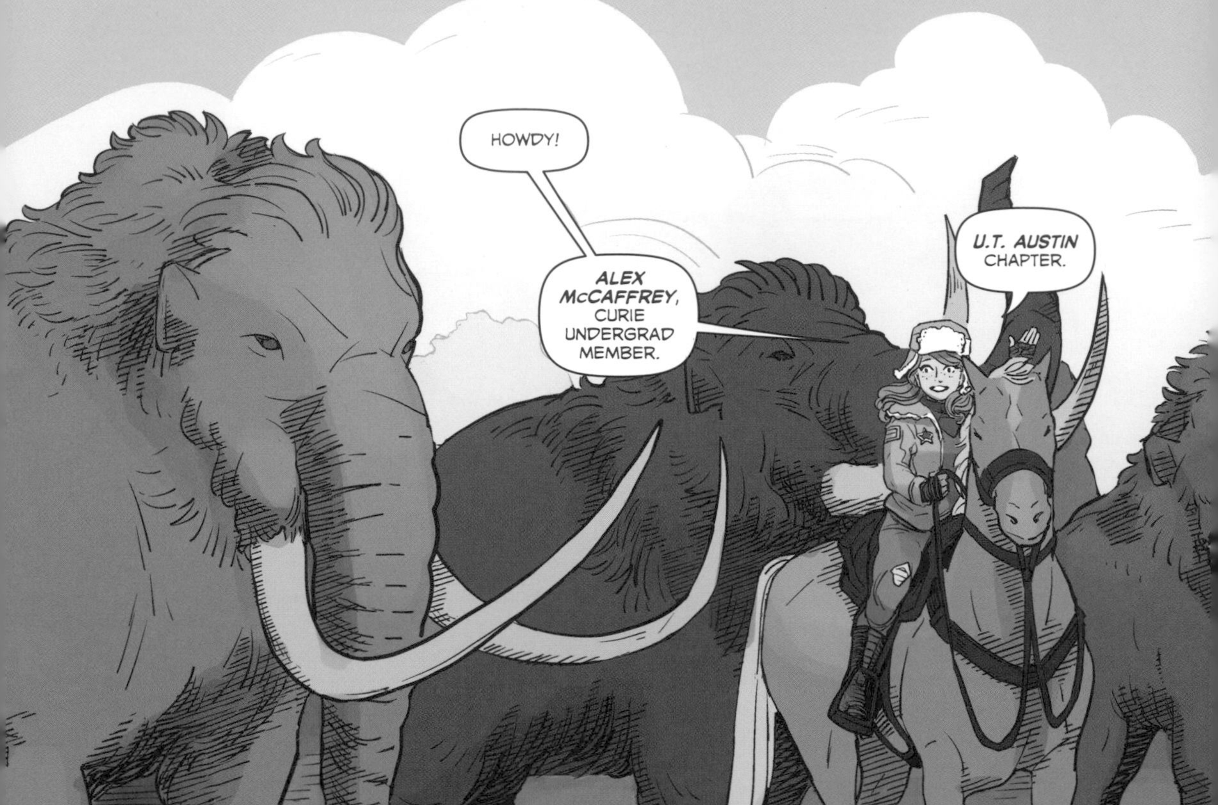
HOWDY!
ALEX McCAFFREY, CURIE UNDERGRAD MEMBER.
U.T. AUSTIN CHAPTER.

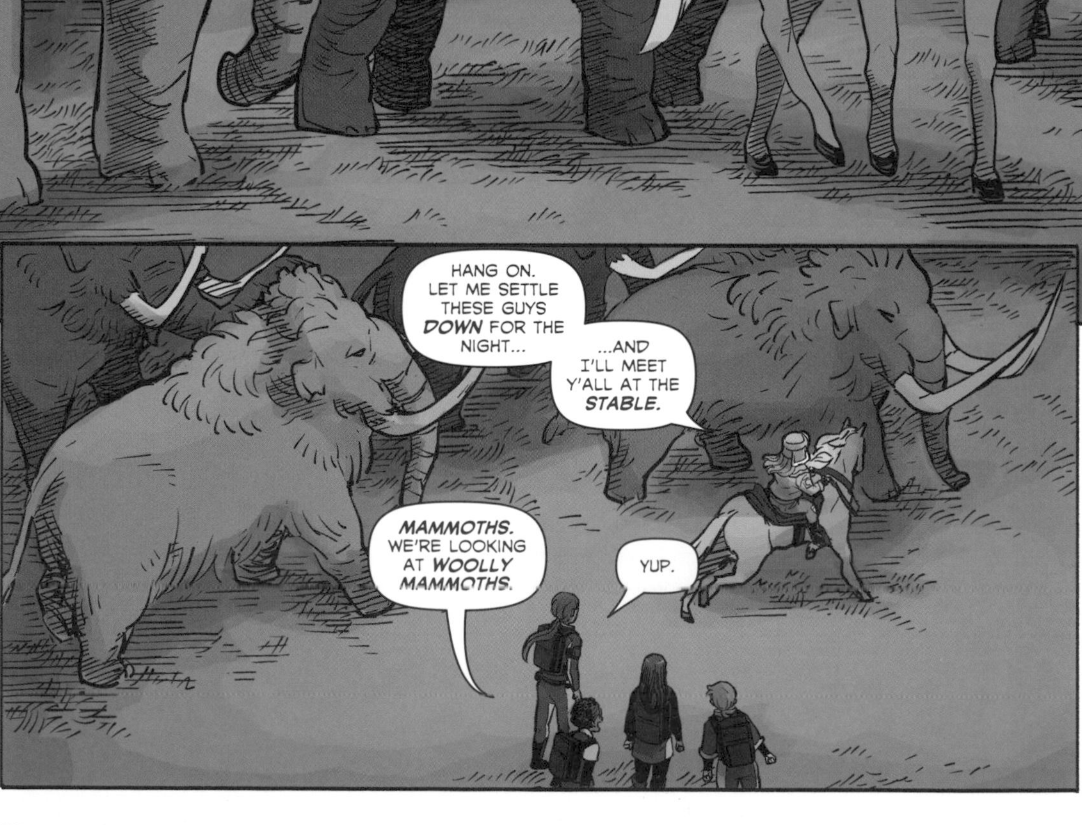
HANG ON. LET ME SETTLE THESE GUYS DOWN FOR THE NIGHT...
...AND I'LL MEET Y'ALL AT THE STABLE.
MAMMOTHS. WE'RE LOOKING AT WOOLLY MAMMOTHS.
YUP.

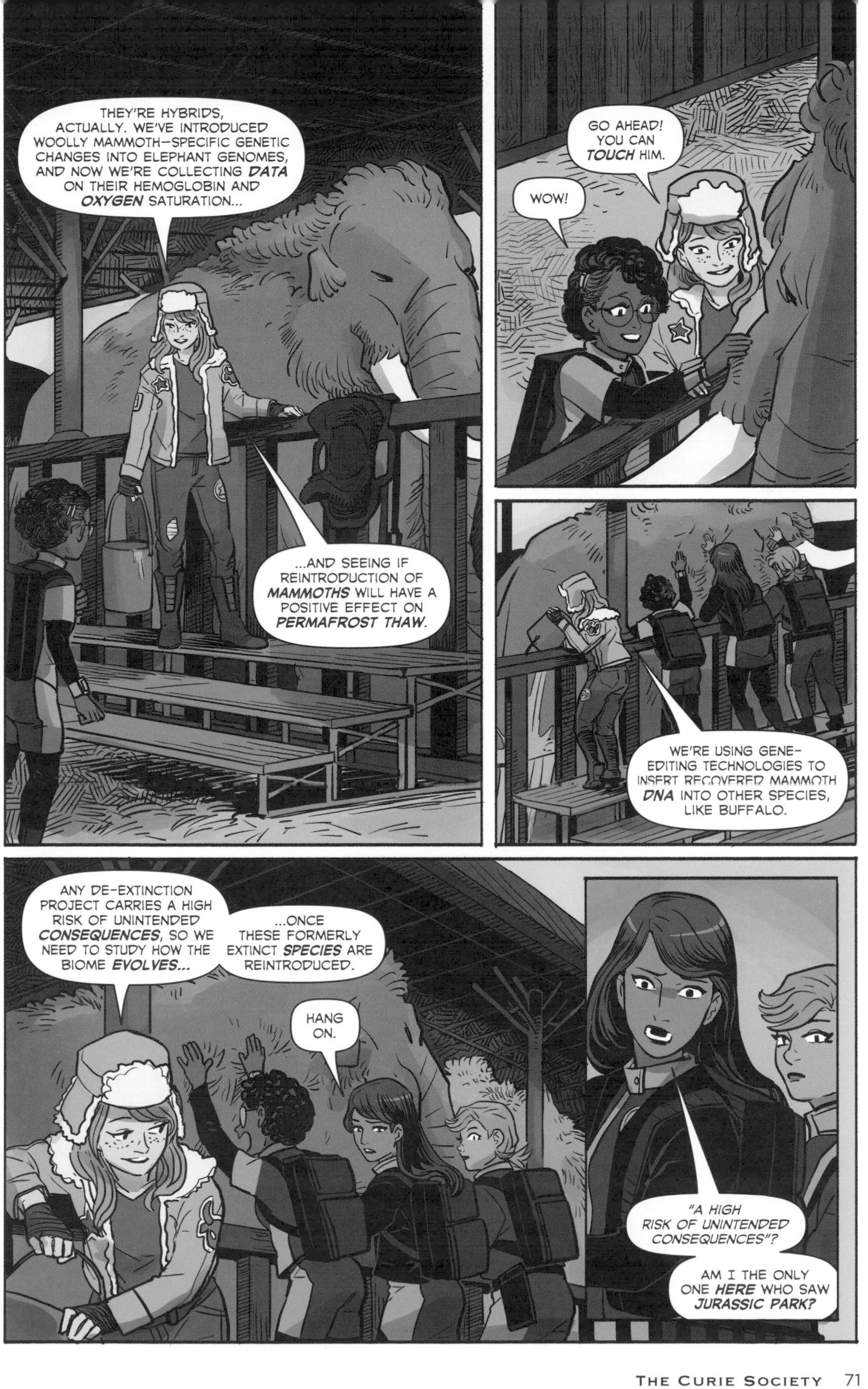
THEY'RE HYBRIDS, ACTUALLY. WE'VE INTRODUCED WOOLLY MAMMOTH–SPECIFIC GENETIC CHANGES INTO ELEPHANT GENOMES, AND NOW WE'RE COLLECTING DATA ON THEIR HEMOGLOBIN AND OXYGEN SATURATION...
...AND SEEING IF REINTRODUCTION OF MAMMOTHS WILL HAVE A POSITIVE EFFECT ON PERMAFROST THAW.
GO AHEAD! YOU CAN TOUCH HIM.
WOW!
WE'RE USING GENE-EDITING TECHNOLOGIES TO INSERT RECOVERED MAMMOTH DNA INTO OTHER SPECIES, LIKE BUFFALO.
ANY DE-EXTINCTION PROJECT CARRIES A HIGH RISK OF UNINTENDED CONSEQUENCES, SO WE NEED TO STUDY HOW THE BIOME EVOLVES...
...ONCE THESE FORMERLY EXTINCT SPECIES ARE REINTRODUCED.
HANG ON.
"A HIGH RISK OF UNINTENDED CONSEQUENCES"?
AM I THE ONLY ONE HERE WHO SAW JURASSIC PARK?

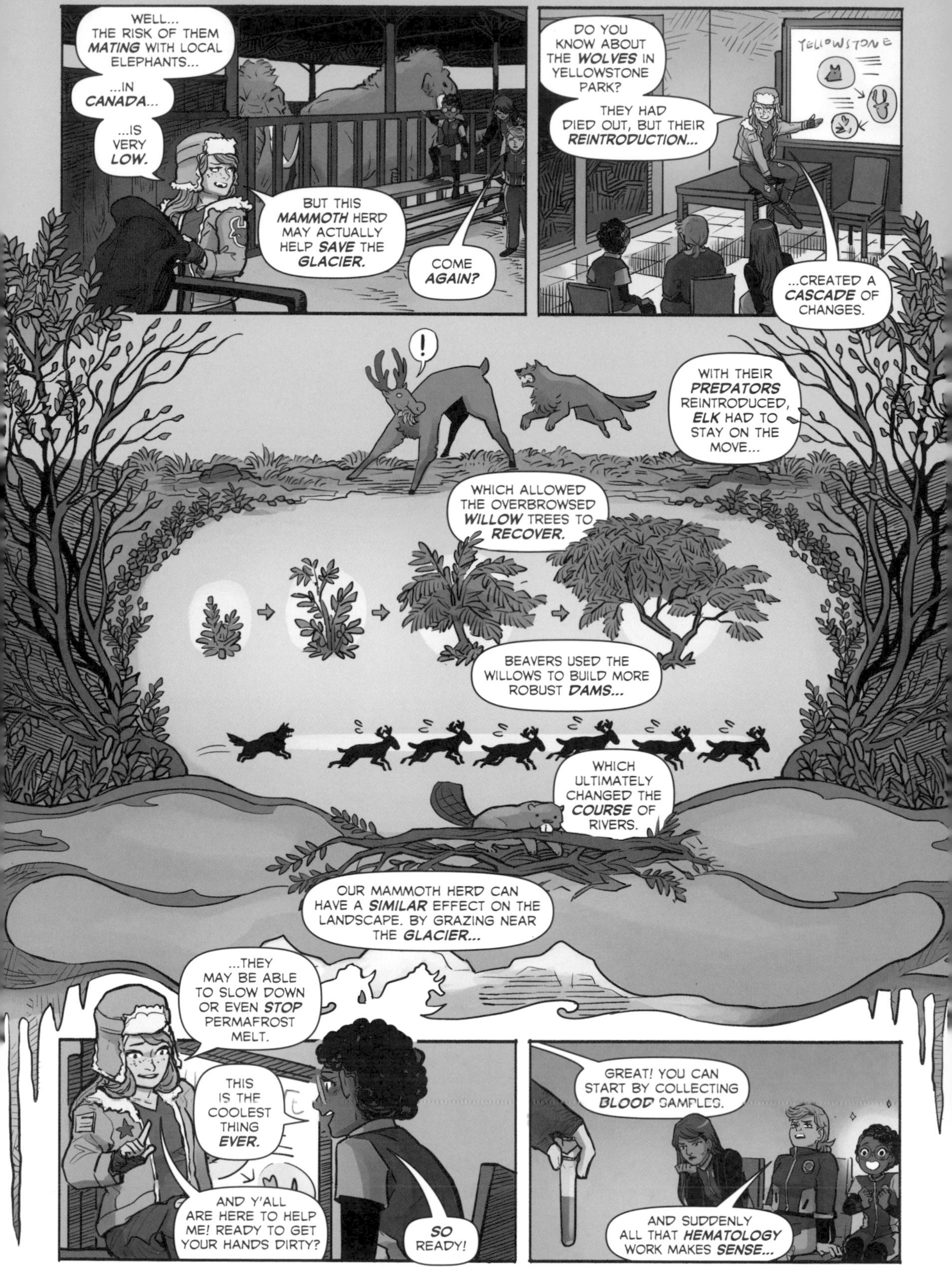
WELL... THE RISK OF THEM MATING WITH LOCAL ELEPHANTS...
...IN CANADA...
...IS VERY LOW.
BUT THIS MAMMOTH HERD MAY ACTUALLY HELP SAVE THE GLACIER.
COME AGAIN?
DO YOU KNOW ABOUT THE WOLVES IN YELLOWSTONE PARK?
THEY HAD DIED OUT, BUT THEIR REINTRODUCTION...
YELLOWSTONE
...CREATED A CASCADE OF CHANGES.
!
WITH THEIR PREDATORS REINTRODUCED, ELK HAD TO STAY ON THE MOVE...
WHICH ALLOWED THE OVERBROWSED WILLOW TREES TO RECOVER.
BEAVERS USED THE WILLOWS TO BUILD MORE ROBUST DAMS...
WHICH ULTIMATELY CHANGED THE COURSE OF RIVERS.
OUR MAMMOTH HERD CAN HAVE A SIMILAR EFFECT ON THE LANDSCAPE. BY GRAZING NEAR THE GLACIER...
...THEY MAY BE ABLE TO SLOW DOWN OR EVEN STOP PERMAFROST MELT.
THIS IS THE COOLEST THING EVER.
AND Y'ALL ARE HERE TO HELP ME! READY TO GET YOUR HANDS DIRTY?
SO READY!
GREAT! YOU CAN START BY COLLECTING BLOOD SAMPLES.
AND SUDDENLY ALL THAT HEMATOLOGY WORK MAKES SENSE...

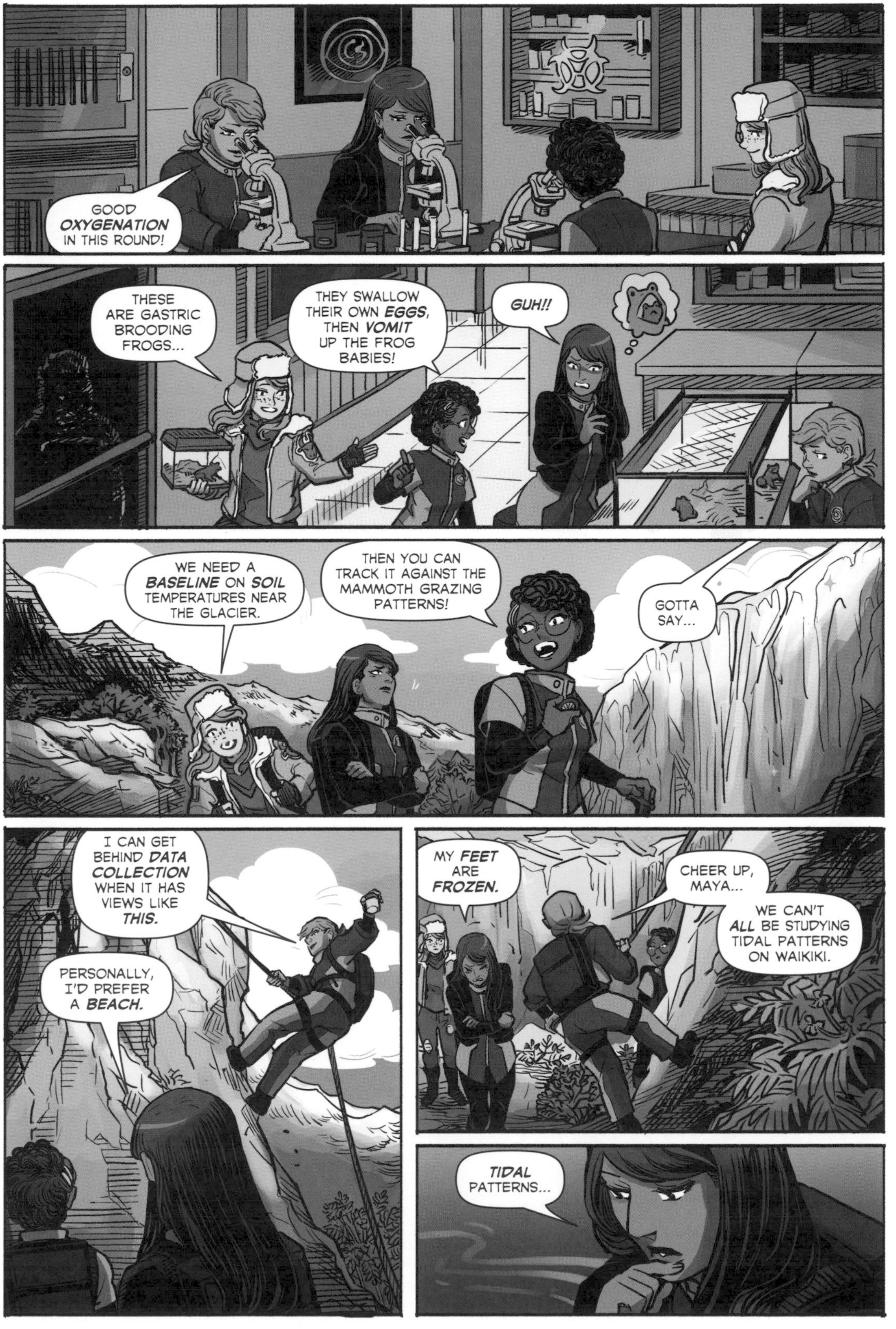
GOOD OXYGENATION IN THIS ROUND!
THESE ARE GASTRIC BROODING FROGS...
THEY SWALLOW THEIR OWN EGGS, THEN VOMIT UP THE FROG BABIES!
GUH!!
WE NEED A BASELINE ON SOIL TEMPERATURES NEAR THE GLACIER.
THEN YOU CAN TRACK IT AGAINST THE MAMMOTH GRAZING PATTERNS!
GOTTA SAY...
I CAN GET BEHIND DATA COLLECTION WHEN IT HAS VIEWS LIKE THIS.
PERSONALLY, I'D PREFER A BEACH.
MY FEET ARE FROZEN.
CHEER UP, MAYA...
WE CAN'T ALL BE STUDYING TIDAL PATTERNS ON WAIKIKI.
TIDAL PATTERNS...

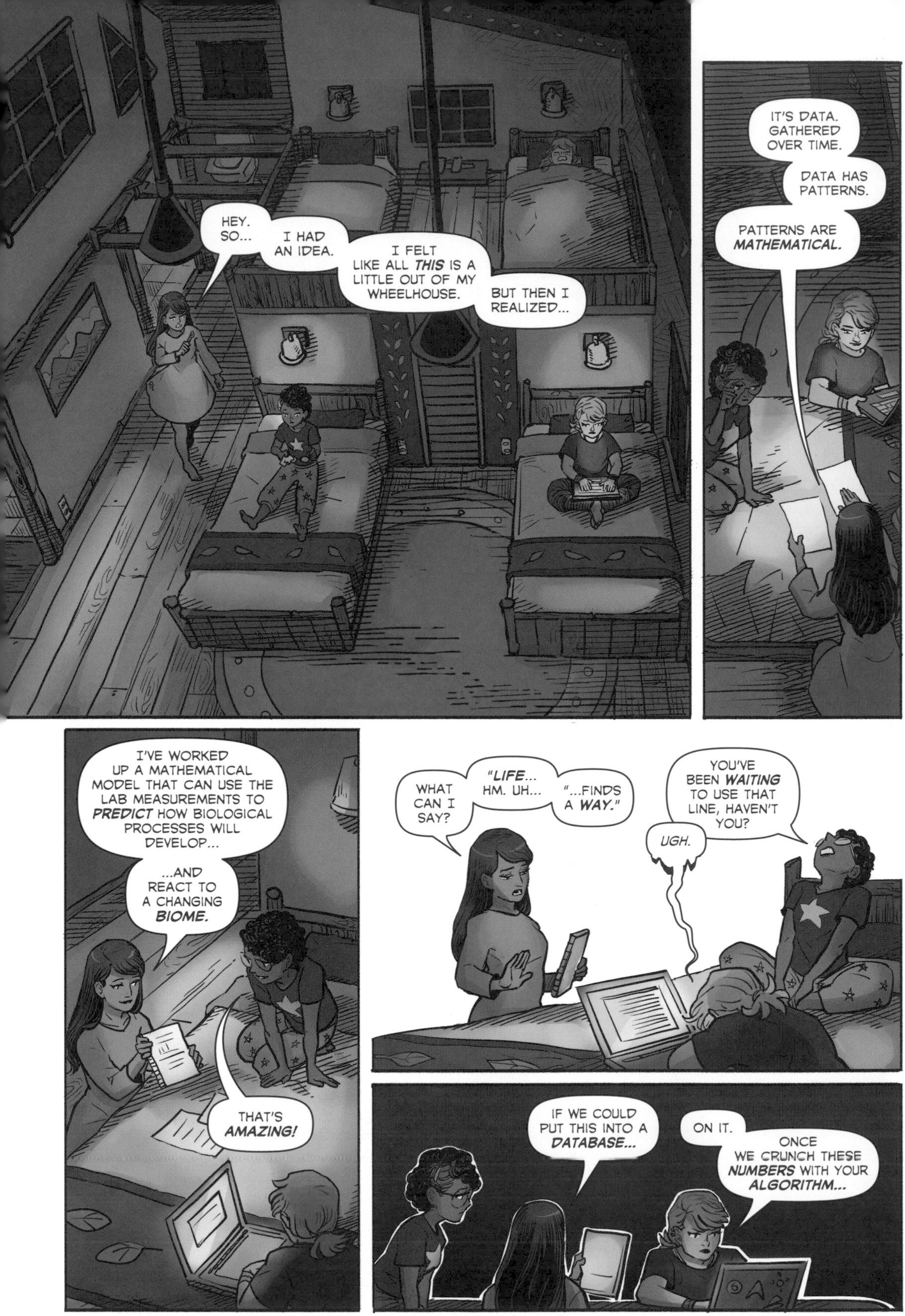

HEY. SO...
I HAD AN IDEA.
I FELT LIKE ALL THIS IS A LITTLE OUT OF MY WHEELHOUSE.
BUT THEN I REALIZED...
IT'S DATA. GATHERED OVER TIME.
DATA HAS PATTERNS.
PATTERNS ARE MATHEMATICAL.
I'VE WORKED UP A MATHEMATICAL MODEL THAT CAN USE THE LAB MEASUREMENTS TO PREDICT HOW BIOLOGICAL PROCESSES WILL DEVELOP...
...AND REACT TO A CHANGING BIOME.
THAT'S AMAZING!
WHAT CAN I SAY?
"LIFE... HM. UH...
"...FINDS A WAY."
UGH.
YOU'VE BEEN WAITING TO USE THAT LINE, HAVEN'T YOU?
IF WE COULD PUT THIS INTO A DATABASE...
ON IT.
ONCE WE CRUNCH THESE NUMBERS WITH YOUR ALGORITHM...

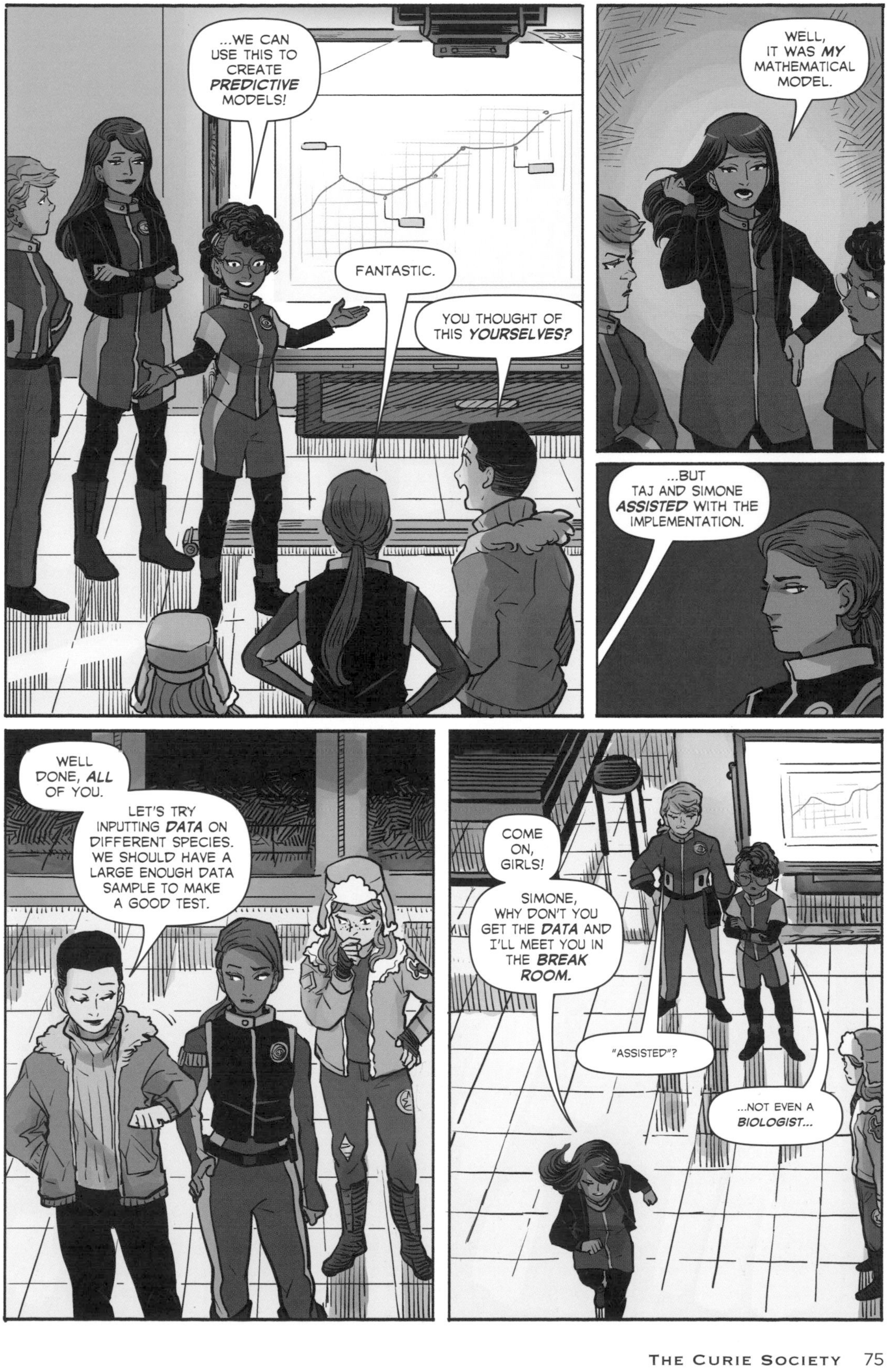
...WE CAN USE THIS TO CREATE *PREDICTIVE* MODELS!
FANTASTIC.
YOU THOUGHT OF THIS *YOURSELVES?*
WELL, IT WAS *MY* MATHEMATICAL MODEL.
...BUT TAJ AND SIMONE *ASSISTED* WITH THE IMPLEMENTATION.
WELL DONE, *ALL* OF YOU.
LET'S TRY INPUTTING *DATA* ON DIFFERENT SPECIES. WE SHOULD HAVE A LARGE ENOUGH DATA SAMPLE TO MAKE A GOOD TEST.
COME ON, GIRLS!
SIMONE, WHY DON'T YOU GET THE *DATA* AND I'LL MEET YOU IN THE *BREAK ROOM.*
"ASSISTED"?
...NOT EVEN A *BIOLOGIST...*

LATER...

THE THYLACINE SEEMS TO BE REALLY LOW-ENERGY.

OH, DON'T WORRY. THYLACINES ARE NOCTURNAL. SHE'S JUST NAPPING.

I DUNNO, I MEAN, I HAVE A DOG...

...AND SHE WOULD NEVER SLEEP THIS SOUNDLY EXCEPT AFTER THE VET WHEN SHE'S BEEN--

--MEDICATED.

...?

SYSTEM: ACTIVATE CODE *SIERRA-ROMEO-ALPHA!*

LOCK DOWN THE LABS AND STABLES AND SCAN THE VALLEY PERIMETER--

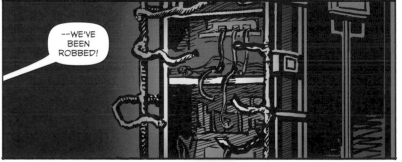

--WE'VE BEEN ROBBED!

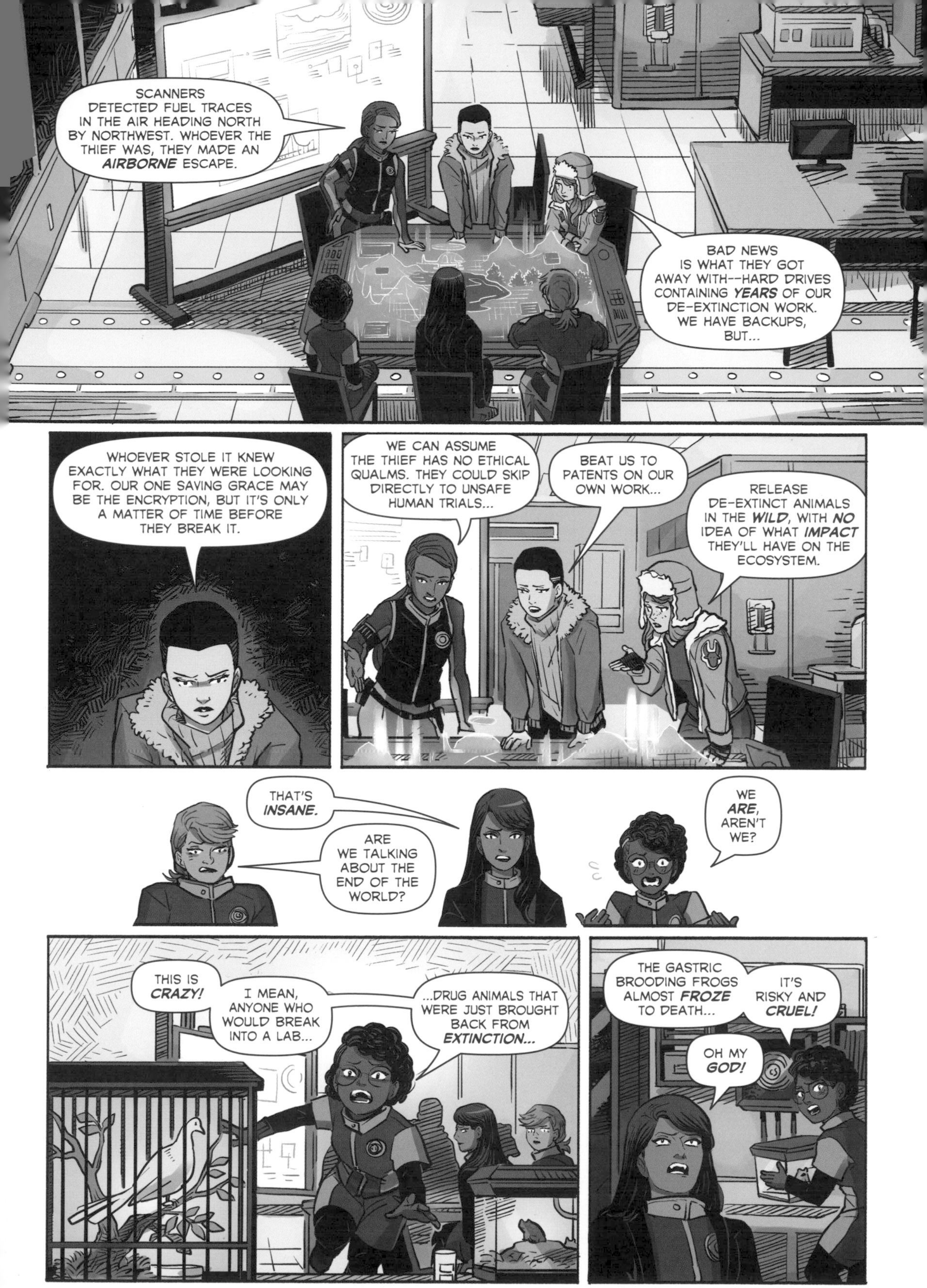

SCANNERS DETECTED FUEL TRACES IN THE AIR HEADING NORTH BY NORTHWEST. WHOEVER THE THIEF WAS, THEY MADE AN ***AIRBORNE*** ESCAPE.
BAD NEWS IS WHAT THEY GOT AWAY WITH--HARD DRIVES CONTAINING ***YEARS*** OF OUR DE-EXTINCTION WORK. WE HAVE BACKUPS, BUT...
WHOEVER STOLE IT KNEW EXACTLY WHAT THEY WERE LOOKING FOR. OUR ONE SAVING GRACE MAY BE THE ENCRYPTION, BUT IT'S ONLY A MATTER OF TIME BEFORE THEY BREAK IT.
WE CAN ASSUME THE THIEF HAS NO ETHICAL QUALMS. THEY COULD SKIP DIRECTLY TO UNSAFE HUMAN TRIALS...
BEAT US TO PATENTS ON OUR OWN WORK...
RELEASE DE-EXTINCT ANIMALS IN THE ***WILD***, WITH ***NO*** IDEA OF WHAT ***IMPACT*** THEY'LL HAVE ON THE ECOSYSTEM.
THAT'S ***INSANE.***
ARE WE TALKING ABOUT THE END OF THE WORLD?
WE ***ARE***, AREN'T WE?
THIS IS ***CRAZY!***
I MEAN, ANYONE WHO WOULD BREAK INTO A LAB...
...DRUG ANIMALS THAT WERE JUST BROUGHT BACK FROM ***EXTINCTION...***
THE GASTRIC BROODING FROGS ALMOST ***FROZE*** TO DEATH...
IT'S RISKY AND ***CRUEL!***
OH MY ***GOD!***

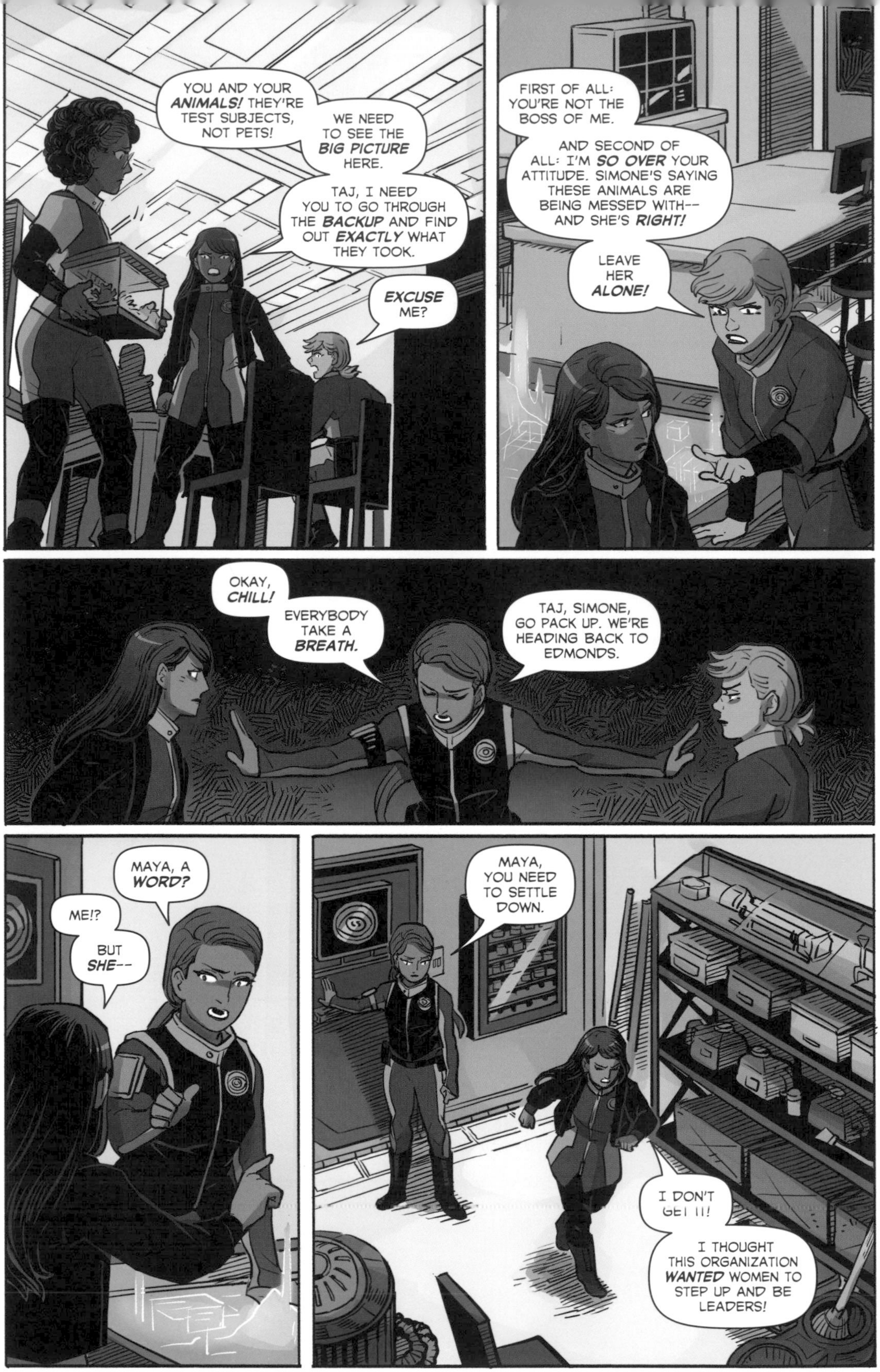
YOU AND YOUR ANIMALS! THEY'RE TEST SUBJECTS, NOT PETS!
WE NEED TO SEE THE BIG PICTURE HERE.
TAJ, I NEED YOU TO GO THROUGH THE BACKUP AND FIND OUT EXACTLY WHAT THEY TOOK.
EXCUSE ME?
FIRST OF ALL: YOU'RE NOT THE BOSS OF ME.
AND SECOND OF ALL: I'M SO OVER YOUR ATTITUDE. SIMONE'S SAYING THESE ANIMALS ARE BEING MESSED WITH-- AND SHE'S RIGHT!
LEAVE HER ALONE!
OKAY, CHILL!
EVERYBODY TAKE A BREATH.
TAJ, SIMONE, GO PACK UP. WE'RE HEADING BACK TO EDMONDS.
MAYA, A WORD?
ME!?
BUT SHE--
MAYA, YOU NEED TO SETTLE DOWN.
I DON'T GET IT!
I THOUGHT THIS ORGANIZATION WANTED WOMEN TO STEP UP AND BE LEADERS!

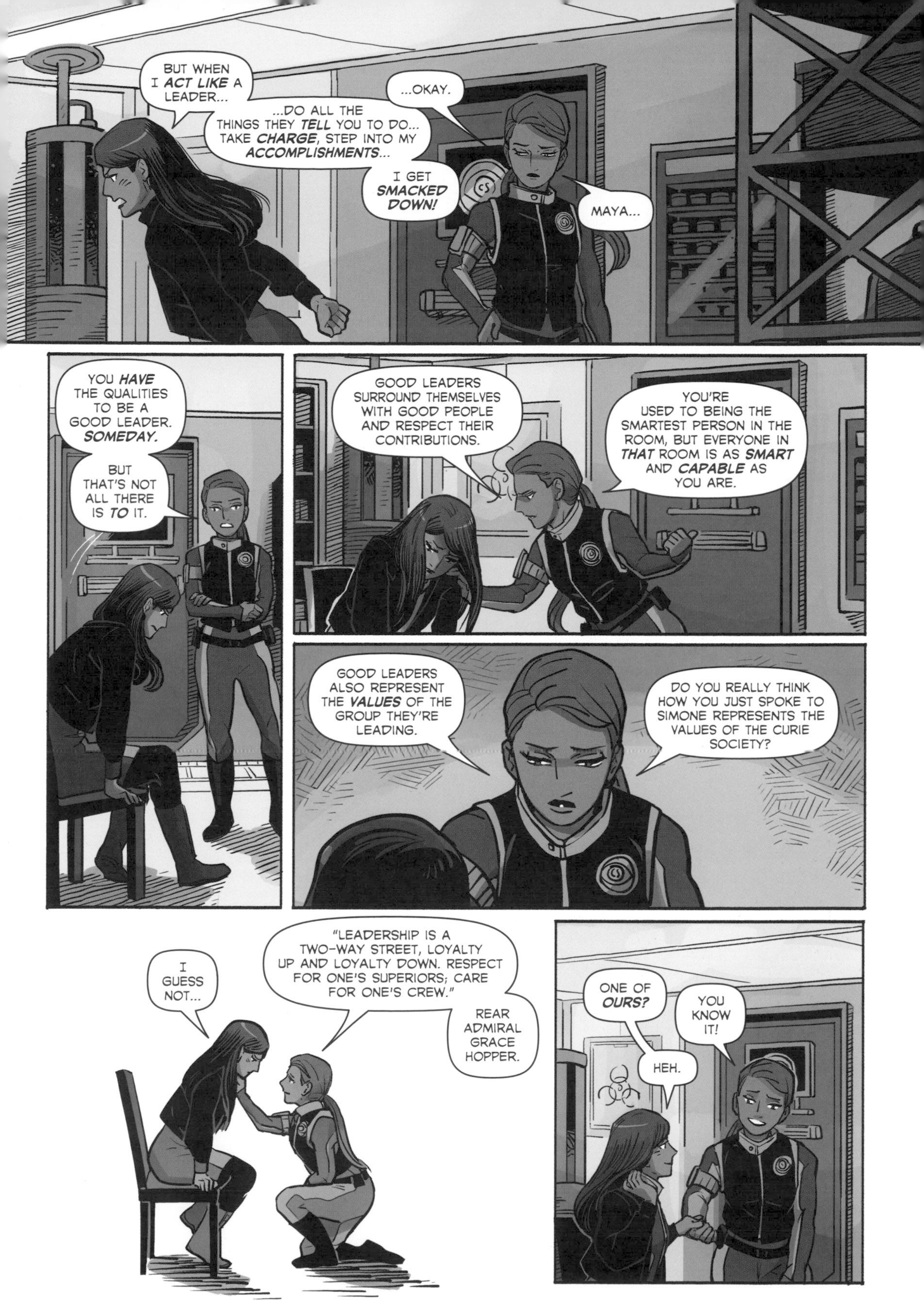
BUT WHEN I ACT LIKE A LEADER...
...DO ALL THE THINGS THEY TELL YOU TO DO... TAKE CHARGE, STEP INTO MY ACCOMPLISHMENTS...
I GET SMACKED DOWN!
...OKAY.
MAYA...
YOU HAVE THE QUALITIES TO BE A GOOD LEADER. SOMEDAY.
BUT THAT'S NOT ALL THERE IS TO IT.
GOOD LEADERS SURROUND THEMSELVES WITH GOOD PEOPLE AND RESPECT THEIR CONTRIBUTIONS.
YOU'RE USED TO BEING THE SMARTEST PERSON IN THE ROOM, BUT EVERYONE IN THAT ROOM IS AS SMART AND CAPABLE AS YOU ARE.
GOOD LEADERS ALSO REPRESENT THE VALUES OF THE GROUP THEY'RE LEADING.
DO YOU REALLY THINK HOW YOU JUST SPOKE TO SIMONE REPRESENTS THE VALUES OF THE CURIE SOCIETY?
I GUESS NOT...
"LEADERSHIP IS A TWO-WAY STREET, LOYALTY UP AND LOYALTY DOWN. RESPECT FOR ONE'S SUPERIORS; CARE FOR ONE'S CREW."
REAR ADMIRAL GRACE HOPPER.
ONE OF OURS?
HEH.
YOU KNOW IT!

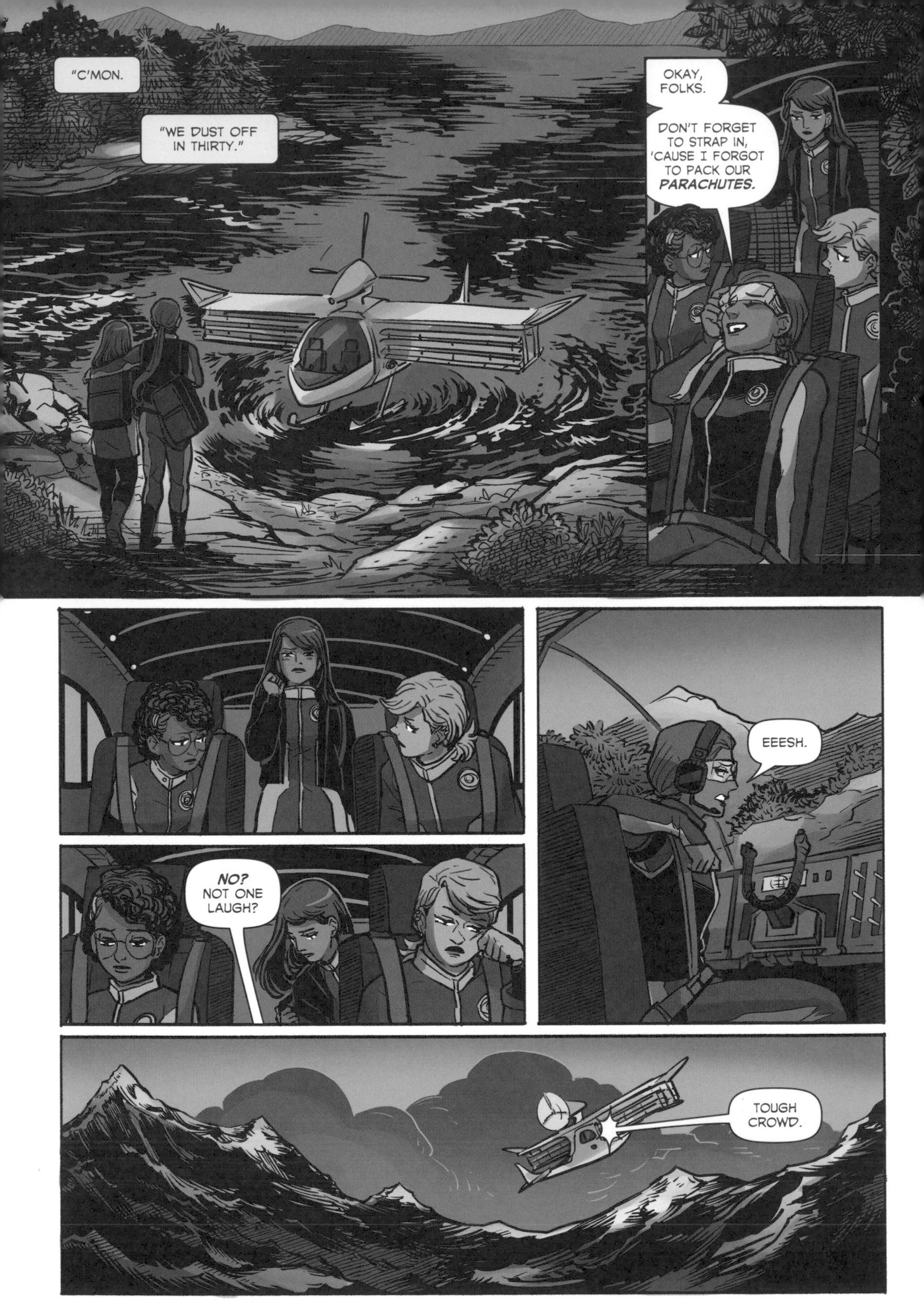
"C'MON.
"WE DUST OFF IN THIRTY."
OKAY, FOLKS.
DON'T FORGET TO STRAP IN, 'CAUSE I FORGOT TO PACK OUR *PARACHUTES.*
NO? NOT ONE LAUGH?
EEESH.
TOUGH CROWD.

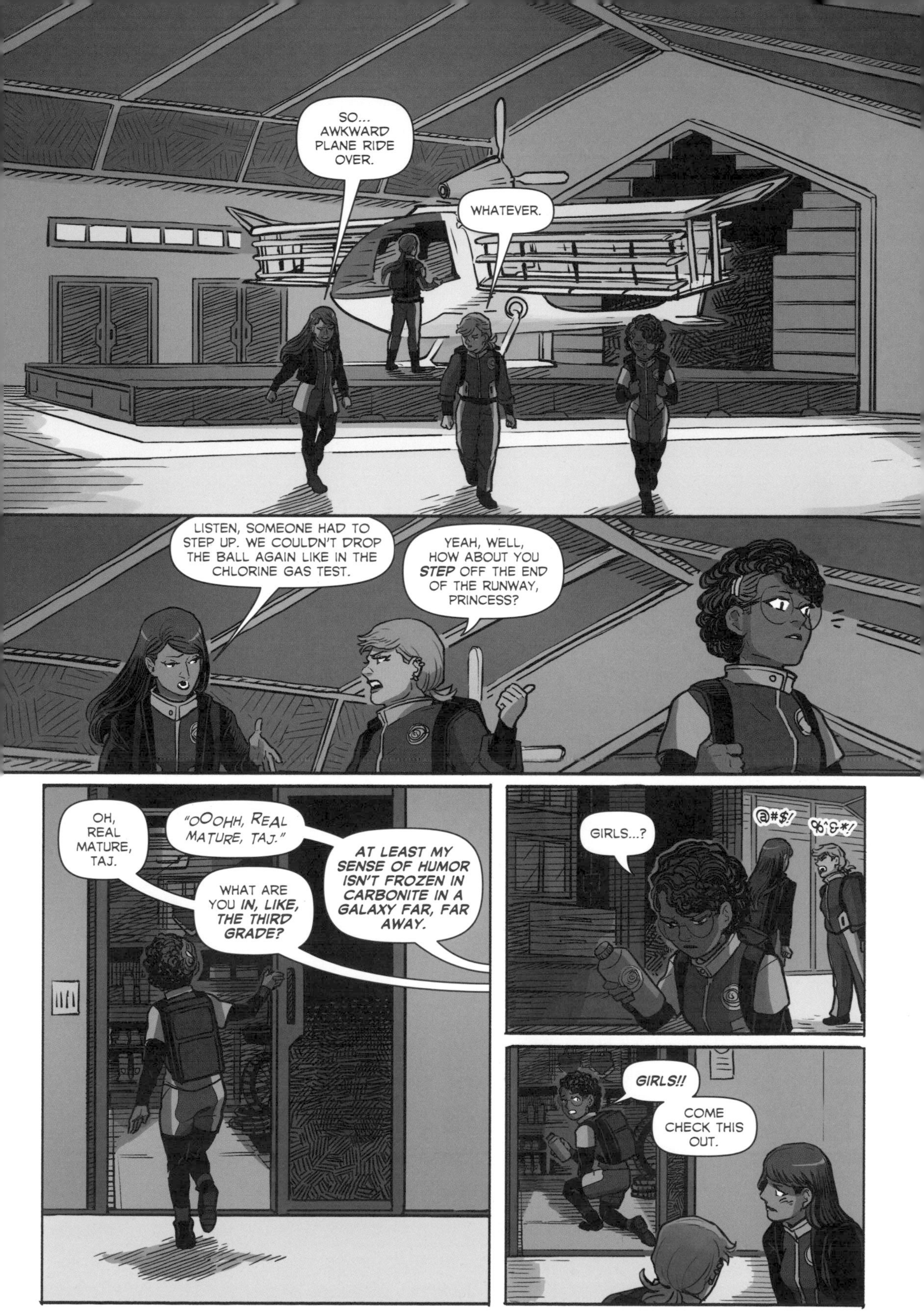
SO... AWKWARD PLANE RIDE OVER.
WHATEVER.
LISTEN, SOMEONE HAD TO STEP UP. WE COULDN'T DROP THE BALL AGAIN LIKE IN THE CHLORINE GAS TEST.
YEAH, WELL, HOW ABOUT YOU STEP OFF THE END OF THE RUNWAY, PRINCESS?
OH, REAL MATURE, TAJ.
"OOOHH, REAL MATURE, TAJ."
WHAT ARE YOU IN, LIKE, THE THIRD GRADE?
AT LEAST MY SENSE OF HUMOR ISN'T FROZEN IN CARBONITE IN A GALAXY FAR, FAR AWAY.
GIRLS...?
@#$!
%^&*!
GIRLS!!
COME CHECK THIS OUT.

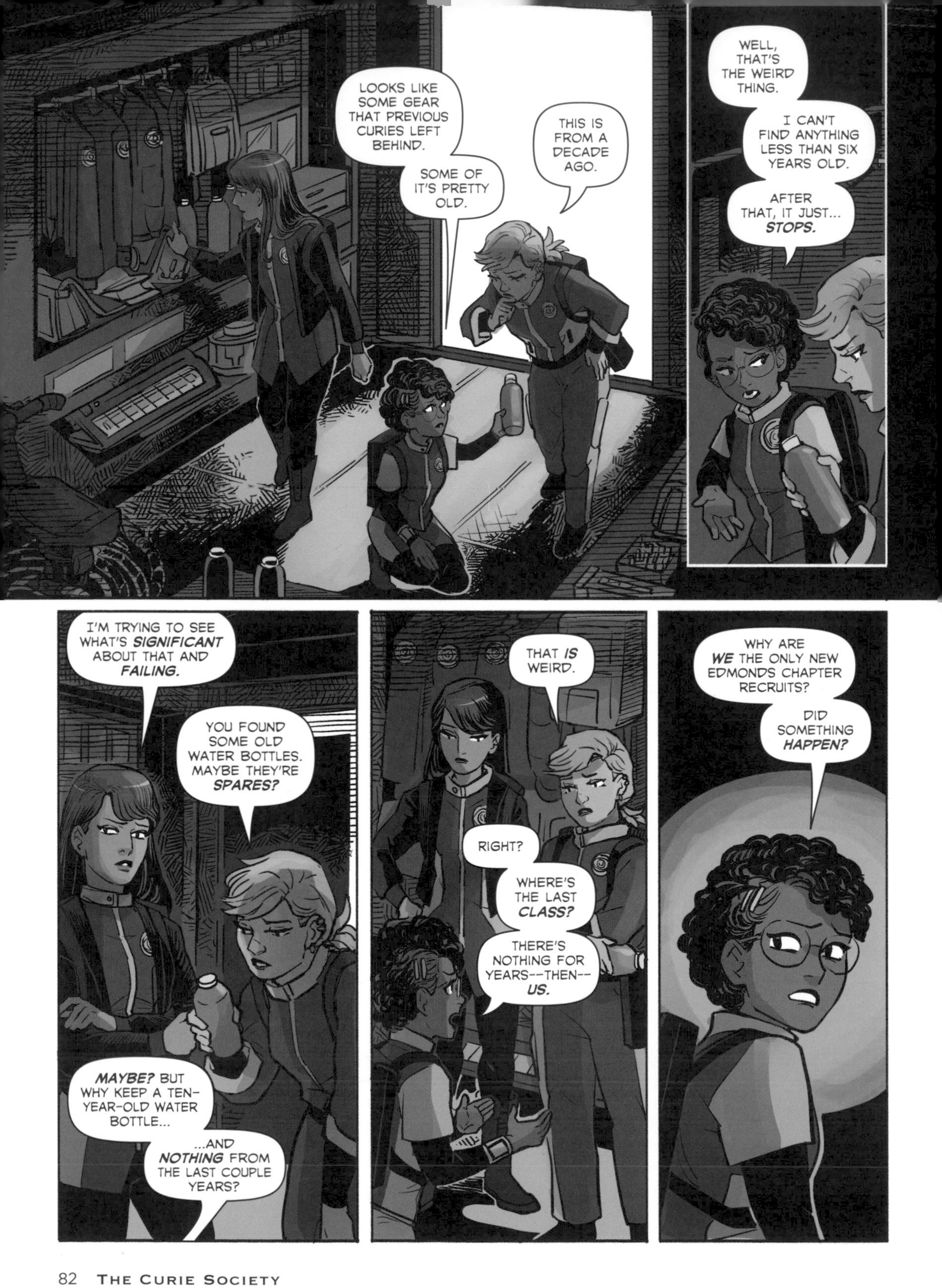
LOOKS LIKE SOME GEAR THAT PREVIOUS CURIES LEFT BEHIND.
SOME OF IT'S PRETTY OLD.
THIS IS FROM A DECADE AGO.
WELL, THAT'S THE WEIRD THING.
I CAN'T FIND ANYTHING LESS THAN SIX YEARS OLD.
AFTER THAT, IT JUST... ***STOPS.***
I'M TRYING TO SEE WHAT'S ***SIGNIFICANT*** ABOUT THAT AND ***FAILING.***
YOU FOUND SOME OLD WATER BOTTLES. MAYBE THEY'RE ***SPARES?***
MAYBE? BUT WHY KEEP A TEN-YEAR-OLD WATER BOTTLE...
...AND ***NOTHING*** FROM THE LAST COUPLE YEARS?
THAT ***IS*** WEIRD.
RIGHT?
WHERE'S THE LAST ***CLASS?***
THERE'S NOTHING FOR YEARS--THEN-- ***US.***
WHY ARE ***WE*** THE ONLY NEW EDMONDS CHAPTER RECRUITS?
DID SOMETHING ***HAPPEN?***

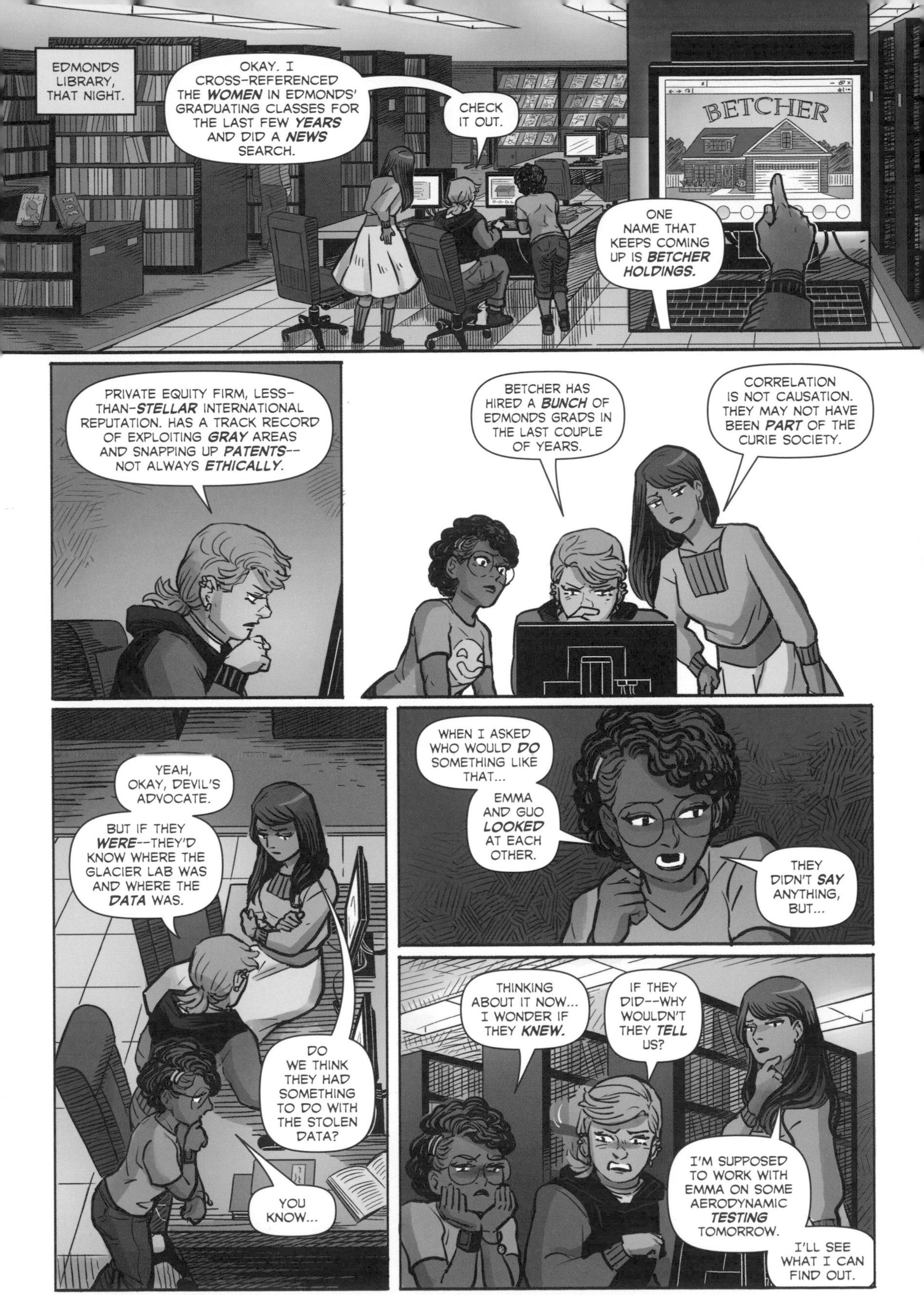
EDMONDS LIBRARY, THAT NIGHT.
OKAY. I CROSS-REFERENCED THE WOMEN IN EDMONDS' GRADUATING CLASSES FOR THE LAST FEW YEARS AND DID A NEWS SEARCH.
CHECK IT OUT.
BETCHER
ONE NAME THAT KEEPS COMING UP IS BETCHER HOLDINGS.
PRIVATE EQUITY FIRM, LESS-THAN-STELLAR INTERNATIONAL REPUTATION. HAS A TRACK RECORD OF EXPLOITING GRAY AREAS AND SNAPPING UP PATENTS--NOT ALWAYS ETHICALLY.
BETCHER HAS HIRED A BUNCH OF EDMONDS GRADS IN THE LAST COUPLE OF YEARS.
CORRELATION IS NOT CAUSATION. THEY MAY NOT HAVE BEEN PART OF THE CURIE SOCIETY.
YEAH, OKAY, DEVIL'S ADVOCATE.
BUT IF THEY WERE--THEY'D KNOW WHERE THE GLACIER LAB WAS AND WHERE THE DATA WAS.
DO WE THINK THEY HAD SOMETHING TO DO WITH THE STOLEN DATA?
YOU KNOW...
WHEN I ASKED WHO WOULD DO SOMETHING LIKE THAT...
EMMA AND GUO LOOKED AT EACH OTHER.
THEY DIDN'T SAY ANYTHING, BUT...
THINKING ABOUT IT NOW... I WONDER IF THEY KNEW.
IF THEY DID--WHY WOULDN'T THEY TELL US?
I'M SUPPOSED TO WORK WITH EMMA ON SOME AERODYNAMIC TESTING TOMORROW.
I'LL SEE WHAT I CAN FIND OUT.

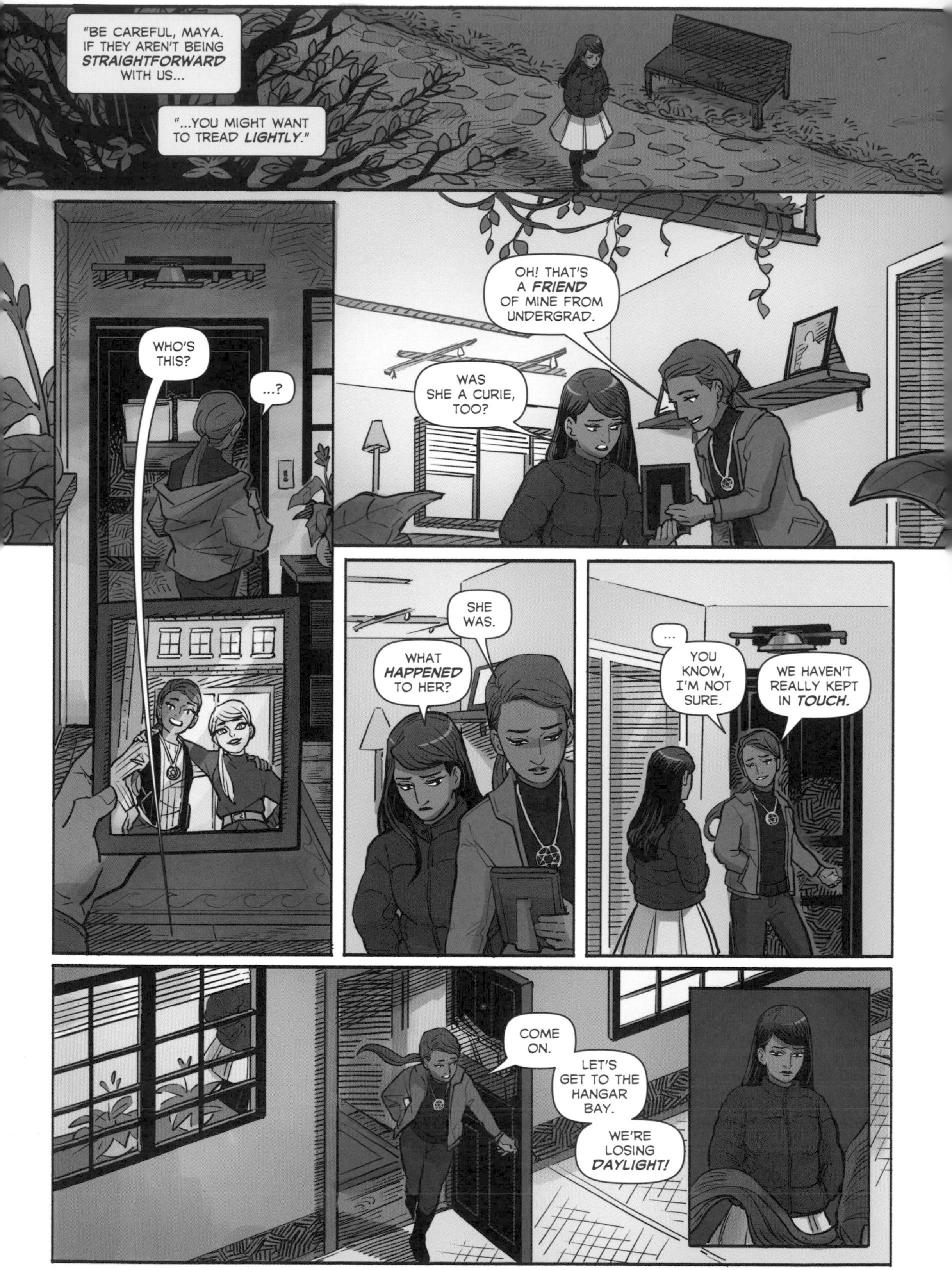

"BE CAREFUL, MAYA. IF THEY AREN'T BEING STRAIGHTFORWARD WITH US...
"...YOU MIGHT WANT TO TREAD LIGHTLY."
WHO'S THIS?
...?
OH! THAT'S A FRIEND OF MINE FROM UNDERGRAD.
WAS SHE A CURIE, TOO?
SHE WAS.
WHAT HAPPENED TO HER?
...
YOU KNOW, I'M NOT SURE.
WE HAVEN'T REALLY KEPT IN TOUCH.
COME ON.
LET'S GET TO THE HANGAR BAY.
WE'RE LOSING DAYLIGHT!

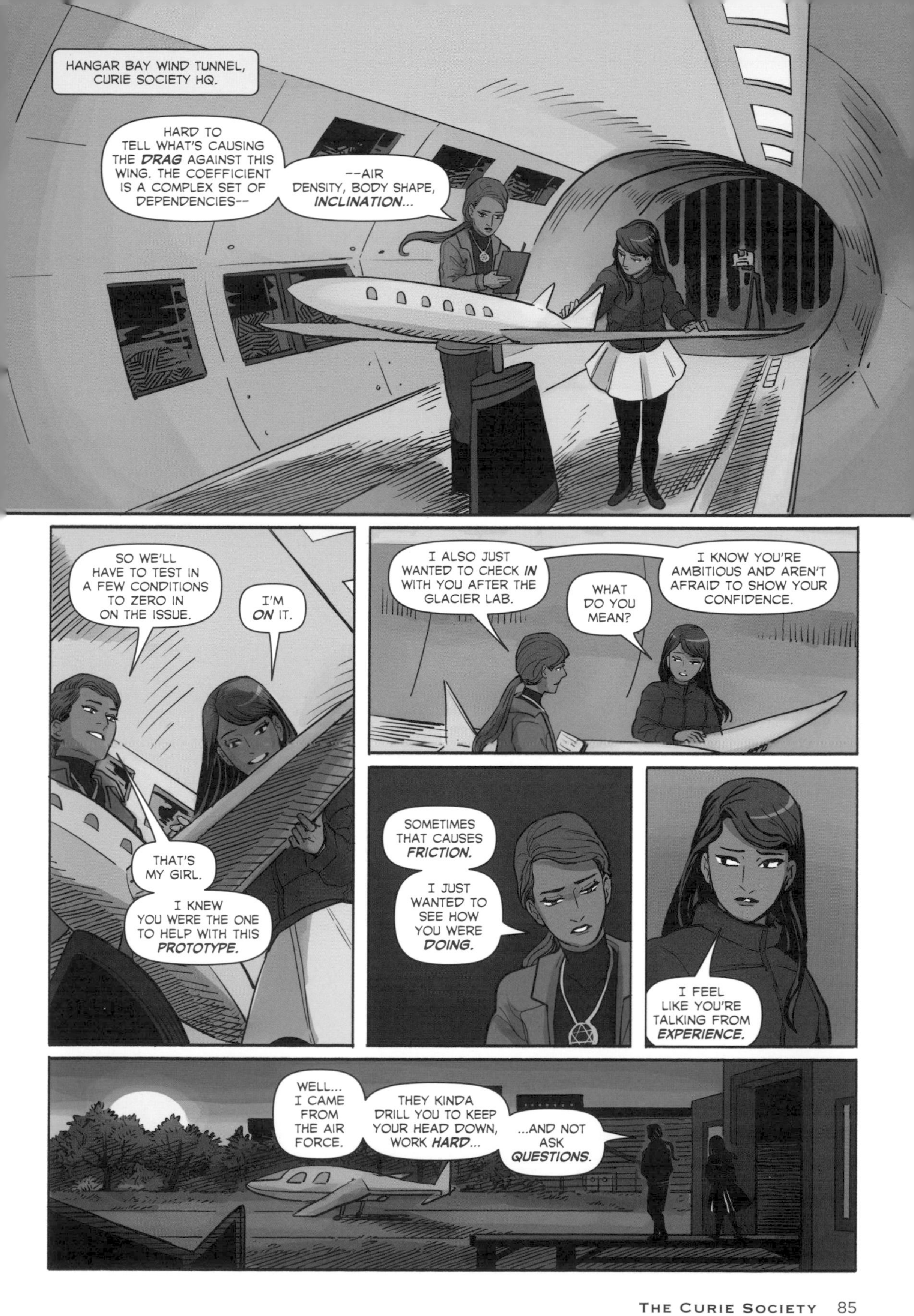
HANGAR BAY WIND TUNNEL, CURIE SOCIETY HQ.
HARD TO TELL WHAT'S CAUSING THE **DRAG** AGAINST THIS WING. THE COEFFICIENT IS A COMPLEX SET OF DEPENDENCIES--
--AIR DENSITY, BODY SHAPE, **INCLINATION**...
SO WE'LL HAVE TO TEST IN A FEW CONDITIONS TO ZERO IN ON THE ISSUE.
I'M **ON** IT.
THAT'S MY GIRL.
I KNEW YOU WERE THE ONE TO HELP WITH THIS **PROTOTYPE.**
I ALSO JUST WANTED TO CHECK **IN** WITH YOU AFTER THE GLACIER LAB.
WHAT DO YOU MEAN?
I KNOW YOU'RE AMBITIOUS AND AREN'T AFRAID TO SHOW YOUR CONFIDENCE.
SOMETIMES THAT CAUSES **FRICTION.**
I JUST WANTED TO SEE HOW YOU WERE **DOING.**
I FEEL LIKE YOU'RE TALKING FROM **EXPERIENCE.**
WELL... I CAME FROM THE AIR FORCE.
THEY KINDA DRILL YOU TO KEEP YOUR HEAD DOWN, WORK **HARD**...
...AND NOT ASK **QUESTIONS**.

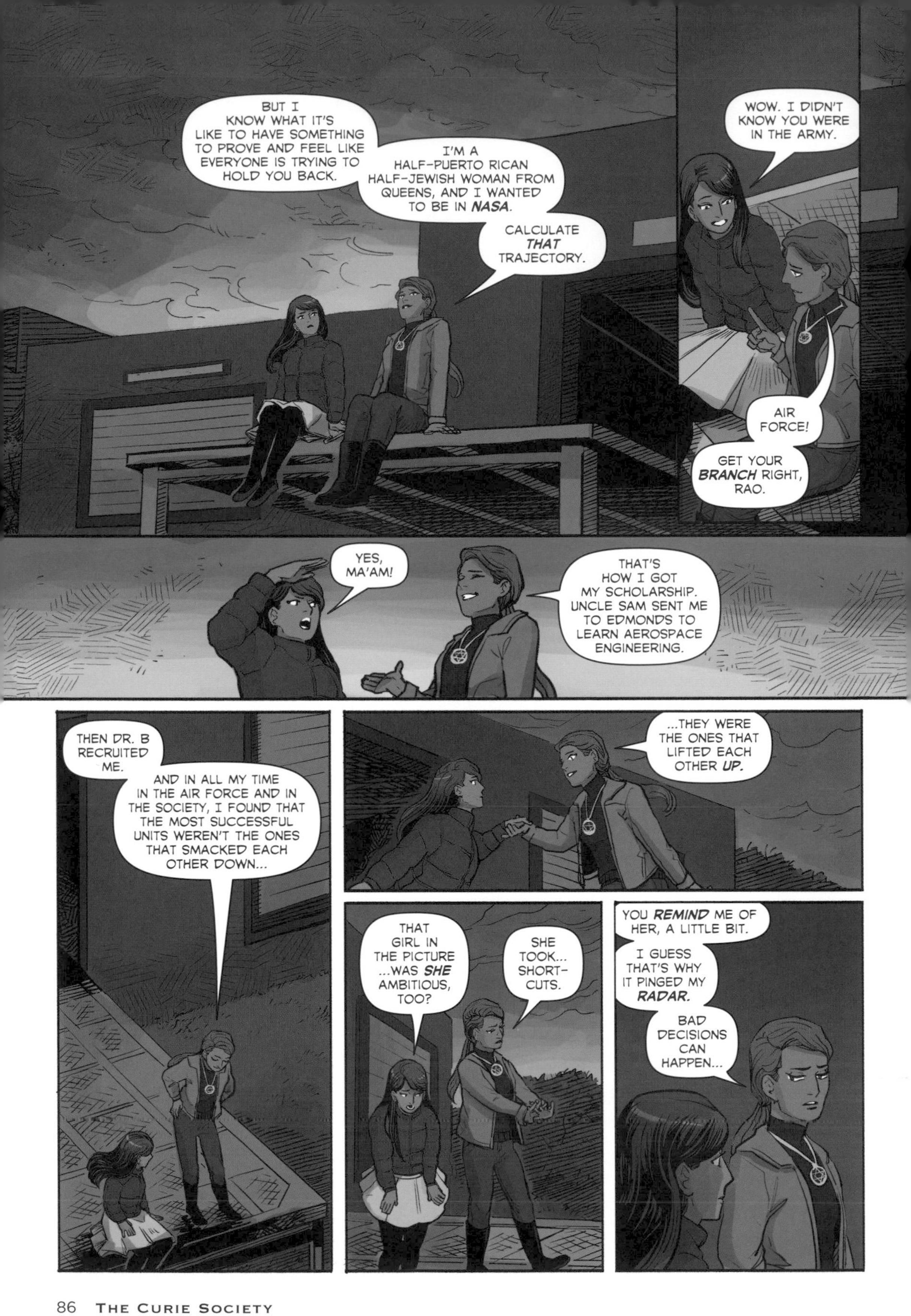
BUT I KNOW WHAT IT'S LIKE TO HAVE SOMETHING TO PROVE AND FEEL LIKE EVERYONE IS TRYING TO HOLD YOU BACK.
I'M A HALF-PUERTO RICAN HALF-JEWISH WOMAN FROM QUEENS, AND I WANTED TO BE IN NASA.
CALCULATE THAT TRAJECTORY.
WOW. I DIDN'T KNOW YOU WERE IN THE ARMY.
AIR FORCE!
GET YOUR BRANCH RIGHT, RAO.
YES, MA'AM!
THAT'S HOW I GOT MY SCHOLARSHIP. UNCLE SAM SENT ME TO EDMONDS TO LEARN AEROSPACE ENGINEERING.
THEN DR. B RECRUITED ME.
AND IN ALL MY TIME IN THE AIR FORCE AND IN THE SOCIETY, I FOUND THAT THE MOST SUCCESSFUL UNITS WEREN'T THE ONES THAT SMACKED EACH OTHER DOWN...
...THEY WERE THE ONES THAT LIFTED EACH OTHER UP.
THAT GIRL IN THE PICTURE ...WAS SHE AMBITIOUS, TOO?
SHE TOOK... SHORT-CUTS.
YOU REMIND ME OF HER, A LITTLE BIT.
I GUESS THAT'S WHY IT PINGED MY RADAR.
BAD DECISIONS CAN HAPPEN...

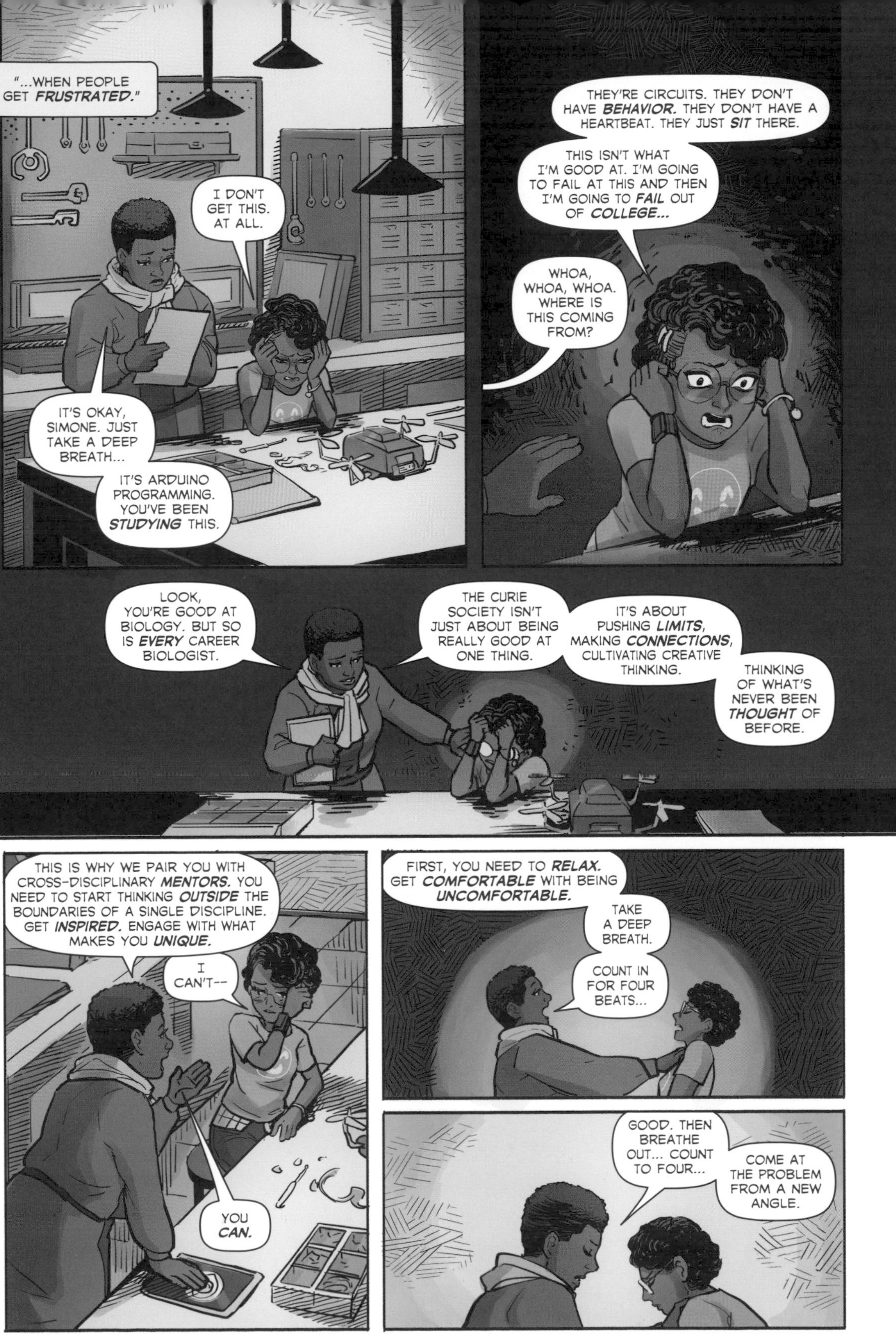
"...WHEN PEOPLE GET FRUSTRATED."
I DON'T GET THIS. AT ALL.
IT'S OKAY, SIMONE. JUST TAKE A DEEP BREATH...
IT'S ARDUINO PROGRAMMING. YOU'VE BEEN STUDYING THIS.
THEY'RE CIRCUITS. THEY DON'T HAVE BEHAVIOR. THEY DON'T HAVE A HEARTBEAT. THEY JUST SIT THERE.
THIS ISN'T WHAT I'M GOOD AT. I'M GOING TO FAIL AT THIS AND THEN I'M GOING TO FAIL OUT OF COLLEGE...
WHOA, WHOA, WHOA. WHERE IS THIS COMING FROM?
LOOK, YOU'RE GOOD AT BIOLOGY. BUT SO IS EVERY CAREER BIOLOGIST.
THE CURIE SOCIETY ISN'T JUST ABOUT BEING REALLY GOOD AT ONE THING.
IT'S ABOUT PUSHING LIMITS, MAKING CONNECTIONS, CULTIVATING CREATIVE THINKING.
THINKING OF WHAT'S NEVER BEEN THOUGHT OF BEFORE.
THIS IS WHY WE PAIR YOU WITH CROSS-DISCIPLINARY MENTORS. YOU NEED TO START THINKING OUTSIDE THE BOUNDARIES OF A SINGLE DISCIPLINE. GET INSPIRED. ENGAGE WITH WHAT MAKES YOU UNIQUE.
I CAN'T--
YOU CAN.
FIRST, YOU NEED TO RELAX. GET COMFORTABLE WITH BEING UNCOMFORTABLE.
TAKE A DEEP BREATH.
COUNT IN FOR FOUR BEATS...
GOOD. THEN BREATHE OUT... COUNT TO FOUR...
COME AT THE PROBLEM FROM A NEW ANGLE.

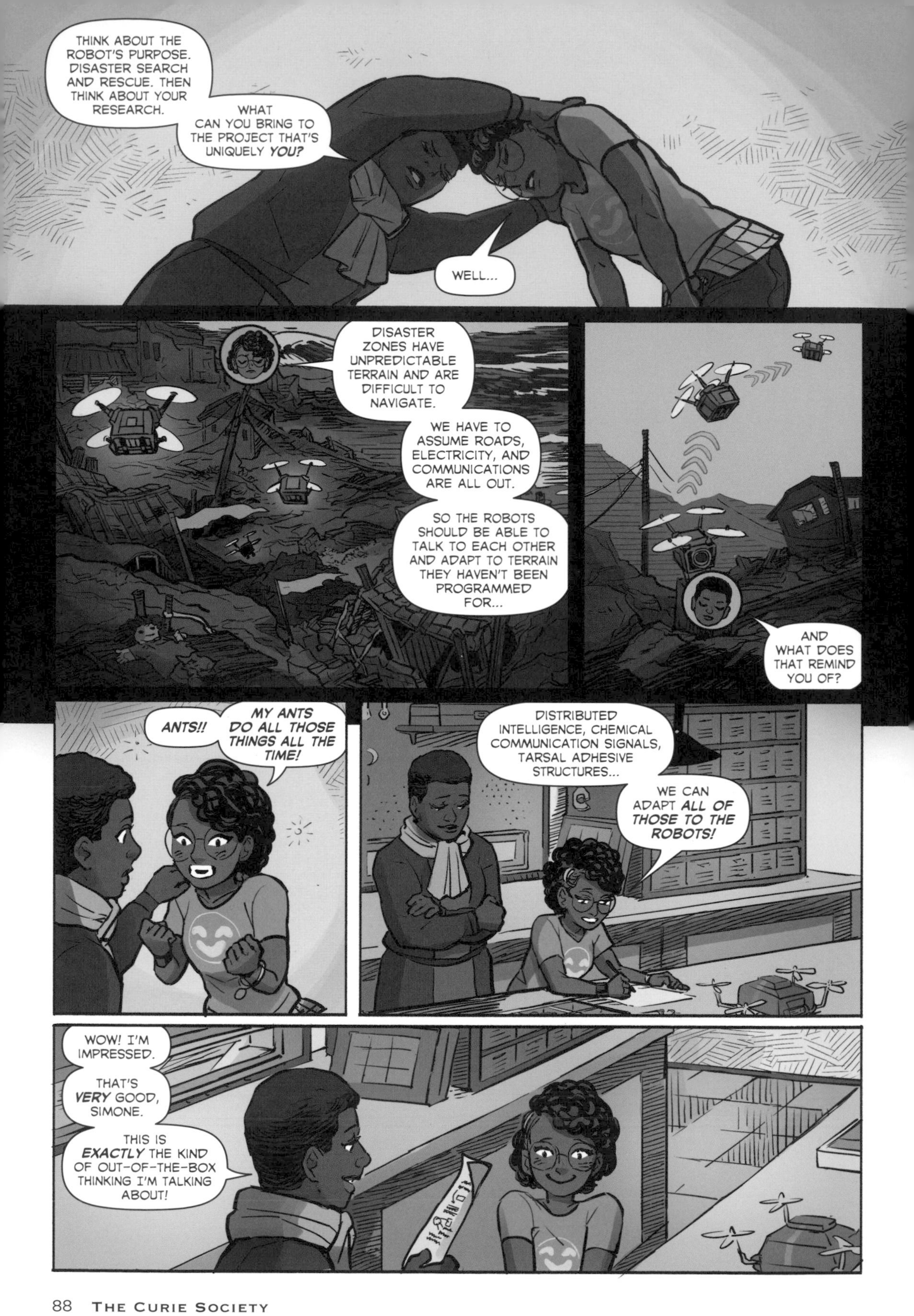
THINK ABOUT THE ROBOT'S PURPOSE. DISASTER SEARCH AND RESCUE. THEN THINK ABOUT YOUR RESEARCH.
WHAT CAN YOU BRING TO THE PROJECT THAT'S UNIQUELY *YOU?*
WELL...
DISASTER ZONES HAVE UNPREDICTABLE TERRAIN AND ARE DIFFICULT TO NAVIGATE.
WE HAVE TO ASSUME ROADS, ELECTRICITY, AND COMMUNICATIONS ARE ALL OUT.
SO THE ROBOTS SHOULD BE ABLE TO TALK TO EACH OTHER AND ADAPT TO TERRAIN THEY HAVEN'T BEEN PROGRAMMED FOR...
AND WHAT DOES THAT REMIND YOU OF?
ANTS!!
MY ANTS DO ALL THOSE THINGS ALL THE TIME!
DISTRIBUTED INTELLIGENCE, CHEMICAL COMMUNICATION SIGNALS, TARSAL ADHESIVE STRUCTURES...
WE CAN ADAPT *ALL OF THOSE TO THE ROBOTS!*
WOW! I'M IMPRESSED.
THAT'S *VERY* GOOD, SIMONE.
THIS IS *EXACTLY* THE KIND OF OUT-OF-THE-BOX THINKING I'M TALKING ABOUT!

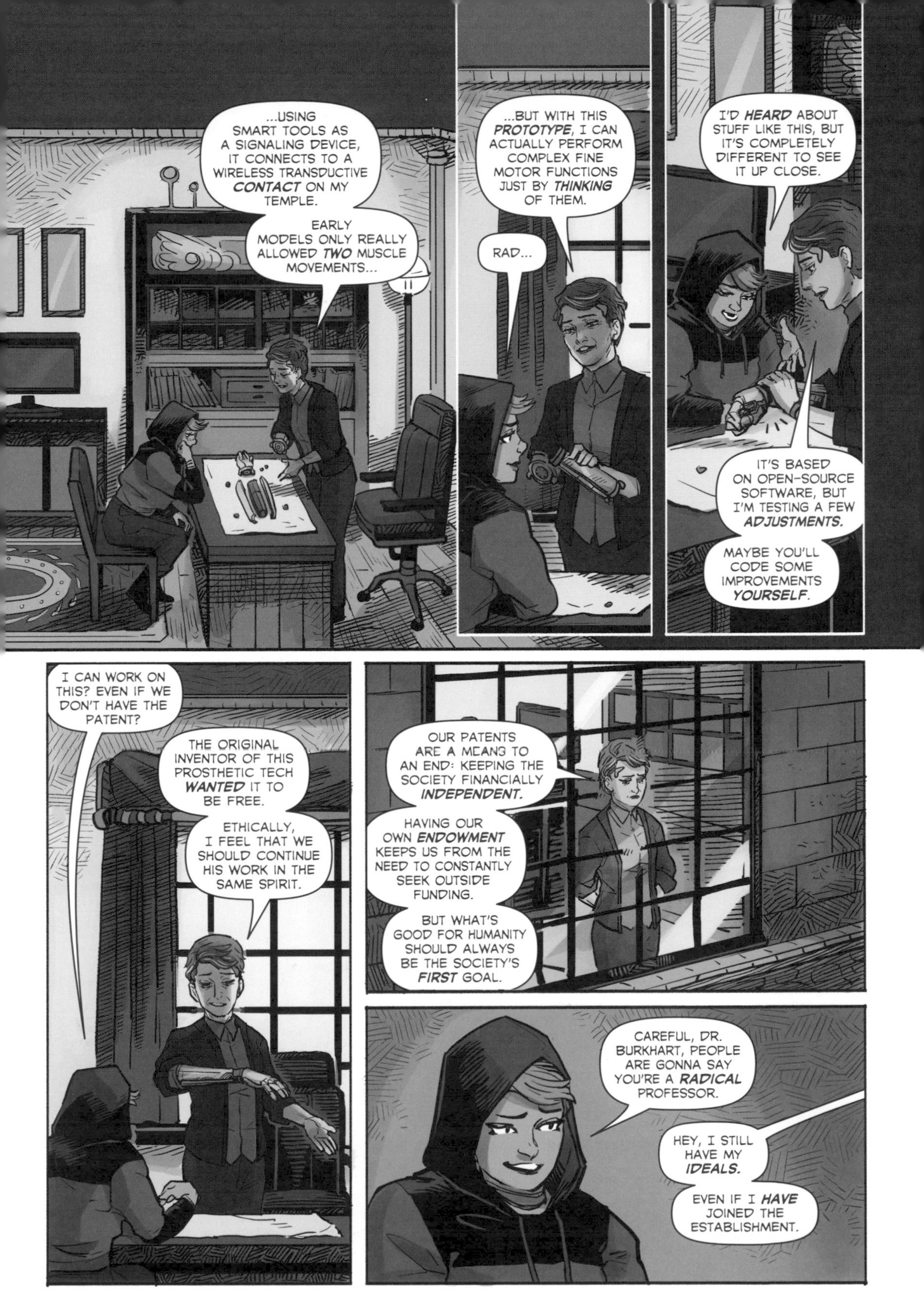

...USING SMART TOOLS AS A SIGNALING DEVICE, IT CONNECTS TO A WIRELESS TRANSDUCTIVE *CONTACT* ON MY TEMPLE.
EARLY MODELS ONLY REALLY ALLOWED *TWO* MUSCLE MOVEMENTS...
...BUT WITH THIS *PROTOTYPE*, I CAN ACTUALLY PERFORM COMPLEX FINE MOTOR FUNCTIONS JUST BY *THINKING* OF THEM.
RAD...
I'D *HEARD* ABOUT STUFF LIKE THIS, BUT IT'S COMPLETELY DIFFERENT TO SEE IT UP CLOSE.
IT'S BASED ON OPEN-SOURCE SOFTWARE, BUT I'M TESTING A FEW *ADJUSTMENTS.*
MAYBE YOU'LL CODE SOME IMPROVEMENTS *YOURSELF*.
I CAN WORK ON THIS? EVEN IF WE DON'T HAVE THE PATENT?
THE ORIGINAL INVENTOR OF THIS PROSTHETIC TECH *WANTED* IT TO BE FREE.
ETHICALLY, I FEEL THAT WE SHOULD CONTINUE HIS WORK IN THE SAME SPIRIT.
OUR PATENTS ARE A MEANS TO AN END: KEEPING THE SOCIETY FINANCIALLY *INDEPENDENT.*
HAVING OUR OWN *ENDOWMENT* KEEPS US FROM THE NEED TO CONSTANTLY SEEK OUTSIDE FUNDING.
BUT WHAT'S GOOD FOR HUMANITY SHOULD ALWAYS BE THE SOCIETY'S *FIRST* GOAL.
CAREFUL, DR. BURKHART, PEOPLE ARE GONNA SAY YOU'RE A *RADICAL* PROFESSOR.
HEY, I STILL HAVE MY *IDEALS.*
EVEN IF I *HAVE* JOINED THE ESTABLISHMENT.

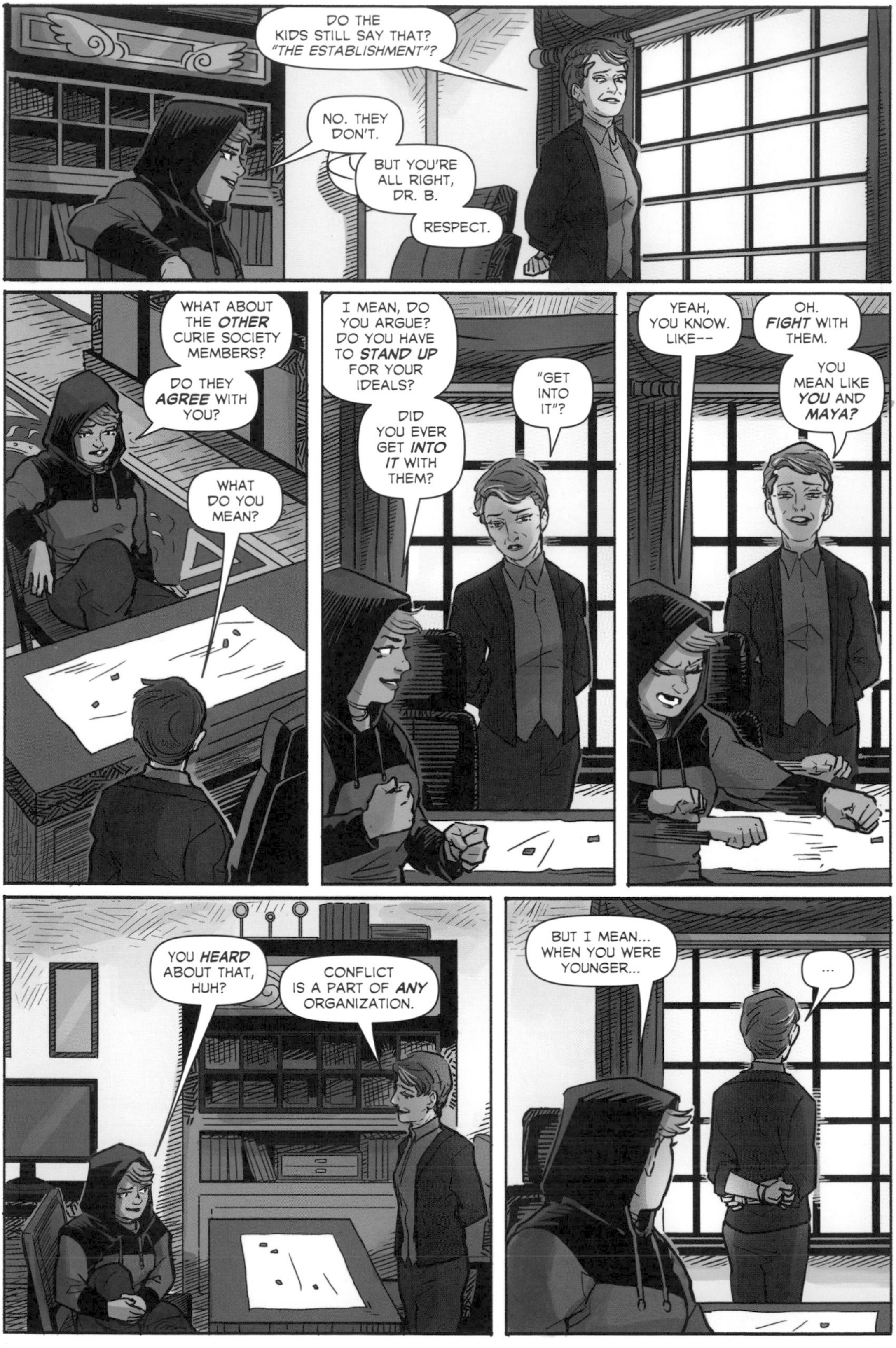
DO THE KIDS STILL SAY THAT? "THE ESTABLISHMENT"?
NO. THEY DON'T.
BUT YOU'RE ALL RIGHT, DR. B.
RESPECT.
WHAT ABOUT THE OTHER CURIE SOCIETY MEMBERS?
DO THEY AGREE WITH YOU?
WHAT DO YOU MEAN?
I MEAN, DO YOU ARGUE? DO YOU HAVE TO STAND UP FOR YOUR IDEALS?
DID YOU EVER GET INTO IT WITH THEM?
"GET INTO IT"?
YEAH, YOU KNOW. LIKE--
OH. FIGHT WITH THEM.
YOU MEAN LIKE YOU AND MAYA?
YOU HEARD ABOUT THAT, HUH?
CONFLICT IS A PART OF ANY ORGANIZATION.
BUT I MEAN... WHEN YOU WERE YOUNGER...
...

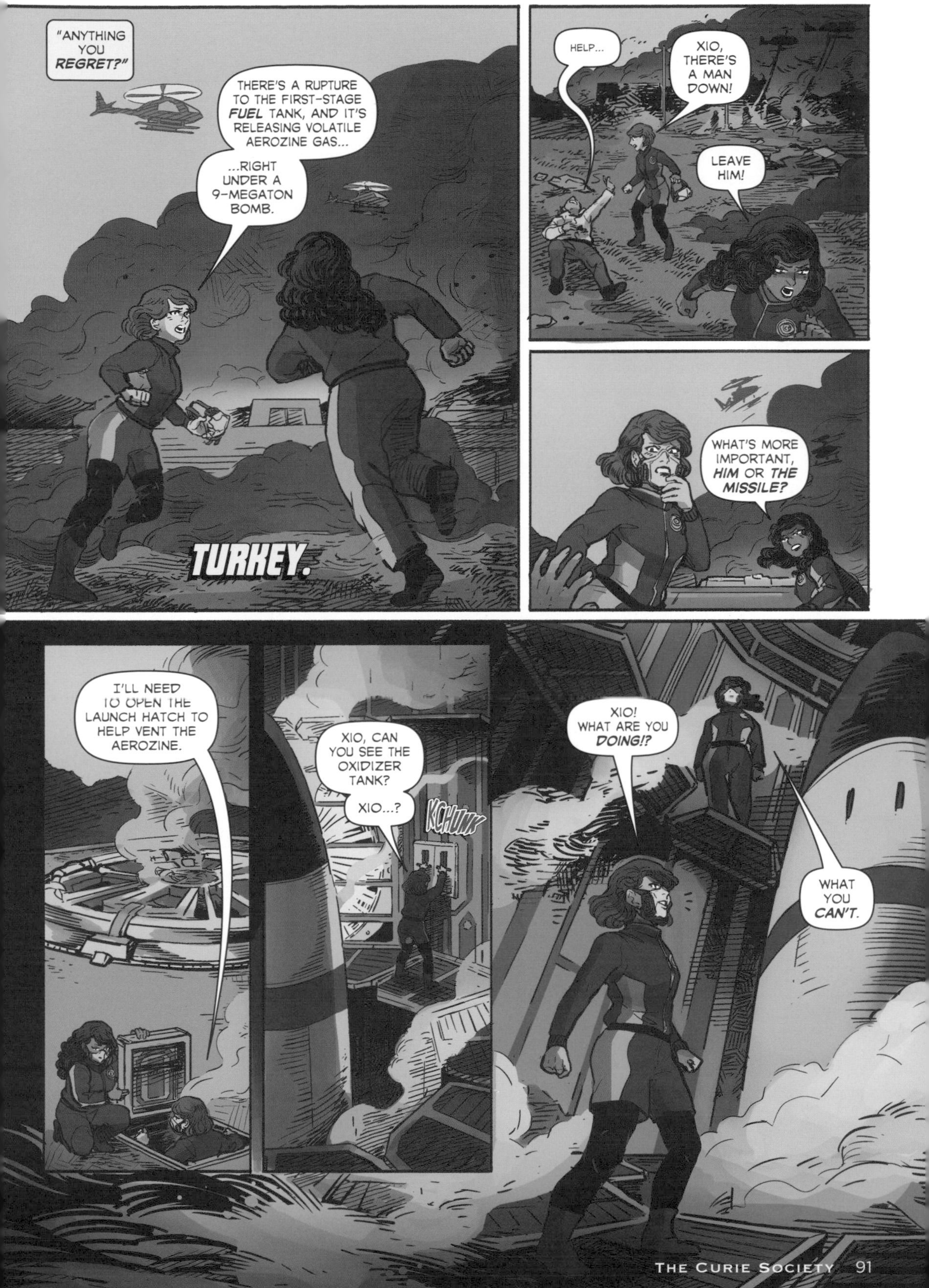
"ANYTHING YOU REGRET?"
THERE'S A RUPTURE TO THE FIRST-STAGE FUEL TANK, AND IT'S RELEASING VOLATILE AEROZINE GAS...
...RIGHT UNDER A 9-MEGATON BOMB.
TURKEY.
HELP...
XIO, THERE'S A MAN DOWN!
LEAVE HIM!
WHAT'S MORE IMPORTANT, HIM OR THE MISSILE?
I'LL NEED TO OPEN THE LAUNCH HATCH TO HELP VENT THE AEROZINE.
XIO, CAN YOU SEE THE OXIDIZER TANK?
XIO...?
KCHUNK
XIO! WHAT ARE YOU DOING!?
WHAT YOU CAN'T.

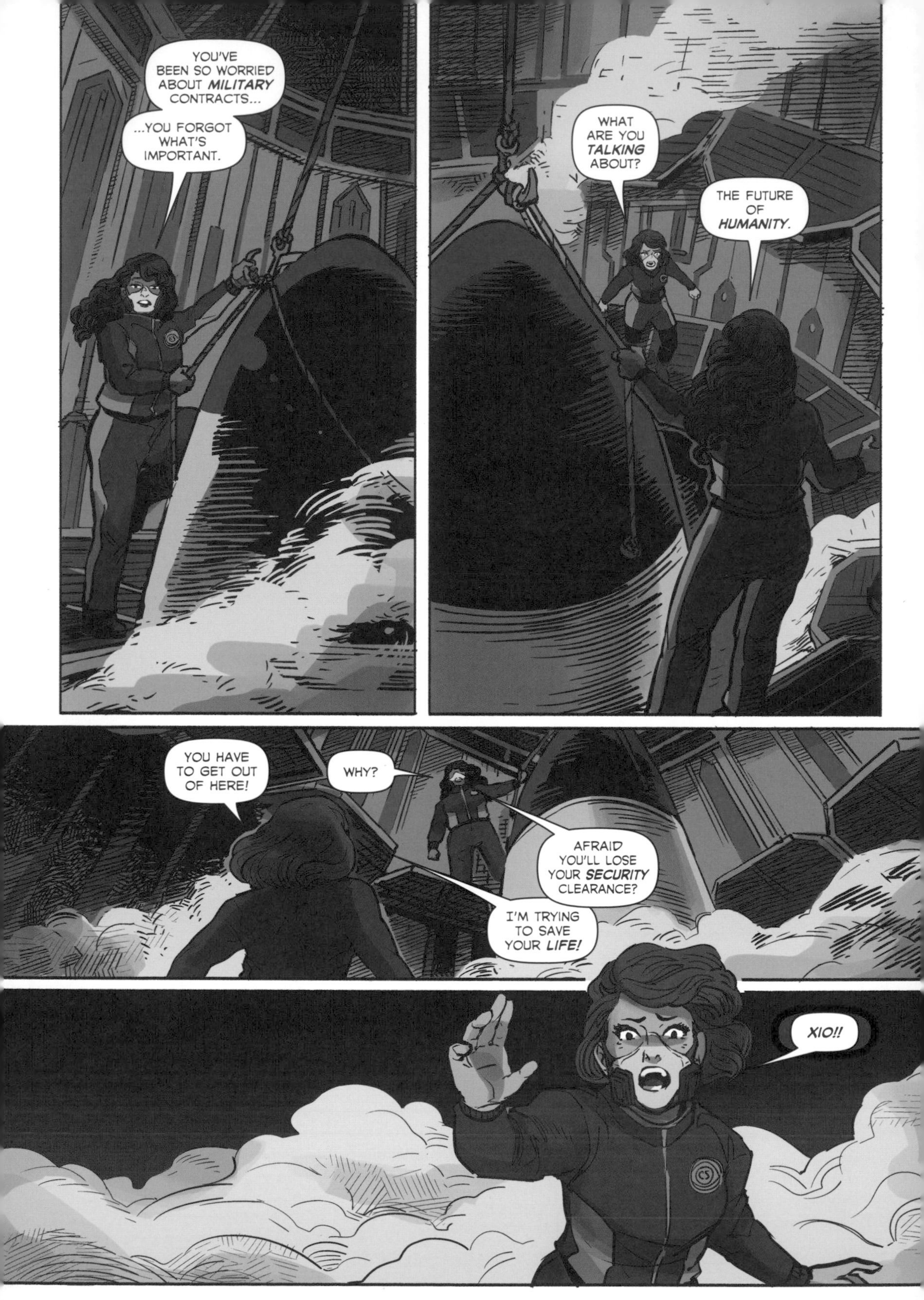
YOU'VE BEEN SO WORRIED ABOUT MILITARY CONTRACTS...
...YOU FORGOT WHAT'S IMPORTANT.
WHAT ARE YOU TALKING ABOUT?
THE FUTURE OF HUMANITY.
YOU HAVE TO GET OUT OF HERE!
WHY?
AFRAID YOU'LL LOSE YOUR SECURITY CLEARANCE?
I'M TRYING TO SAVE YOUR LIFE!
XIO!!

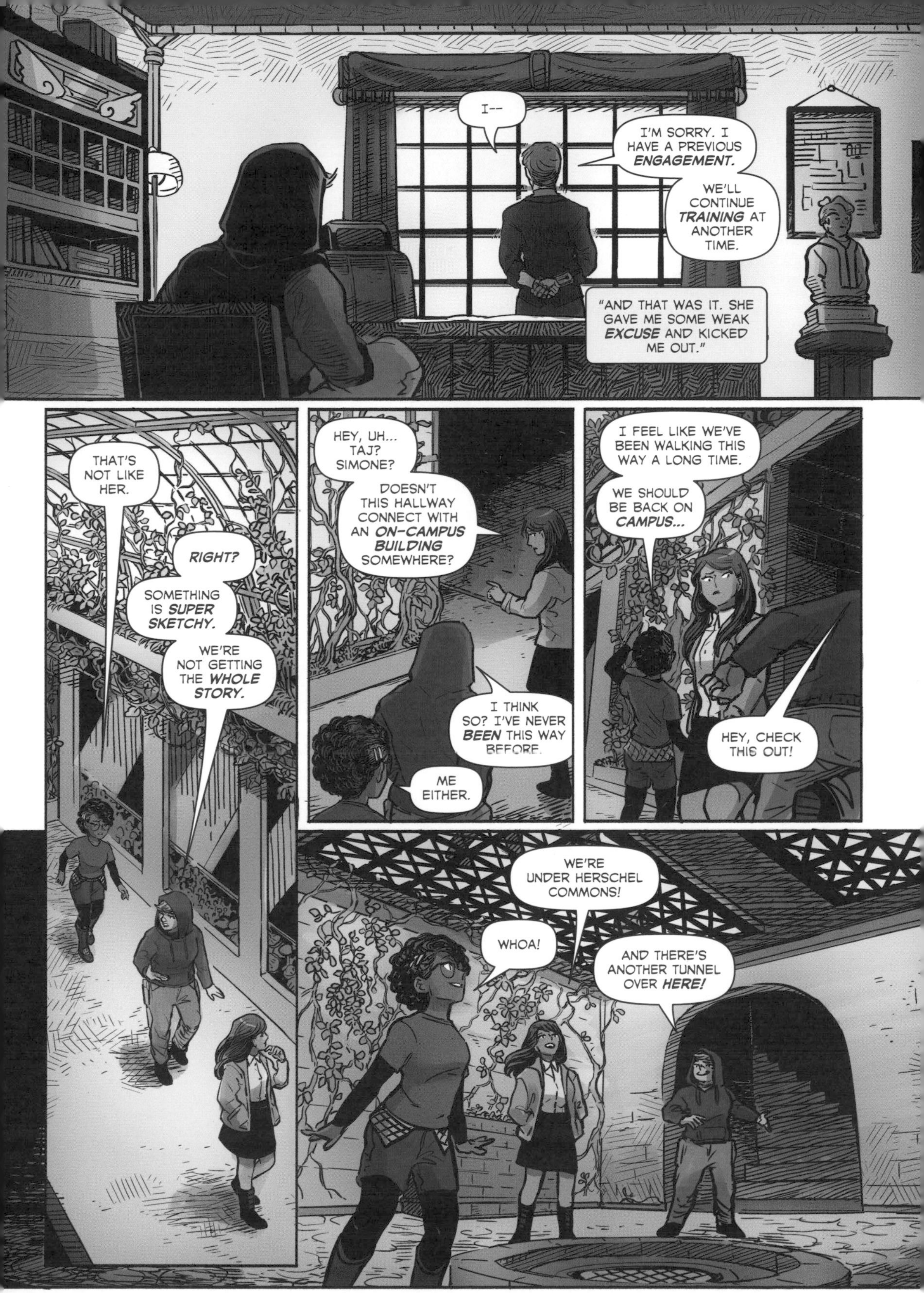
I--
I'M SORRY. I HAVE A PREVIOUS ENGAGEMENT.
WE'LL CONTINUE TRAINING AT ANOTHER TIME.
"AND THAT WAS IT. SHE GAVE ME SOME WEAK EXCUSE AND KICKED ME OUT."
THAT'S NOT LIKE HER.
RIGHT?
SOMETHING IS SUPER SKETCHY.
WE'RE NOT GETTING THE WHOLE STORY.
HEY, UH... TAJ? SIMONE?
DOESN'T THIS HALLWAY CONNECT WITH AN ON-CAMPUS BUILDING SOMEWHERE?
I THINK SO? I'VE NEVER BEEN THIS WAY BEFORE.
ME EITHER.
I FEEL LIKE WE'VE BEEN WALKING THIS WAY A LONG TIME.
WE SHOULD BE BACK ON CAMPUS...
HEY, CHECK THIS OUT!
WE'RE UNDER HERSCHEL COMMONS!
WHOA!
AND THERE'S ANOTHER TUNNEL OVER HERE!

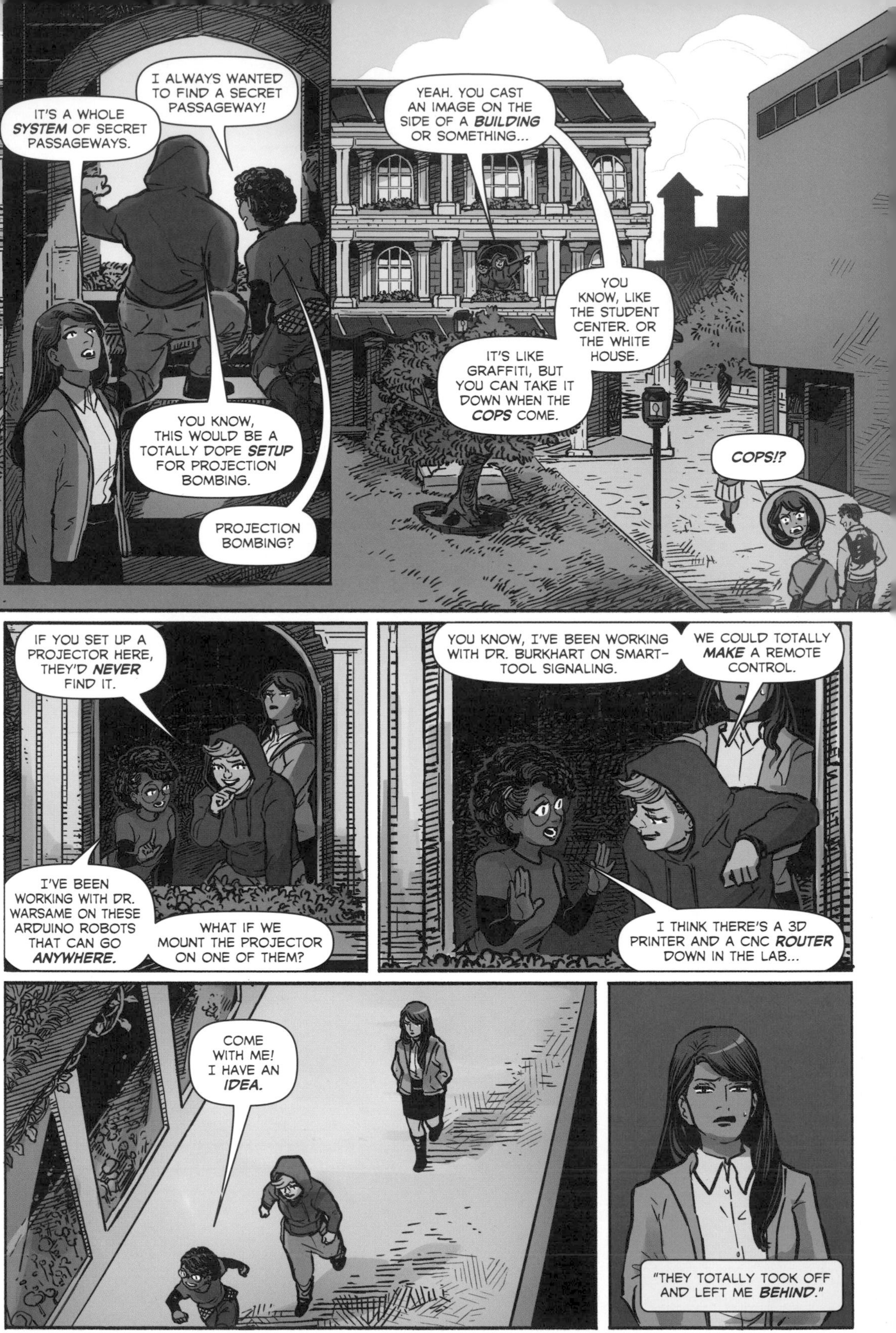
I ALWAYS WANTED TO FIND A SECRET PASSAGEWAY!
IT'S A WHOLE SYSTEM OF SECRET PASSAGEWAYS.
YOU KNOW, THIS WOULD BE A TOTALLY DOPE SETUP FOR PROJECTION BOMBING.
PROJECTION BOMBING?
YEAH. YOU CAST AN IMAGE ON THE SIDE OF A BUILDING OR SOMETHING...
YOU KNOW, LIKE THE STUDENT CENTER. OR THE WHITE HOUSE.
IT'S LIKE GRAFFITI, BUT YOU CAN TAKE IT DOWN WHEN THE COPS COME.
COPS!?
IF YOU SET UP A PROJECTOR HERE, THEY'D NEVER FIND IT.
I'VE BEEN WORKING WITH DR. WARSAME ON THESE ARDUINO ROBOTS THAT CAN GO ANYWHERE.
WHAT IF WE MOUNT THE PROJECTOR ON ONE OF THEM?
YOU KNOW, I'VE BEEN WORKING WITH DR. BURKHART ON SMART-TOOL SIGNALING.
WE COULD TOTALLY MAKE A REMOTE CONTROL.
I THINK THERE'S A 3D PRINTER AND A CNC ROUTER DOWN IN THE LAB...
COME WITH ME! I HAVE AN IDEA.
"THEY TOTALLY TOOK OFF AND LEFT ME BEHIND."

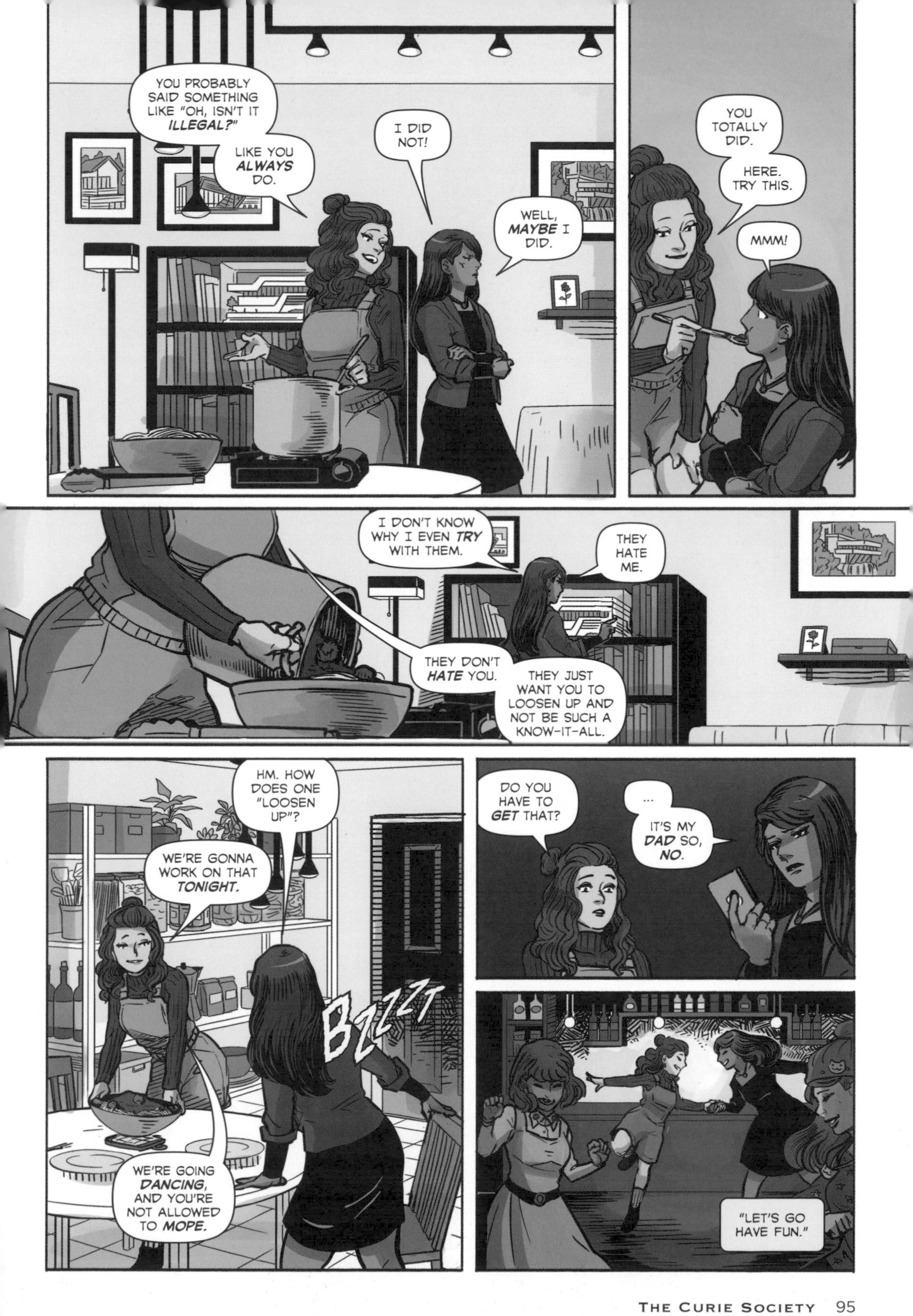
YOU PROBABLY SAID SOMETHING LIKE "OH, ISN'T IT ILLEGAL?"
LIKE YOU ALWAYS DO.
I DID NOT!
WELL, MAYBE I DID.
YOU TOTALLY DID.
HERE. TRY THIS.
MMM!
I DON'T KNOW WHY I EVEN TRY WITH THEM.
THEY HATE ME.
THEY DON'T HATE YOU.
THEY JUST WANT YOU TO LOOSEN UP AND NOT BE SUCH A KNOW-IT-ALL.
HM. HOW DOES ONE "LOOSEN UP"?
WE'RE GONNA WORK ON THAT TONIGHT.
WE'RE GOING DANCING, AND YOU'RE NOT ALLOWED TO MOPE.
BZZZZT
DO YOU HAVE TO GET THAT?
...
IT'S MY DAD SO, NO.
"LET'S GO HAVE FUN."

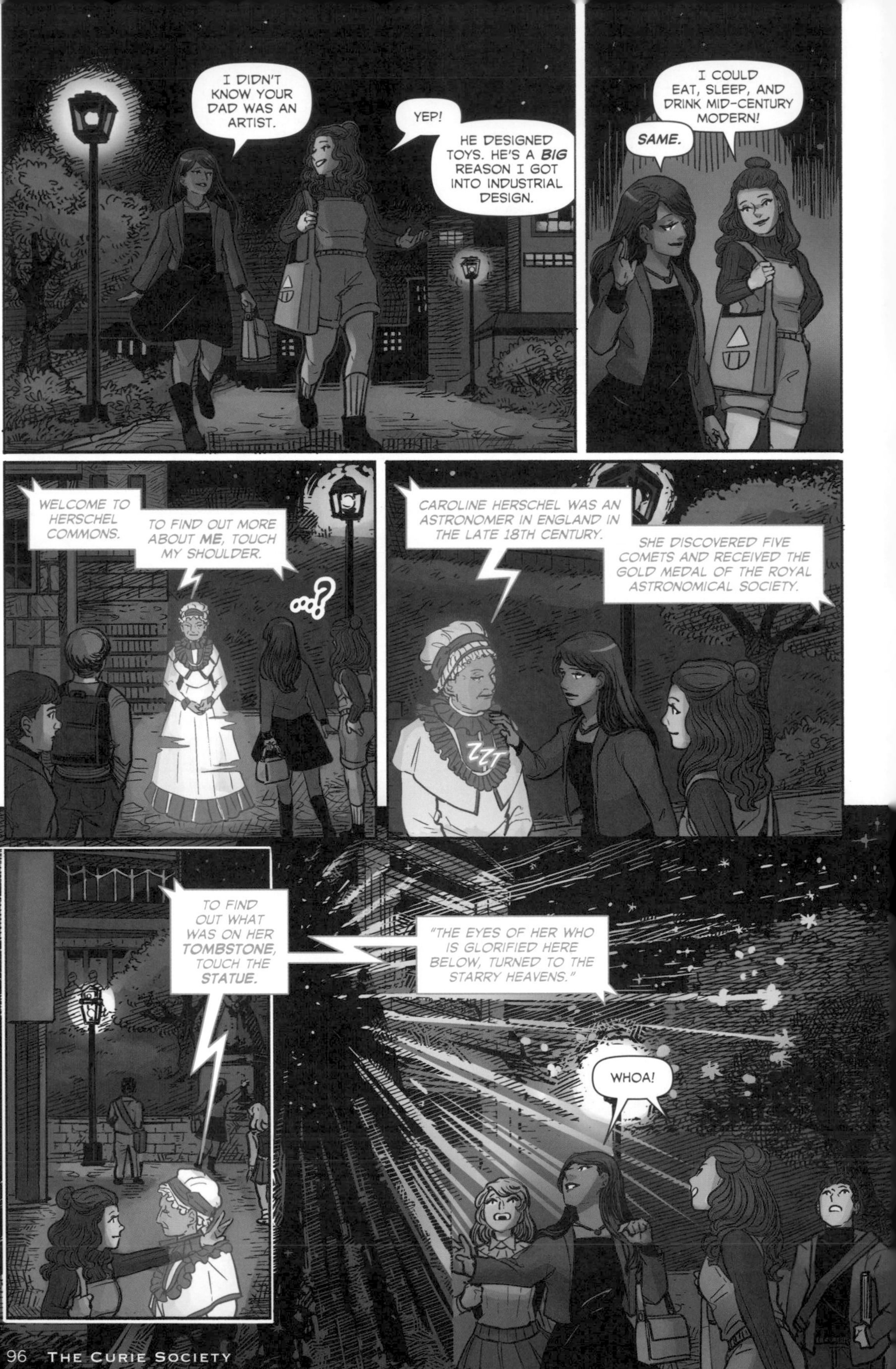
I DIDN'T KNOW YOUR DAD WAS AN ARTIST.
YEP!
HE DESIGNED TOYS. HE'S A BIG REASON I GOT INTO INDUSTRIAL DESIGN.
I COULD EAT, SLEEP, AND DRINK MID-CENTURY MODERN!
SAME.
WELCOME TO HERSCHEL COMMONS.
TO FIND OUT MORE ABOUT ME, TOUCH MY SHOULDER.
...?
CAROLINE HERSCHEL WAS AN ASTRONOMER IN ENGLAND IN THE LATE 18TH CENTURY.
SHE DISCOVERED FIVE COMETS AND RECEIVED THE GOLD MEDAL OF THE ROYAL ASTRONOMICAL SOCIETY.
ZZT
TO FIND OUT WHAT WAS ON HER TOMBSTONE, TOUCH THE STATUE.
"THE EYES OF HER WHO IS GLORIFIED HERE BELOW, TURNED TO THE STARRY HEAVENS."
WHOA!

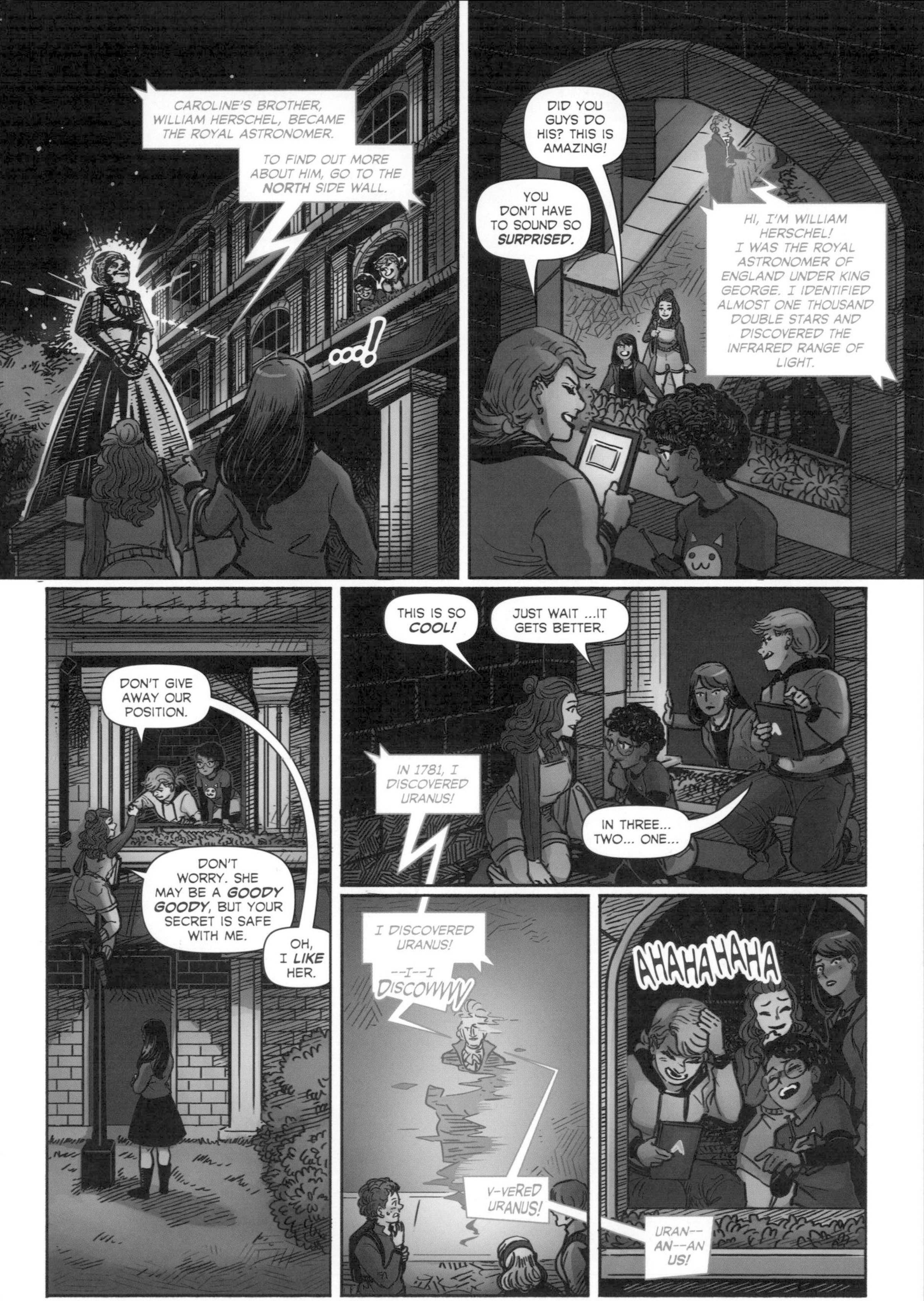

CAROLINE'S BROTHER, WILLIAM HERSCHEL, BECAME THE ROYAL ASTRONOMER.
TO FIND OUT MORE ABOUT HIM, GO TO THE NORTH SIDE WALL.
...!
DID YOU GUYS DO HIS? THIS IS AMAZING!
YOU DON'T HAVE TO SOUND SO SURPRISED.
HI, I'M WILLIAM HERSCHEL! I WAS THE ROYAL ASTRONOMER OF ENGLAND UNDER KING GEORGE. I IDENTIFIED ALMOST ONE THOUSAND DOUBLE STARS AND DISCOVERED THE INFRARED RANGE OF LIGHT.
DON'T GIVE AWAY OUR POSITION.
DON'T WORRY. SHE MAY BE A GOODY GOODY, BUT YOUR SECRET IS SAFE WITH ME.
OH, I LIKE HER.
THIS IS SO COOL!
JUST WAIT ...IT GETS BETTER.
IN 1781, I DISCOVERED URANUS!
IN THREE... TWO... ONE...
I DISCOVERED URANUS!
--I--I DISCOWVVV
V-VERED URANUS!
AHAHAHAHA
URAN-- AN--AN US!

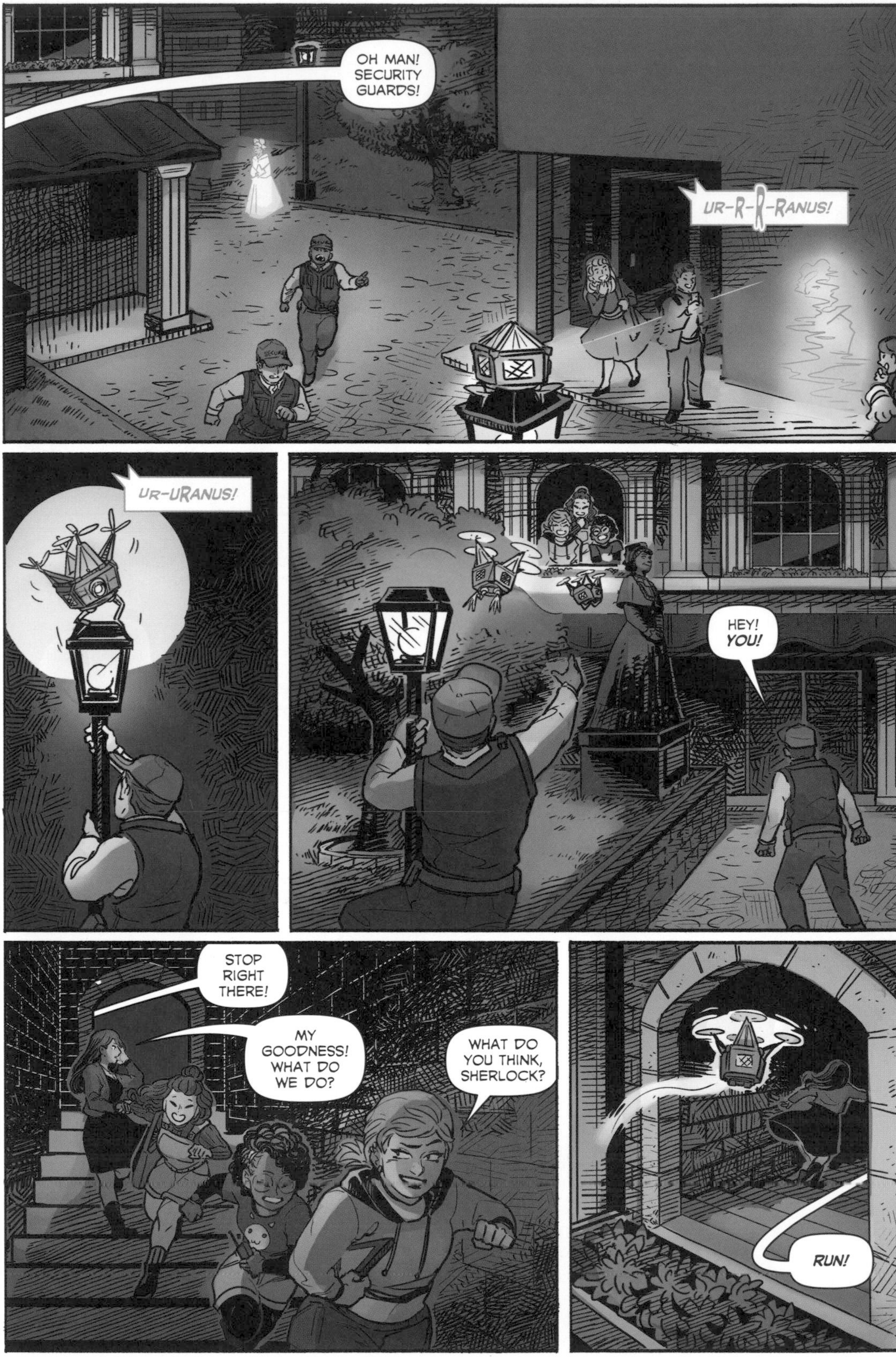
OH MAN! SECURITY GUARDS!
UR-R-R-RANUS!
UR-URANUS!
HEY! YOU!
STOP RIGHT THERE!
MY GOODNESS! WHAT DO WE DO?
WHAT DO YOU THINK, SHERLOCK?
RUN!

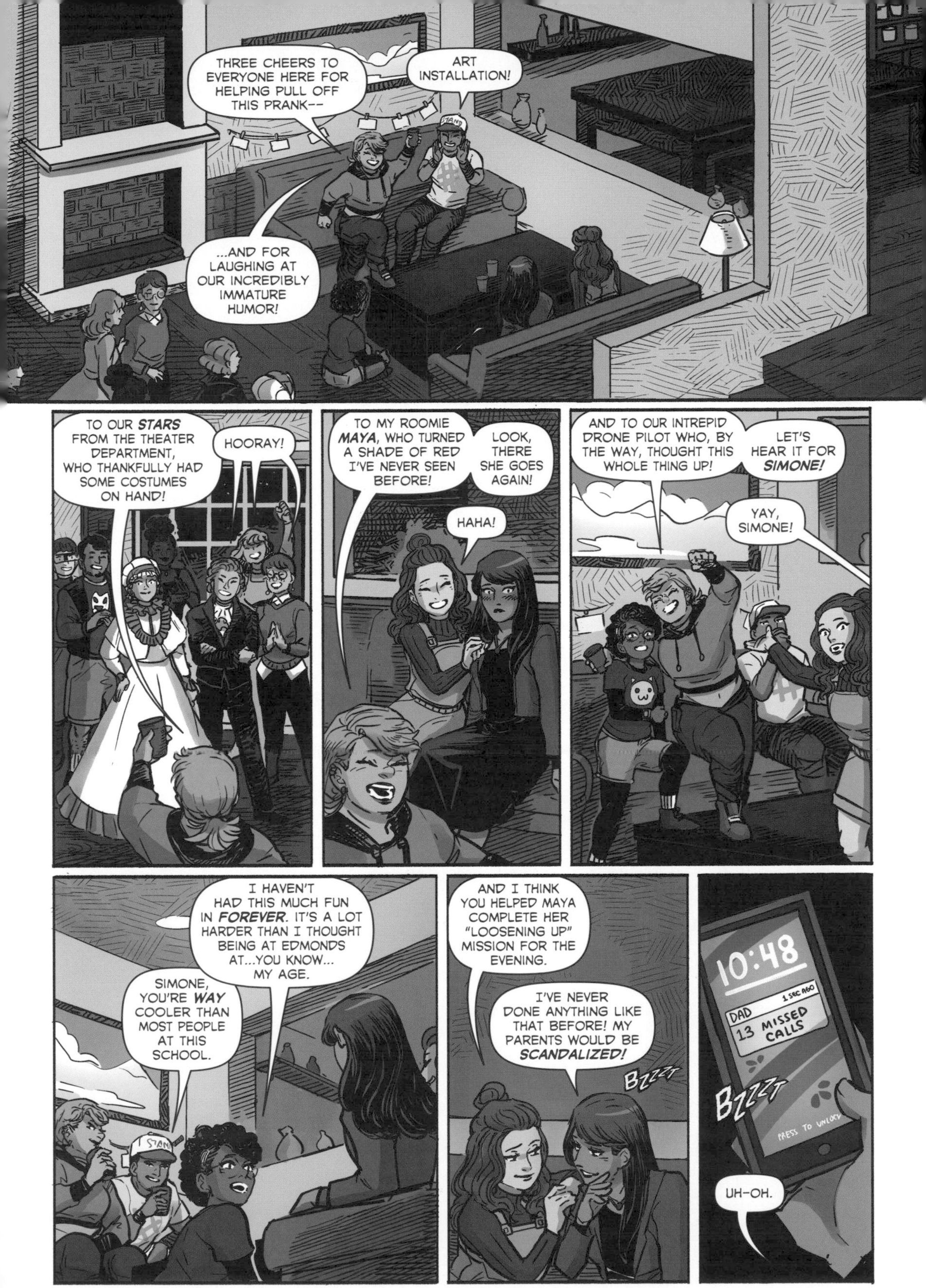
THREE CHEERS TO EVERYONE HERE FOR HELPING PULL OFF THIS PRANK--
ART INSTALLATION!
STAND
...AND FOR LAUGHING AT OUR INCREDIBLY IMMATURE HUMOR!
TO OUR STARS FROM THE THEATER DEPARTMENT, WHO THANKFULLY HAD SOME COSTUMES ON HAND!
HOORAY!
TO MY ROOMIE MAYA, WHO TURNED A SHADE OF RED I'VE NEVER SEEN BEFORE!
LOOK, THERE SHE GOES AGAIN!
HAHA!
AND TO OUR INTREPID DRONE PILOT WHO, BY THE WAY, THOUGHT THIS WHOLE THING UP!
LET'S HEAR IT FOR SIMONE!
YAY, SIMONE!
I HAVEN'T HAD THIS MUCH FUN IN FOREVER. IT'S A LOT HARDER THAN I THOUGHT BEING AT EDMONDS AT...YOU KNOW... MY AGE.
SIMONE, YOU'RE WAY COOLER THAN MOST PEOPLE AT THIS SCHOOL.
STAN
AND I THINK YOU HELPED MAYA COMPLETE HER "LOOSENING UP" MISSION FOR THE EVENING.
I'VE NEVER DONE ANYTHING LIKE THAT BEFORE! MY PARENTS WOULD BE SCANDALIZED!
BZZZT
10:48
DAD
1 SEC AGO
13 MISSED CALLS
BZZZT
PRESS TO UNLOCK
UH-OH.

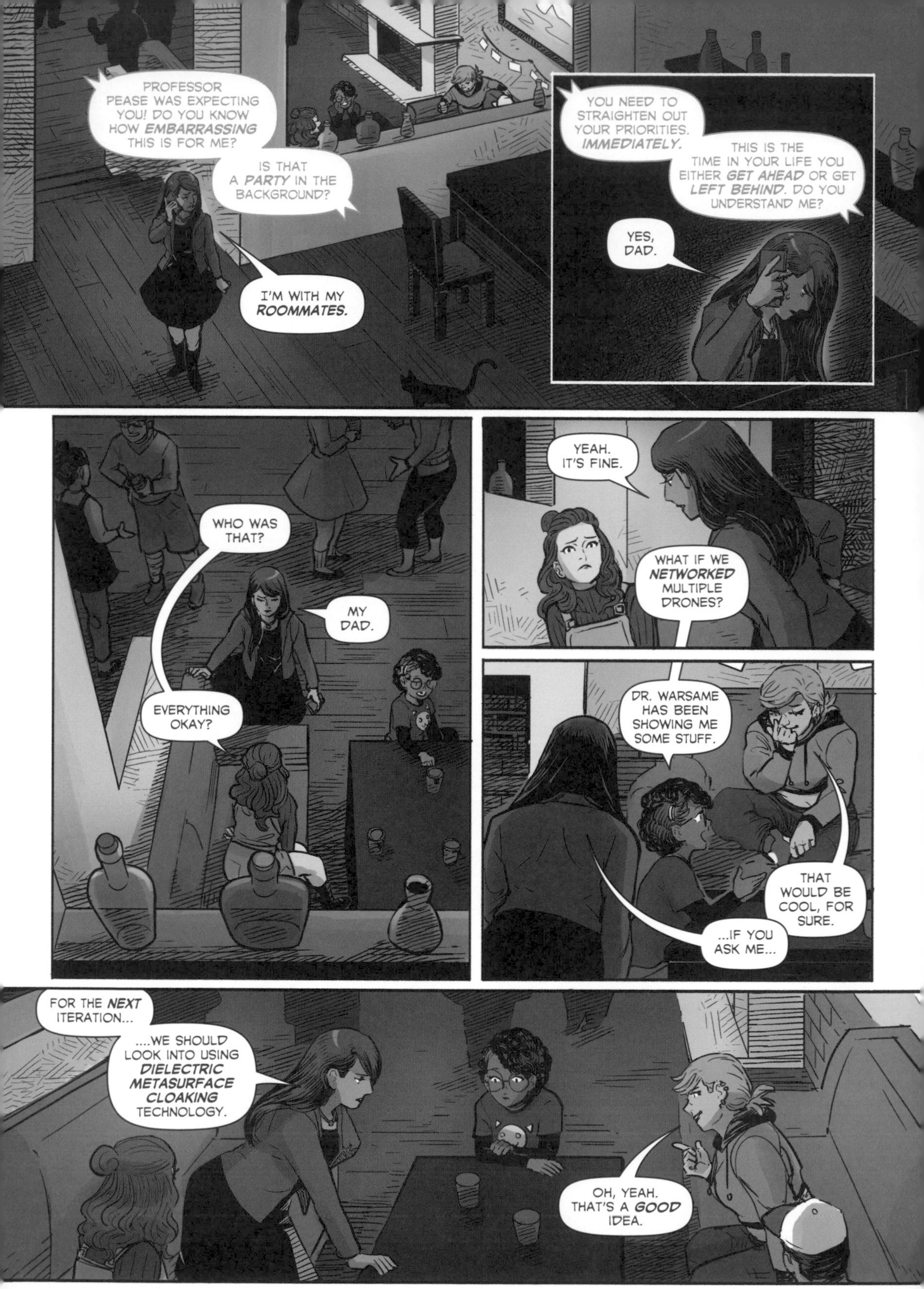
PROFESSOR PEASE WAS EXPECTING YOU! DO YOU KNOW HOW EMBARRASSING THIS IS FOR ME?
IS THAT A PARTY IN THE BACKGROUND?
I'M WITH MY ROOMMATES.
YOU NEED TO STRAIGHTEN OUT YOUR PRIORITIES. IMMEDIATELY.
THIS IS THE TIME IN YOUR LIFE YOU EITHER GET AHEAD OR GET LEFT BEHIND. DO YOU UNDERSTAND ME?
YES, DAD.
WHO WAS THAT?
MY DAD.
EVERYTHING OKAY?
YEAH. IT'S FINE.
WHAT IF WE NETWORKED MULTIPLE DRONES?
DR. WARSAME HAS BEEN SHOWING ME SOME STUFF.
THAT WOULD BE COOL, FOR SURE.
...IF YOU ASK ME...
FOR THE NEXT ITERATION...
....WE SHOULD LOOK INTO USING DIELECTRIC METASURFACE CLOAKING TECHNOLOGY.
OH, YEAH. THAT'S A GOOD IDEA.

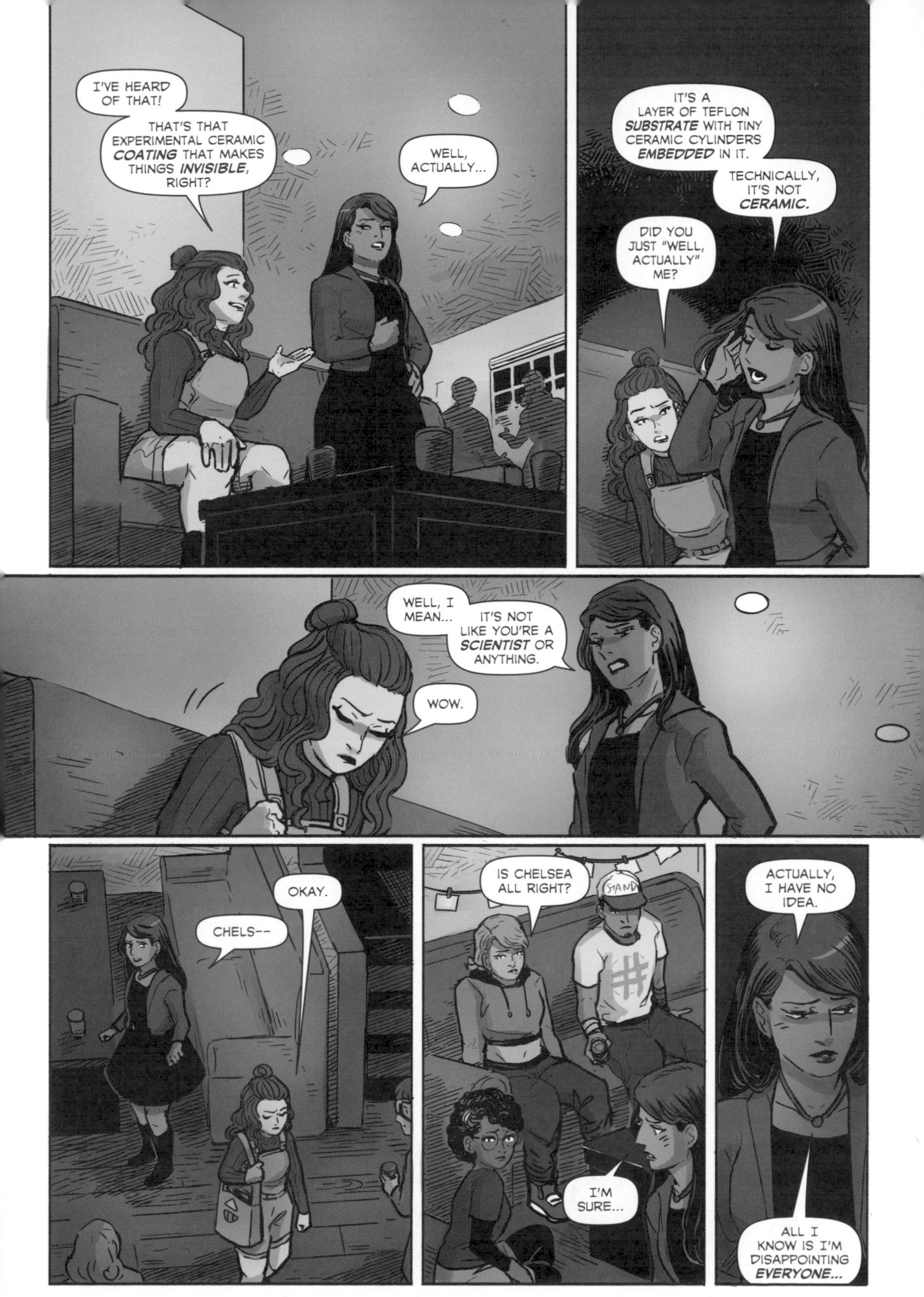
I'VE HEARD OF THAT!
THAT'S THAT EXPERIMENTAL CERAMIC **COATING** THAT MAKES THINGS **INVISIBLE**, RIGHT?
WELL, ACTUALLY...
IT'S A LAYER OF TEFLON **SUBSTRATE** WITH TINY CERAMIC CYLINDERS **EMBEDDED** IN IT.
TECHNICALLY, IT'S NOT **CERAMIC.**
DID YOU JUST "WELL, ACTUALLY" ME?
WELL, I MEAN...
IT'S NOT LIKE YOU'RE A **SCIENTIST** OR ANYTHING.
WOW.
CHELS--
OKAY.
IS CHELSEA ALL RIGHT?
I'M SURE...
ACTUALLY, I HAVE NO IDEA.
ALL I KNOW IS I'M DISAPPOINTING **EVERYONE...**

BZZZT
BZZZT
BZZZT

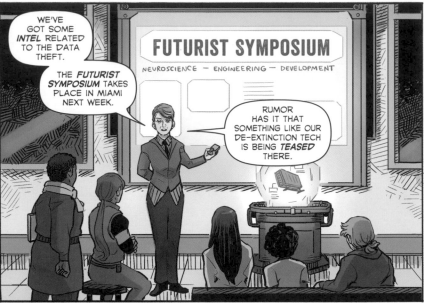

WE'VE GOT SOME *INTEL* RELATED TO THE DATA THEFT.

THE *FUTURIST SYMPOSIUM* TAKES PLACE IN MIAMI NEXT WEEK.

FUTURIST SYMPOSIUM

NEUROSCIENCE — ENGINEERING — DEVELOPMENT

RUMOR HAS IT THAT SOMETHING LIKE OUR DE-EXTINCTION TECH IS BEING *TEASED* THERE.

LOOKS LIKE A REGULAR *ACADEMIC CONFERENCE.*

ON THE SURFACE, *YES.*

BUT BEHIND CLOSED DOORS, THERE'S SOME HIGH-STAKES BLACK MARKET *TRADING* GOING ON.

PROTOTYPES, *PROPRIETARY* INFORMATION... MOSTLY ACQUIRED THROUGH CORPORATE *ESPIONAGE.* LIKE OUR STOLEN RESEARCH.

ANY BUYERS?

WE'VE IDENTIFIED A FEW POTENTIAL *TARGETS.*

THE MAIN ONE OF INTEREST IS *HARVEY BETCHER* OF BETCHER HOLDINGS.

HARVEY BETCHER

BETCHER IS A VENTURE *CAPITALIST* WITH A PARTICULAR INTEREST IN *BIOTECH.*

BETCHER!?

IT'S AN ADVANCED MISSION FOR RECRUITS, BUT WE THINK YOU'RE READY.

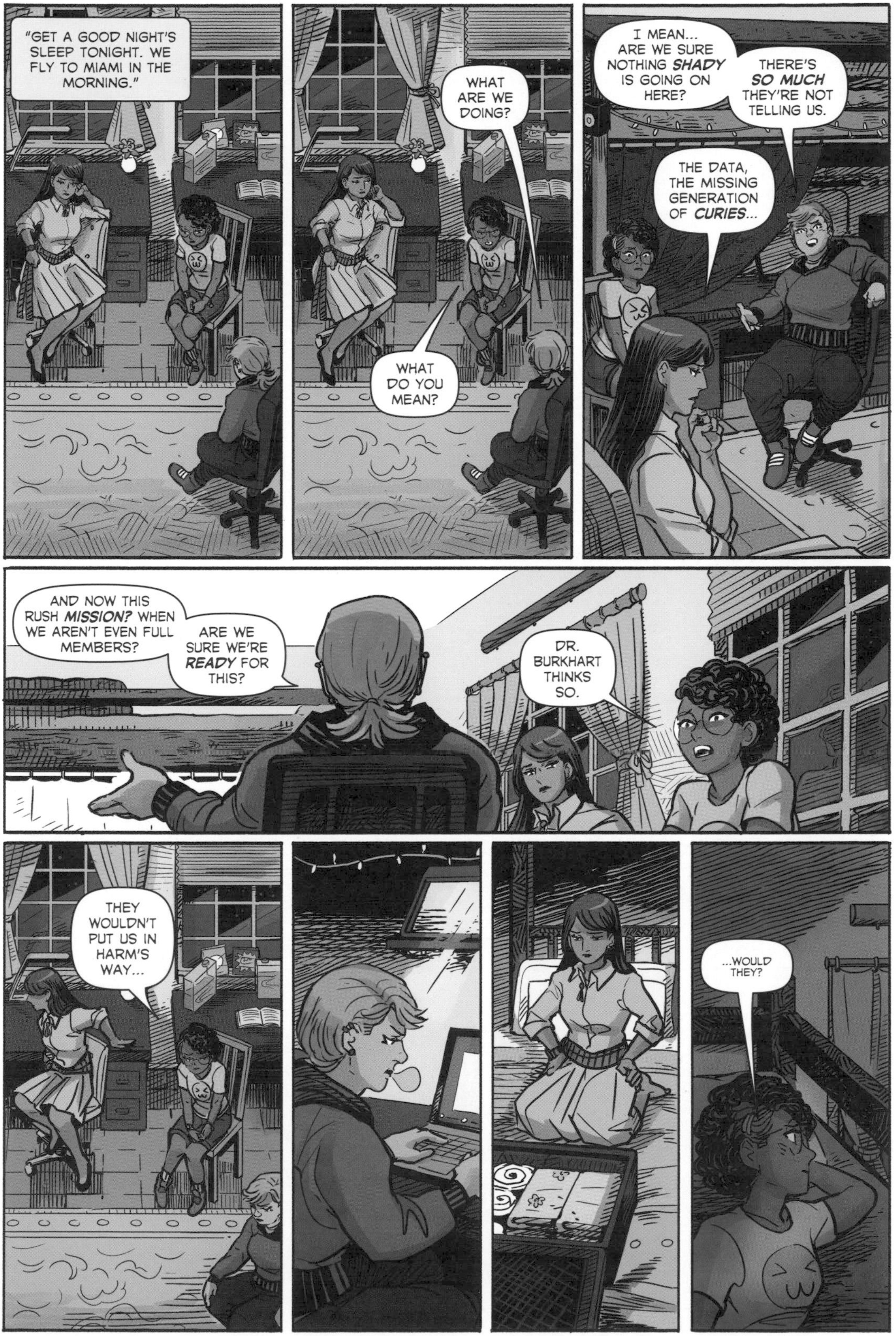
"GET A GOOD NIGHT'S SLEEP TONIGHT. WE FLY TO MIAMI IN THE MORNING."
WHAT ARE WE DOING?
WHAT DO YOU MEAN?
I MEAN... ARE WE SURE NOTHING SHADY IS GOING ON HERE?
THERE'S SO MUCH THEY'RE NOT TELLING US.
THE DATA, THE MISSING GENERATION OF CURIES...
AND NOW THIS RUSH MISSION? WHEN WE AREN'T EVEN FULL MEMBERS?
ARE WE SURE WE'RE READY FOR THIS?
DR. BURKHART THINKS SO.
THEY WOULDN'T PUT US IN HARM'S WAY...
...WOULD THEY?

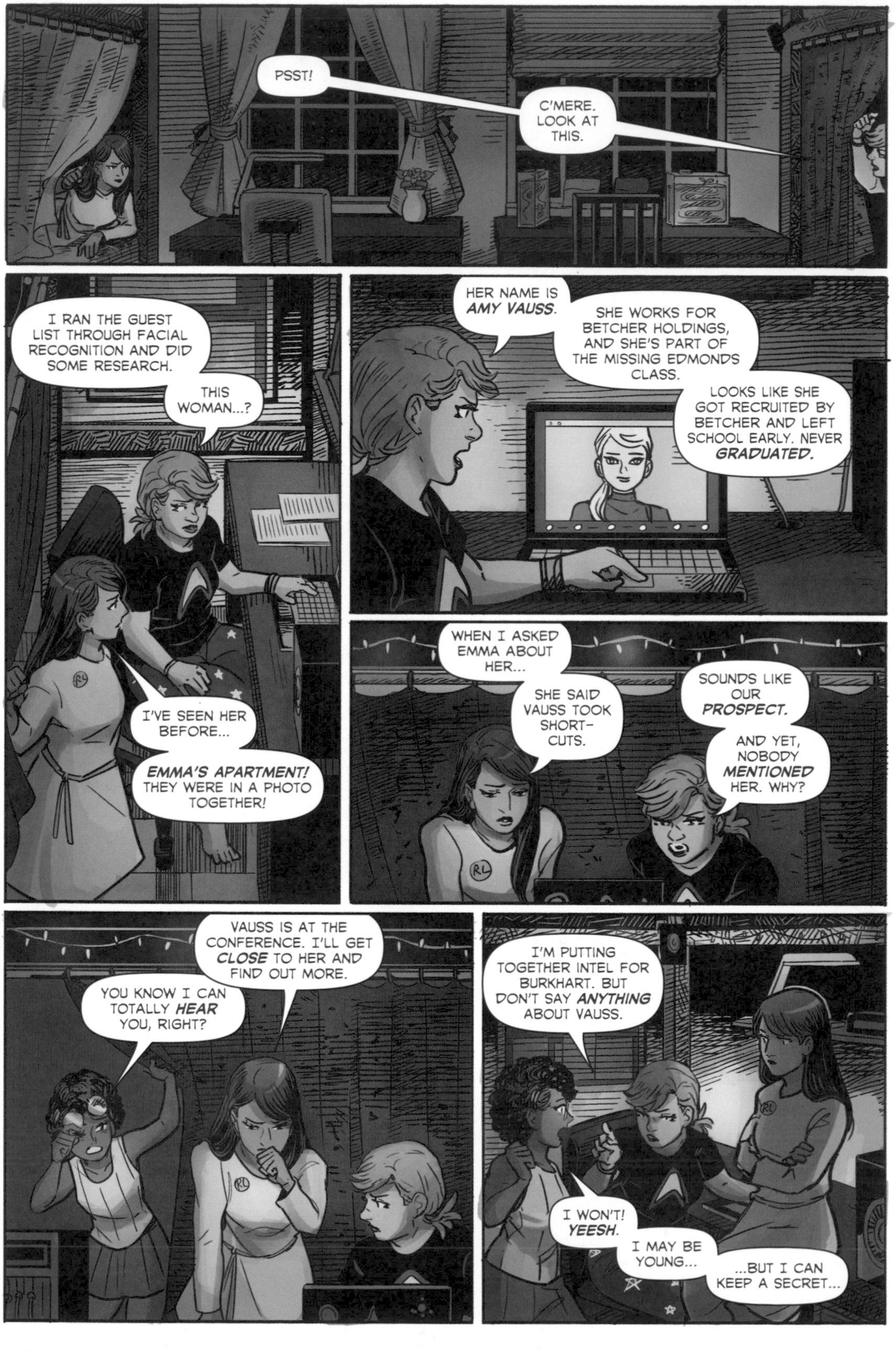
PSST!
C'MERE. LOOK AT THIS.
I RAN THE GUEST LIST THROUGH FACIAL RECOGNITION AND DID SOME RESEARCH.
THIS WOMAN...?
I'VE SEEN HER BEFORE...
EMMA'S APARTMENT! THEY WERE IN A PHOTO TOGETHER!
HER NAME IS AMY VAUSS.
SHE WORKS FOR BETCHER HOLDINGS, AND SHE'S PART OF THE MISSING EDMONDS CLASS.
LOOKS LIKE SHE GOT RECRUITED BY BETCHER AND LEFT SCHOOL EARLY. NEVER GRADUATED.
WHEN I ASKED EMMA ABOUT HER...
SHE SAID VAUSS TOOK SHORT-CUTS.
SOUNDS LIKE OUR PROSPECT.
AND YET, NOBODY MENTIONED HER. WHY?
VAUSS IS AT THE CONFERENCE. I'LL GET CLOSE TO HER AND FIND OUT MORE.
YOU KNOW I CAN TOTALLY HEAR YOU, RIGHT?
I'M PUTTING TOGETHER INTEL FOR BURKHART. BUT DON'T SAY ANYTHING ABOUT VAUSS.
I WON'T! YEESH.
I MAY BE YOUNG...
...BUT I CAN KEEP A SECRET...

STRAP IN, LADIES.

NEXT STOP: *MIAMI.*

"DR. BURKHART WAS ABLE TO WRANGLE US AN *INVITATION* AS GUESTS OF THE UNIVERSITY, AND SHE'S BEEN ADDED AS A LAST-MINUTE SPEAKER.

"WE WILL FLY OUT *TOGETHER,* MEET HER AT THE CONFERENCE, AND THEN RETRIEVE THE HARD DRIVE."

TAJ AND I ASSEMBLED THIS *DOSSIER* DOCUMENTING POSSIBLE BUYERS AT THE CONFERENCE WHO MIGHT BE IN THE MARKET FOR OUR DATA.

HERE'S THE *PLAN:*

"MAYA, YOU'LL BE ON THE FLOOR OF THE CONFERENCE.

"BETCHER IS THE MAIN *TARGET,* SO WE'LL NEED YOU TO GET CLOSE TO HIM AND PLANT A *BUG.*"

MAYA FINALLY GETS TO USE HER SUPER-POWER--*SCHMOOZING.*

THANKS! ...I *THINK.*

YOU'LL ALSO BE WEARING *THIS.*

IT'S A LIMITED-USE *STUN GUN* DISGUISED AS A RING.

NICE! I GET THE JAMES BOND TECH!

BE CAREFUL, 007. EMERGENCIES ONLY. YOU ONLY HAVE *ONE* CHARGE.

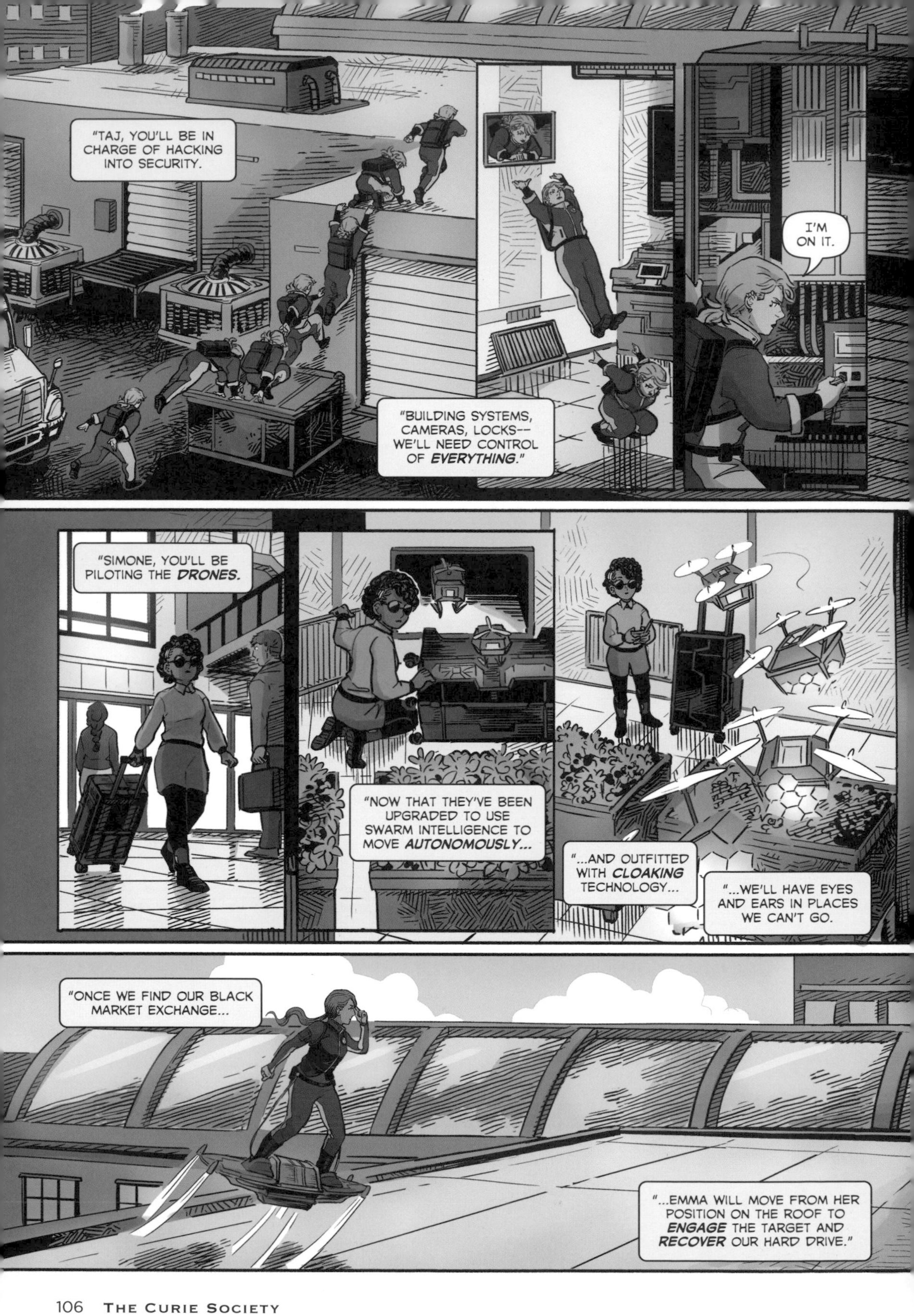
"TAJ, YOU'LL BE IN CHARGE OF HACKING INTO SECURITY.
"BUILDING SYSTEMS, CAMERAS, LOCKS-- WE'LL NEED CONTROL OF EVERYTHING."
I'M ON IT.
"SIMONE, YOU'LL BE PILOTING THE DRONES.
"NOW THAT THEY'VE BEEN UPGRADED TO USE SWARM INTELLIGENCE TO MOVE AUTONOMOUSLY...
"...AND OUTFITTED WITH CLOAKING TECHNOLOGY...
"...WE'LL HAVE EYES AND EARS IN PLACES WE CAN'T GO.
"ONCE WE FIND OUR BLACK MARKET EXCHANGE...
"...EMMA WILL MOVE FROM HER POSITION ON THE ROOF TO ENGAGE THE TARGET AND RECOVER OUR HARD DRIVE."

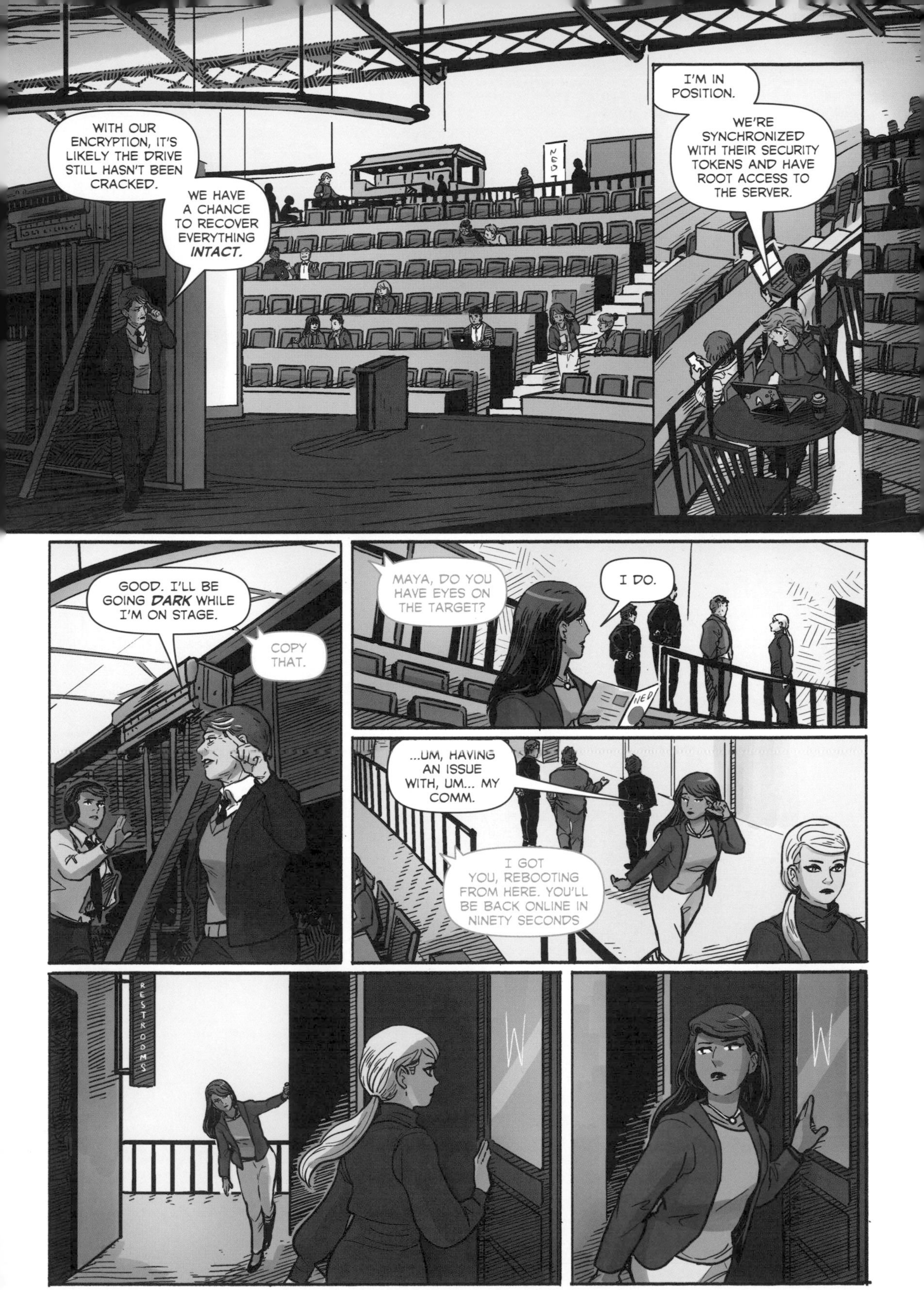
WITH OUR ENCRYPTION, IT'S LIKELY THE DRIVE STILL HASN'T BEEN CRACKED.
WE HAVE A CHANCE TO RECOVER EVERYTHING ***INTACT.***
NED
I'M IN POSITION.
WE'RE SYNCHRONIZED WITH THEIR SECURITY TOKENS AND HAVE ROOT ACCESS TO THE SERVER.
GOOD. I'LL BE GOING ***DARK*** WHILE I'M ON STAGE.
COPY THAT.
MAYA, DO YOU HAVE EYES ON THE TARGET?
I DO.
NED
...UM, HAVING AN ISSUE WITH, UM... MY COMM.
I GOT YOU, REBOOTING FROM HERE. YOU'LL BE BACK ONLINE IN NINETY SECONDS
RESTROOMS
W
W

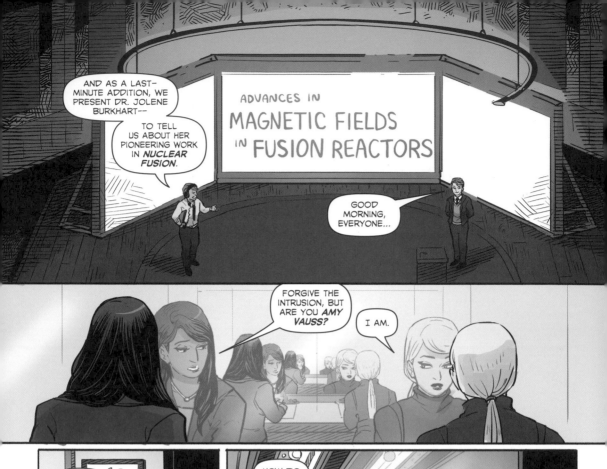

AND AS A LAST-MINUTE ADDITION, WE PRESENT DR. JOLENE BURKHART--

TO TELL US ABOUT HER PIONEERING WORK IN *NUCLEAR FUSION.*

ADVANCES IN
MAGNETIC FIELDS IN FUSION REACTORS

GOOD MORNING, EVERYONE...

FORGIVE THE INTRUSION, BUT ARE YOU *AMY VAUSS?*

I AM.

CAN I HELP YOU?

I UNDERSTAND WE HAVE SOMETHING IN COMMON.

MAYA RAO. *EDMONDS* UNIVERSITY.

HOW DO YOU LIKE IT?

WELL...

...IT HAS A STELLAR REPUTATION. BUT NOW I'M NOTICING A LOT OF PEOPLE ...LEAVE EARLY. HOW ABOUT YOU?

WELL, I...*LEFT EARLY.*

I'M ALREADY FEELING LIKE THE SCHOOL IS BECOMING...

AN ALBATROSS?

AROUND MY *NECK.*

SOUNDS FAMILIAR.

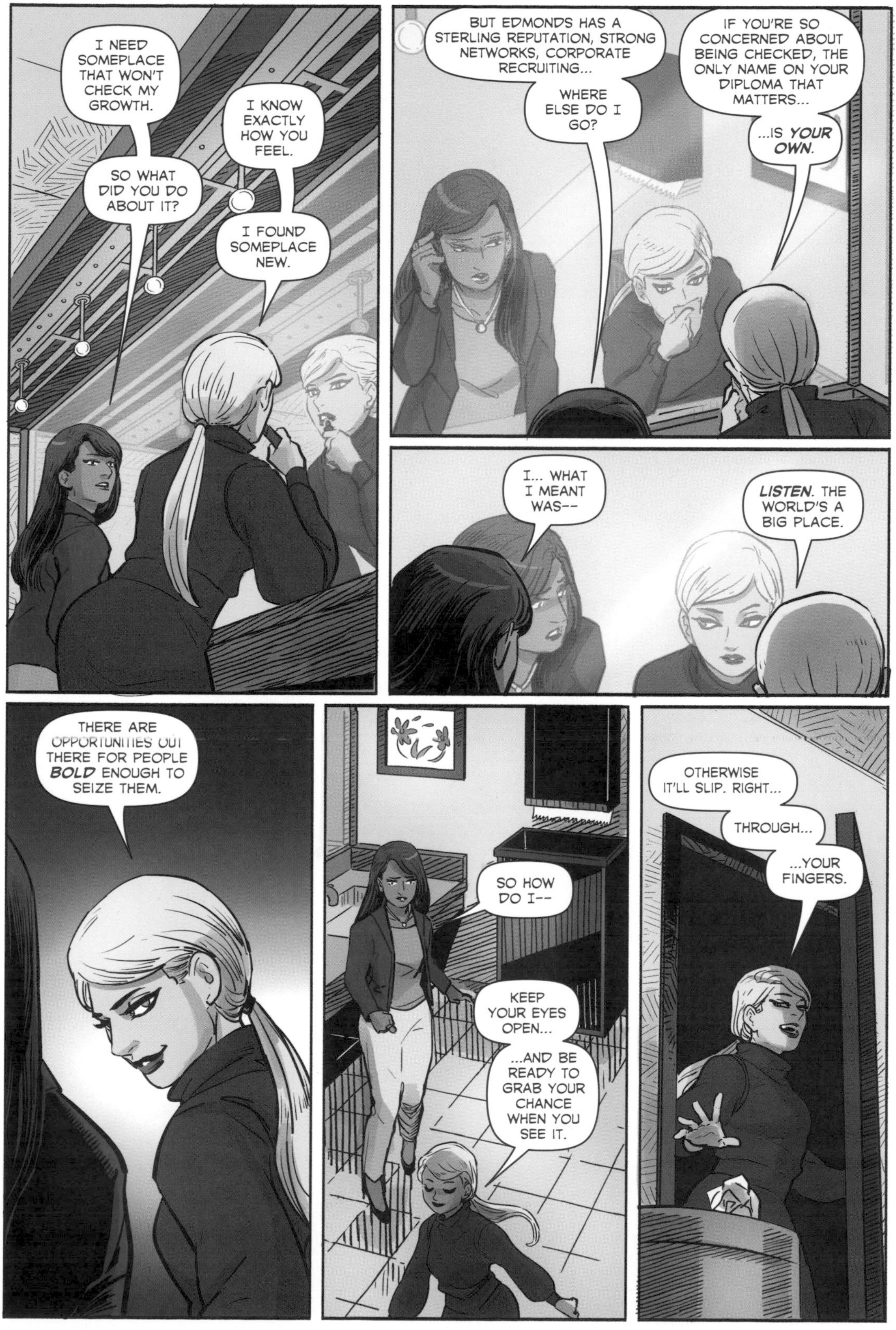
I NEED SOMEPLACE THAT WON'T CHECK MY GROWTH.
I KNOW EXACTLY HOW YOU FEEL.
SO WHAT DID YOU DO ABOUT IT?
I FOUND SOMEPLACE NEW.
BUT EDMONDS HAS A STERLING REPUTATION, STRONG NETWORKS, CORPORATE RECRUITING...
WHERE ELSE DO I GO?
IF YOU'RE SO CONCERNED ABOUT BEING CHECKED, THE ONLY NAME ON YOUR DIPLOMA THAT MATTERS...
...IS *YOUR OWN*.
I... WHAT I MEANT WAS--
LISTEN. THE WORLD'S A BIG PLACE.
THERE ARE OPPORTUNITIES OUT THERE FOR PEOPLE *BOLD* ENOUGH TO SEIZE THEM.
SO HOW DO I--
KEEP YOUR EYES OPEN...
...AND BE READY TO GRAB YOUR CHANCE WHEN YOU SEE IT.
OTHERWISE IT'LL SLIP. RIGHT...
THROUGH...
...YOUR FINGERS.

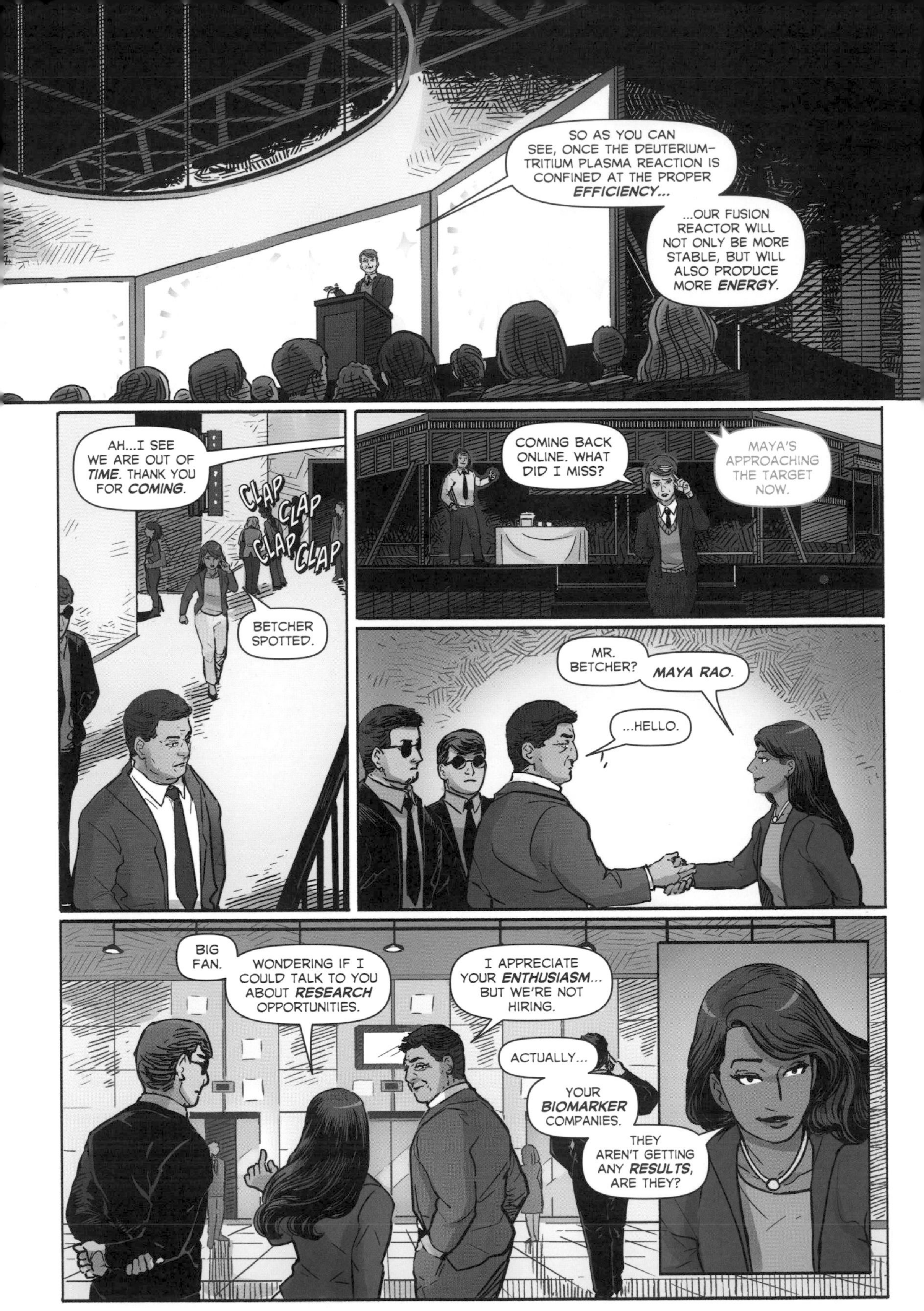
SO AS YOU CAN SEE, ONCE THE DEUTERIUM-TRITIUM PLASMA REACTION IS CONFINED AT THE PROPER EFFICIENCY...
...OUR FUSION REACTOR WILL NOT ONLY BE MORE STABLE, BUT WILL ALSO PRODUCE MORE ENERGY.
AH...I SEE WE ARE OUT OF TIME. THANK YOU FOR COMING.
CLAP CLAP CLAP CLAP
BETCHER SPOTTED.
COMING BACK ONLINE. WHAT DID I MISS?
MAYA'S APPROACHING THE TARGET NOW.
MR. BETCHER?
MAYA RAO.
...HELLO.
BIG FAN.
WONDERING IF I COULD TALK TO YOU ABOUT RESEARCH OPPORTUNITIES.
I APPRECIATE YOUR ENTHUSIASM... BUT WE'RE NOT HIRING.
ACTUALLY...
YOUR BIOMARKER COMPANIES.
THEY AREN'T GETTING ANY RESULTS, ARE THEY?

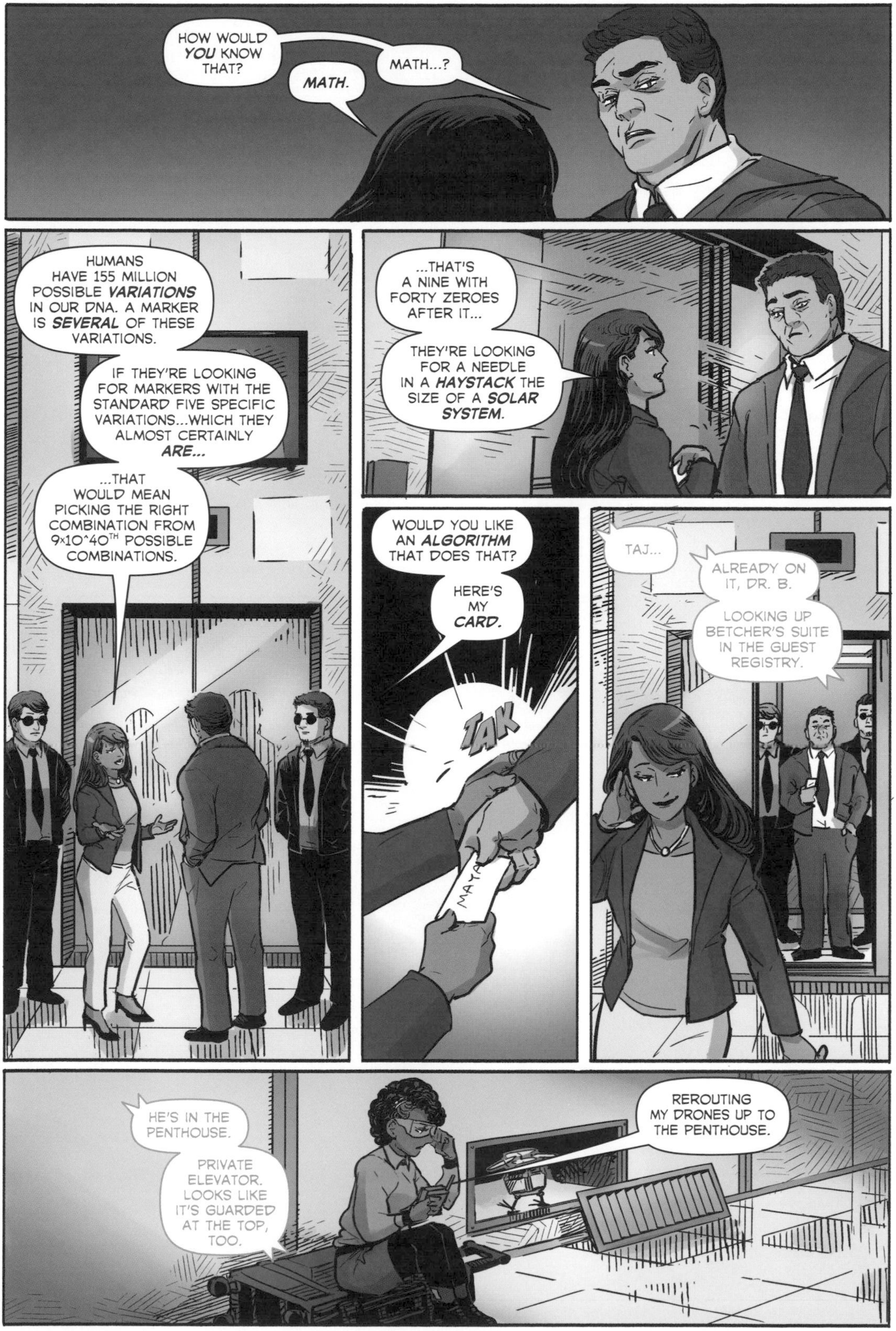
HOW WOULD YOU KNOW THAT?
MATH.
MATH...?
HUMANS HAVE 155 MILLION POSSIBLE VARIATIONS IN OUR DNA. A MARKER IS SEVERAL OF THESE VARIATIONS.
IF THEY'RE LOOKING FOR MARKERS WITH THE STANDARD FIVE SPECIFIC VARIATIONS...WHICH THEY ALMOST CERTAINLY ARE...
...THAT WOULD MEAN PICKING THE RIGHT COMBINATION FROM 9x10^40TH POSSIBLE COMBINATIONS.
...THAT'S A NINE WITH FORTY ZEROES AFTER IT...
THEY'RE LOOKING FOR A NEEDLE IN A HAYSTACK THE SIZE OF A SOLAR SYSTEM.
WOULD YOU LIKE AN ALGORITHM THAT DOES THAT?
HERE'S MY CARD.
TAK
MAYA
TAJ...
ALREADY ON IT, DR. B.
LOOKING UP BETCHER'S SUITE IN THE GUEST REGISTRY.
HE'S IN THE PENTHOUSE.
PRIVATE ELEVATOR. LOOKS LIKE IT'S GUARDED AT THE TOP, TOO.
REROUTING MY DRONES UP TO THE PENTHOUSE.

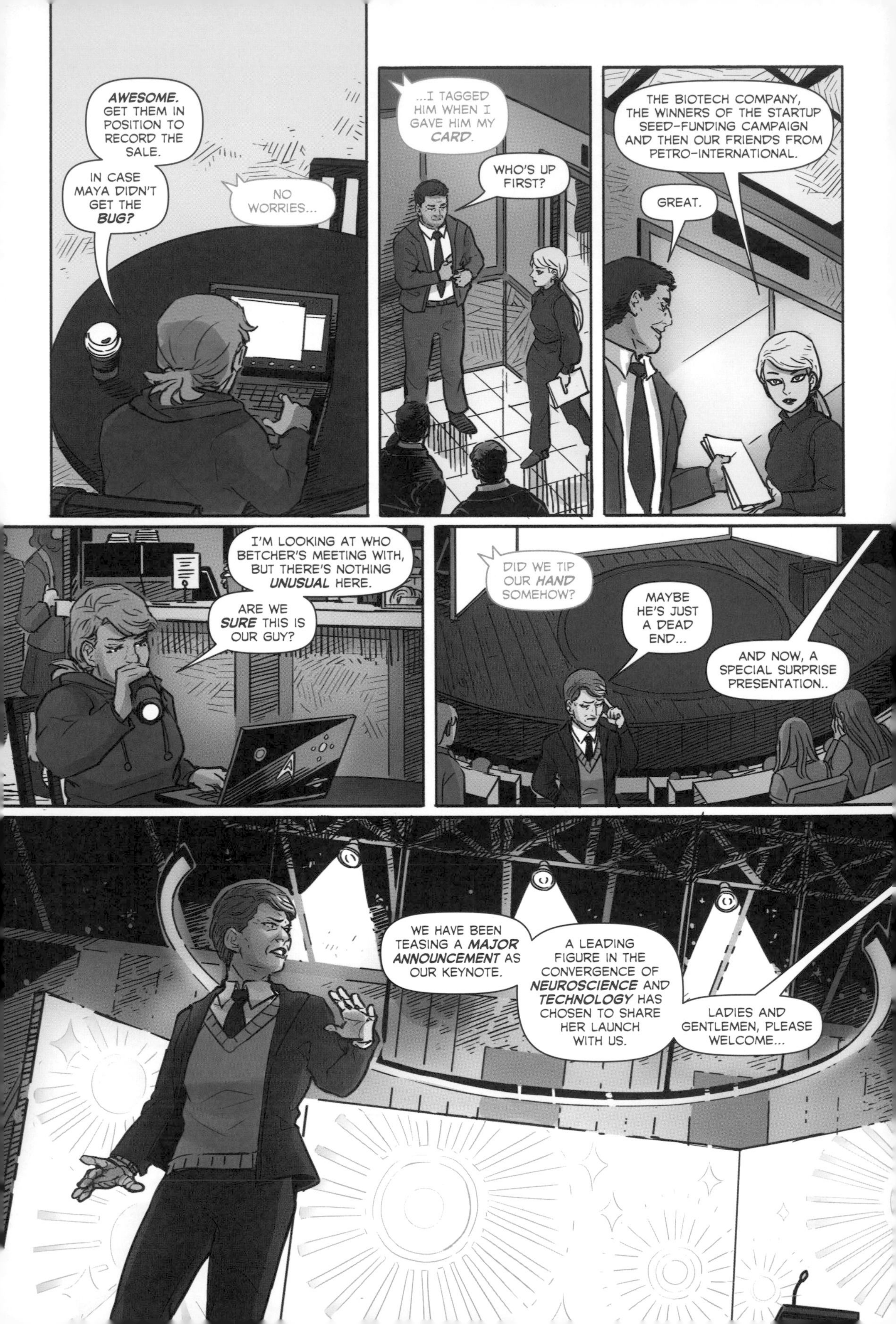

AWESOME. GET THEM IN POSITION TO RECORD THE SALE.
IN CASE MAYA DIDN'T GET THE BUG?
NO WORRIES...
...I TAGGED HIM WHEN I GAVE HIM MY CARD.
WHO'S UP FIRST?
THE BIOTECH COMPANY, THE WINNERS OF THE STARTUP SEED-FUNDING CAMPAIGN AND THEN OUR FRIENDS FROM PETRO-INTERNATIONAL.
GREAT.
I'M LOOKING AT WHO BETCHER'S MEETING WITH, BUT THERE'S NOTHING UNUSUAL HERE.
ARE WE SURE THIS IS OUR GUY?
DID WE TIP OUR HAND SOMEHOW?
MAYBE HE'S JUST A DEAD END...
AND NOW, A SPECIAL SURPRISE PRESENTATION..
WE HAVE BEEN TEASING A MAJOR ANNOUNCEMENT AS OUR KEYNOTE.
A LEADING FIGURE IN THE CONVERGENCE OF NEUROSCIENCE AND TECHNOLOGY HAS CHOSEN TO SHARE HER LAUNCH WITH US.
LADIES AND GENTLEMEN, PLEASE WELCOME...

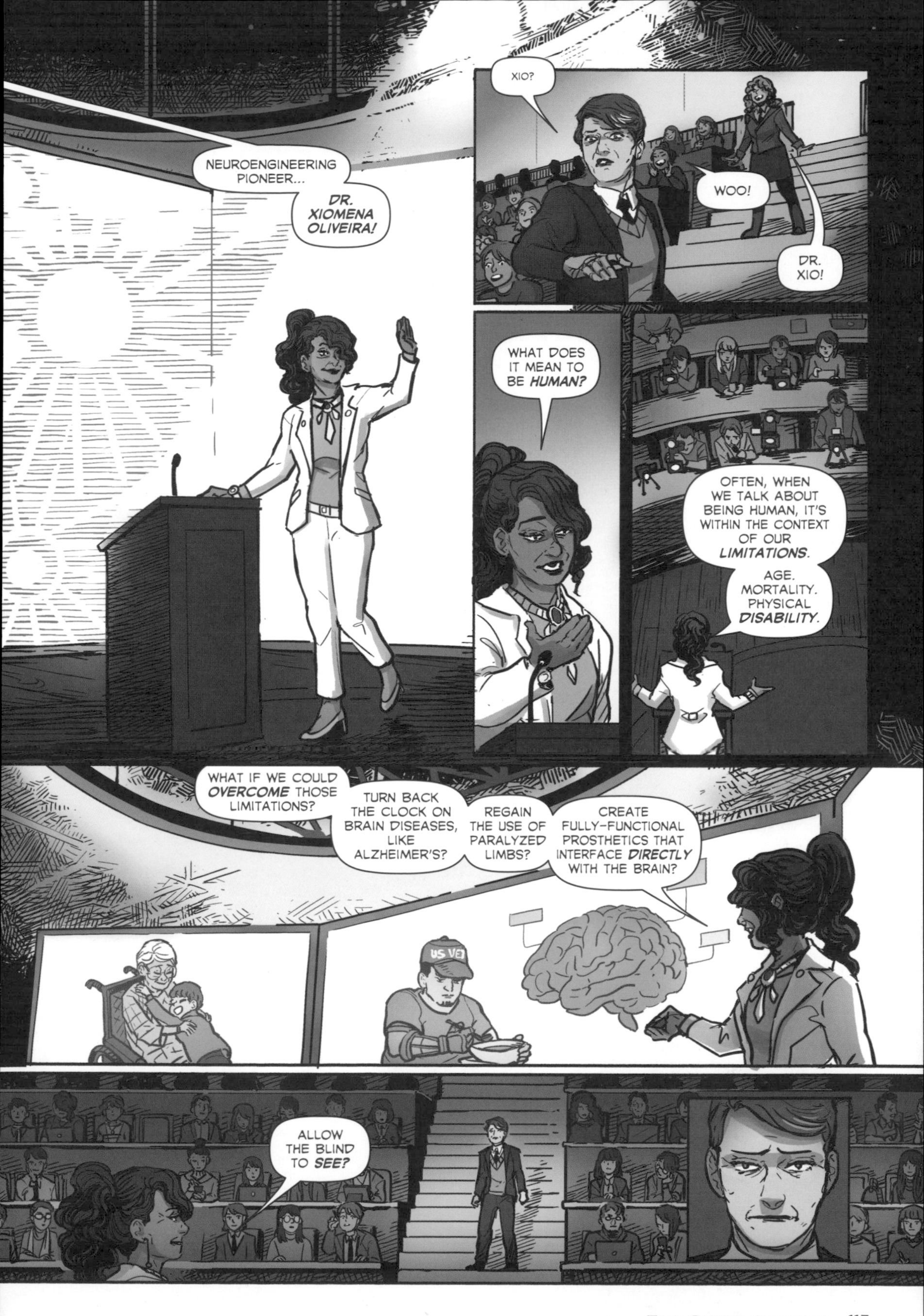
NEUROENGINEERING PIONEER...
DR. XIOMENA OLIVEIRA!
XIO?
WOO!
DR. XIO!
WHAT DOES IT MEAN TO BE HUMAN?
OFTEN, WHEN WE TALK ABOUT BEING HUMAN, IT'S WITHIN THE CONTEXT OF OUR LIMITATIONS.
AGE. MORTALITY. PHYSICAL DISABILITY.
WHAT IF WE COULD OVERCOME THOSE LIMITATIONS?
TURN BACK THE CLOCK ON BRAIN DISEASES, LIKE ALZHEIMER'S?
REGAIN THE USE OF PARALYZED LIMBS?
CREATE FULLY-FUNCTIONAL PROSTHETICS THAT INTERFACE DIRECTLY WITH THE BRAIN?
US VET
ALLOW THE BLIND TO SEE?

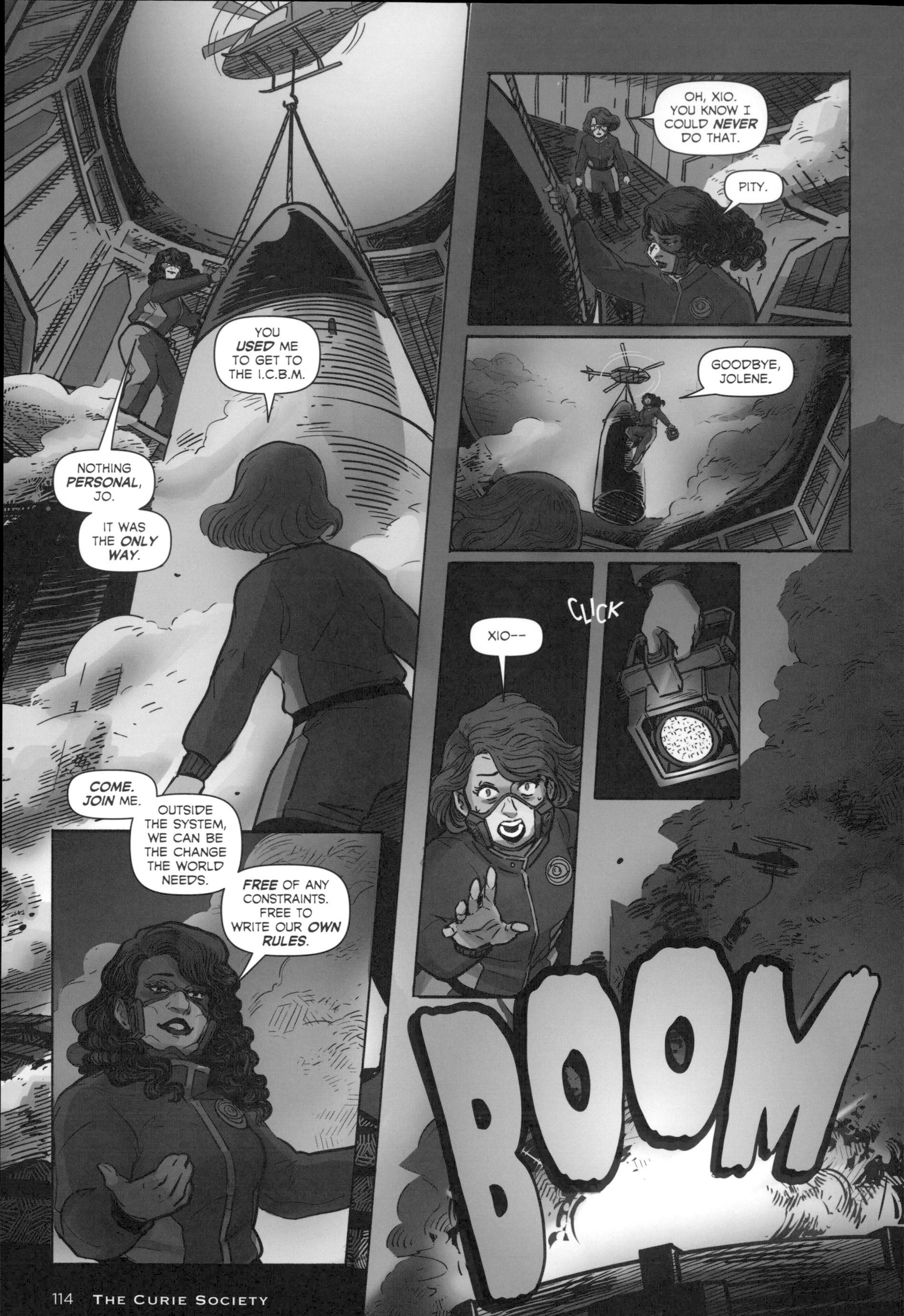
YOU USED ME TO GET TO THE I.C.B.M.
NOTHING PERSONAL, JO.
IT WAS THE ONLY WAY.
COME. JOIN ME.
OUTSIDE THE SYSTEM, WE CAN BE THE CHANGE THE WORLD NEEDS.
FREE OF ANY CONSTRAINTS. FREE TO WRITE OUR OWN RULES.
OH, XIO. YOU KNOW I COULD NEVER DO THAT.
PITY.
GOODBYE, JOLENE.
CLICK
XIO--
BOOM

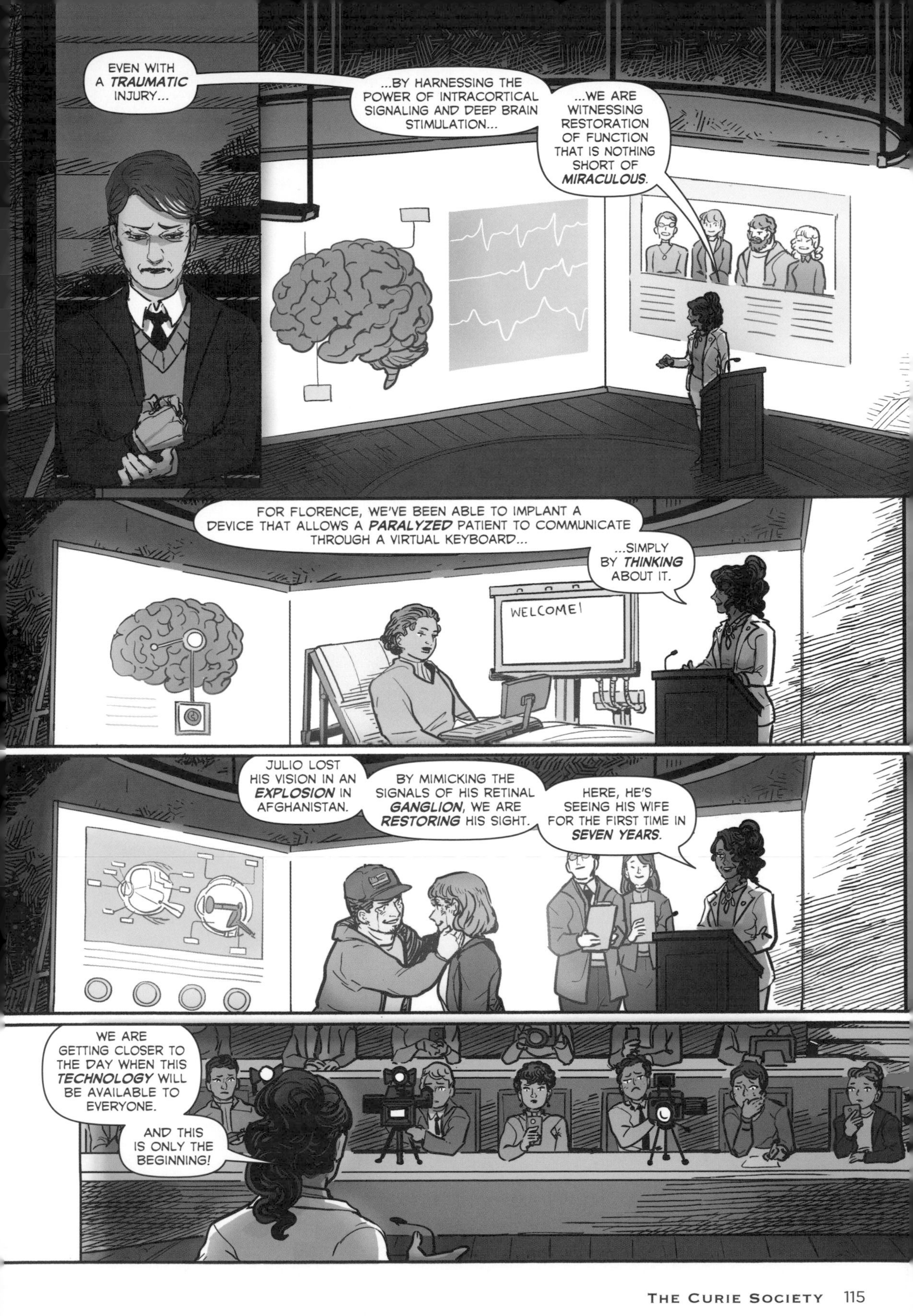

EVEN WITH A *TRAUMATIC* INJURY...
...BY HARNESSING THE POWER OF INTRACORTICAL SIGNALING AND DEEP BRAIN STIMULATION...
...WE ARE WITNESSING RESTORATION OF FUNCTION THAT IS NOTHING SHORT OF *MIRACULOUS*.
FOR FLORENCE, WE'VE BEEN ABLE TO IMPLANT A DEVICE THAT ALLOWS A *PARALYZED* PATIENT TO COMMUNICATE THROUGH A VIRTUAL KEYBOARD...
...SIMPLY BY *THINKING* ABOUT IT.
WELCOME!
JULIO LOST HIS VISION IN AN *EXPLOSION* IN AFGHANISTAN.
BY MIMICKING THE SIGNALS OF HIS RETINAL *GANGLION*, WE ARE *RESTORING* HIS SIGHT.
HERE, HE'S SEEING HIS WIFE FOR THE FIRST TIME IN *SEVEN YEARS*.
WE ARE GETTING CLOSER TO THE DAY WHEN THIS *TECHNOLOGY* WILL BE AVAILABLE TO EVERYONE.
AND THIS IS ONLY THE BEGINNING!

AND THAT'S THE MISSION OF MY NEW COMPANY.

AXIOTHEA.

WE EXIST AT THE INTERSECTION OF *ENGINEERING* AND *NEUROSCIENCE.*

BETWEEN *ARTIFICIAL INTELLIGENCE...* AND *HUMAN* INTELLIGENCE.

IF WE'VE DONE OUR JOB RIGHT...

...YOU WON'T BE ABLE TO TELL THE *DIFFERENCE.*

CLAP CLAP CLAP CLAP CLAP CLAP CLAP CLAP CLAP CLAP CLAP CLAP CLAP CLAP CLAP CLAP CLAP CLAP CLAP

EXHIBIT HALL

DR. OLIVEIRA!

XIOMENA!

WILL AXIOTHEA BE A PUBLICLY TRADED COMPANY?

THAT'S ALL FOR TODAY, EVERYONE!

PLEASE EXCUSE ME.

HEY, GIRLS?

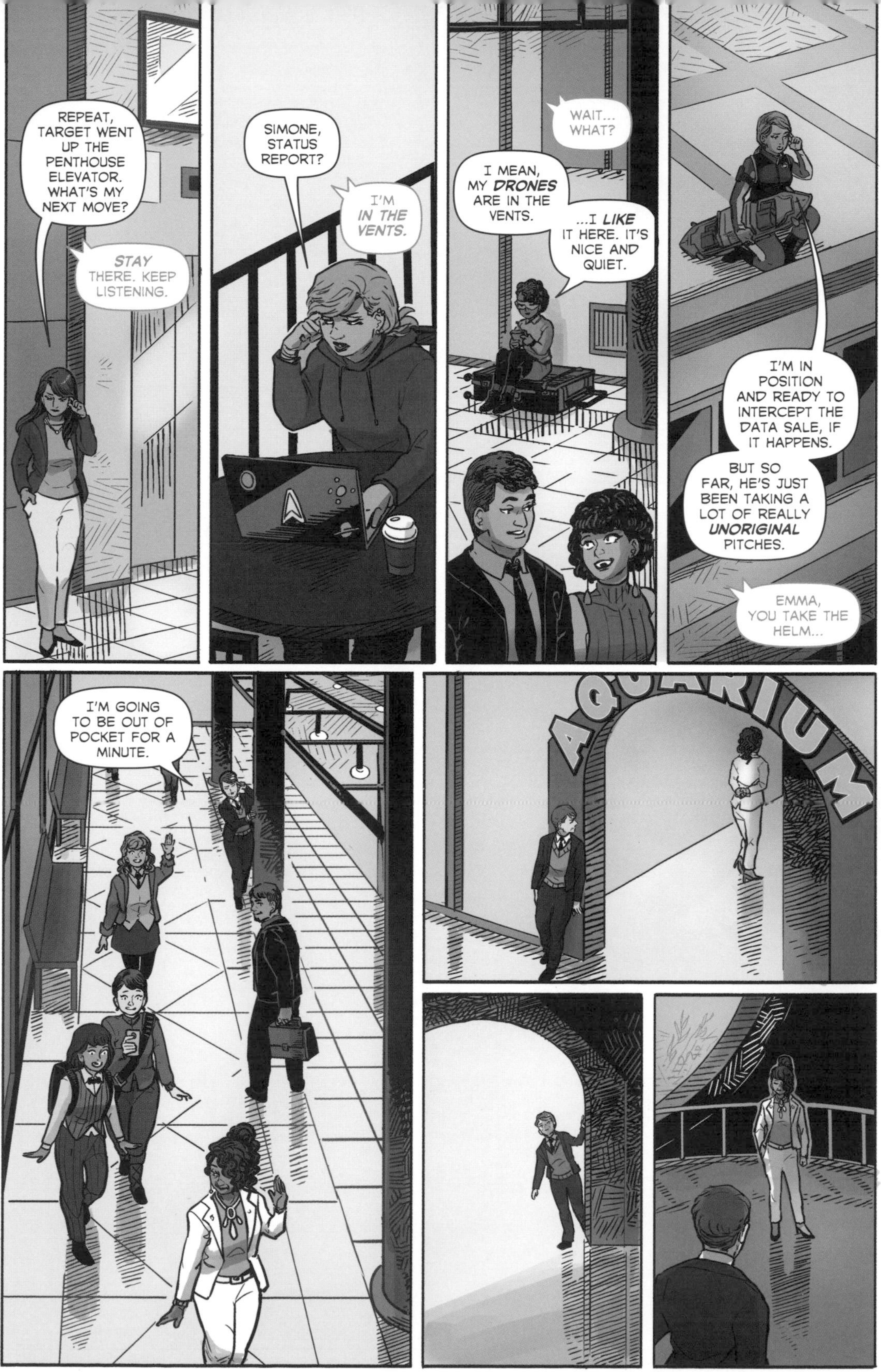
REPEAT, TARGET WENT UP THE PENTHOUSE ELEVATOR. WHAT'S MY NEXT MOVE?
STAY THERE. KEEP LISTENING.
SIMONE, STATUS REPORT?
I'M IN THE VENTS.
WAIT... WHAT?
I MEAN, MY DRONES ARE IN THE VENTS.
...I LIKE IT HERE. IT'S NICE AND QUIET.
I'M IN POSITION AND READY TO INTERCEPT THE DATA SALE, IF IT HAPPENS.
BUT SO FAR, HE'S JUST BEEN TAKING A LOT OF REALLY UNORIGINAL PITCHES.
EMMA, YOU TAKE THE HELM...
I'M GOING TO BE OUT OF POCKET FOR A MINUTE.
AQUARIUM

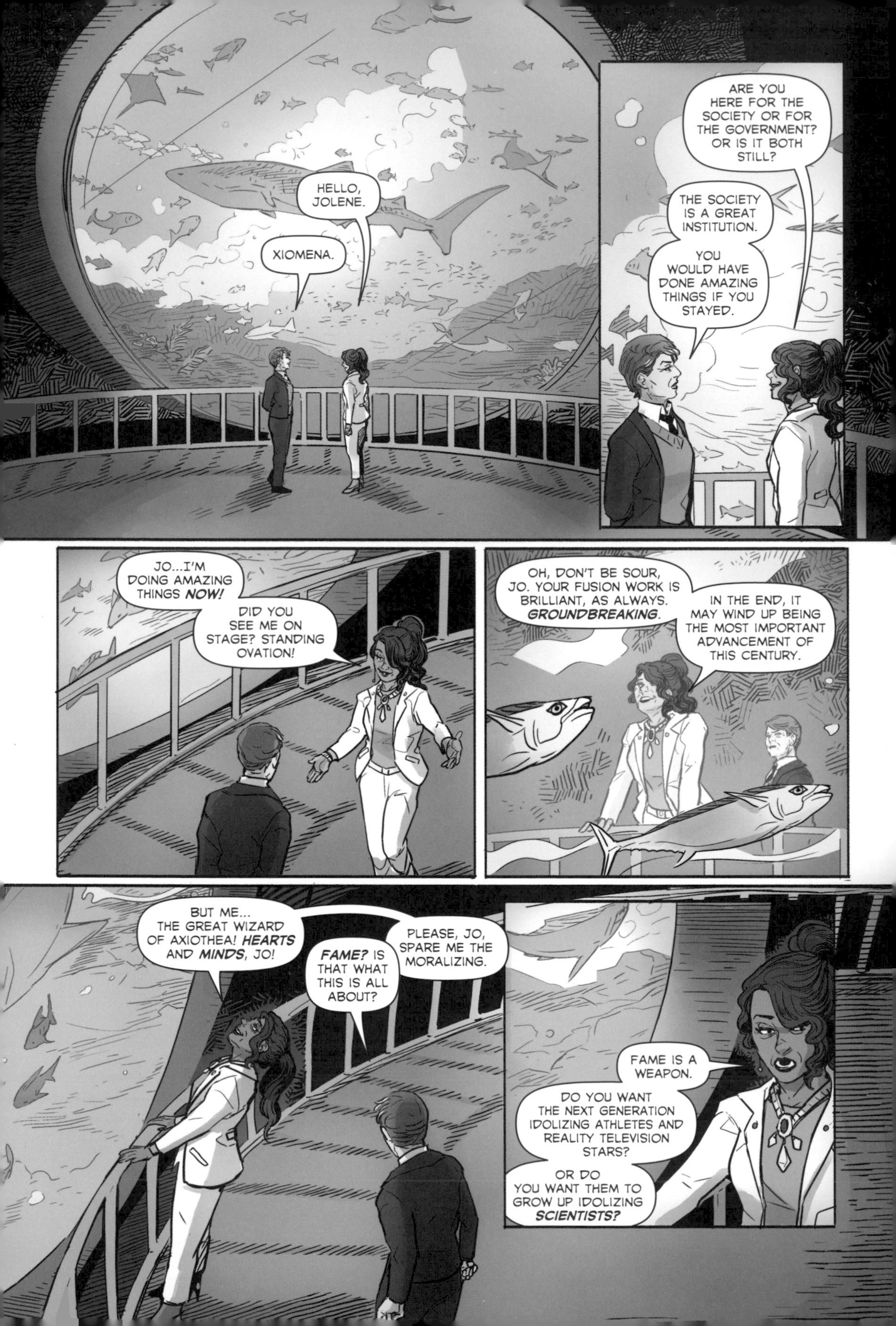

HELLO, JOLENE.
XIOMENA.
ARE YOU HERE FOR THE SOCIETY OR FOR THE GOVERNMENT? OR IS IT BOTH STILL?
THE SOCIETY IS A GREAT INSTITUTION.
YOU WOULD HAVE DONE AMAZING THINGS IF YOU STAYED.
JO...I'M DOING AMAZING THINGS NOW!
DID YOU SEE ME ON STAGE? STANDING OVATION!
OH, DON'T BE SOUR, JO. YOUR FUSION WORK IS BRILLIANT, AS ALWAYS. GROUNDBREAKING.
IN THE END, IT MAY WIND UP BEING THE MOST IMPORTANT ADVANCEMENT OF THIS CENTURY.
BUT ME... THE GREAT WIZARD OF AXIOTHEA! HEARTS AND MINDS, JO!
FAME? IS THAT WHAT THIS IS ALL ABOUT?
PLEASE, JO, SPARE ME THE MORALIZING.
FAME IS A WEAPON.
DO YOU WANT THE NEXT GENERATION IDOLIZING ATHLETES AND REALITY TELEVISION STARS?
OR DO YOU WANT THEM TO GROW UP IDOLIZING SCIENTISTS?

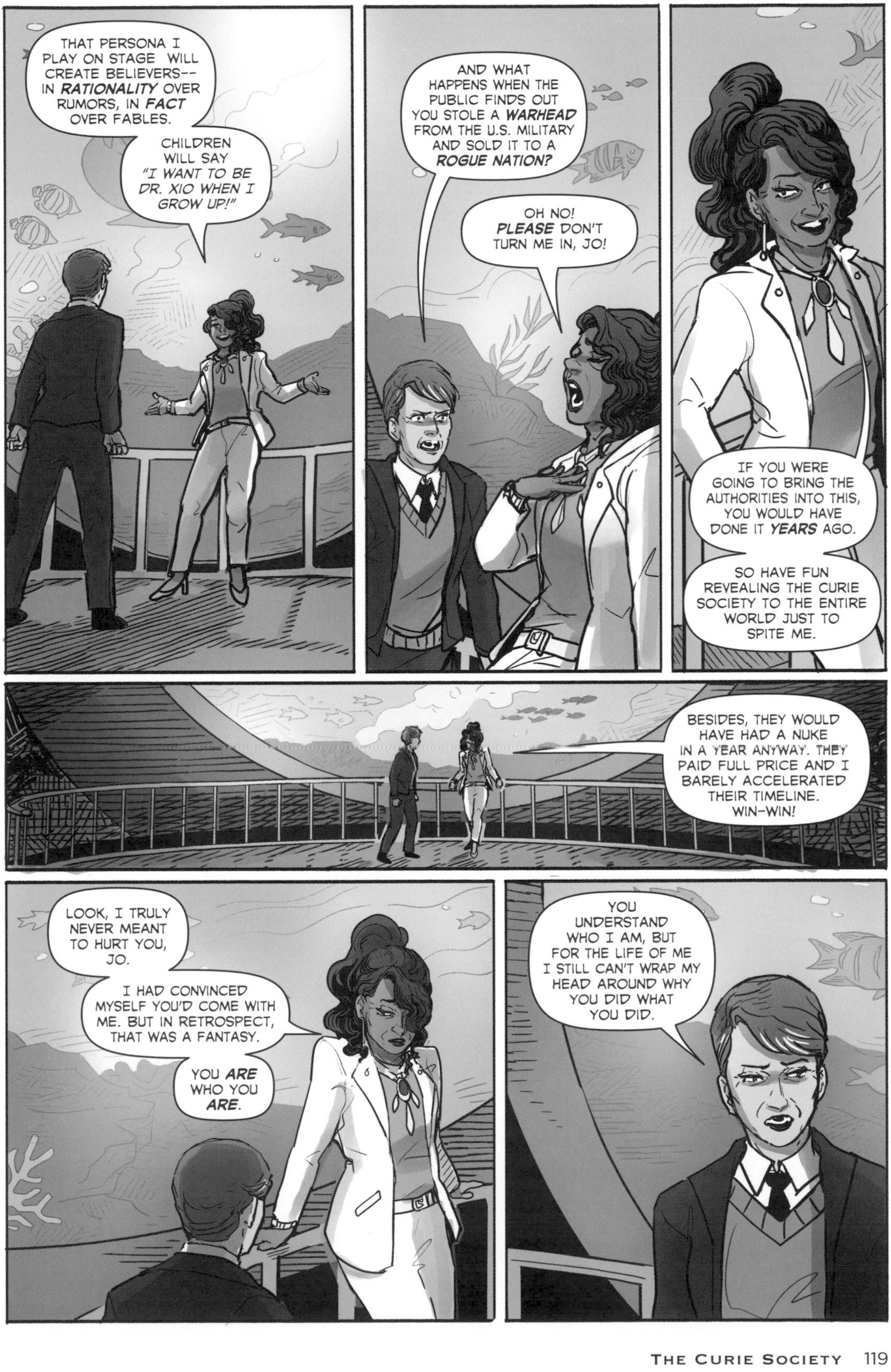
THAT PERSONA I PLAY ON STAGE WILL CREATE BELIEVERS-- IN ***RATIONALITY*** OVER RUMORS, IN ***FACT*** OVER FABLES.
CHILDREN WILL SAY *"I WANT TO BE DR. XIO WHEN I GROW UP!"*
AND WHAT HAPPENS WHEN THE PUBLIC FINDS OUT YOU STOLE A ***WARHEAD*** FROM THE U.S. MILITARY AND SOLD IT TO A ***ROGUE NATION?***
OH NO! ***PLEASE*** DON'T TURN ME IN, JO!
IF YOU WERE GOING TO BRING THE AUTHORITIES INTO THIS, YOU WOULD HAVE DONE IT ***YEARS*** AGO.
SO HAVE FUN REVEALING THE CURIE SOCIETY TO THE ENTIRE WORLD JUST TO SPITE ME.
BESIDES, THEY WOULD HAVE HAD A NUKE IN A YEAR ANYWAY. THEY PAID FULL PRICE AND I BARELY ACCELERATED THEIR TIMELINE. WIN-WIN!
LOOK, I TRULY NEVER MEANT TO HURT YOU, JO.
I HAD CONVINCED MYSELF YOU'D COME WITH ME. BUT IN RETROSPECT, THAT WAS A FANTASY.
YOU ***ARE*** WHO YOU ***ARE***.
YOU UNDERSTAND WHO I AM, BUT FOR THE LIFE OF ME I STILL CAN'T WRAP MY HEAD AROUND WHY YOU DID WHAT YOU DID.

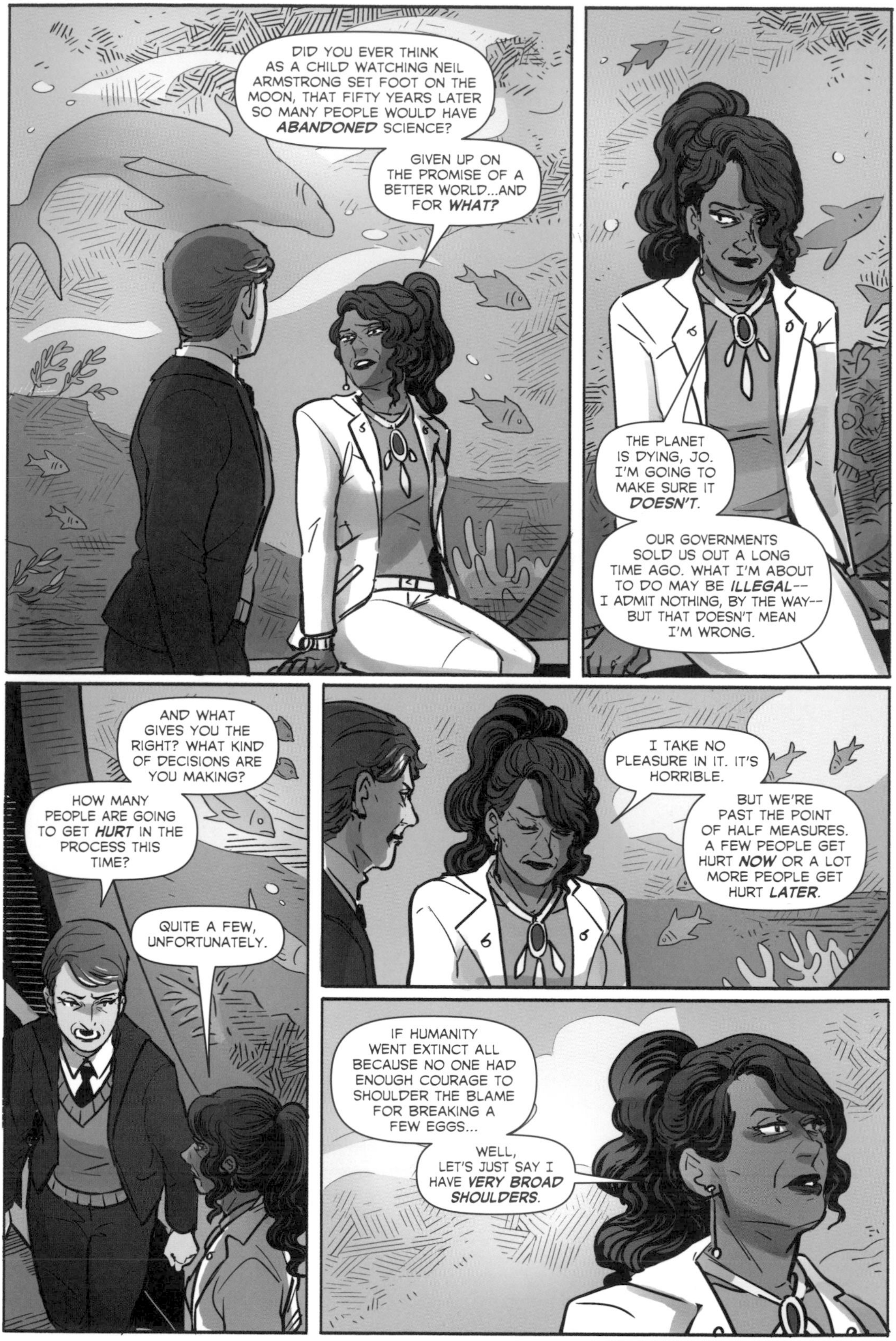
DID YOU EVER THINK AS A CHILD WATCHING NEIL ARMSTRONG SET FOOT ON THE MOON, THAT FIFTY YEARS LATER SO MANY PEOPLE WOULD HAVE ABANDONED SCIENCE?
GIVEN UP ON THE PROMISE OF A BETTER WORLD...AND FOR WHAT?
THE PLANET IS DYING, JO. I'M GOING TO MAKE SURE IT DOESN'T.
OUR GOVERNMENTS SOLD US OUT A LONG TIME AGO. WHAT I'M ABOUT TO DO MAY BE ILLEGAL-- I ADMIT NOTHING, BY THE WAY-- BUT THAT DOESN'T MEAN I'M WRONG.
AND WHAT GIVES YOU THE RIGHT? WHAT KIND OF DECISIONS ARE YOU MAKING?
HOW MANY PEOPLE ARE GOING TO GET HURT IN THE PROCESS THIS TIME?
QUITE A FEW, UNFORTUNATELY.
I TAKE NO PLEASURE IN IT. IT'S HORRIBLE.
BUT WE'RE PAST THE POINT OF HALF MEASURES. A FEW PEOPLE GET HURT NOW OR A LOT MORE PEOPLE GET HURT LATER.
IF HUMANITY WENT EXTINCT ALL BECAUSE NO ONE HAD ENOUGH COURAGE TO SHOULDER THE BLAME FOR BREAKING A FEW EGGS...
WELL, LET'S JUST SAY I HAVE VERY BROAD SHOULDERS.

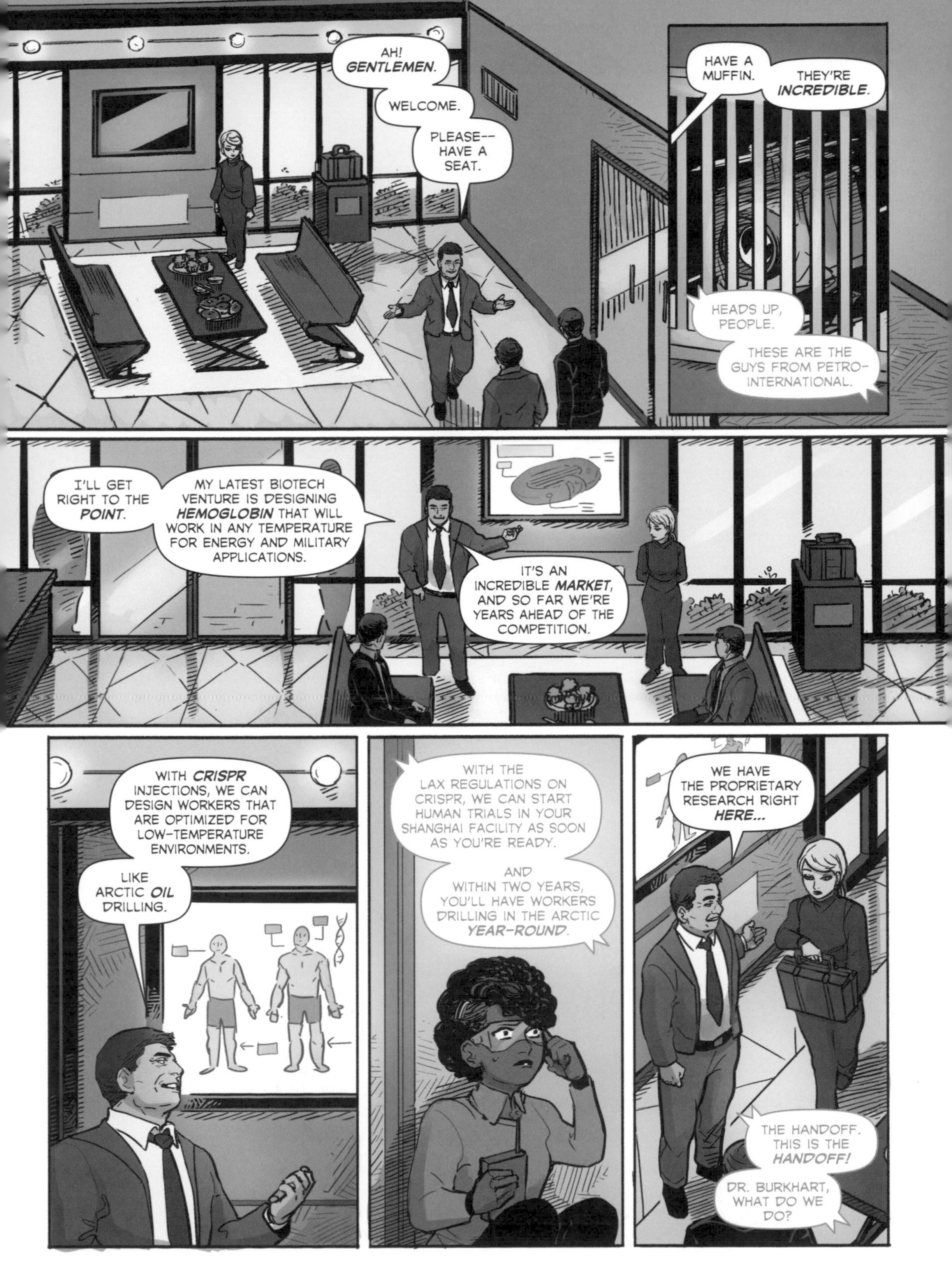
AH! *GENTLEMEN.*
WELCOME.
PLEASE-- HAVE A SEAT.
HAVE A MUFFIN.
THEY'RE *INCREDIBLE.*
HEADS UP, PEOPLE.
THESE ARE THE GUYS FROM PETRO-INTERNATIONAL.
I'LL GET RIGHT TO THE *POINT.*
MY LATEST BIOTECH VENTURE IS DESIGNING *HEMOGLOBIN* THAT WILL WORK IN ANY TEMPERATURE FOR ENERGY AND MILITARY APPLICATIONS.
IT'S AN INCREDIBLE *MARKET,* AND SO FAR WE'RE YEARS AHEAD OF THE COMPETITION.
WITH *CRISPR* INJECTIONS, WE CAN DESIGN WORKERS THAT ARE OPTIMIZED FOR LOW-TEMPERATURE ENVIRONMENTS.
LIKE ARCTIC *OIL* DRILLING.
WITH THE LAX REGULATIONS ON CRISPR, WE CAN START HUMAN TRIALS IN YOUR SHANGHAI FACILITY AS SOON AS YOU'RE READY.
AND WITHIN TWO YEARS, YOU'LL HAVE WORKERS DRILLING IN THE ARCTIC *YEAR-ROUND.*
WE HAVE THE PROPRIETARY RESEARCH RIGHT *HERE...*
THE HANDOFF. THIS IS THE *HANDOFF!*
DR. BURKHART, WHAT DO WE DO?

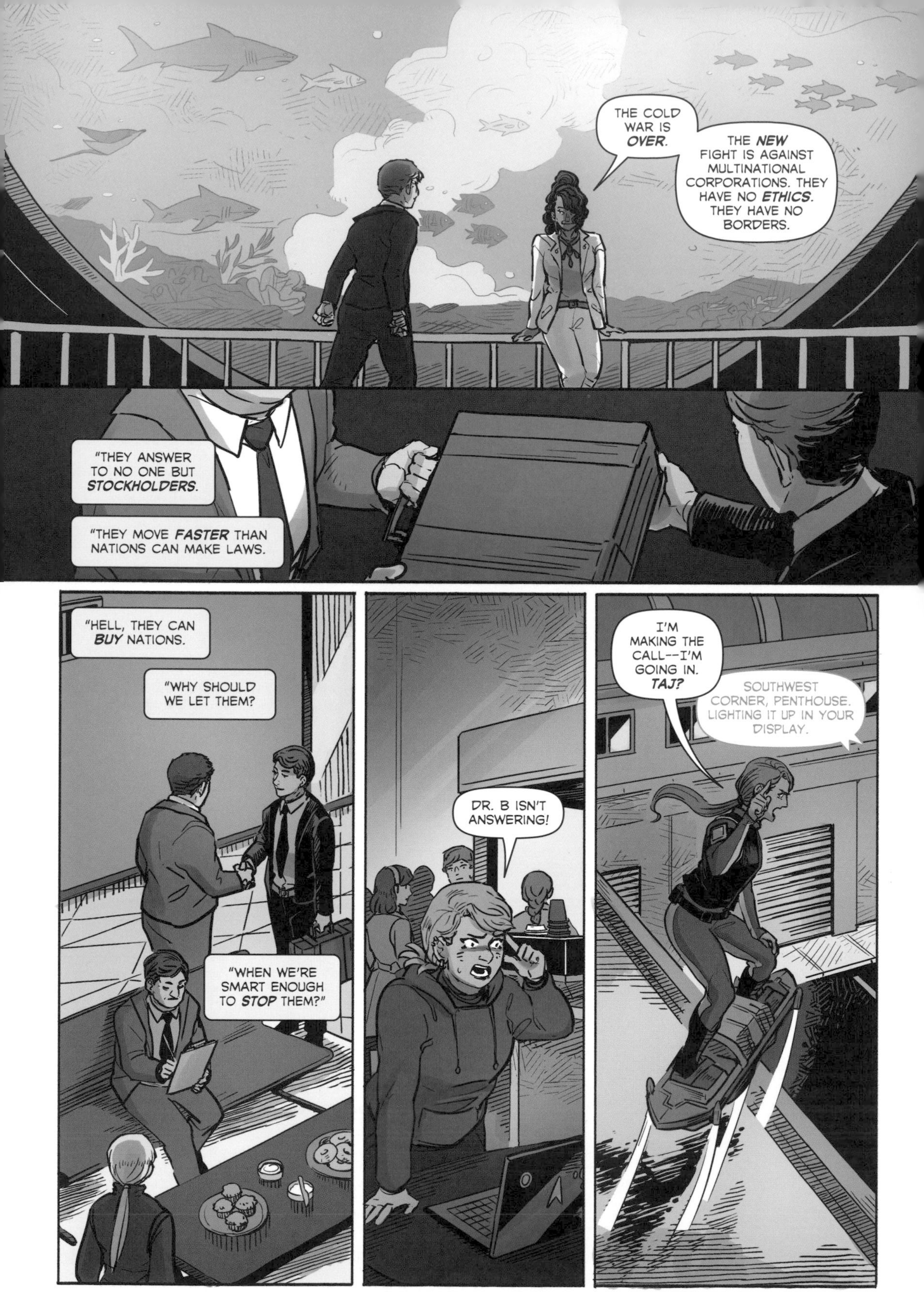
THE COLD WAR IS *OVER*.
THE *NEW* FIGHT IS AGAINST MULTINATIONAL CORPORATIONS. THEY HAVE NO *ETHICS*. THEY HAVE NO BORDERS.
"THEY ANSWER TO NO ONE BUT *STOCKHOLDERS*.
"THEY MOVE *FASTER* THAN NATIONS CAN MAKE LAWS.
"HELL, THEY CAN *BUY* NATIONS.
"WHY SHOULD WE LET THEM?
"WHEN WE'RE SMART ENOUGH TO *STOP* THEM?"
DR. B ISN'T ANSWERING!
I'M MAKING THE CALL--I'M GOING IN. *TAJ?*
SOUTHWEST CORNER, PENTHOUSE. LIGHTING IT UP IN YOUR DISPLAY.

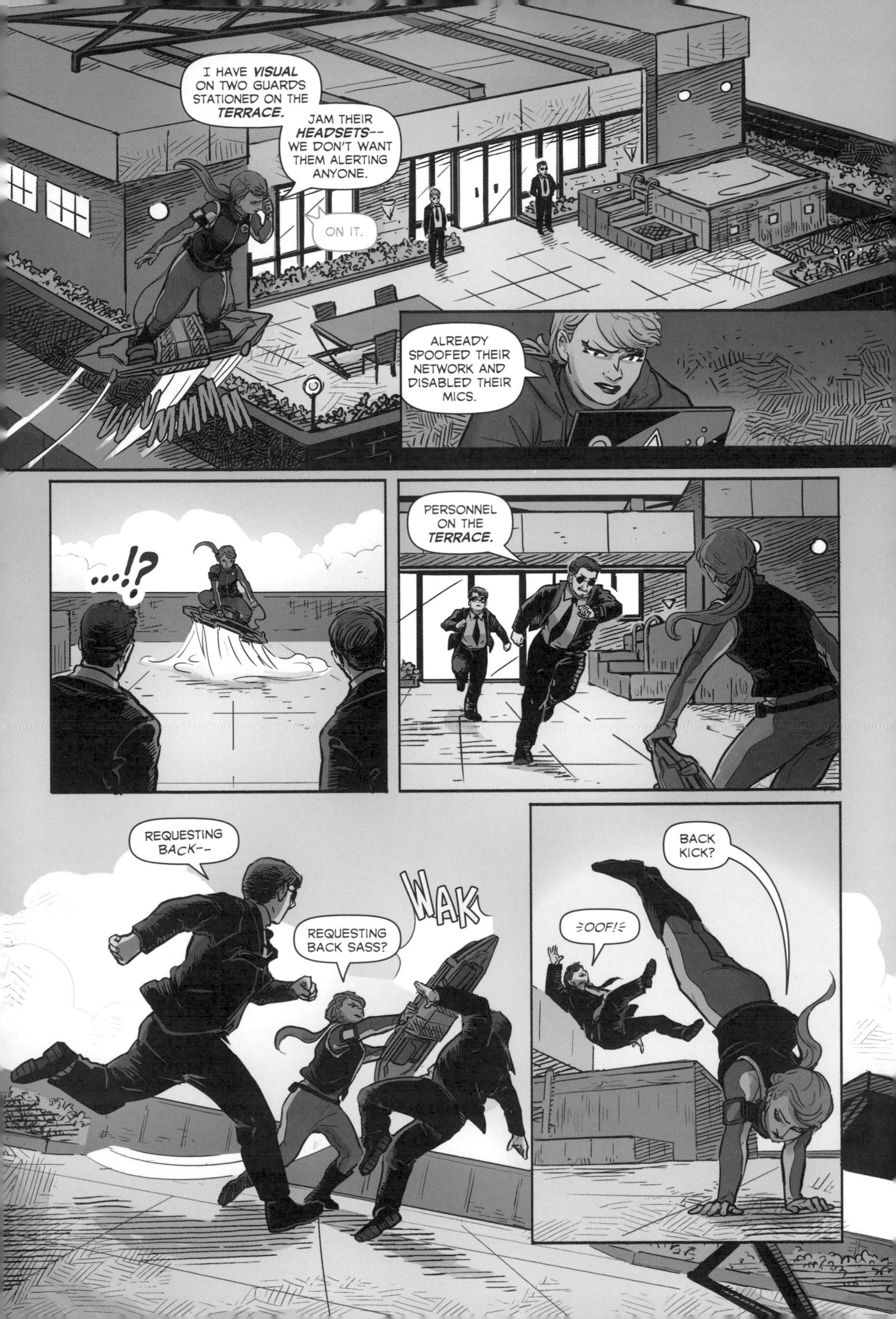

I HAVE VISUAL ON TWO GUARDS STATIONED ON THE TERRACE.
JAM THEIR HEADSETS-- WE DON'T WANT THEM ALERTING ANYONE.
ON IT.
VVVMMMMM
ALREADY SPOOFED THEIR NETWORK AND DISABLED THEIR MICS.
...!?
PERSONNEL ON THE TERRACE.
REQUESTING BACK--
WAK
REQUESTING BACK SASS?
BACK KICK?
OOF!

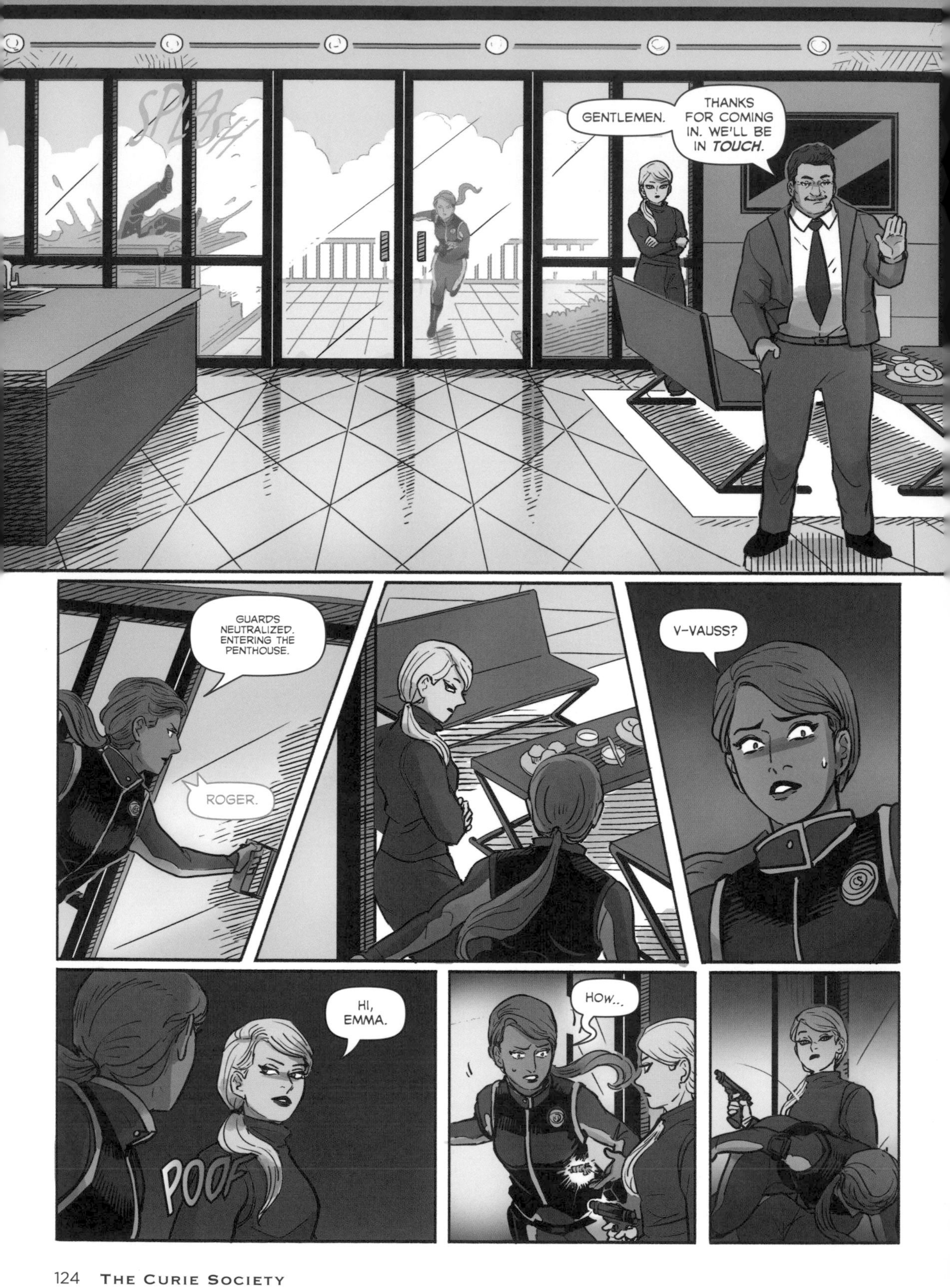
SPLASH
GENTLEMEN.
THANKS FOR COMING IN. WE'LL BE IN *TOUCH*.
GUARDS NEUTRALIZED. ENTERING THE PENTHOUSE.
ROGER.
V-VAUSS?
HI, EMMA.
POOF
HOW...

WHAT'S GOING ON!? I DON'T HAVE VISUAL!
SIMONE, GET EYES ON EMMA RIGHT NOW!
WHAT'S GOING ON UP THERE? EMMA, TELL US SOMETHING!
THEY... THEY...
F12
ZOOM 2.1X
THEY SHOT EMMA!
THEY SHOT EMMA!!

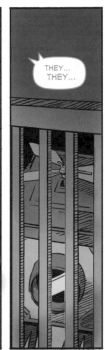

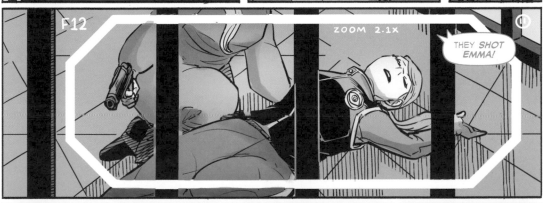

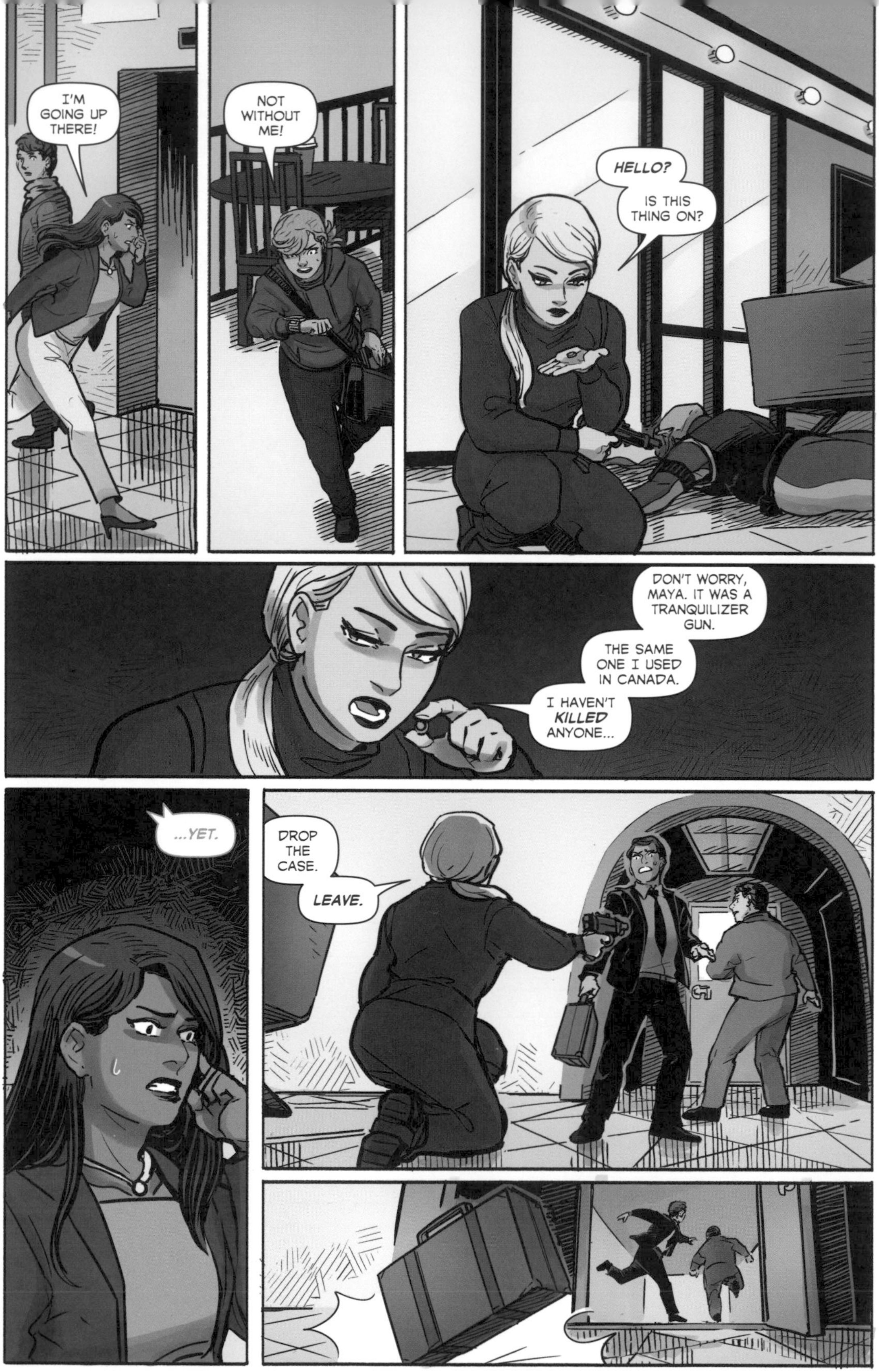
I'M GOING UP THERE!
NOT WITHOUT ME!
HELLO?
IS THIS THING ON?
DON'T WORRY, MAYA. IT WAS A TRANQUILIZER GUN.
THE SAME ONE I USED IN CANADA.
I HAVEN'T KILLED ANYONE...
...YET.
DROP THE CASE.
LEAVE.

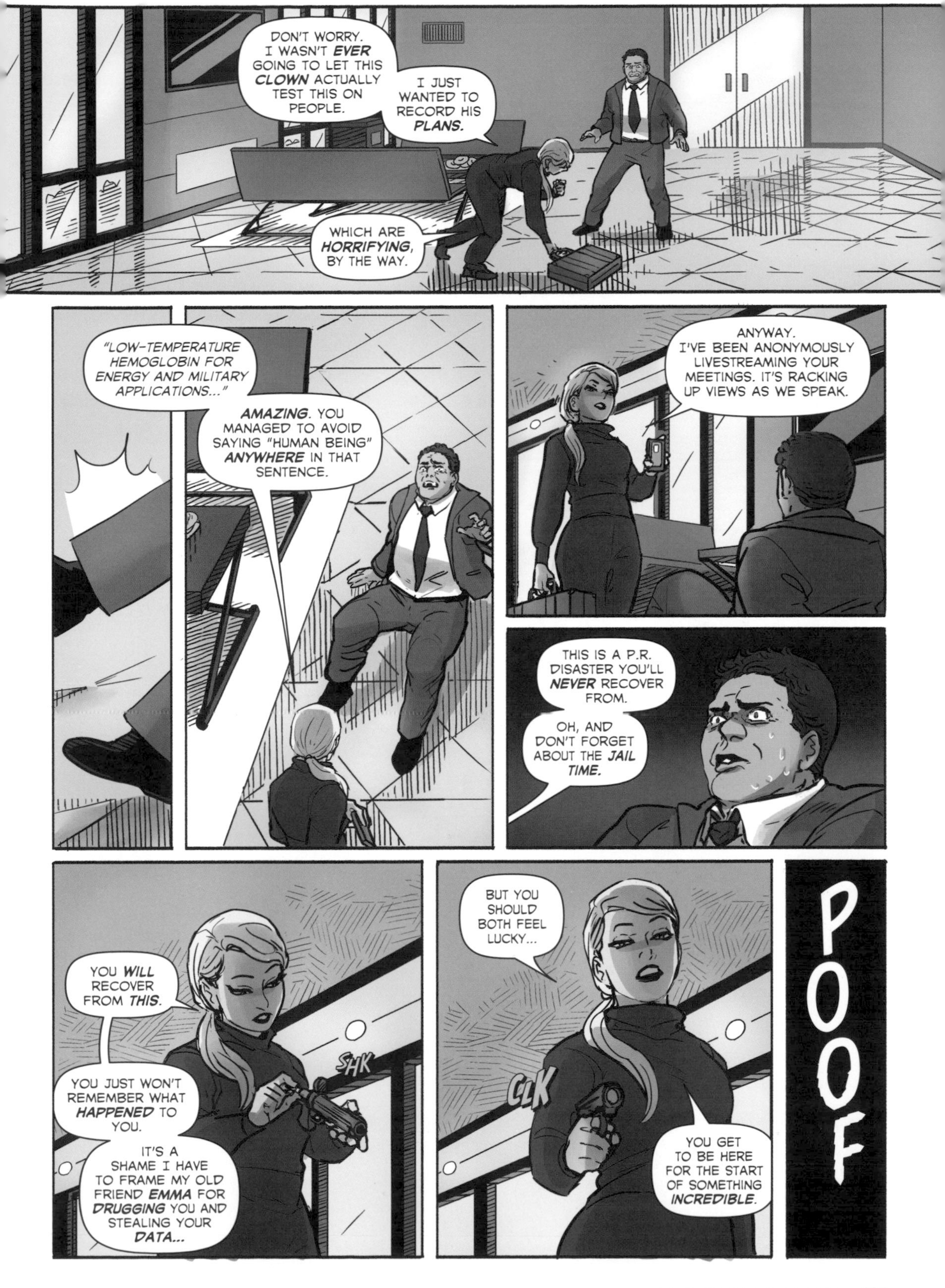
DON'T WORRY. I WASN'T EVER GOING TO LET THIS CLOWN ACTUALLY TEST THIS ON PEOPLE.
I JUST WANTED TO RECORD HIS PLANS.
WHICH ARE HORRIFYING, BY THE WAY.
"LOW-TEMPERATURE HEMOGLOBIN FOR ENERGY AND MILITARY APPLICATIONS..."
AMAZING. YOU MANAGED TO AVOID SAYING "HUMAN BEING" ANYWHERE IN THAT SENTENCE.
ANYWAY. I'VE BEEN ANONYMOUSLY LIVESTREAMING YOUR MEETINGS. IT'S RACKING UP VIEWS AS WE SPEAK.
THIS IS A P.R. DISASTER YOU'LL NEVER RECOVER FROM.
OH, AND DON'T FORGET ABOUT THE JAIL TIME.
YOU WILL RECOVER FROM THIS.
SHK
YOU JUST WON'T REMEMBER WHAT HAPPENED TO YOU.
IT'S A SHAME I HAVE TO FRAME MY OLD FRIEND EMMA FOR DRUGGING YOU AND STEALING YOUR DATA...
BUT YOU SHOULD BOTH FEEL LUCKY...
CLK
YOU GET TO BE HERE FOR THE START OF SOMETHING INCREDIBLE.
POOF

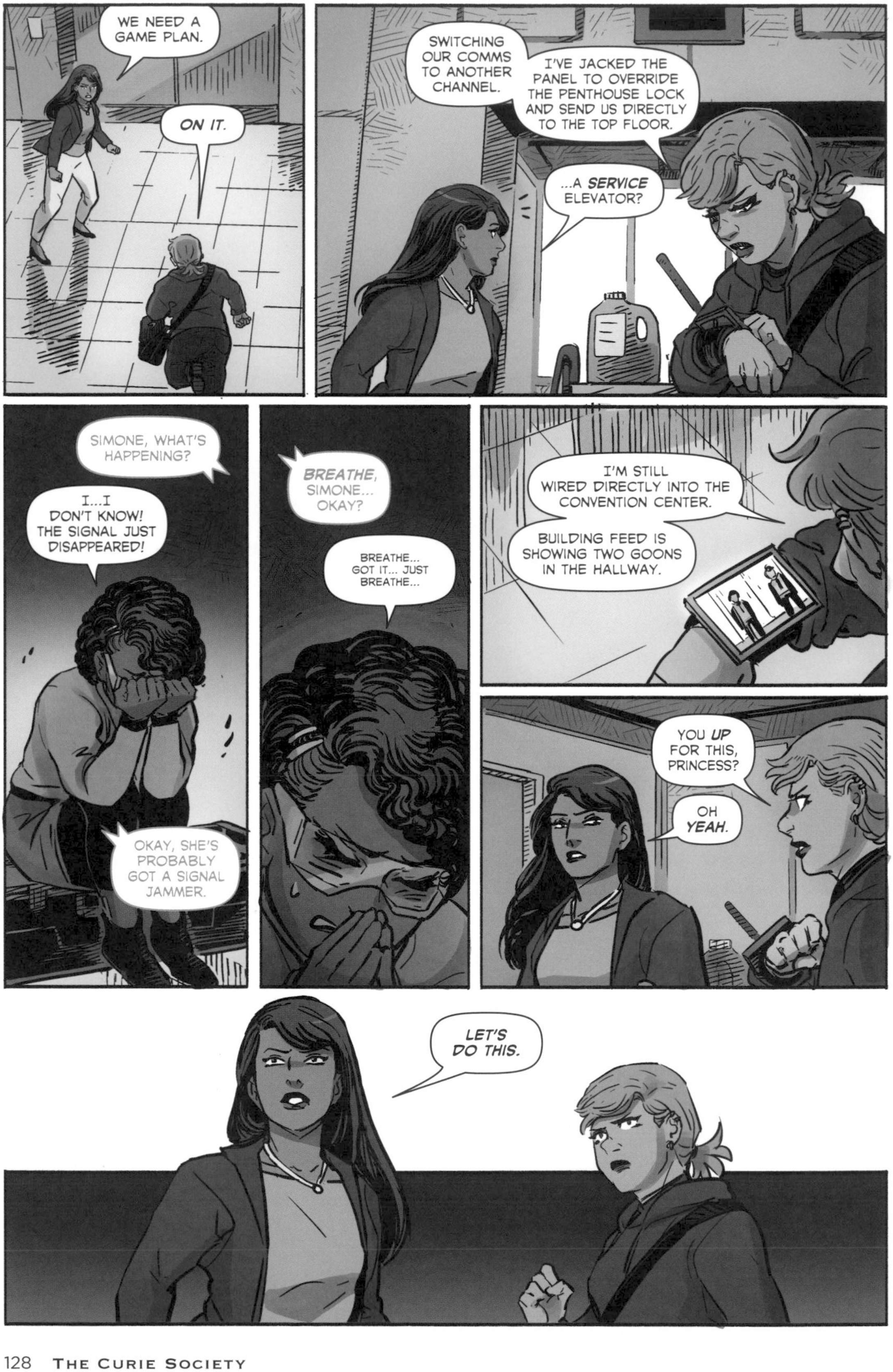
WE NEED A GAME PLAN.
ON IT.
SWITCHING OUR COMMS TO ANOTHER CHANNEL.
I'VE JACKED THE PANEL TO OVERRIDE THE PENTHOUSE LOCK AND SEND US DIRECTLY TO THE TOP FLOOR.
...A SERVICE ELEVATOR?
SIMONE, WHAT'S HAPPENING?
I...I DON'T KNOW! THE SIGNAL JUST DISAPPEARED!
OKAY, SHE'S PROBABLY GOT A SIGNAL JAMMER.
BREATHE, SIMONE... OKAY?
BREATHE... GOT IT... JUST BREATHE...
I'M STILL WIRED DIRECTLY INTO THE CONVENTION CENTER.
BUILDING FEED IS SHOWING TWO GOONS IN THE HALLWAY.
YOU UP FOR THIS, PRINCESS?
OH YEAH.
LET'S DO THIS.

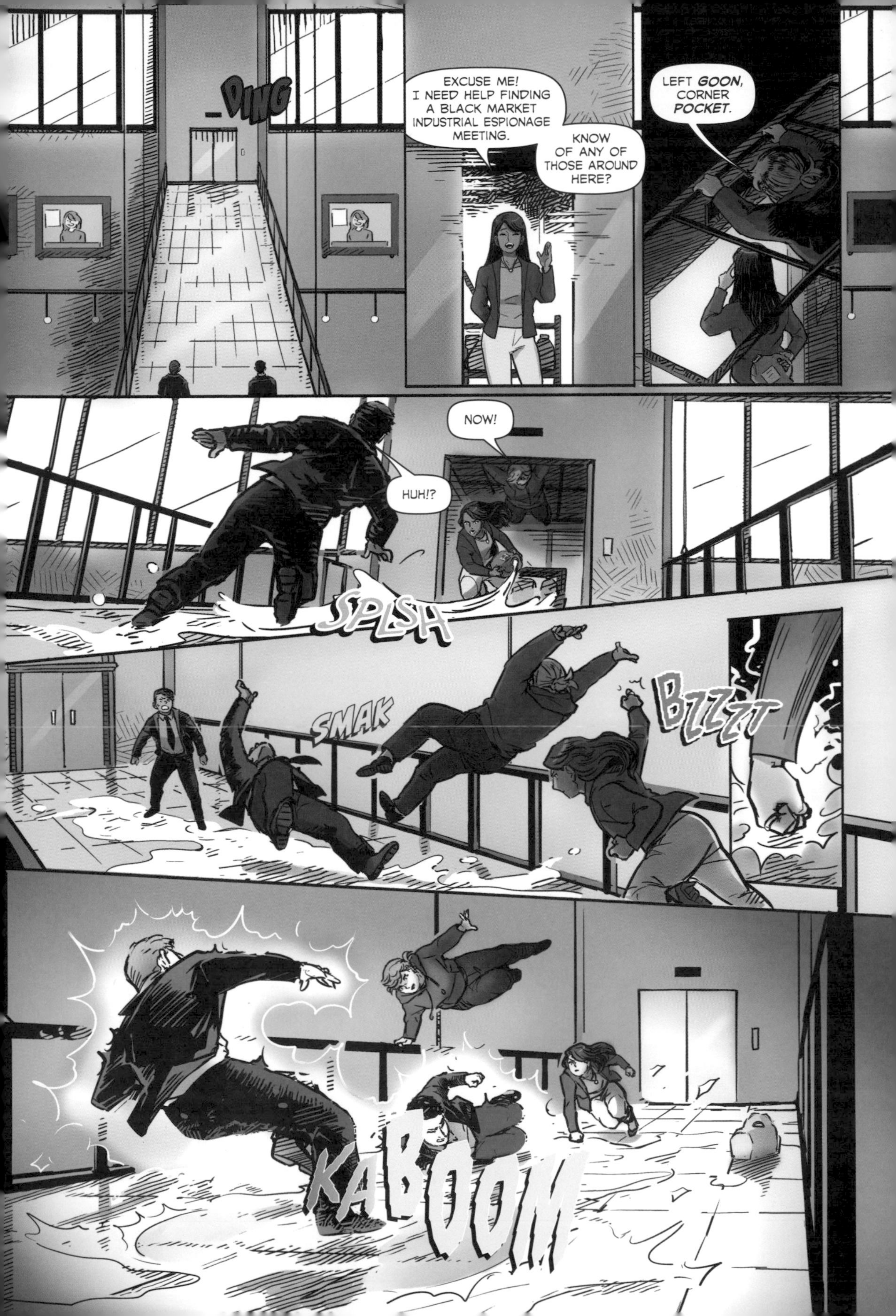
DING
EXCUSE ME! I NEED HELP FINDING A BLACK MARKET INDUSTRIAL ESPIONAGE MEETING.
KNOW OF ANY OF THOSE AROUND HERE?
LEFT *GOON*, CORNER *POCKET*.
NOW!
HUH!?
SPLSH
SMAK
BZZZT
KABOOM

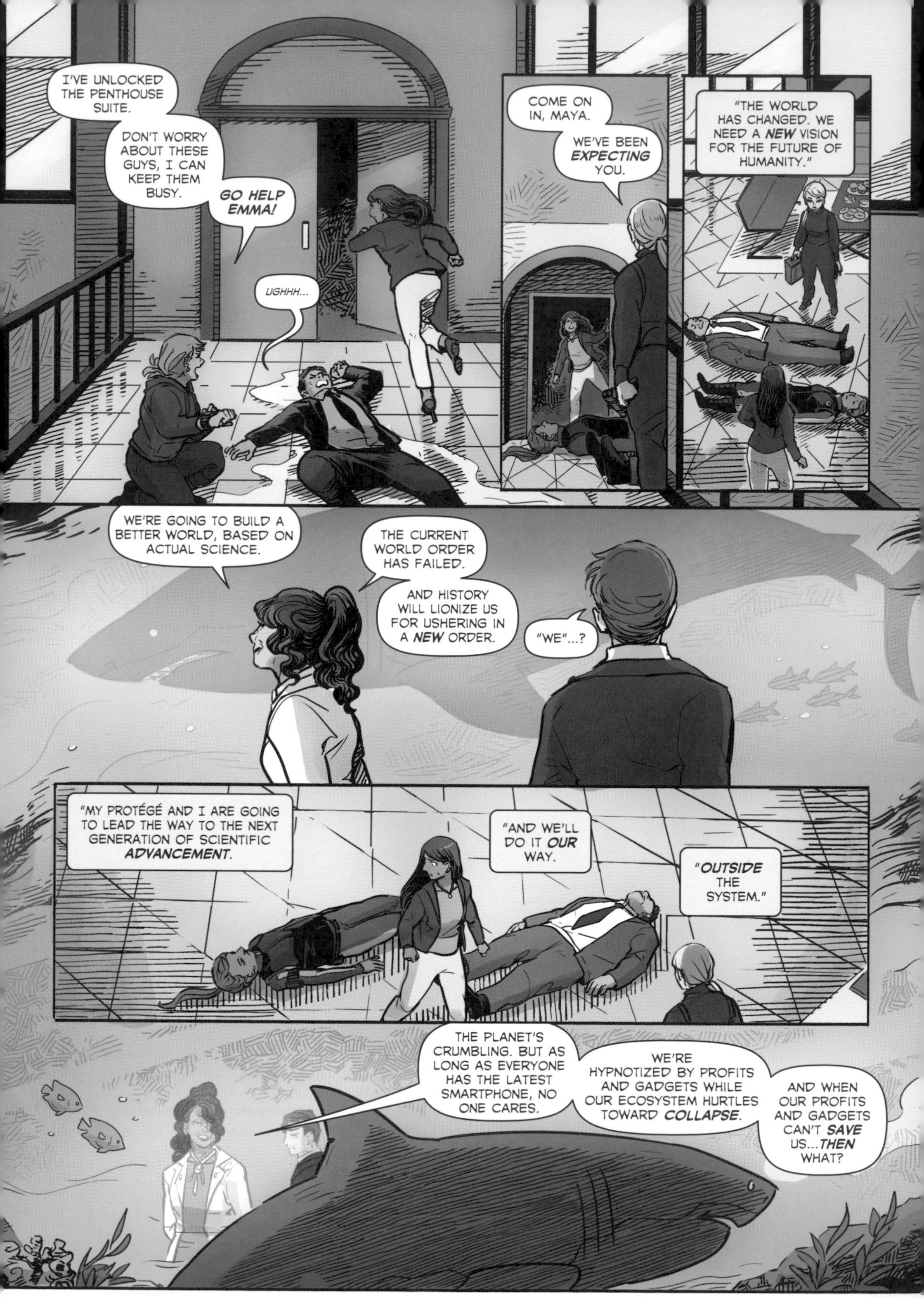
I'VE UNLOCKED THE PENTHOUSE SUITE.
DON'T WORRY ABOUT THESE GUYS, I CAN KEEP THEM BUSY.
GO HELP EMMA!
UGHHH...
COME ON IN, MAYA.
WE'VE BEEN EXPECTING YOU.
"THE WORLD HAS CHANGED. WE NEED A NEW VISION FOR THE FUTURE OF HUMANITY."
WE'RE GOING TO BUILD A BETTER WORLD, BASED ON ACTUAL SCIENCE.
THE CURRENT WORLD ORDER HAS FAILED.
AND HISTORY WILL LIONIZE US FOR USHERING IN A NEW ORDER.
"WE"...?
"MY PROTÉGÉ AND I ARE GOING TO LEAD THE WAY TO THE NEXT GENERATION OF SCIENTIFIC ADVANCEMENT.
"AND WE'LL DO IT OUR WAY.
"OUTSIDE THE SYSTEM."
THE PLANET'S CRUMBLING. BUT AS LONG AS EVERYONE HAS THE LATEST SMARTPHONE, NO ONE CARES.
WE'RE HYPNOTIZED BY PROFITS AND GADGETS WHILE OUR ECOSYSTEM HURTLES TOWARD COLLAPSE.
AND WHEN OUR PROFITS AND GADGETS CAN'T SAVE US...THEN WHAT?

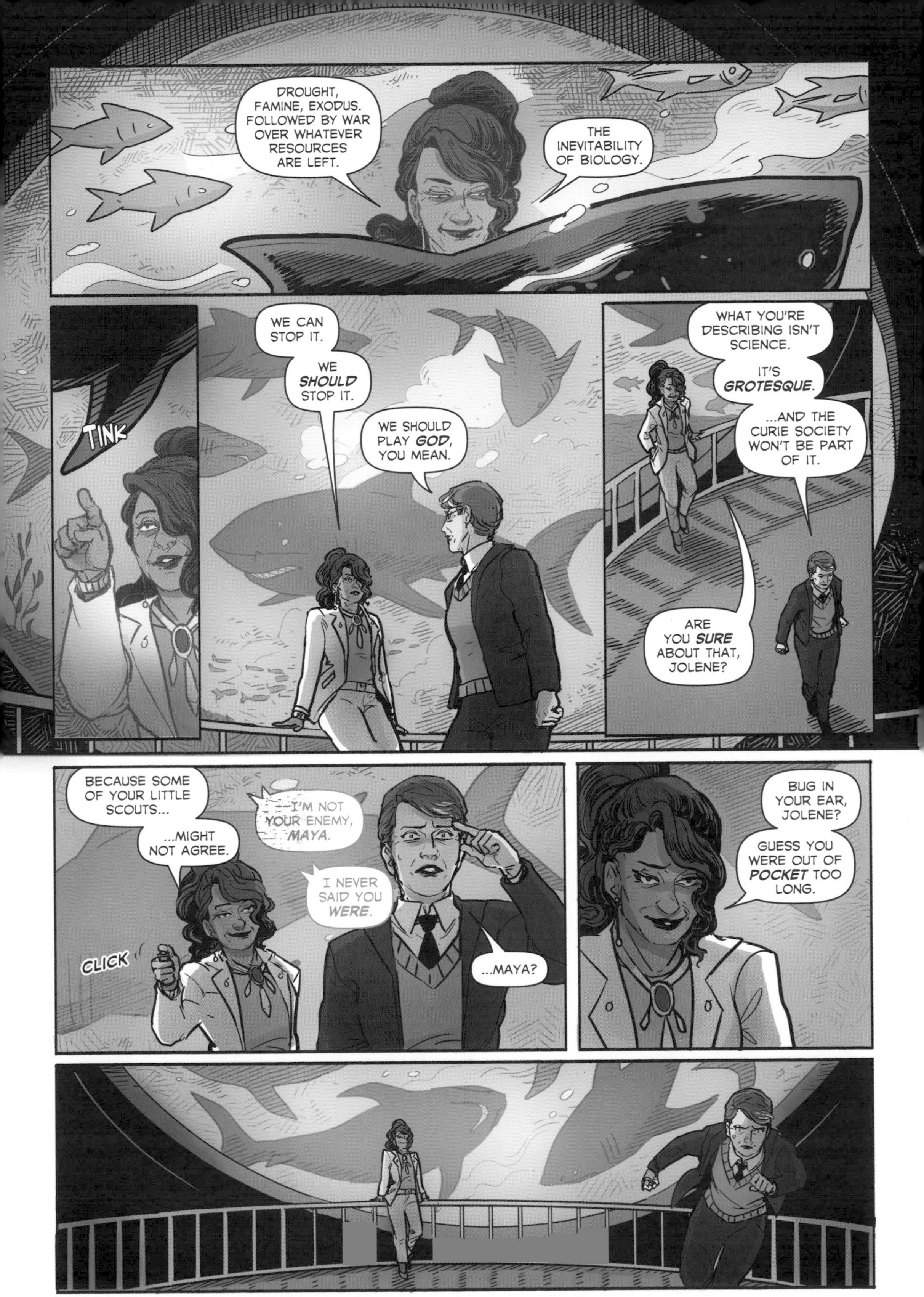
DROUGHT, FAMINE, EXODUS. FOLLOWED BY WAR OVER WHATEVER RESOURCES ARE LEFT.
THE INEVITABILITY OF BIOLOGY.
TINK
WE CAN STOP IT.
WE *SHOULD* STOP IT.
WE SHOULD PLAY *GOD*, YOU MEAN.
WHAT YOU'RE DESCRIBING ISN'T SCIENCE.
IT'S *GROTESQUE*.
...AND THE CURIE SOCIETY WON'T BE PART OF IT.
ARE YOU *SURE* ABOUT THAT, JOLENE?
BECAUSE SOME OF YOUR LITTLE SCOUTS...
...MIGHT NOT AGREE.
--I'M NOT YOUR ENEMY, *MAYA*.
I NEVER SAID YOU *WERE*.
CLICK
...MAYA?
BUG IN YOUR EAR, JOLENE?
GUESS YOU WERE OUT OF *POCKET* TOO LONG.

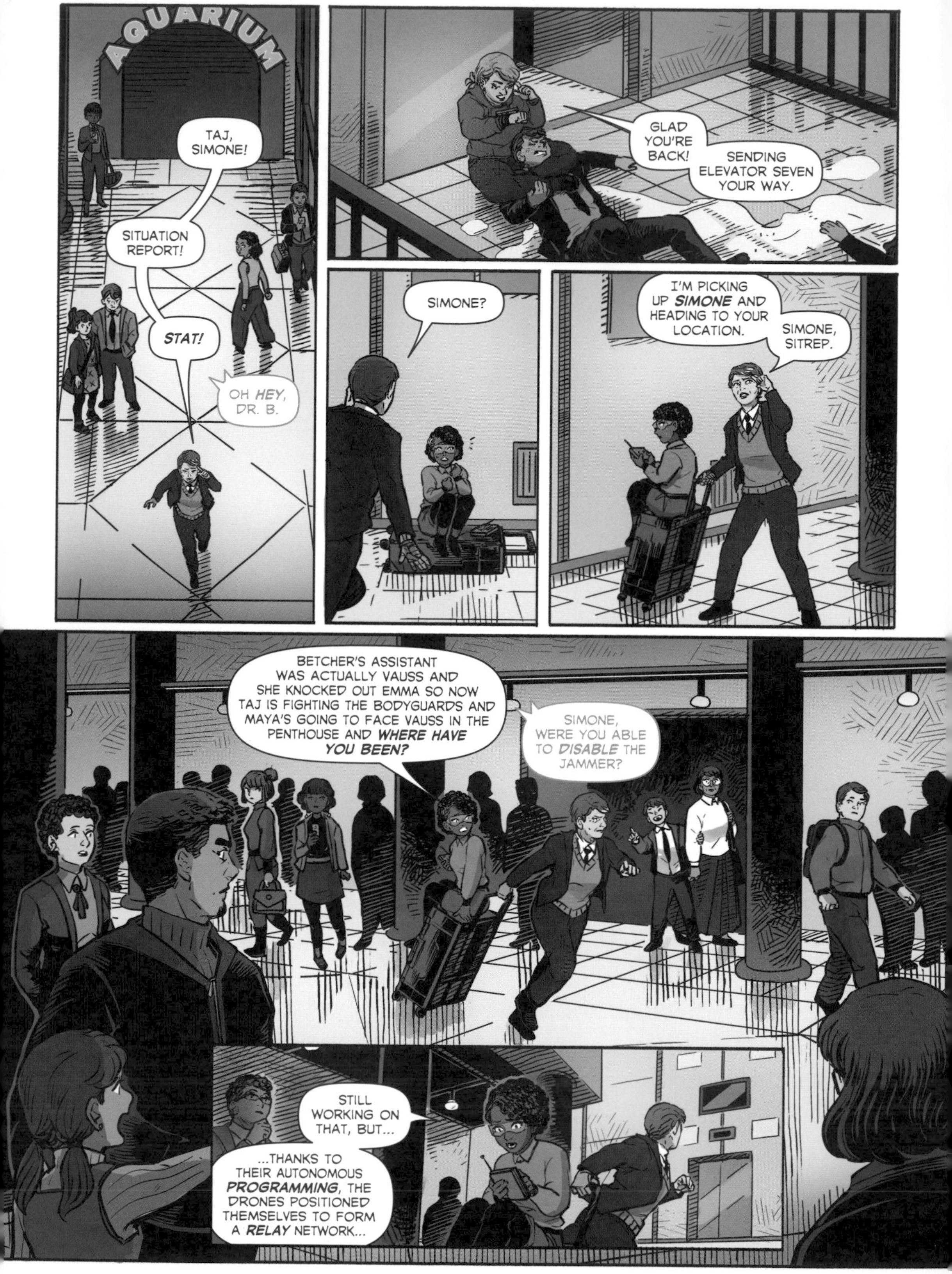
AQUARIUM
TAJ, SIMONE!
SITUATION REPORT!
STAT!
OH HEY, DR. B.
GLAD YOU'RE BACK!
SENDING ELEVATOR SEVEN YOUR WAY.
SIMONE?
I'M PICKING UP SIMONE AND HEADING TO YOUR LOCATION.
SIMONE, SITREP.
BETCHER'S ASSISTANT WAS ACTUALLY VAUSS AND SHE KNOCKED OUT EMMA SO NOW TAJ IS FIGHTING THE BODYGUARDS AND MAYA'S GOING TO FACE VAUSS IN THE PENTHOUSE AND WHERE HAVE YOU BEEN?
SIMONE, WERE YOU ABLE TO DISABLE THE JAMMER?
STILL WORKING ON THAT, BUT...
...THANKS TO THEIR AUTONOMOUS PROGRAMMING, THE DRONES POSITIONED THEMSELVES TO FORM A RELAY NETWORK...

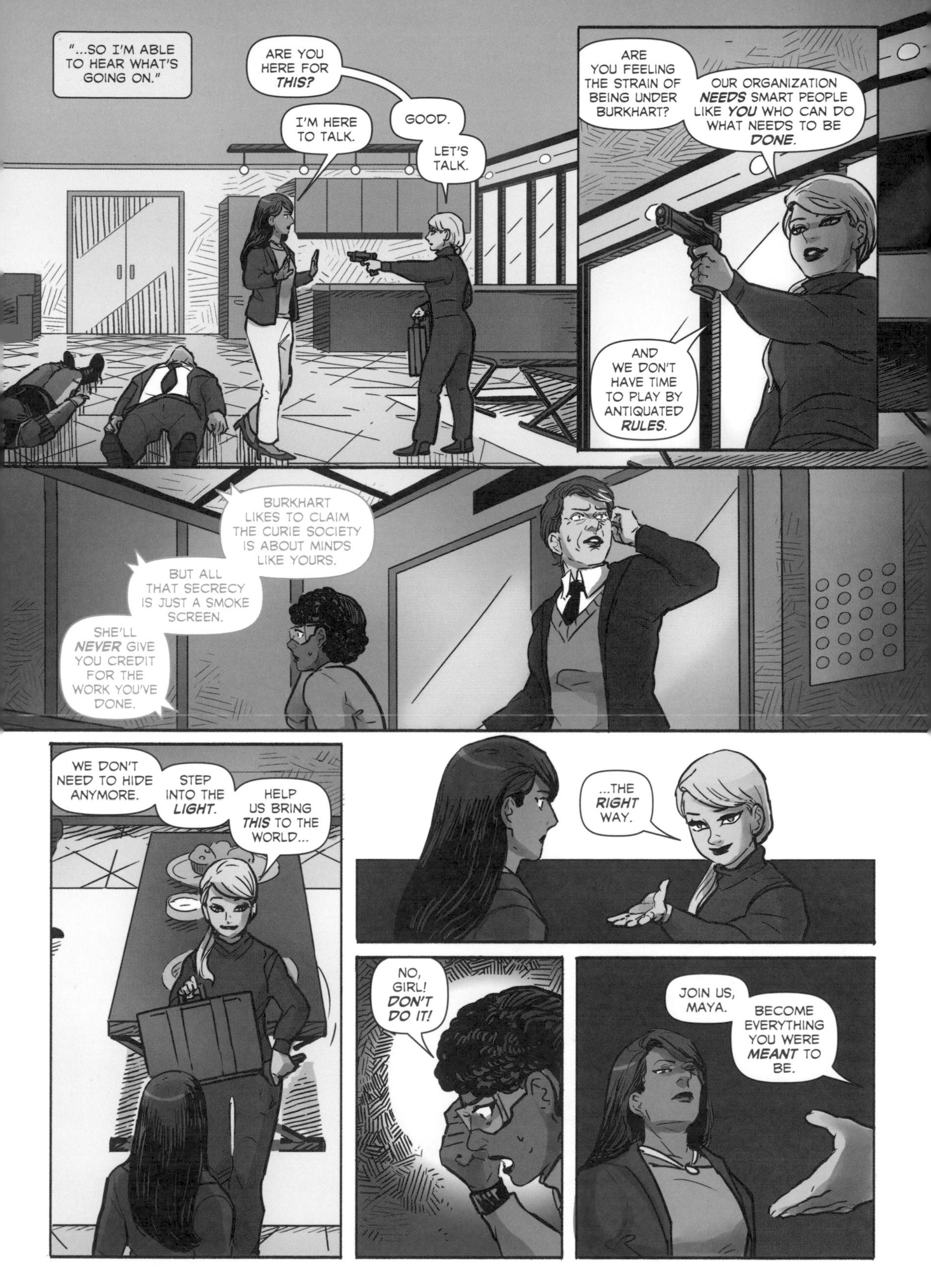
"...SO I'M ABLE TO HEAR WHAT'S GOING ON."
ARE YOU HERE FOR THIS?
I'M HERE TO TALK.
GOOD.
LET'S TALK.
ARE YOU FEELING THE STRAIN OF BEING UNDER BURKHART?
OUR ORGANIZATION NEEDS SMART PEOPLE LIKE YOU WHO CAN DO WHAT NEEDS TO BE DONE.
AND WE DON'T HAVE TIME TO PLAY BY ANTIQUATED RULES.
BURKHART LIKES TO CLAIM THE CURIE SOCIETY IS ABOUT MINDS LIKE YOURS.
BUT ALL THAT SECRECY IS JUST A SMOKE SCREEN.
SHE'LL NEVER GIVE YOU CREDIT FOR THE WORK YOU'VE DONE.
WE DON'T NEED TO HIDE ANYMORE.
STEP INTO THE LIGHT.
HELP US BRING THIS TO THE WORLD...
...THE RIGHT WAY.
NO, GIRL! DON'T DO IT!
JOIN US, MAYA.
BECOME EVERYTHING YOU WERE MEANT TO BE.

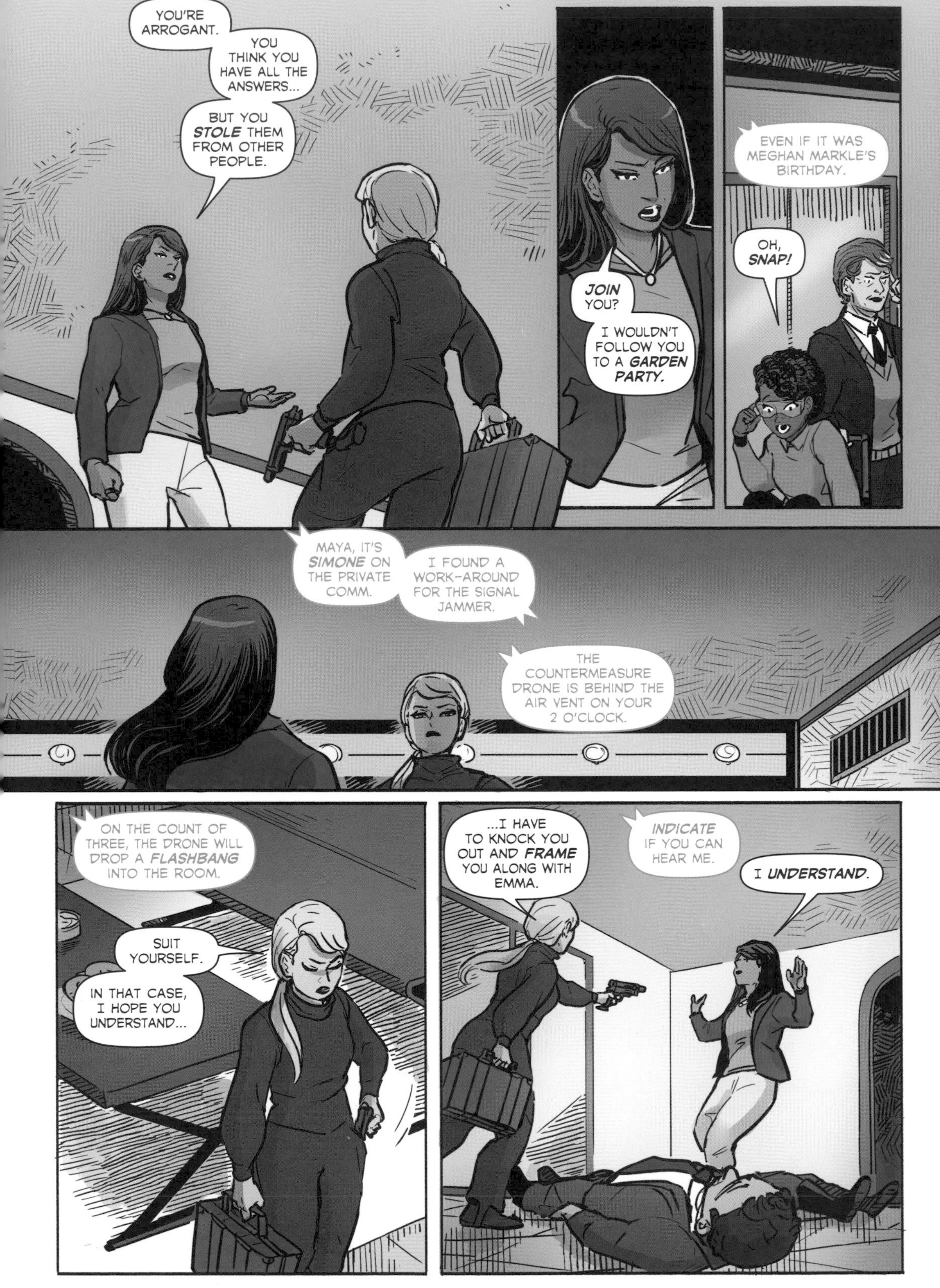
YOU'RE ARROGANT.
YOU THINK YOU HAVE ALL THE ANSWERS...
BUT YOU STOLE THEM FROM OTHER PEOPLE.
JOIN YOU?
I WOULDN'T FOLLOW YOU TO A GARDEN PARTY.
EVEN IF IT WAS MEGHAN MARKLE'S BIRTHDAY.
OH, SNAP!
MAYA, IT'S SIMONE ON THE PRIVATE COMM.
I FOUND A WORK-AROUND FOR THE SIGNAL JAMMER.
THE COUNTERMEASURE DRONE IS BEHIND THE AIR VENT ON YOUR 2 O'CLOCK.
ON THE COUNT OF THREE, THE DRONE WILL DROP A FLASHBANG INTO THE ROOM.
SUIT YOURSELF.
IN THAT CASE, I HOPE YOU UNDERSTAND...
...I HAVE TO KNOCK YOU OUT AND FRAME YOU ALONG WITH EMMA.
INDICATE IF YOU CAN HEAR ME.
I UNDERSTAND.

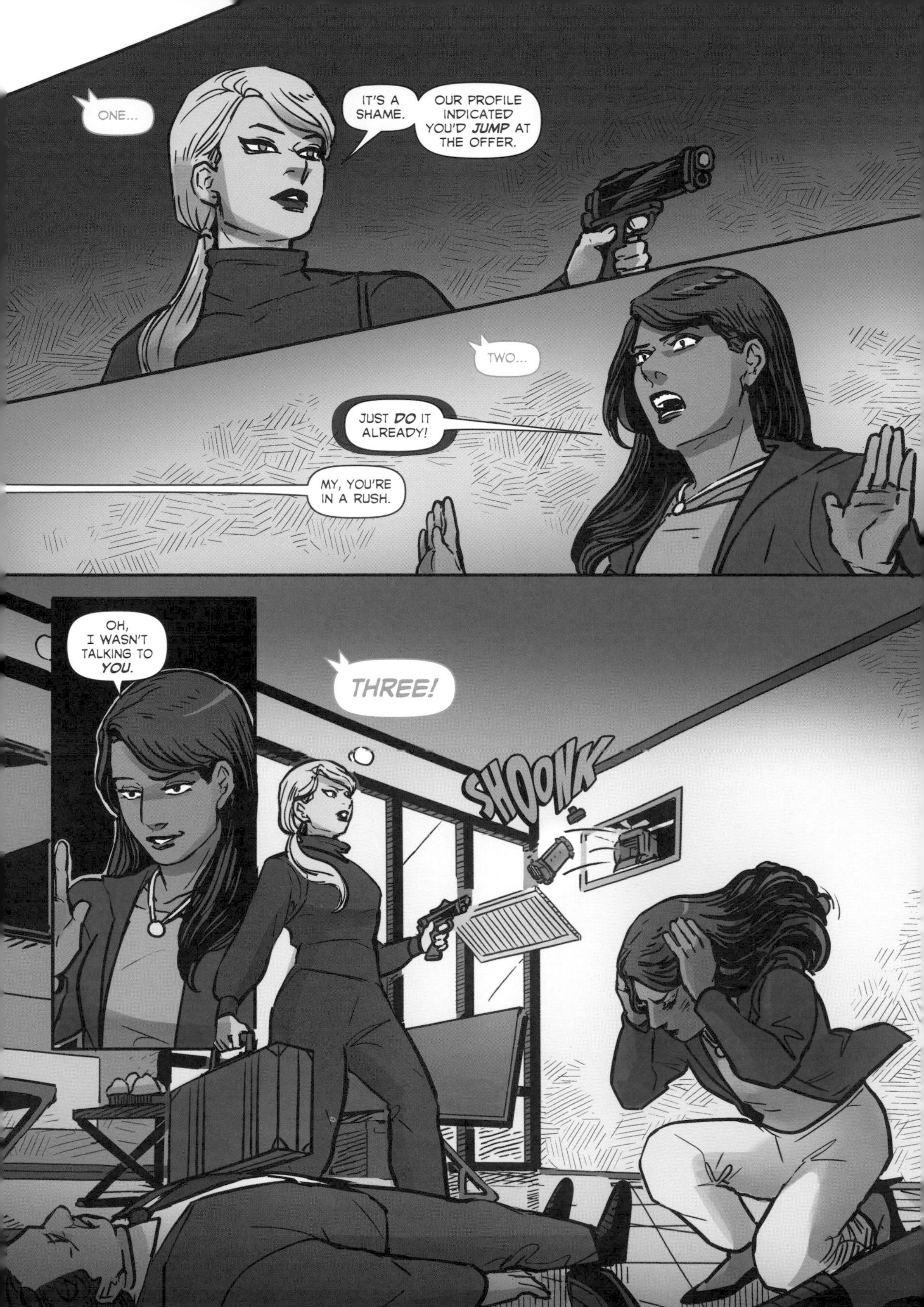
ONE...
IT'S A SHAME.
OUR PROFILE INDICATED YOU'D *JUMP* AT THE OFFER.
TWO...
JUST *DO* IT ALREADY!
MY, YOU'RE IN A RUSH.
OH, I WASN'T TALKING TO *YOU*.
THREE!
SHOONK

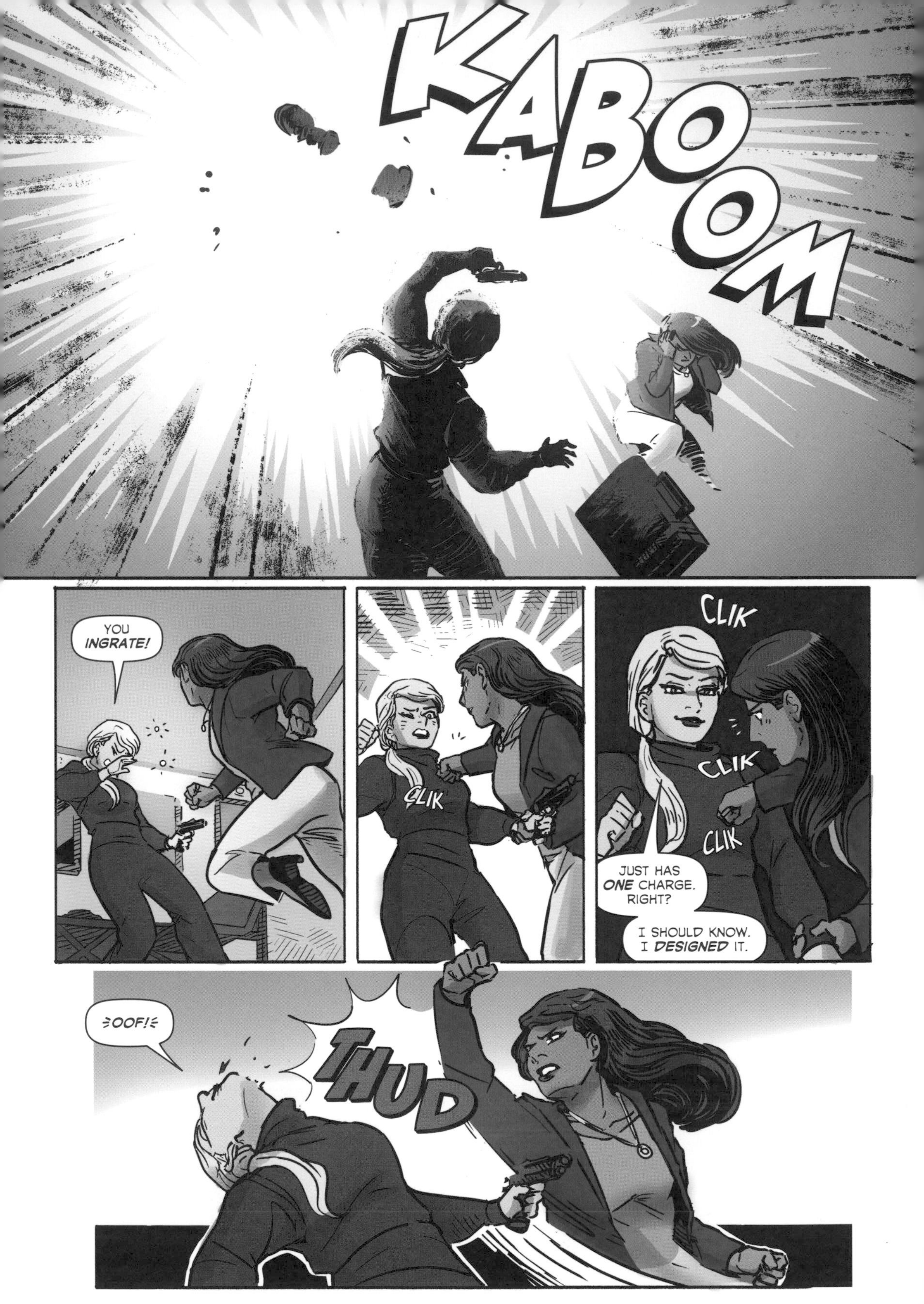
KABOOM
YOU INGRATE!
CLIK
CLIK
CLIK
CLIK
JUST HAS ONE CHARGE. RIGHT?
I SHOULD KNOW. I DESIGNED IT.
OOF!
THUD

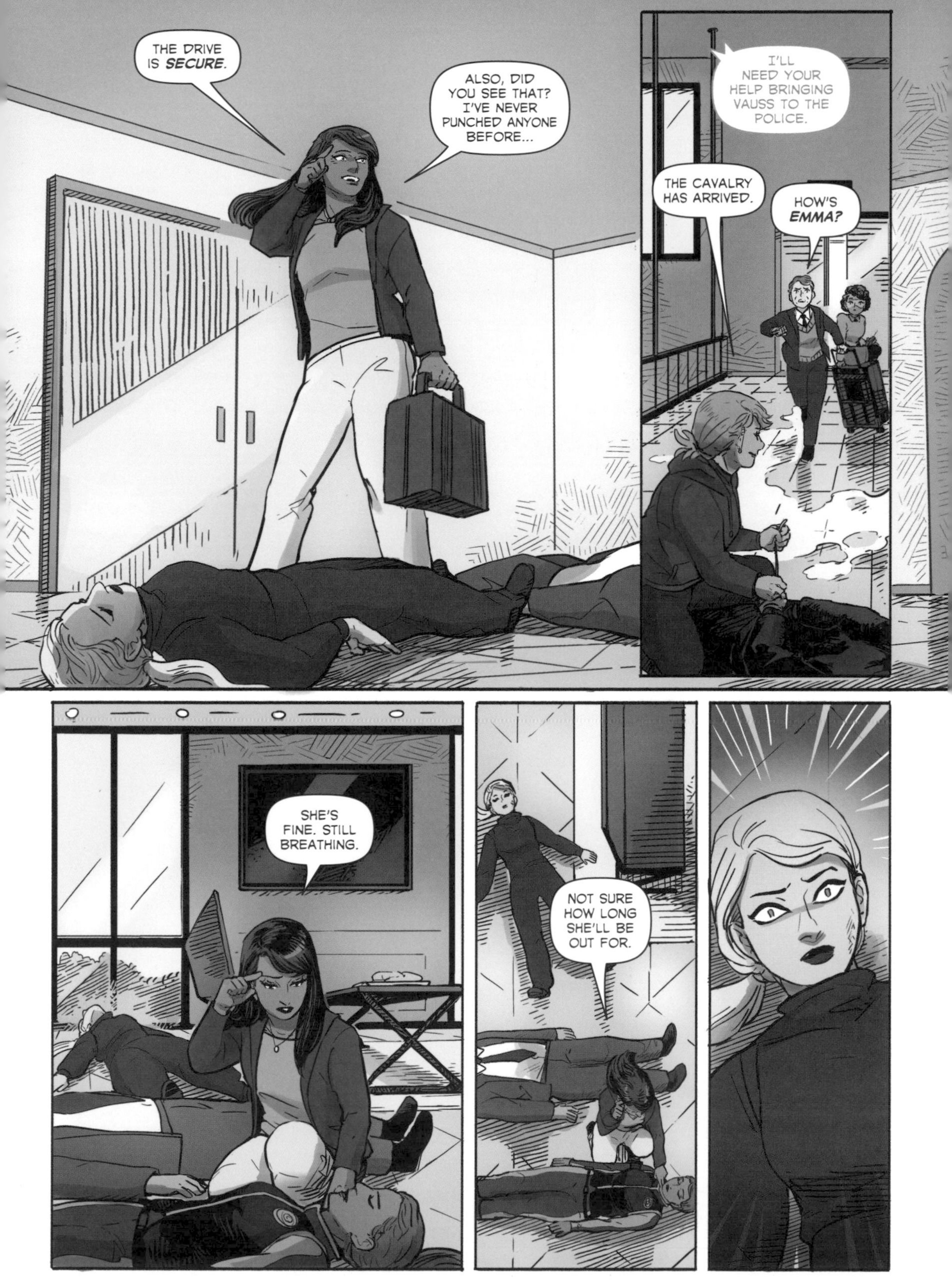
THE DRIVE IS SECURE.
ALSO, DID YOU SEE THAT? I'VE NEVER PUNCHED ANYONE BEFORE...
I'LL NEED YOUR HELP BRINGING VAUSS TO THE POLICE.
THE CAVALRY HAS ARRIVED.
HOW'S EMMA?
SHE'S FINE. STILL BREATHING.
NOT SURE HOW LONG SHE'LL BE OUT FOR.

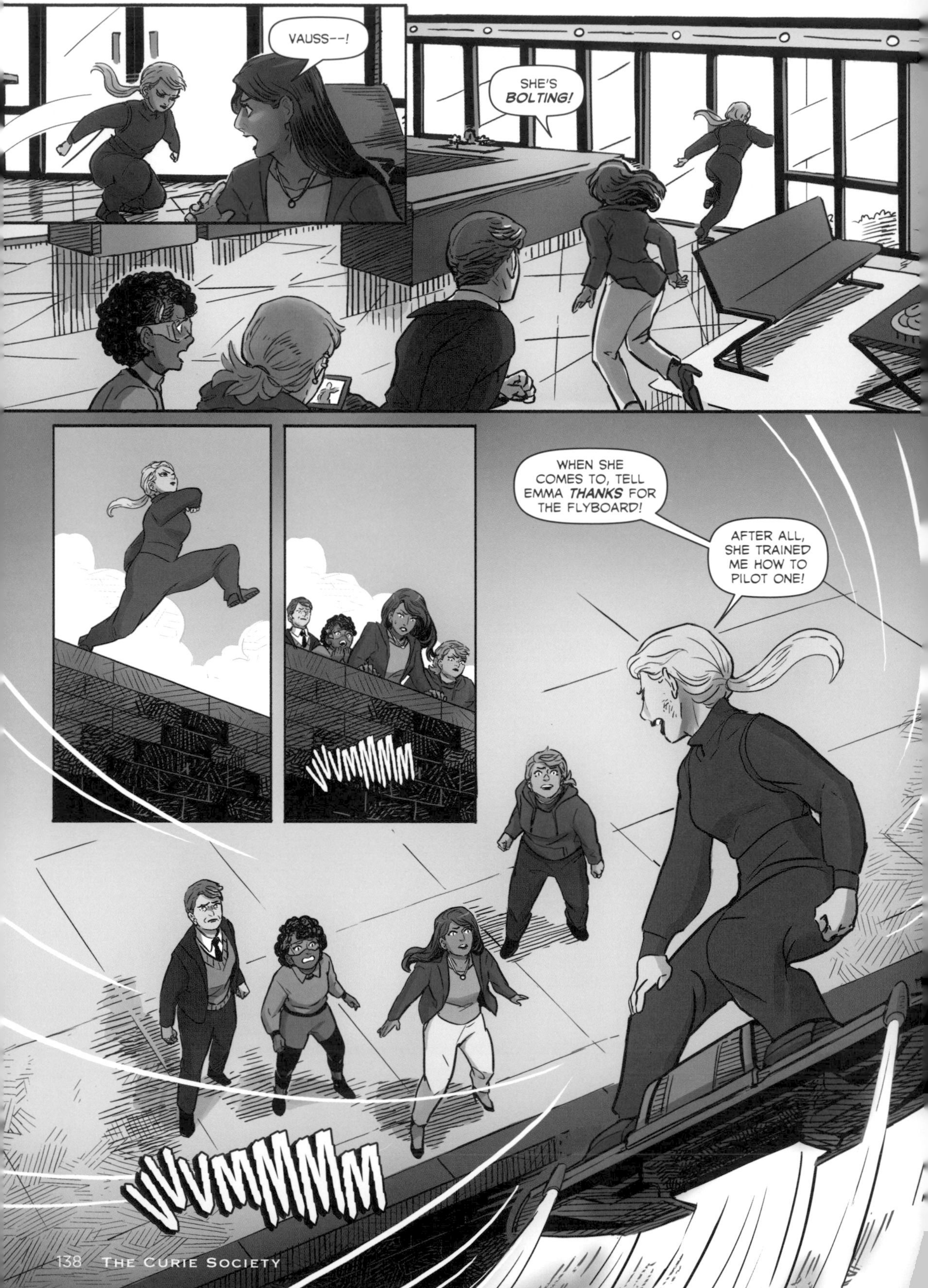
VAUSS--!
SHE'S *BOLTING!*
WHEN SHE COMES TO, TELL EMMA ***THANKS*** FOR THE FLYBOARD!
AFTER ALL, SHE TRAINED ME HOW TO PILOT ONE!
VVVMMMM
VVVMMMMM

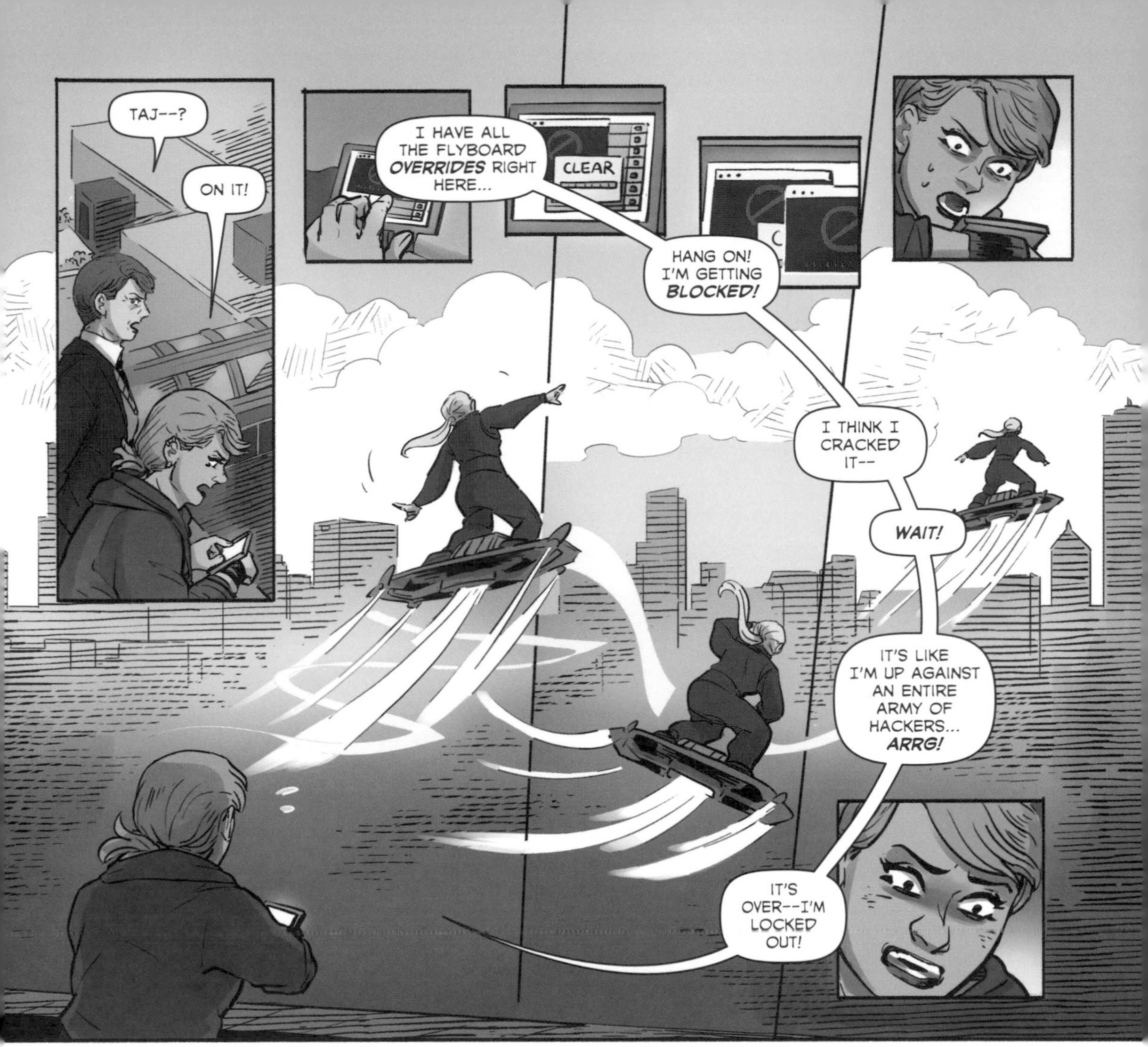
TAJ--?
ON IT!
I HAVE ALL THE FLYBOARD OVERRIDES RIGHT HERE...
CLEAR
HANG ON! I'M GETTING BLOCKED!
I THINK I CRACKED IT--
WAIT!
IT'S LIKE I'M UP AGAINST AN ENTIRE ARMY OF HACKERS... ARRG!
IT'S OVER--I'M LOCKED OUT!

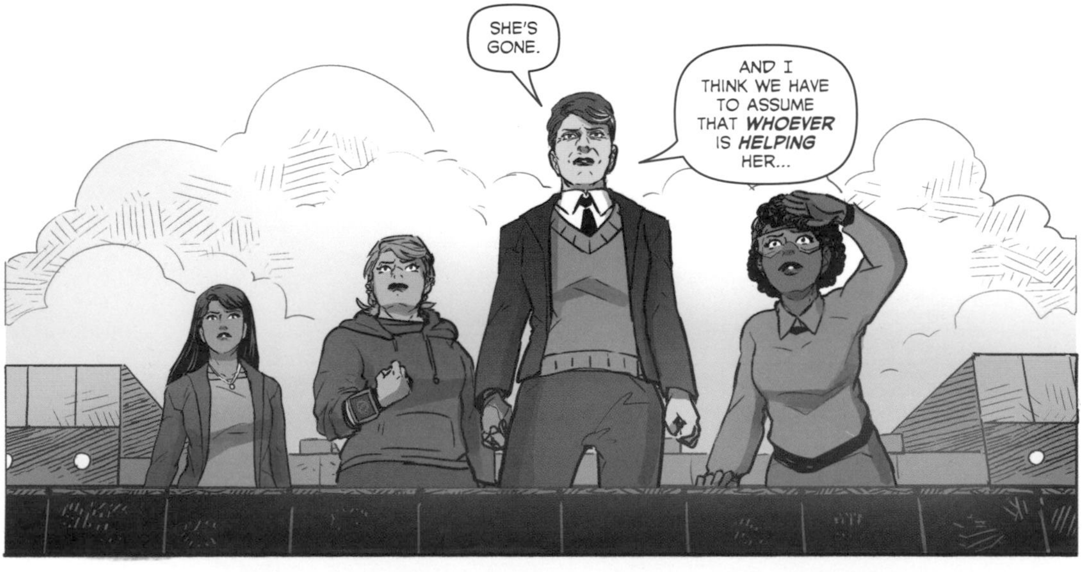
SHE'S GONE.
AND I THINK WE HAVE TO ASSUME THAT WHOEVER IS HELPING HER...

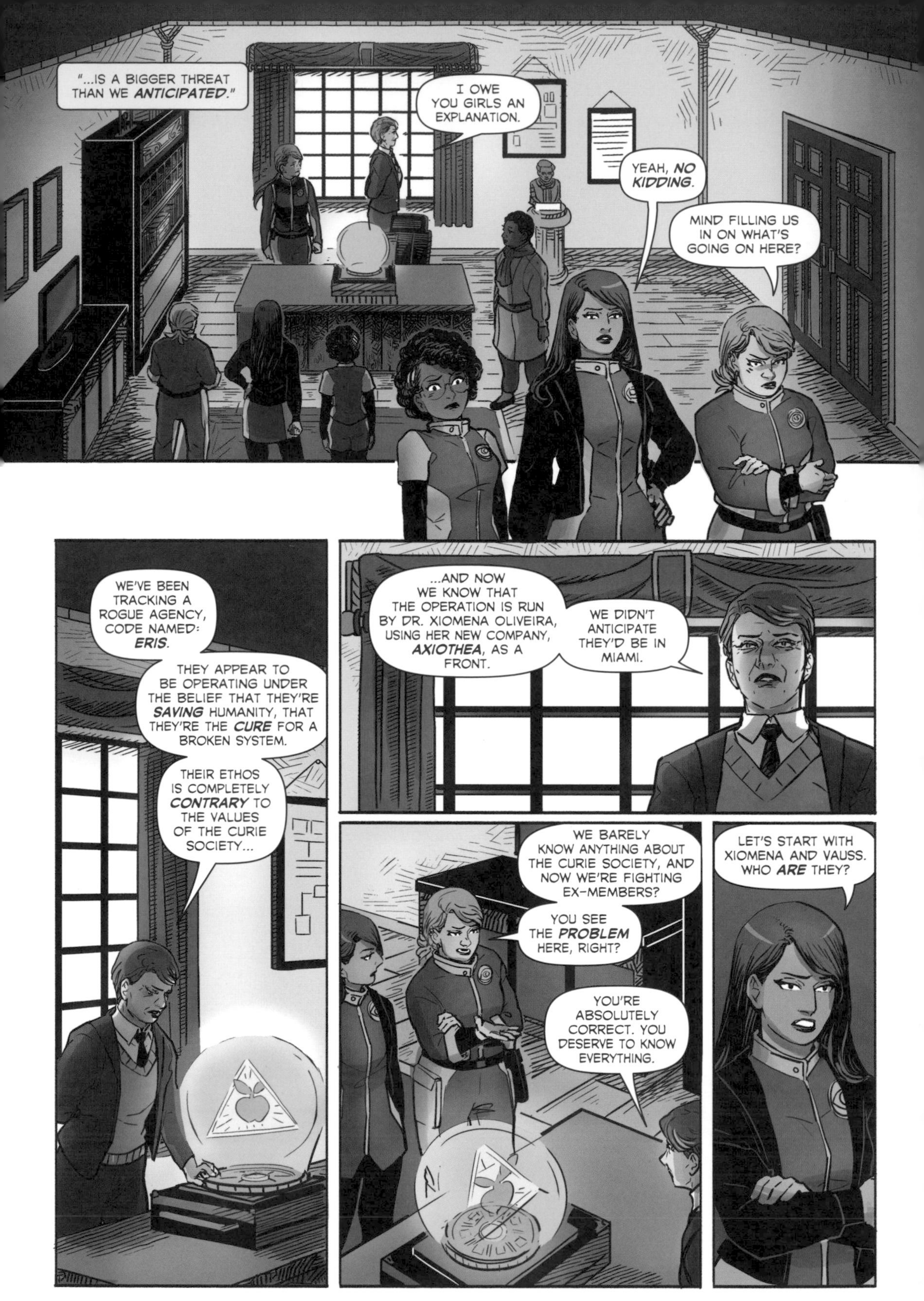

"...IS A BIGGER THREAT THAN WE *ANTICIPATED*."
I OWE YOU GIRLS AN EXPLANATION.
YEAH, *NO KIDDING*.
MIND FILLING US IN ON WHAT'S GOING ON HERE?
WE'VE BEEN TRACKING A ROGUE AGENCY, CODE NAMED: *ERIS*.
THEY APPEAR TO BE OPERATING UNDER THE BELIEF THAT THEY'RE *SAVING* HUMANITY, THAT THEY'RE THE *CURE* FOR A BROKEN SYSTEM.
THEIR ETHOS IS COMPLETELY *CONTRARY* TO THE VALUES OF THE CURIE SOCIETY...
...AND NOW WE KNOW THAT THE OPERATION IS RUN BY DR. XIOMENA OLIVEIRA, USING HER NEW COMPANY, *AXIOTHEA*, AS A FRONT.
WE DIDN'T ANTICIPATE THEY'D BE IN MIAMI.
WE BARELY KNOW ANYTHING ABOUT THE CURIE SOCIETY, AND NOW WE'RE FIGHTING EX-MEMBERS?
YOU SEE THE *PROBLEM* HERE, RIGHT?
YOU'RE ABSOLUTELY CORRECT. YOU DESERVE TO KNOW EVERYTHING.
LET'S START WITH XIOMENA AND VAUSS. WHO *ARE* THEY?

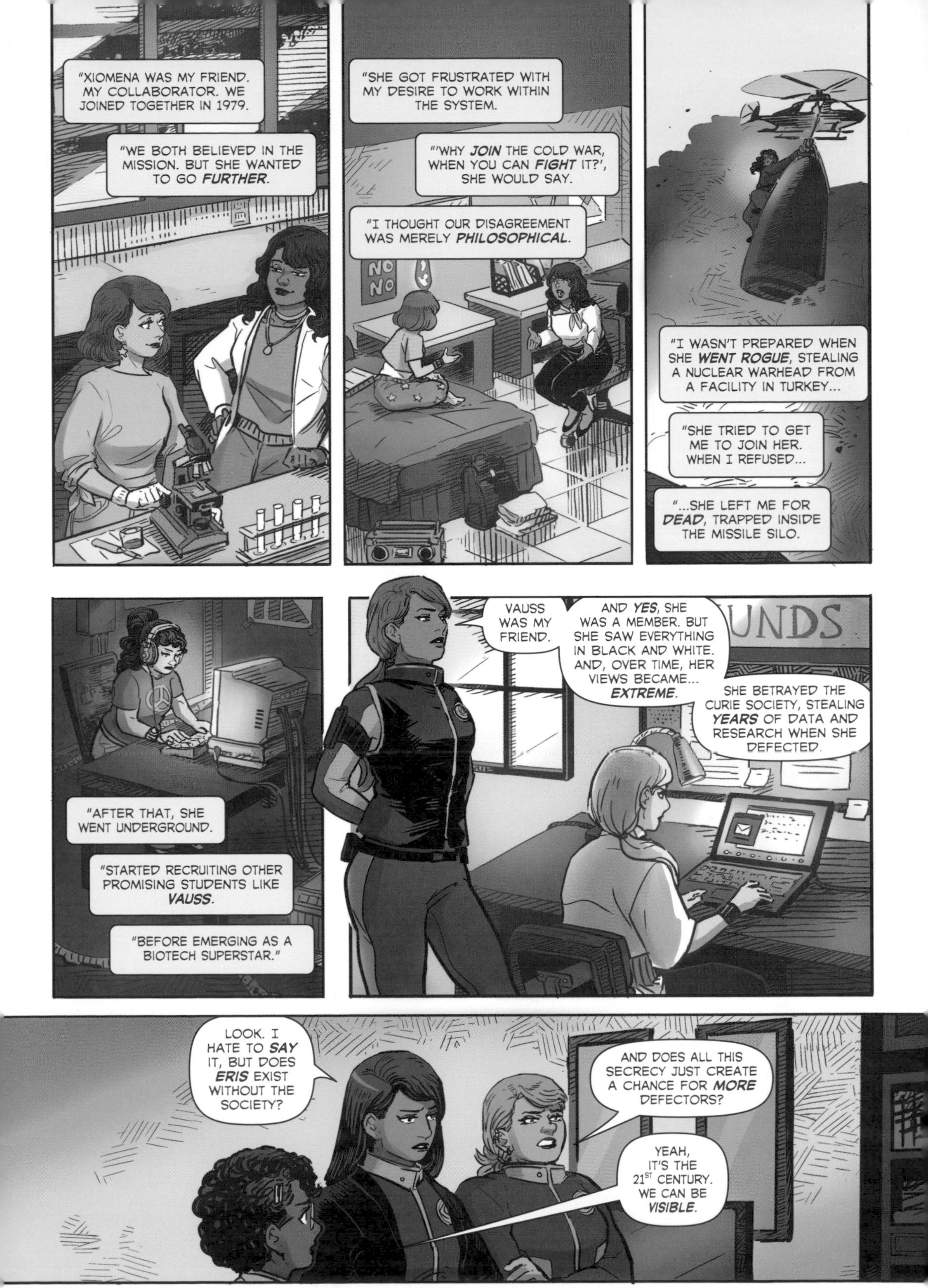
"XIOMENA WAS MY FRIEND. MY COLLABORATOR. WE JOINED TOGETHER IN 1979.
"WE BOTH BELIEVED IN THE MISSION. BUT SHE WANTED TO GO FURTHER.
"SHE GOT FRUSTRATED WITH MY DESIRE TO WORK WITHIN THE SYSTEM.
"'WHY JOIN THE COLD WAR, WHEN YOU CAN FIGHT IT?', SHE WOULD SAY.
"I THOUGHT OUR DISAGREEMENT WAS MERELY PHILOSOPHICAL.
NO NO
"I WASN'T PREPARED WHEN SHE WENT ROGUE, STEALING A NUCLEAR WARHEAD FROM A FACILITY IN TURKEY...
"SHE TRIED TO GET ME TO JOIN HER. WHEN I REFUSED...
"...SHE LEFT ME FOR DEAD, TRAPPED INSIDE THE MISSILE SILO.
"AFTER THAT, SHE WENT UNDERGROUND.
"STARTED RECRUITING OTHER PROMISING STUDENTS LIKE VAUSS.
"BEFORE EMERGING AS A BIOTECH SUPERSTAR."
VAUSS WAS MY FRIEND.
AND YES, SHE WAS A MEMBER. BUT SHE SAW EVERYTHING IN BLACK AND WHITE. AND, OVER TIME, HER VIEWS BECAME... EXTREME.
SHE BETRAYED THE CURIE SOCIETY, STEALING YEARS OF DATA AND RESEARCH WHEN SHE DEFECTED.
UNDS
LOOK. I HATE TO SAY IT, BUT DOES ERIS EXIST WITHOUT THE SOCIETY?
AND DOES ALL THIS SECRECY JUST CREATE A CHANCE FOR MORE DEFECTORS?
YEAH, IT'S THE 21ST CENTURY. WE CAN BE VISIBLE.

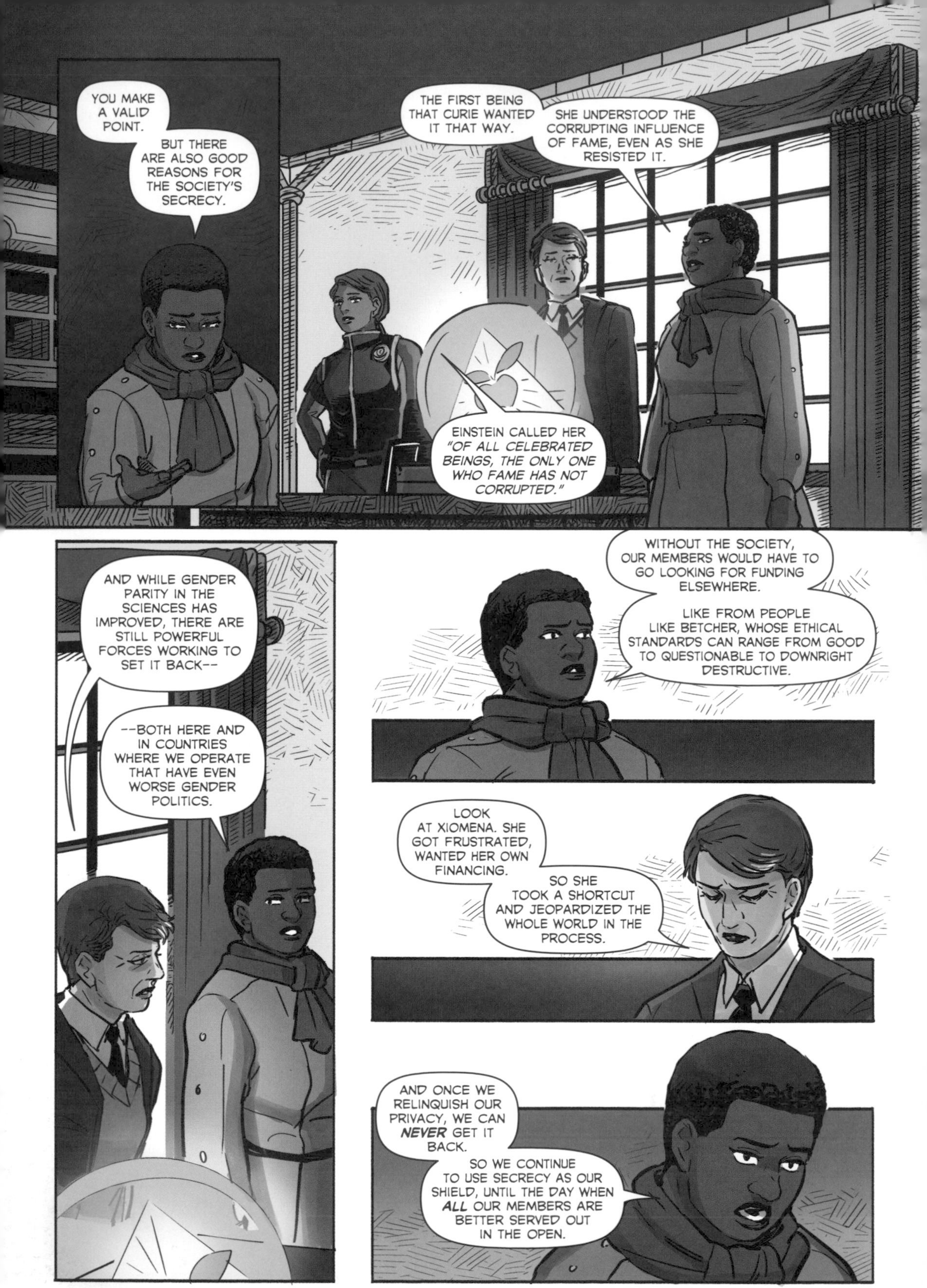
YOU MAKE A VALID POINT.
BUT THERE ARE ALSO GOOD REASONS FOR THE SOCIETY'S SECRECY.
THE FIRST BEING THAT CURIE WANTED IT THAT WAY.
SHE UNDERSTOOD THE CORRUPTING INFLUENCE OF FAME, EVEN AS SHE RESISTED IT.
EINSTEIN CALLED HER *"OF ALL CELEBRATED BEINGS, THE ONLY ONE WHO FAME HAS NOT CORRUPTED."*
AND WHILE GENDER PARITY IN THE SCIENCES HAS IMPROVED, THERE ARE STILL POWERFUL FORCES WORKING TO SET IT BACK--
--BOTH HERE AND IN COUNTRIES WHERE WE OPERATE THAT HAVE EVEN WORSE GENDER POLITICS.
WITHOUT THE SOCIETY, OUR MEMBERS WOULD HAVE TO GO LOOKING FOR FUNDING ELSEWHERE.
LIKE FROM PEOPLE LIKE BETCHER, WHOSE ETHICAL STANDARDS CAN RANGE FROM GOOD TO QUESTIONABLE TO DOWNRIGHT DESTRUCTIVE.
LOOK AT XIOMENA. SHE GOT FRUSTRATED, WANTED HER OWN FINANCING.
SO SHE TOOK A SHORTCUT AND JEOPARDIZED THE WHOLE WORLD IN THE PROCESS.
AND ONCE WE RELINQUISH OUR PRIVACY, WE CAN ***NEVER*** GET IT BACK.
SO WE CONTINUE TO USE SECRECY AS OUR SHIELD, UNTIL THE DAY WHEN ***ALL*** OUR MEMBERS ARE BETTER SERVED OUT IN THE OPEN.

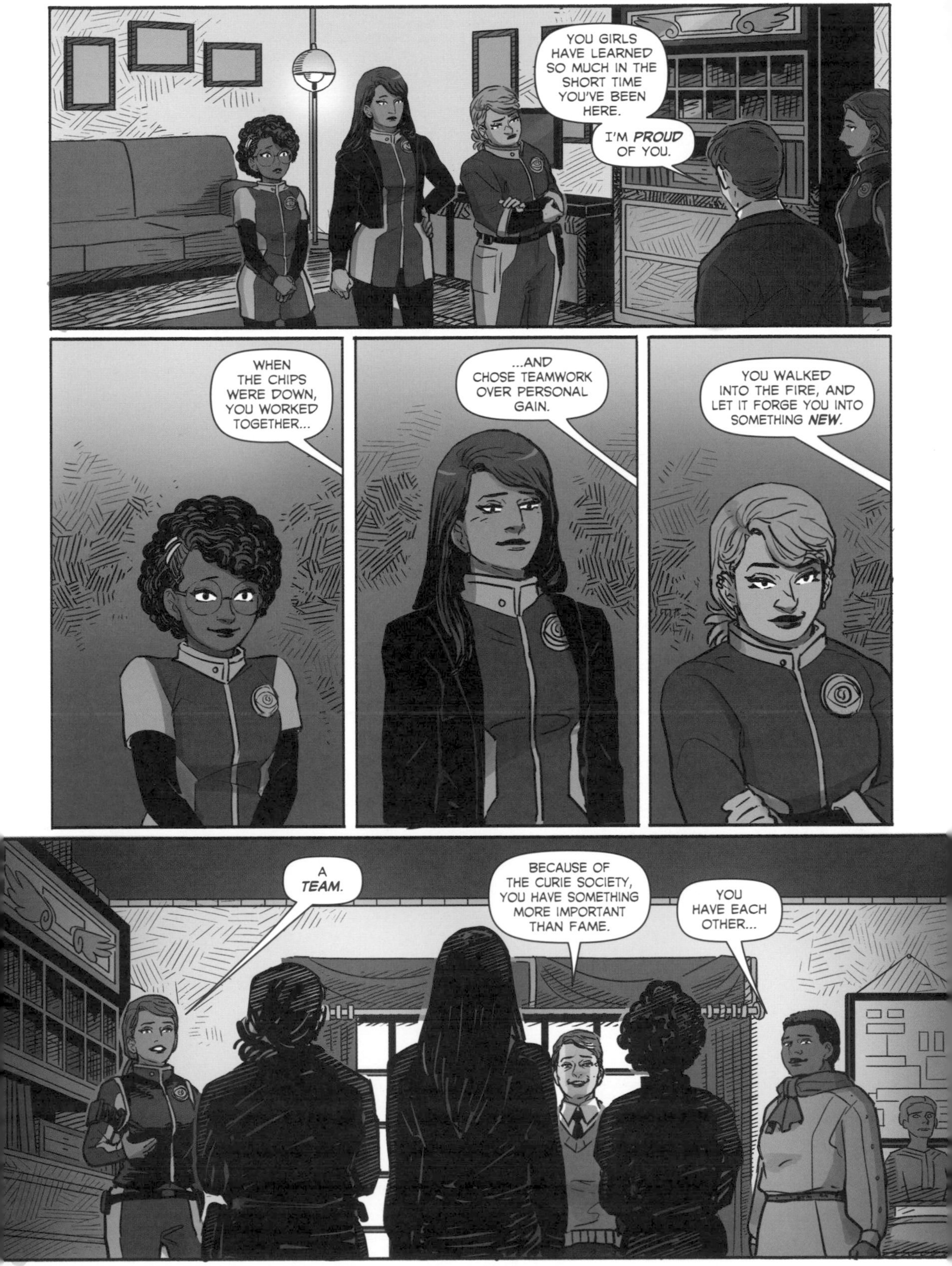
YOU GIRLS HAVE LEARNED SO MUCH IN THE SHORT TIME YOU'VE BEEN HERE.
I'M **PROUD** OF YOU.
WHEN THE CHIPS WERE DOWN, YOU WORKED TOGETHER...
...AND CHOSE TEAMWORK OVER PERSONAL GAIN.
YOU WALKED INTO THE FIRE, AND LET IT FORGE YOU INTO SOMETHING **NEW**.
A **TEAM**.
BECAUSE OF THE CURIE SOCIETY, YOU HAVE SOMETHING MORE IMPORTANT THAN FAME.
YOU HAVE EACH OTHER...

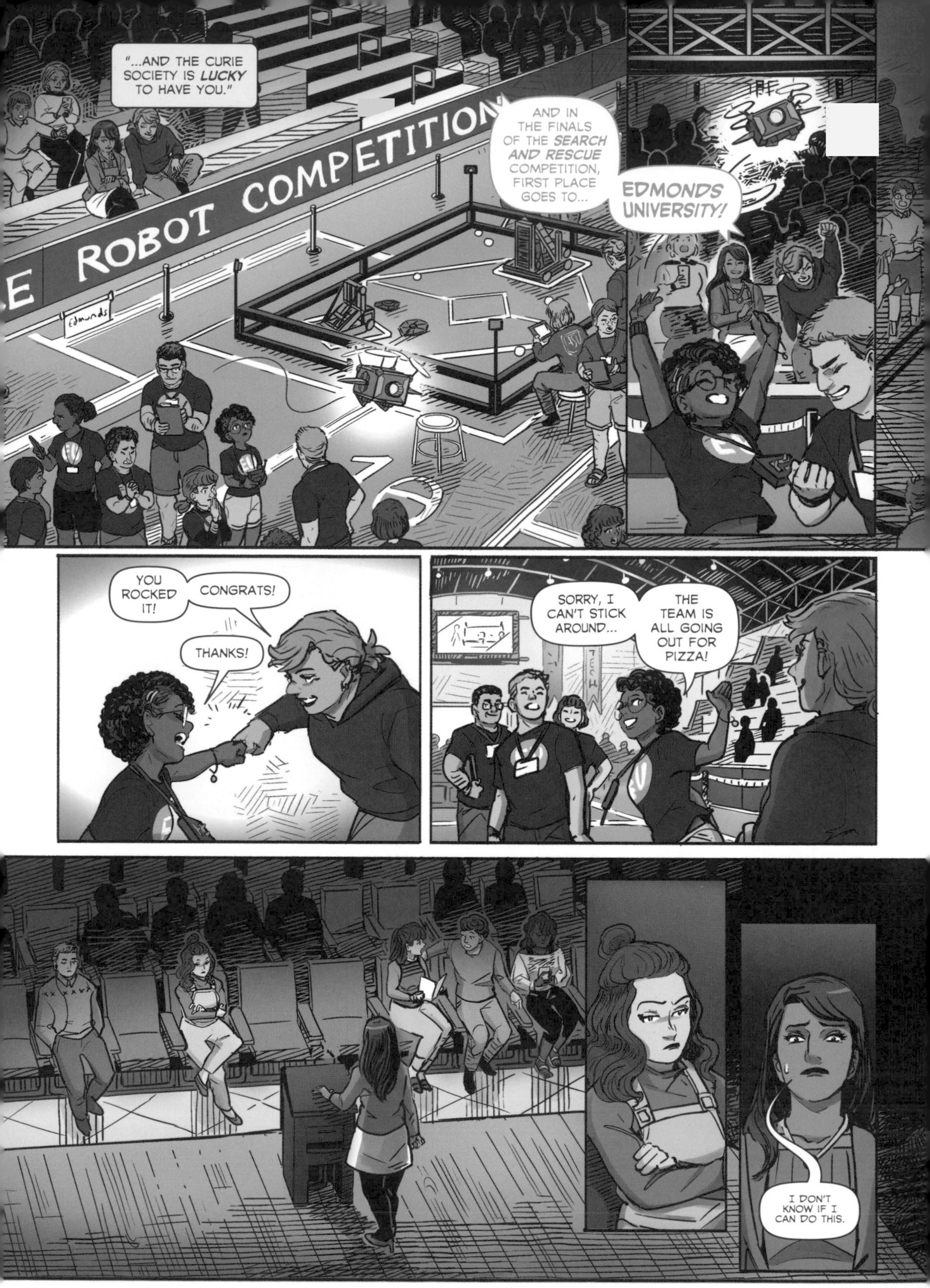
"...AND THE CURIE SOCIETY IS *LUCKY* TO HAVE YOU."
ROBOT COMPETITION
Edmonds
AND IN THE FINALS OF THE *SEARCH AND RESCUE* COMPETITION, FIRST PLACE GOES TO...
EDMONDS UNIVERSITY!
YOU ROCKED IT!
CONGRATS!
THANKS!
SORRY, I CAN'T STICK AROUND...
THE TEAM IS ALL GOING OUT FOR PIZZA!
I DON'T KNOW IF I CAN DO THIS.

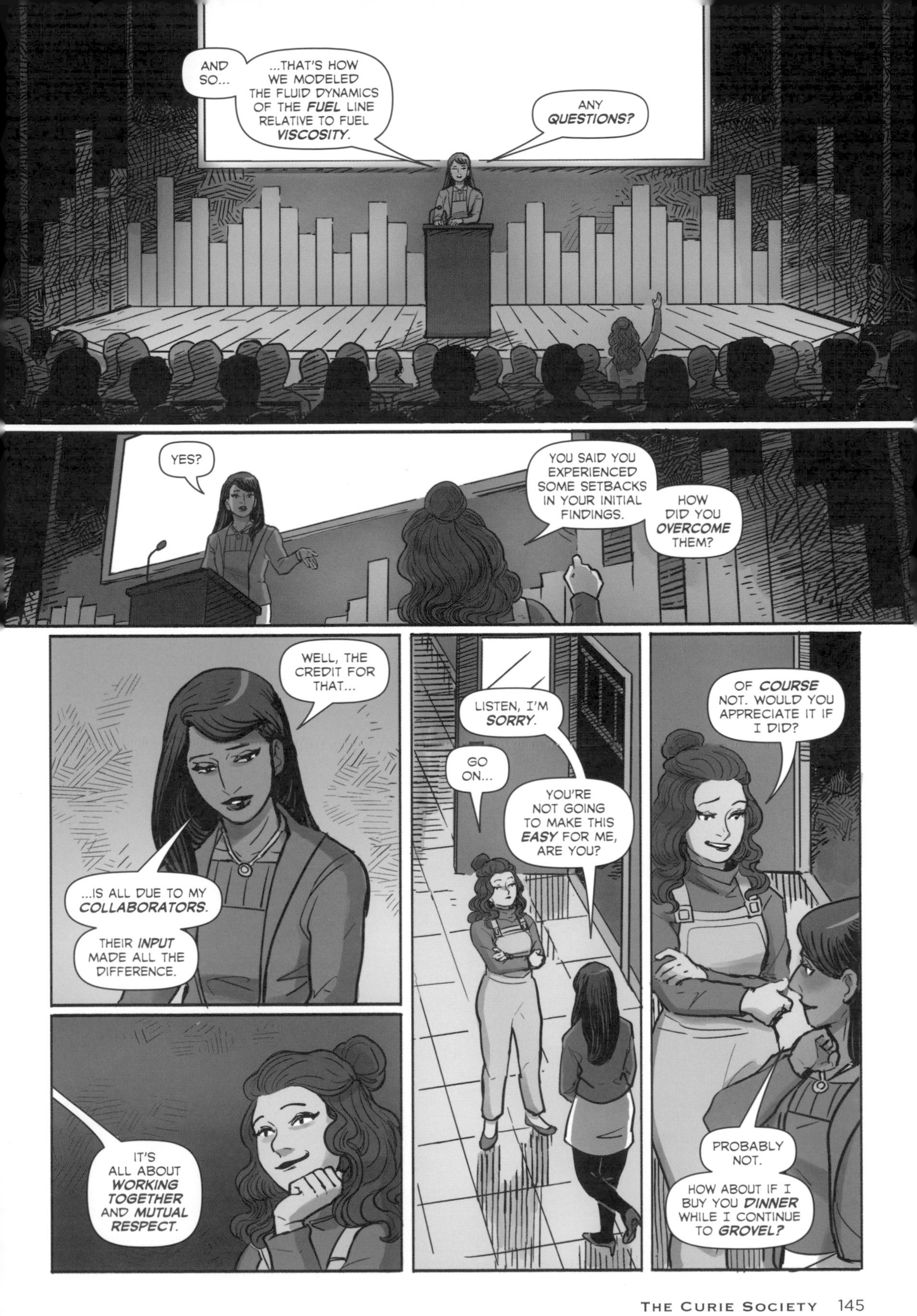
AND SO...
...THAT'S HOW WE MODELED THE FLUID DYNAMICS OF THE **FUEL** LINE RELATIVE TO FUEL **VISCOSITY**.
ANY **QUESTIONS?**
YES?
YOU SAID YOU EXPERIENCED SOME SETBACKS IN YOUR INITIAL FINDINGS.
HOW DID YOU **OVERCOME** THEM?
WELL, THE CREDIT FOR THAT...
...IS ALL DUE TO MY **COLLABORATORS**.
THEIR **INPUT** MADE ALL THE DIFFERENCE.
IT'S ALL ABOUT **WORKING TOGETHER** AND **MUTUAL RESPECT**.
LISTEN, I'M **SORRY**.
GO ON...
YOU'RE NOT GOING TO MAKE THIS **EASY** FOR ME, ARE YOU?
OF **COURSE** NOT. WOULD YOU APPRECIATE IT IF I DID?
PROBABLY NOT.
HOW ABOUT IF I BUY YOU **DINNER** WHILE I CONTINUE TO **GROVEL?**

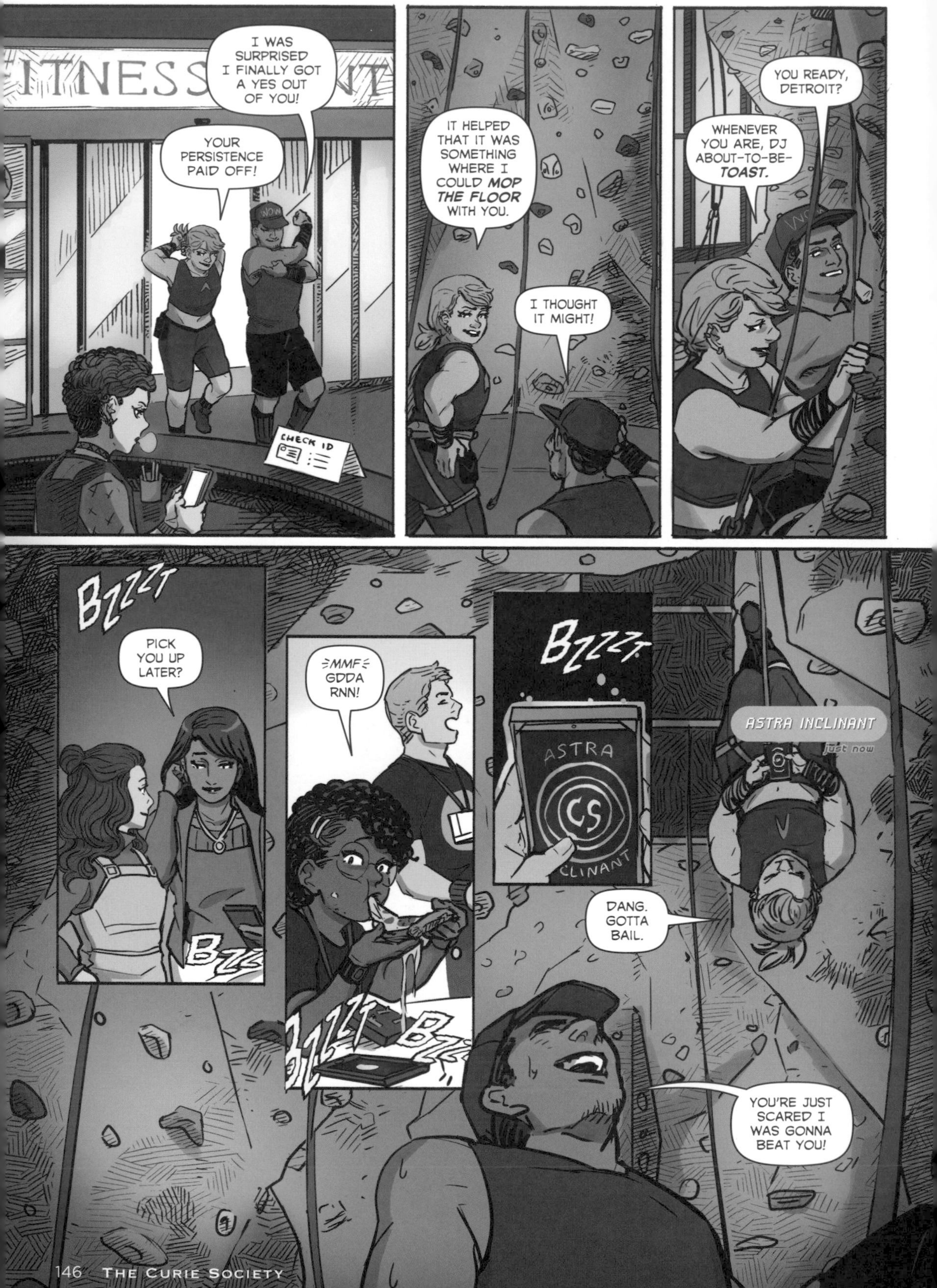
ITNESS NT
I WAS SURPRISED I FINALLY GOT A YES OUT OF YOU!
YOUR PERSISTENCE PAID OFF!
CHECK ID
IT HELPED THAT IT WAS SOMETHING WHERE I COULD ***MOP THE FLOOR*** WITH YOU.
I THOUGHT IT MIGHT!
YOU READY, DETROIT?
WHENEVER YOU ARE, DJ ABOUT-TO-BE-***TOAST.***
BZZZZT
PICK YOU UP LATER?
BZZ
MMF GDDA RNN!
BZZZZT
BZZ
BZZZZT.
ASTRA
CS
CLINANT
ASTRA INCLINANT
just now
DANG. GOTTA BAIL.
YOU'RE JUST SCARED I WAS GONNA BEAT YOU!

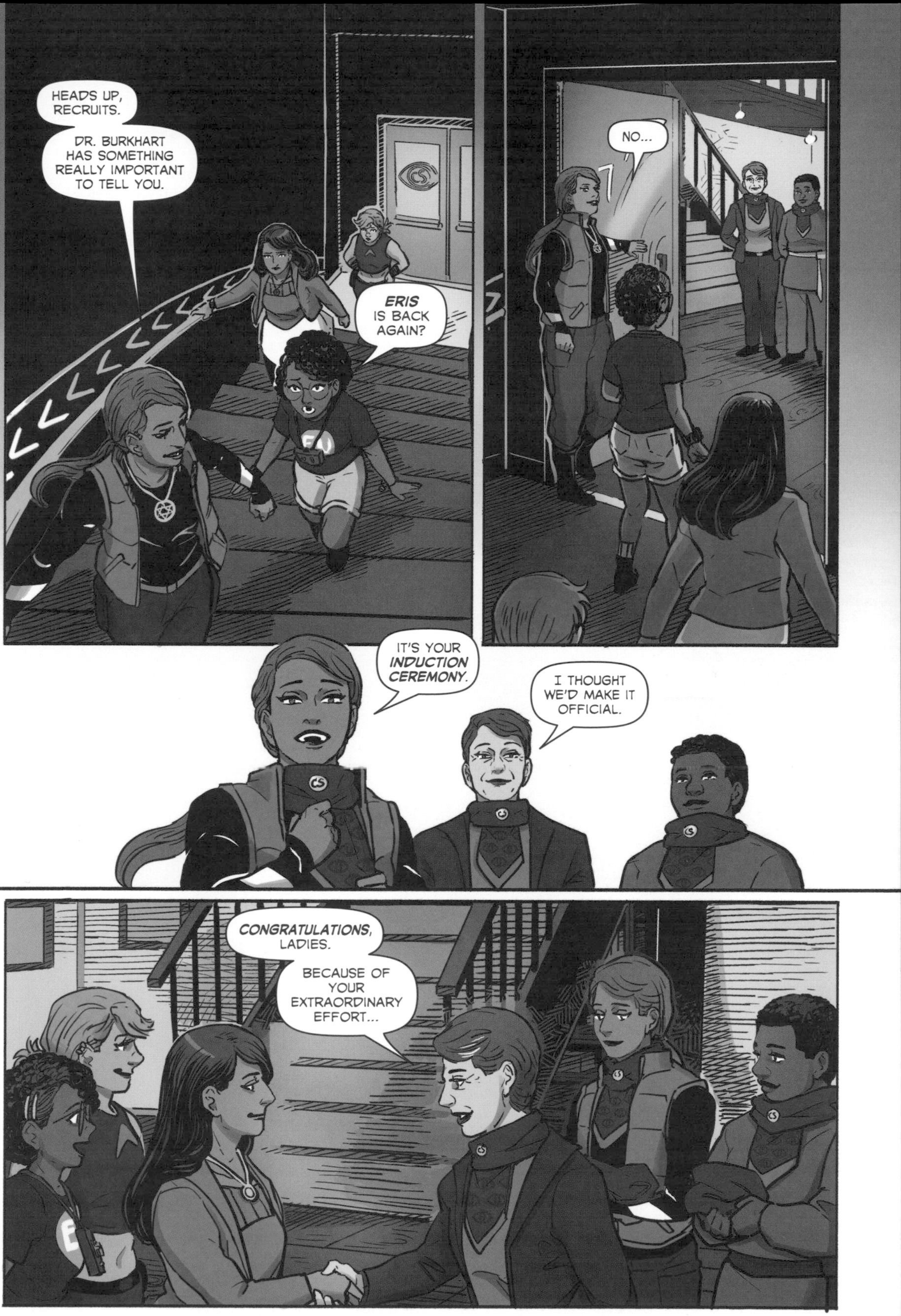
HEADS UP, RECRUITS.
DR. BURKHART HAS SOMETHING REALLY IMPORTANT TO TELL YOU.
ERIS IS BACK AGAIN?
NO...
IT'S YOUR INDUCTION CEREMONY.
I THOUGHT WE'D MAKE IT OFFICIAL.
CONGRATULATIONS, LADIES.
BECAUSE OF YOUR EXTRAORDINARY EFFORT...

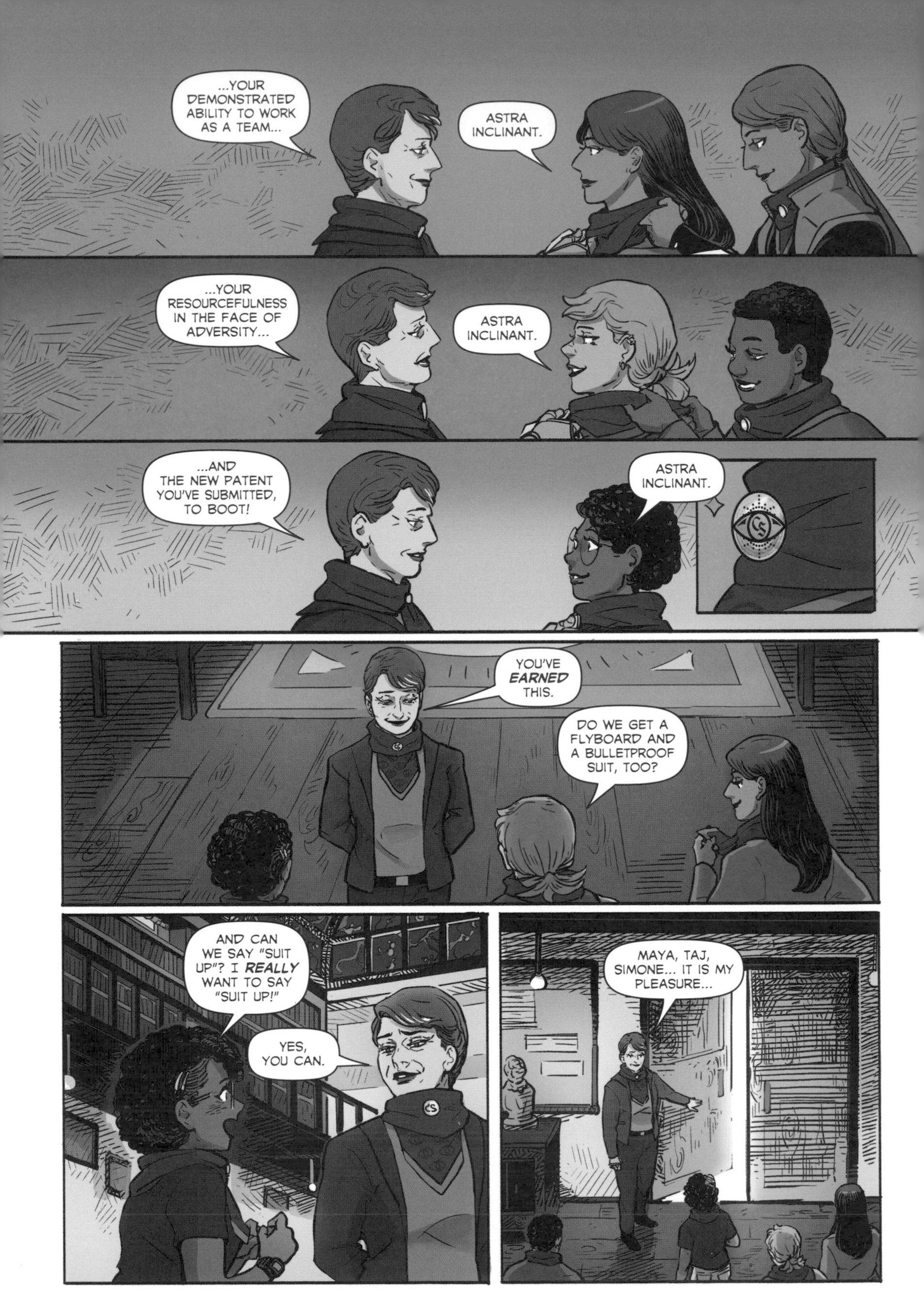
...YOUR DEMONSTRATED ABILITY TO WORK AS A TEAM...
ASTRA INCLINANT.
...YOUR RESOURCEFULNESS IN THE FACE OF ADVERSITY...
ASTRA INCLINANT.
...AND THE NEW PATENT YOU'VE SUBMITTED, TO BOOT!
ASTRA INCLINANT.
YOU'VE *EARNED* THIS.
DO WE GET A FLYBOARD AND A BULLETPROOF SUIT, TOO?
AND CAN WE SAY "SUIT UP"? I *REALLY* WANT TO SAY "SUIT UP!"
YES, YOU CAN.
MAYA, TAJ, SIMONE... IT IS MY PLEASURE...

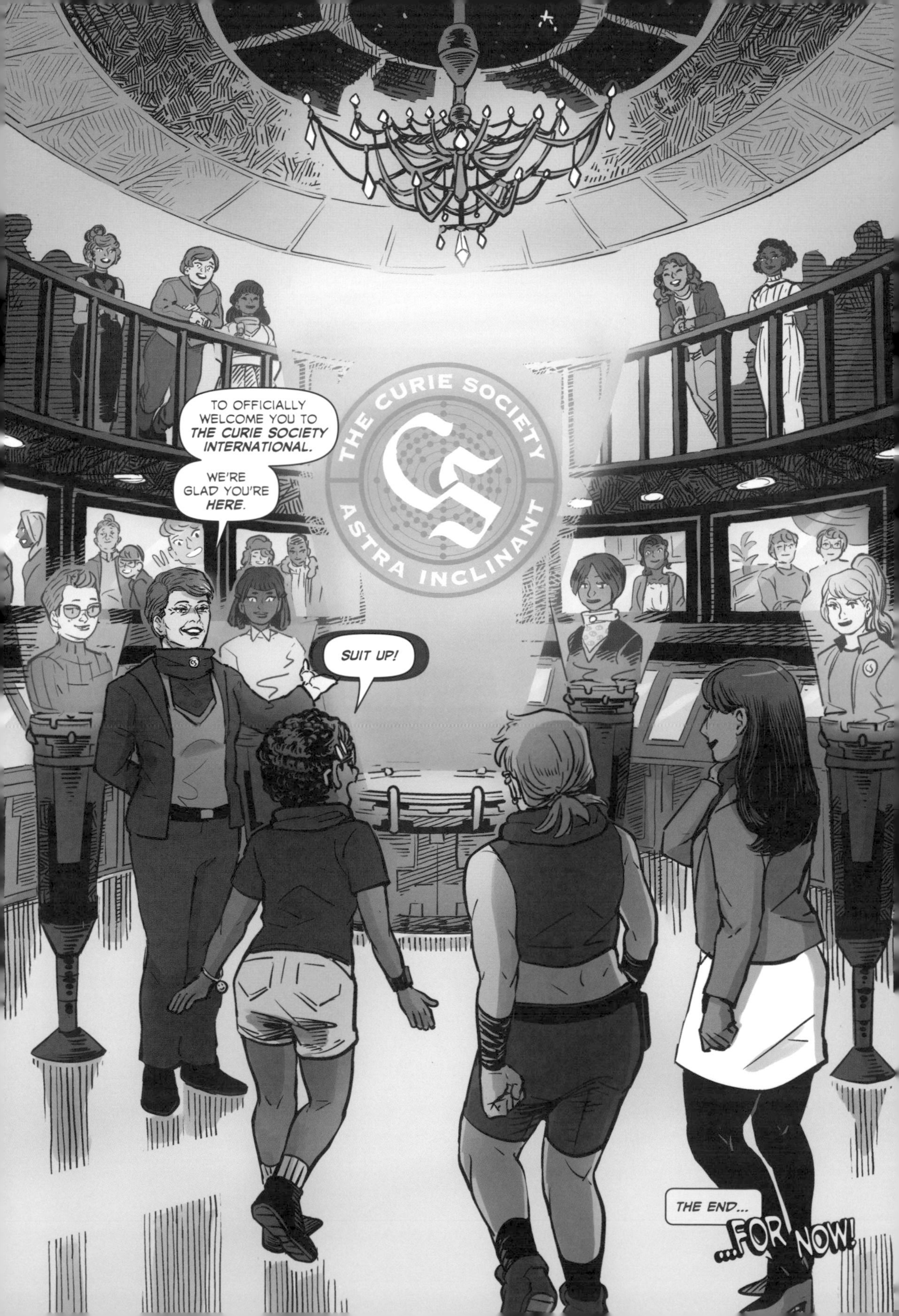
THE CURIE SOCIETY
ASTRA INCLINANT
TO OFFICIALLY WELCOME YOU TO *THE CURIE SOCIETY INTERNATIONAL.*
WE'RE GLAD YOU'RE *HERE.*
SUIT UP!
THE END...
...FOR NOW!

THE CURIE SOCIETY

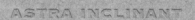

ASTRA INCLINANT

SCIENTIST BIOGRAPHIES

DANBEE "TAUNTAUN" KIM
NEUROSCIENTIST

DANBEE "TAUNTAUN" KIM is a neuroscientist and teacher based in London, UK. Her research combines studies of cuttlefish, storytelling, philosophy of science, and the evolution of brain architecture throughout time and across species. In collaboration with NeuroGEARS, she builds interactive experiences that both communicate science in accessible ways and allow people to participate in Field Neuroscience experiments. Tauntaun believes that art has an important role in organizing and building knowledge, as a tool for experts to collaborate and share insights. Her dream future is to train and play as a musician, capoeirista, and Vigilante Intergalactic Roustabout Scholar (VIRS, pronounced "verse").

DR. RITU RAMAN is an engineer, writer, and educator with a passion for biohybrid design—building machines powered by biological materials. She develops implantable robots that dynamically sense and adapt to the human body and help fight disease and damage. Ritu grew up in India, Kenya, and the United States. This taught her to thrive in dynamic environments and inspires her to diversify STEM education. Ritu is currently a postdoctoral fellow at MIT. She received her BS from Cornell University, and her MS and PhD from the University of Illinois at Urbana-Champaign. Website: RituRaman.com | Twitter: @DrRituRaman

DR. RITU RAMAN
ENGINEER, WRITER

KASIA CHMIELINSKI
TECHNOLOGIST

KASIA CHMIELINSKI is the co-founder of the Data Nutrition Project, an initiative that builds tools to improve the health of artificial intelligence through better data. Kasia is also a technologist at McKinsey & Company and previously worked at the U.S. Digital Service (Executive Office of the President) and Scratch, a project of the MIT Media Lab (Lifelong Kindergarten Group). They are an affiliate at The Berkman Klein Center for Internet & Society at Harvard University, where they also studied physics. When not in front of a whiteboard or a keyboard, Kasia can be found cycling uncomfortably long distances.

SCIENTIST BIOGRAPHIES

DR. JANE ZELIKOVA
ECOSYSTEM SCIENTIST

DR. JANE ZELIKOVA is an ecosystem scientist working at the intersection of climate change science and policy. From a young age, Jane has loved spending time outside and getting her hands dirty, which is one of the reasons she fell in love with ecology. She earned a PhD from the University of Colorado and has worked across the Western US and abroad examining the effects of global change in natural and managed systems. She is now a researcher at the University of Wyoming and the Chief Scientist at Carbon180, a nonprofit organization that brings together scientists, policymakers, and businesses to fundamentally rethink carbon. Jane also cofounded 500 Women Scientists and Hey Girl Productions.

After a few years working in a crime lab, **DR. RAYCHELLE BURKS** returned to academia. An analytical chemist, she enjoys the challenge of developing detection methods for a wide variety of analytes including regulated drugs, explosives, and chemical weapons. Dr. Burks is a popular science communicator, appearing on TV, in podcasts, and at large-genre conventions such as DragonCon and GeekGirlCon, in addition to writing a science-meets-true crime column called "Trace Analysis" for *Chemistry World*. She is a member of a number of local, national, and international committees, task forces, and projects focused on social justice and STEM.

DR. RAYCHELLE BURKS
ANALYTICAL CHEMIST

DEBORAH BLUM
SCIENCE JOURNALIST

DEBORAH BLUM, director of the Knight Science Journalism Program at MIT, is a Pulitzer Prize-winning American science journalist, columnist, and author of six books, including the 2018 *New York Times* Notable Book *The Poison Squad*, and the *New York Times* best-seller, *The Poisoner's Handbook* (2010). She has written for publications including the *New York Times*, the *Washington Post*, the *Wall Street Journal*, *Scientific American*, and *Wired*. She is currently publisher of the award winning digital science magazine *Undark* and serves on the advisory boards of *Chemical & Engineering News* and *The Scientist*.

CHRISTINE CORBETT MORAN
NASA / JPL

CHRISTINE CORBETT MORAN is the technical group supervisor of the Cyber Defense Engineering and Research group at NASA's Jet Propulsion Laboratory. She has a PhD in astrophysics and spent nearly one year in Antarctica running the South Pole Telescope. She's also an aspiring astronaut, an author, and a mom.

BRITT WRAY, PhD., science communicator is the author of the books *Rise of the Necrofauna: The Science, Ethics, and Risks of De-Extinction* and *Generation Dread* as well as a broadcaster who has hosted and produced science programs with the BBC and CBC.

BRITT WRAY, PHD
SCIENCE COMMUNICATOR

MAIA WEINSTOCK
EDITOR, WRITER, PRODUCER

MAIA WEINSTOCK is an editor, writer, and producer of science and children's media. She is the deputy editorial director at MIT News and has been on staff at BrainPOP, Discover, SPACE. com, and Science World. Maia writes on diversity in STEM media and on the history of women in STEM. She is the author of *Carbon Queen*, a biography of physicist Mildred Dresselhaus, and is known for LEGO projects including Women of NASA, a LEGO Ideas-winning and Amazon best-selling toy. Maia has been an MIT lecturer on the history of women in STEM and led efforts to increase diversity on Wikipedia.

SCIENTIST BIOGRAPHIES

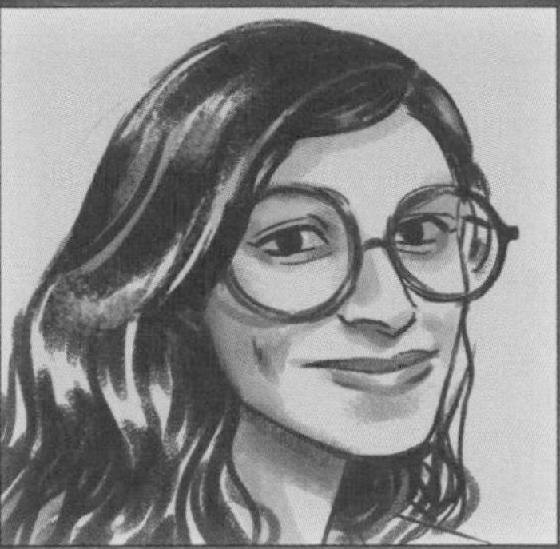

NADJA OERTELT
CO-FOUNDER OF MASSIVE SCIENCE

NADJA OERTELT is a co-founder of Massive Science, a science media company that aims to engage the public and scientists in new ways. She is a former research neuroscientist and works as a digital, educational, interactive, and event media producer and documentary filmmaker. She graduated from MIT in 2007 and has worked in labs at MIT, Harvard, and Cambridge University.

DR. CHANDA PRESCOD-WEINSTEIN is an assistant professor of physics and core faculty in women's and gender studies at the University of New Hampshire. One of fewer than 100 Black American women to earn a PhD from a department of physics, Dr. Prescod-Weinstein is a theoretical particle cosmologist with an expertise in dark matter, and a feminist theorist with a focus on Black women's social location in STEM.

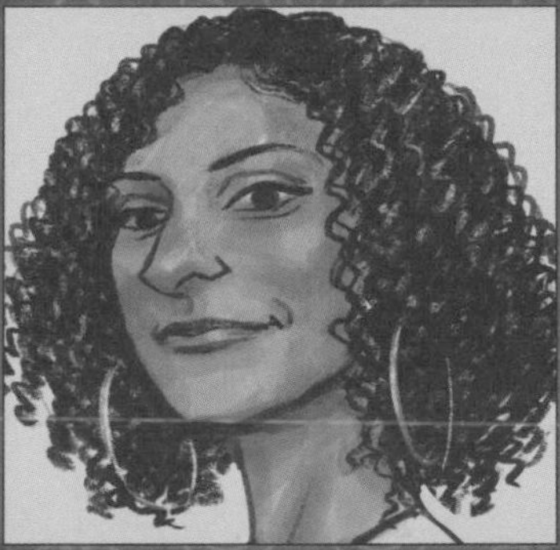

DR. CHANDA PRESCOD-WEINSTEIN
ASST. PROFESSOR OF PHYSICS

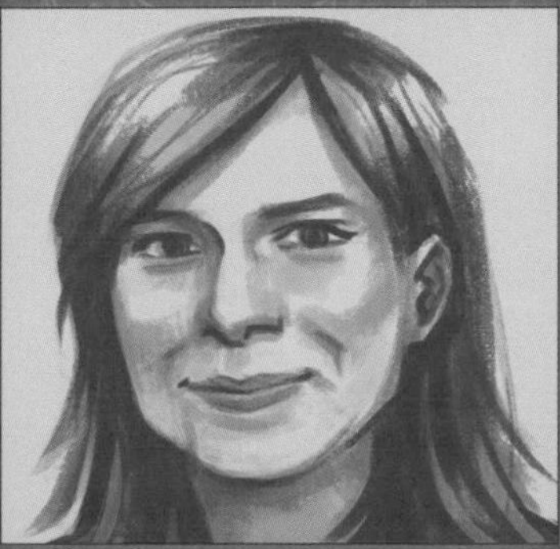

DR. ANGELA BELCHER
PROFESSOR, MIT

DR. ANGELA BELCHER
Professor Angela Belcher is the James Mason Crafts Professor of Biological Engineering, Materials Science, and the Koch Institute for Integrative Cancer Medicine at MIT and the head of the Department of Biological Engineering at MIT. She is a biological and materials engineer with expertise in the fields of biomaterials, biomolecular materials, organic-inorganic interfaces, and solid-state chemistry and devices. Her primary research focus is evolving new materials for energy, electronics, the environment, and medicine. She received her BS in Creative Studies from the University of California, Santa Barbara. She earned a PhD in inorganic chemistry at UCSB in 1997.

Glossary

Pg 1 - Missile Silo

The missile silo in *Curie Society* is inspired by the "Titan II Missile Explosion" in Damascus, Arkansas (1980), in which a wrench was dropped onto a fuel tank, causing it to leak. The Titan II exploded because of the accident.

Pg 2 - Radio Frequencies

Radio communication devices, like two-way radios, receive information from electromagnetic waves. Each of those waves has a specific frequency. Radio channels operate at fixed frequencies. Changing the channel means that the user is selecting a different frequency of radio transmission.

Pg 9 - Control Groups

When testing a hypothesis, it's important to have a group that is not experimented on for comparison. This is called a control group.

Pg 10-11 - Simone's Ant Experiment

Scientists have discerned 12 different kinds of ant communication including touch, body language, sound, and scent. Ants antennae are key in detecting pheromones and can "smell" the difference between an ant from one colony versus another. Ants can also communicate by touching antennae and have communicated nearby food by letting a fellow ant take a bite out of its mouth.

Pg 18-19 - Lagrangian Physics and Noether's Theorem

In physics, you can use different kinds of math. "Classical" physics uses algebra and some calculus. Lagrangian physics uses more complex calculus called differential equations. If the problem is relatively simple, the math can be simple, too, and classical physics works. But if the problem has a lot of parts, Lagrangian physics works better. Noether's Theorem comes from mathematician Emmy Noether, who proved that laws of physics come from symmetry.

Pg 24-25 - The Science of Laundry

"Colorfast clothing" (or the trait of colorfastness) is used to describe how well a fabric can hold dye through wash and wear. The effectiveness of colorfast clothing is dependent on a number of factors, including the type of fabric, dyes used, and any chemicals used to help color bond to the material.

Pg 26 - Computer Algorithms Syncing Light and Color to Sound

Scientists have created computer algorithms to synchronize music and visuals automatically. The algorithm analyzes the volume and pitch of digital soundwaves from a music on a DJ's computer and automatically translates that sound into a specific display of lights. Some have even made programs that synchronize music to images of landscapes.

Pg 30 - The Science of Baking

Baking relies heavily on chemistry. Eggs add structure, binding ingredients together, and variants on the ratio of ingredients can drastically alter the texture of a chocolate chip cookie. Another variant is how long dough is allowed to rest before baking, with some bakers suggesting 24 hours.

Pg 40 - IP Addresses

An IP address is a unique identifier that every machine on a network possesses. It functions in the same way that a person's home address does when you're mailing them a letter. IP stands for "Internet Protocol," the series of rules that machines follow when they communicate on the Internet. For those who know where to look, they may hold more than meets the *eye*.

Pg 42 - Orienteering, Compasses, and Topography

Orienteering began as an exercise for the Swedish military in the late 1800s and describes the navigation of an unknown region with only a compass and a map. Orienteering maps use an internationally agreed-upon set of symbols — for example, vegetation is represented by greens and yellows, while human-made features are black.

Pg 47-48 - Neutralizing Chlorine Gas

Chlorine gas is a poison that appears yellow-green in color and has a pungent odor similar to bleach. On its own it is not flammable, but it can react explosively with other chemicals, such as turpentine and ammonia. Sodium bicarbonate and urea have both been proposed as ways to neutralize chlorine gas: in WWI, soldiers were told to soak socks in urine and tie them around their faces during gas attacks.

Pg 54 - Aerozine 50 Gas

Aerozine 50 is a rocket fuel developed in the 1950s and still used today. It is a 50:50 combination of two extremely flammable compounds, unsymmetrical dimethylhydrazine and hydrazine. When a start cartridge combined Aerozine 50 with an oxidizer during the launches of the Titan II rockets, the rockets produced a distinctive "bwoop" sound.

Pg 56-57 - Marie Curie

Most know of Marie Curie's contributions to physics and chemistry through her research on radiation and discovery of polonium and radium, but Curie also developed mobile radiography units for WWI soldiers called "Petites Curies." In 2014, an analysis found that a notebook and papers belonging to Curie were still radioactive.

Pg 61 - Best Lab Practices for Hematology and Pathology

Best practices ensure that researchers do not introduce contaminants into their experiments or put themselves in harm's way through improper protection. When handling animals and their parts, such as a section of a frozen frog, best practices entail wearing personal protective equipment (PPE), such as gloves and a lab coat.

Pg 87 - Arduino Circuitry

Created in 2005, Arduino is an open-source software and related set of hardware devices that provide the backbone for art and design projects. Users on Arduino's Project Hub have posted designs for greenhouses, music-reactive LED lights, and punch-activated flamethrowers that all use the software and an Arduino board.

Pg 62-63 - Nanofiber Bulletproof Suits

Nanofiber garments can stop bullets in real life! These tiny, man-made fibers have properties that allow them to convert pressure into an electric charge. One nanofiber was even found to be tougher than Kevlar, the material used to make bulletproof vests.

Pg 64-65 - Ionic Plane

UNDER THE WING
aero foils
high voltage wire
+20K VOLTAGE
-20K VOLTAGE
IONS FLOW TOWARDS NEGATIVE VOLTAGE
WIND
FOLDING PROPELLER
WIND

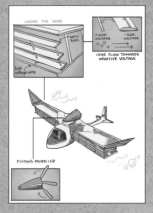

The plane seen in *Curie Society* is based off of a plane in development by MIT engineers, inspired by *Star Trek*. The plane is powered by "ionic wind" — a silent but mighty flow of ions that is produced aboard the plane and generates enough thrust to propel the plane over sustained flight. It does not rely on fossil fuels and is completely silent.

Pg 68-71 - Extinct Species Such as Passenger Pigeons, Gastric Brooding Frogs, Thylacines, Mammoths etc.

The passenger pigeon, once the most abundant bird in North America, went extinct in 1914 after it was hunted out of existence. The gastric brooding frog was known for its unique reproductive behavior: female frogs would swallow fertilized eggs and regurgitate offspring once hatched. De-extinction has not yet been used to resurrect either species (as of the printing of this book).

Pg 72 - Studies into Permafrost and Global Warming

As temperatures rise in the coldest places, frozen layers of soil called permafrost are permanently melting. The liquid water is reshaping how land looks, even causing landslides. Some of the permafrost even contains greenhouse gases. When the permafrost melts, those gases go up into the atmosphere and contribute to more global warming.

Pg 72 - Wolves Trophic Cascade in Yellowstone Ecosystem

The gray wolf was on the road to extinction in Yellowstone National Park until 1995, when a few dozen wolves were reintroduced. By releasing wolves into the wild of the park, the entire ecosystem changed — there were fewer elk, so willows grew healthy and tall. With new trees to munch on, beavers began building dams. Eventually, even the paths of rivers changed.

Pg 73 - Tidal Patterns

Tides are the large-scale movement of water in the ocean and are experienced onshore as periods when the water line is high or low. Different places in the world have different numbers of high and low tides each month. Tidal patterns are caused by interactions of the gravitational forces of the Sun, Moon, and Earth.

Pg 74-75 - Mathematical Patterns to create Predictive Models

Scientists can use statistics to find patterns in a data set and then use those patterns to create mathematical equations to predict other values not included in the data set. As a very simple example, if you saw that the average height of players on a basketball team was 7 feet tall, you would predict that a newly recruited player would probably also be around 7 feet tall.

Pg 76 - NATO Phonetic Alphabet

An alphabet based off English that assigns distinct code words to each letter. This system is used across radio and telephone to make sure that spelling is enunciated clearly. For example: "b" and "p" can often sound familiar, and are instead represented with "bravo" and "papa."

Pg 85 - Wind Tunnels

Huge tunnels with winds blowing through them. Researchers use wind tunnels to test and measure how aircraft or spacecraft will perform in flight, which helps them design safer and more aerodynamic vehicles.

Pg 87 - The Science of Meditation and Anxiety

Studies of meditation and mindfulness (focusing on your present surroundings, slowly breathing in and out) have had mixed results — some studies show that these techniques have greatly aided people with anxiety, but other studies have not found any clear connection.

Pg 88 - Adapting Biological Processes to Robotics: Tarsal Pads, Communication Signals, etc.

A form of biomimetics where materials and machines are designed to mimic features found in nature. Through evolution, plants and animals have developed a wide variety of abilities and characteristics, and applying these to human-created products, including robots, can help improve their function.

Pg 88 - Scientific Method: Problem, Hypothesis, and Testing

A set of steps by which science is performed. The basic steps are to ask a question, form a hypothesis or prediction about the answer based on background research and your own observations, do an experiment to test your hypothesis, analyze data, and repeat the experiment with a new hypothesis.

Pg 89 - Modern Prosthetics

Devices worn to replace lost limbs. Modern prosthetics are more realistic than their predecessors and may incorporate robotics or electronics that enable them to function more like biological limbs. Scientists are even developing artificial skin, complete with sensors, to cover prosthetics!

Pg 94 – Projection Bombing
Putting words, artwork, graffiti, or other kinds of temporary messages on a building using a high-powered projector, instead of using permanent paints.

Pg 96 (also Pg 30) – Industrial Design
The process of inventing physical products that will be manufactured at a large scale, not made by hand. It's an applied art that considers how a product will look, how it will be used, and how it will be made.

Pg 97 – William Herschel
The brother of astronomer Caroline Herschel, William discovered infrared radiation, seasons in Mars's ice caps, the planet Uranus as well as two of its moons, and several moons of Saturn, among other achievements.

Pg 100 – Dielectric Metasurface Cloaking Technology
A metasurface is an extremely thin sheet — so thin that it is considered two-dimensional. Dielectric metasurfaces interact with light at the nanometer scale to scatter waves of light. This technology shields objects from visual and radar detection.

Pg 104 – Facial Recognition Technology

Several different kinds of technology that can identify people by comparing their faces to a database of already known and cataloged people. They can work by scanning and analyzing the 3D shape of a face (measuring things like distance between eyes and nose) or by recognizing features like birthmarks.

Pg 108 – Advances in Magnetic Fields in Fusion Reactors
Fusion reactors often use powerful magnetic fields to keep hydrogen atoms close together, helping them stay in place and fuse together. Instead of adding outside magnetic fields, some new approaches try to use the superhot hydrogen to generate its own magnetic field.

Pg 115 – Brain Interface Technology / Xiomena's AXIOTHEA Presentation

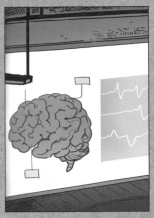

Brain-machine interfaces (BMI) link a human mind with a computer. This way, the computer can read signals from the human, transmit information back and forth (for example: allowing a blind person to see by stimulating the appropriate region of the brain), or precisely measure brain activity.

Pg 121 – CRISPR: CRISPR in Humans; Trials in China
Clustered Regularly Interspersed Palindromic Repeats (CRISPR) is gene-editing technology adapted from bacteria. A protein that cuts DNA is guided to specific spots in a genome. The hope is that it can remove mutations or disease-causing genes. Several people have tried to use CRISPR in humans, but only one, in China, resulted in the birth of children.

Pg 126-127 – Tranquilizer Gun
A device for shooting sedatives, usually at wild animals so they can be approached safely by humans to give medical aid or to move the animals. Often takes the form of a gun shooting a dart-carrying needle that injects a drug on impact.

Pg 132 – Hacking Elevators
The practice of calling into remote elevators or hacking their emergency phones. A hacker can change what an elevator's phone does when someone inside the elevator dials the emergency number or even speak with people who are on board.

Pg 138 – Flyboard
The flyboard seen in the Curie Society is inspired by a real flying platform, or hoverboard, with five jet turbines powered by kerosene. This personal aerial vehicle can reach speeds of 90–100 miles per hour and has been used to cross the English Channel. It has limited fuel capacity, but the rider can carry extra fuel in a backpack.

CREATIVE TEAM

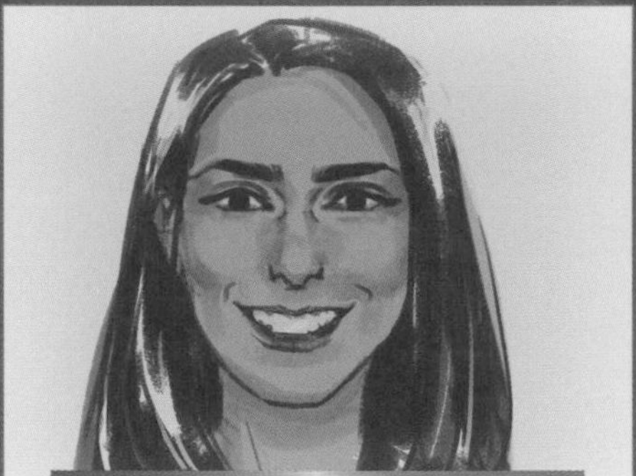

HEATHER EINHORN
CO-CREATOR

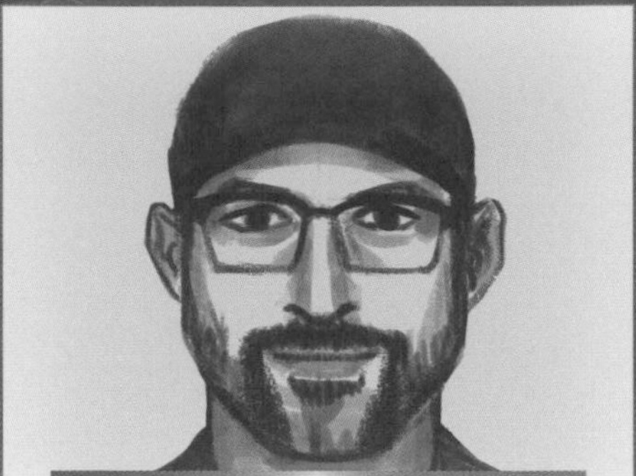

ADAM STAFFARONI
CO-CREATOR

HEATHER EINHORN was born and raised in New York City. She grew up loving *Teenage Mutant Ninja Turtles*, Batgirl, female detective stories, and teen spy thrillers. She'd be happy to eat cookies for every meal of the day. After many years as an executive in the entertainment industry, Heather made the leap to co-found EEP so she could create stories showcasing heroic women characters. Heather co-created the popular scripted podcasts *Daughters of DC* and *Lethal Lit: A Tig Torres Mystery*, which was listed as a NY Times Great Podcast and was the first Young Adult scripted podcast. She still lives in New York City with her husband and creative partner, Adam Staffaroni.

ADAM STAFFARONI is a lifelong fan of comics in all forms — newspaper strips, comic books, graphic novels — and has been creating comics in one form or another for the past fifteen years. He's a graduate of Dartmouth College and received an MFA as part of the first-ever graduating class at The Center for Cartoon Studies. He lives in New York City where he creates all sorts of stories, including the scripted podcasts *Daughters of DC* and *Lethal Lit: A Tig Torres Mystery*, which he co-created with his wife, Heather Einhorn.

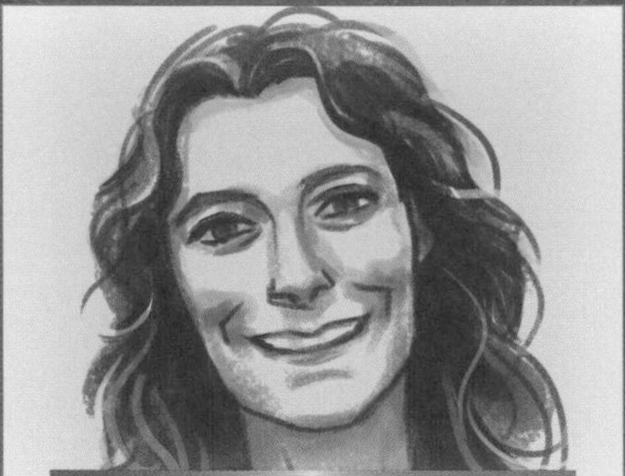

JOAN HILTY
CO-FOUNDER OF PAGETURNER

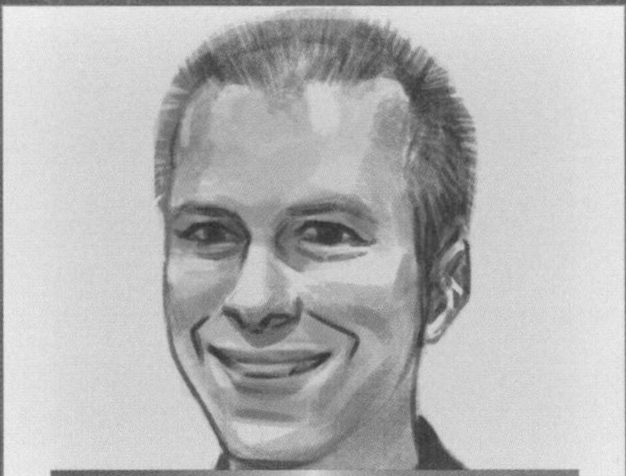

PETE FRIEDRICH
CO-FOUNDER OF PAGETURNER

JOAN HILTY is a former syndicated cartoonist and longtime DC Comics/Vertigo editor; she continues to work as an editor with most of the top publishers of graphic novels and comics. She co-chairs comics programming for Miami Book Fair and the Brooklyn Book Festival, and teaches at the School of Visual Arts in NYC. She would like to own a flyboard.

PETE FRIEDRICH has designed and packaged print and web content for Chronicle Books, Rizzoli, Disney, Harper, Wired Books, and many more. He has worked as a magazine designer for *Rolling Stone*, *Fortune*, and *Sports Illustrated*. He cofounded Pageturner with Joan Hilty in 2013 and directs its graphic design work for publishers, agencies, media companies, nonprofits, and authors.

CREATIVE TEAM

JANET HARVEY
WRITER

SONIA LIAO
ARTIST

JANET HARVEY is an award-winning writer of comic books, movies, and games. She has written for Oni Press, Image Comics, and DC Comics, including the first full-length adventure of Cassandra Cain. Her graphic novel *Angel City* is out from Oni Press. Her first feature film, *A Million Hits*, is available to watch on Amazon Prime.

SONIA LIAO is an illustrator and comic artist based in Westford, Massachusetts. She graduated with her BFA in Illustration from MICA in 2014 and has since drawn comics for publishers like BOOM! Studios, Sourcebook Fire, and Red 5 Comics. Her hobbies include watching crime procedurals, DC television shows, and reading. She is a huge nerd.

JOHANNA TAYLOR
COLORIST

MORGAN MARTINEZ
LETTERER

ANNETTE FANZHU
ART ASSISTANT

JOHANNA TAYLOR is a freelance illustrator and concept artist working in video games and comics. Her love of Zelda, Lord of the Rings, and Dungeons & Dragons inspired her passion for fantasy and collaborative storytelling. She is an avid player of RPGs and contributed artwork to Lion Forge Comics' *Rolled & Told*, the ENnie Award-nominated *Uncaged Anthology*, and other RPG-based publications. She enjoys Bollywood dancing and feeding crows.

MORGAN MARTINEZ has lettered books such as Natasha Alterici's *Heathen*, John Leguizamo's *Freak*, Cullen Bunn's *Night Trap*, and Brandon Easton's *Andre the Giant: Closer to Heaven*. Morgan's interests include writing, drawing, computers, intersectional feminism and trans rights, Nintendo Switch, and being as unserious as circumstances allow. She lives in the South Bronx with her wife and their cat, Darcy.

ANNETTE FANZHU is a Chinese-Canadian illustrator with a BFA in cartooning from the School of Visual Arts. She enjoys exploring narrative through her art and looking to historical aesthetics for inspiration. She hopes to expand her career in illustration and publishing. Her life goals include doing a food tour of Asia with friends and becoming a cat owner.

CURIE SOCIETY HEADQUARTERS, EDMONDS CHAPTER

EDMONDS UNIVERSITY WAS CHOSEN AS THE SITE OF THE CURIE SOCIETY'S FIRST EXPANSION INTO NORTH AMERICA, WITH THE CHAPTER OPENING IN 1910. SUBSEQUENT EXPANSIONS OF THE UNDERGROUND CAMPUS WERE COMPLETED IN 1954 AND 1992, WITH SENIOR CURIE MEMBERS DR. JOLENE BURKHART AND DR. RUUNE WARSAME CO-LEADING THE CHAPTER FOR THE PAST DECADE.

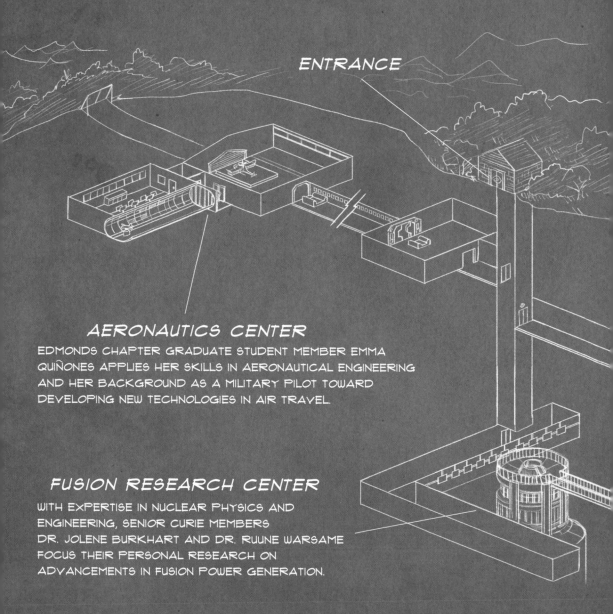

ENTRANCE

AERONAUTICS CENTER

EDMONDS CHAPTER GRADUATE STUDENT MEMBER EMMA QUIÑONES APPLIES HER SKILLS IN AERONAUTICAL ENGINEERING AND HER BACKGROUND AS A MILITARY PILOT TOWARD DEVELOPING NEW TECHNOLOGIES IN AIR TRAVEL.

FUSION RESEARCH CENTER

WITH EXPERTISE IN NUCLEAR PHYSICS AND ENGINEERING, SENIOR CURIE MEMBERS DR. JOLENE BURKHART AND DR. RUUNE WARSAME FOCUS THEIR PERSONAL RESEARCH ON ADVANCEMENTS IN FUSION POWER GENERATION.

ON-CAMPUS BUILDING

THE ORIGINAL EDMONDS CHAPTER BUILDING, NOW DISGUISED AS A DISUSED SORORITY. DUE TO EDMONDS' PROXIMITY TO WASHINGTON, D.C., THIS SITE NOW IS OFTEN USED AS A MEETING HALL FOR INTERNATIONAL CURIE SOCIETY MEMBERS.

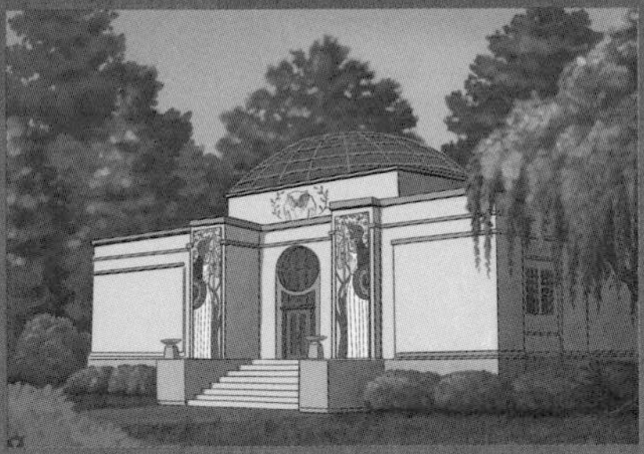

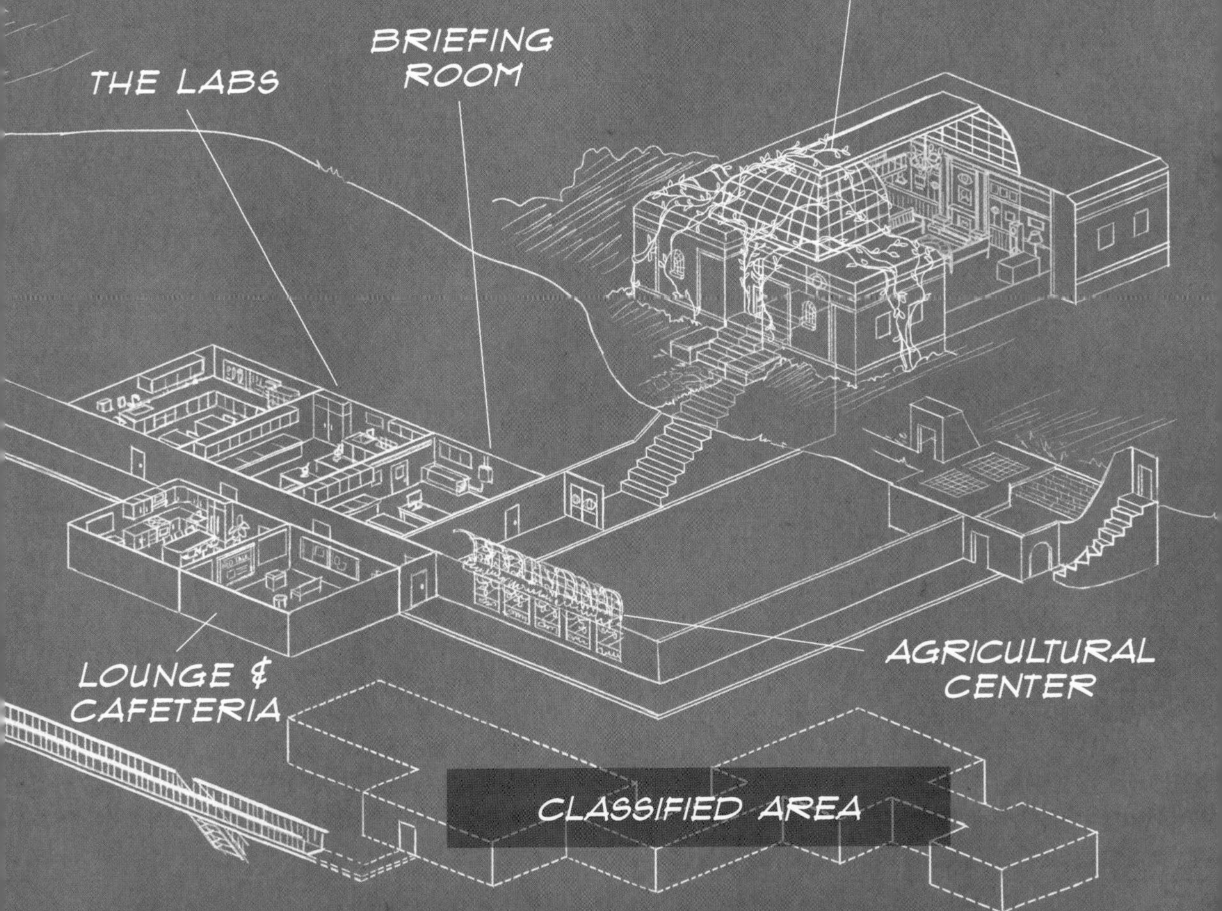
BRIEFING ROOM
THE LABS
LOUNGE & CAFETERIA
AGRICULTURAL CENTER
CLASSIFIED AREA

"I was taught that the way of progress was neither swift nor easy."
—Marie Curie

ACKNOWLEDGMENTS

We never could have imagined what an incredible journey creating The Curie Society would be. There are so many amazing, smart, heroic, courageous people who contributed to this book. Dr. B would be so proud - it truly was a team effort!

First, we'd like to thank the Staffaroni and Einhorn families for supporting us in our creative endeavors. We love you!

Joan Hilty & Pete Friedrich, from day one, we could not have imagined a more wonderful team to go on this journey with. As we said in our very first meeting, "we had a short list of one" for The Curie Society. Your steady hands have guided this ship into port!!

Nadja Oertelt & Allan Lasser, you are the smartest people we know! This was just an ambitious idea when we brought it to you, and we could have never realized it without your expertise.

Jermey Matthews, Amy Brand & the team at The MIT Press, what incredible partners you've been. Thank you for the opportunity to push the boundaries, and for your guidance and support throughout the entire process. We are so happy The Curie Society found such a wonderful home at The MIT Press.

And to the EEP team, thank you for always having our backs and believing in this project: Laura Martin, Ryan McCann, Aroop Sanakkayala, Greg Lockard, Gayle Artino, Jesse Post, and the Shadow Unicorn.

And Special Thanks to everyone else who has contributed and inspired along the way: Andy Weir for giving us confidence in our vision, Pia Guerra for your inspiration, Britt Wray and Kasia Chmielinski for your insight, Aria Kydd and Kera Matthews for your keen eyes.

Joan & Pete would also like to thank: Ellie Wright, Mike Cavallaro, Frank Reynoso, Nick Bertozzi, Cardinal Rae, Deron Bennett, Janet Rossi, Jacque Porte, Jeff Yerkey, Asa and Pamela Geismar.

And, above all, we all want to thank the amazing creative team who embraced the mission of this book and supported it with their brilliance, hard work, and immense talent: Janet Harvey, Sonia Liao, Johanna Taylor, Morgan Martinez, and Annette Fanzhu, thank you.

Did you find the clue?
Uncover more secrets of *The Curie Society* at
thecuriesociety.com

THE CURIE SOCIETY
CS
ASTRA INCLINANT
™